CHANCE

CLARE E. ADKIN JR.

ISBN: 978-1-960146-83-0 (hard cover)
      978-1-960146-84-7 (soft cover)

Edited by: Melisa Graham

Published by Warren Publishing
Charlotte, NC
www.warrenpublishing.net
Printed in the United States

PREFACE

I've started this journey a thousand times. As a young boy growing up on a fruit farm in southern Michigan, I was fascinated with stories about the Wild West, gold prospectors, cattle rustlers, gun fights, wagon trains, Buffalo Bill, and Sweet Betsy from Pike. While I was attending a rural one-room grade school, our music teacher visited for half a day every other week. Among other lessons, she taught us folk and country and western songs. I became determined to light out for the West when I grew up, not forgetting a banjo on my knee and a six-shooter on my hip.

The weekly children's programs on the radio and then later on TV set me on fire. My mother threatened a lynching to get me to turn it off and come to supper, "Now!"

Reminiscing today about those old programs brings a smile to my face. I can still recite lines from the introduction to *The Lone Ranger*, set to the tune of the "William Tell Overture," and sing several verses of Frankie Laine's musical rendition of "Mule Train."

As a teenager, the song "Riders in the Sky" made me shiver as I visualized a herd of wild, red eyed cows thundering up a cloudy draw. I never missed an episode of *Gunsmoke* with Matt Dillon and Miss Kitty. When *Rawhide* debuted in 1959, and I heard those opening lines of the theme song, "Rollin', rollin', rollin'," I rocked in the saddle and coughed trail dust from my throat. I *was* Rowdy Yates—Clint Eastwood—and to the present day, I maintain that Clint Eastwood is the best hero who ever galloped out of Hollywood to right a wrong.

After my dad graduated from high school in 1939, he spent a couple of years working on a ranch in central California. Much as I tried, I could never get him to tell me enough about his experiences in the Wild West. Of course, I was forced to enliven his story more than he knew. Once, Dad told me that, before he returned home to Michigan, he was offered a job as a forest ranger in the Sierra Nevada Mountains. "You should have taken it!" I reprimanded him, never once thinking that if he had taken the job, I wouldn't be here to write about it.

Somewhere along the trail from high school through college, I read Mark Twain's *Roughing It* and John Steinbeck's *Travels with Charley* and *The Grapes of Wrath*. I also read *On the Road* and *The Catcher in the Rye*. Jack Kerouac's need to roam struck my wanderlust fancy, and I was intrigued by J. D. Salinger's main character, teenager Holden Caulfield, with whom I felt a common bond. However, it was the Great Depression's poor, uprooted Okies following Route 66 west that most captured my writer's imagination. Determined to travel the time-worn highway's entire course while experiencing the many attractions despite its crumbling roadways provided, real or imagined, has been my fictive dream for more years than I care to divulge.

My brother, Les, passed away in the fall of 2010 at the end of a three-year struggle with cancer. Because I was five years older than my brother, I thought of myself as more of an authority figure to him than a blood brother. I suspect I treated him accordingly, as was evidenced on a Canadian fishing trip with our parents when I shouted at him, "Stop with the foul mouth and grow up!" which he did not receive well. During adulthood, my brother and I were at odds on several occasions—never extreme quarrels, but sibling rivalry aged right along with us.

Two years before Les's passing, I read *Three Weeks with My Brother* by Nicholas Sparks. While sharing Sparks's story of his brother and him traveling around the world, I posed to Les that we plan a trip together following Route 66 from Chicago to Los Angeles. The idea sparked something in each of us and immediately took on a life of its own. We couldn't wait to go and soon agreed on a launch date. However, our departure time had to be amended twice because of unforeseen medical difficulties and necessary procedures. Postponements did not dampen either of our spirits though. Each time we talked by phone, our plan grew.

We finally agreed to meet at Chicago's Midway Airport on April 20, 2010. Les would drive in from his home in Cadillac, Michigan, and I would fly in from mine in Durham, North Carolina. We had decided to take my brother's car, a bright-red Camaro convertible. Perfect!

Before boarding a plane to Chicago, my cellphone vibrated. It was Les. He told me he had become physically unable to make such a trip. Les never said so, but I could tell the cancellation broke his heart, as it did mine. Route 66 was never mentioned between us again.

However, my desire to travel Route 66 continued to glow brighter, fueled by memories of my diseased brother. Writing this novel provided me a vehicle to reflect on personal experiences, as well as observations of contentious adult siblings. To tell the story while traveling from west to east may seem a juxtaposition, but I wanted to emphasize a Western flavor while tracing the mythical, well-worn highway. Old Route 66 provided the appropriate settings, and there were many of them for long-estranged brothers to reconnect while revealing their most secret selves to one another.

Traveling US Route 66 with David and Larry, the story's main characters, has been a wonderful ride. Thus, as Roy and Dale sang at the end of each episode of *The Roy Rogers Show*, "happy trails to you" as you read onward.

When passing through Oklahoma City on a research trip in June of 1985, my wife and I decided to visit the National Cowboy & Western Heritage Museum. There, we pondered a large bronze sculpture of a weary Indigenous American seated limply atop his exhausted horse. The sculpture's title was *End of the Trail*. Ironically, on June 27, 1985, right about that same time, Route 66 was decertified.

Clare E. Adkin Jr.

CHAPTER I
Seven Days Ago

He had been staring into the mirror above the fireplace mantel for several minutes. Road signs, bridges, narrow mountain passes and sparse desert expanses roll by in slow motion. He's thought about it, mapped, researched and hoped. Only two more days until he departs.

Pain pierces his left shoulder and penetrates deep into his upper chest cavity. He buckles at the waist, gasping for breath. Tumbling forward, he instinctively reaches down with his right hand in a futile attempt to catch himself. Everything goes black before he hits the floor.

Later … maybe seconds, maybe days … a rolling sensation beneath his buttocks runs the entire length of both legs all the way to the soles of his feet. Hurried movements and urgent, hushed voices encircled him, and their panicked tone frightens him. He lay stone still, unable to do more. Light passes over his closed eyelids, and an antiseptic smell floats above his face.

Two distraught women stand next to one another close behind his hospital gurney. The older of the two puts an arm around the younger one to help steady her. "Please, I want to stay with my husband," the trembling woman says.

A physician turns to her and says, "Please take a seat in the lobby. We'll send for you shortly."

The patient is pushed through a tall metal door that opens automatically. "Is he going to make it?" a nurse whispers. Quiet voices grow distant ... become faint ... and then there is only dead silence.

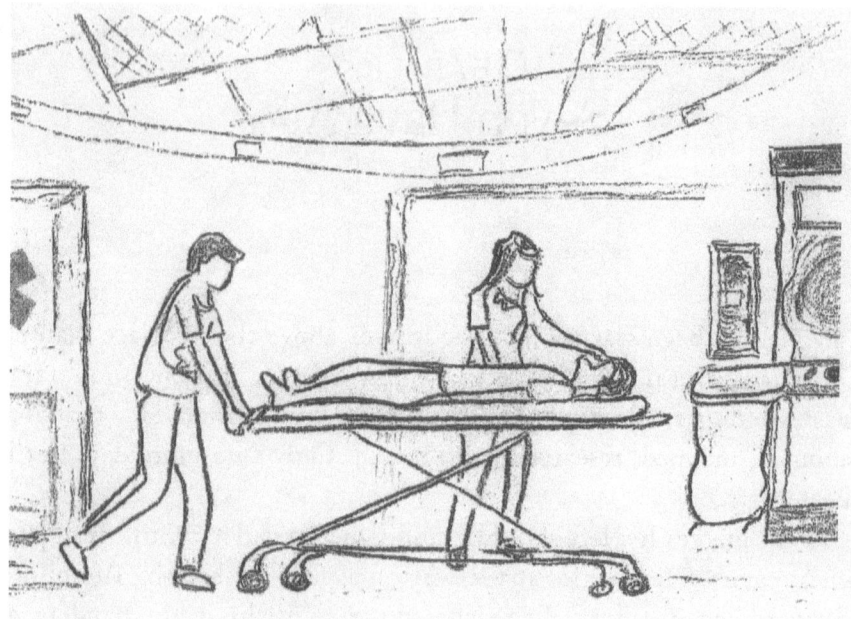

CHAPTER 2
Avalon, California

David had not moved a muscle for several minutes, birddog still, statue straight. His emotions were concealed beneath his gaze, which fixed directly on the two-story townhouse across the street. A variety of paint colors and front door casings were all that differentiated each townhouse from the next. They lined the street on both sides. Several late-model cars were parked beside gray granite curbs that separated the sidewalks from the street. David's prized five-year-old 1958 Chevy would fit right into the neighborhood. Without the four-inch, black, metal numbers affixed above each main entrance, an individual's home would be next to impossible to locate. David pulled a slip of paper from his pants pocket to confirm the address his mother had given him before he left home for California.

Although the townhouses were neat and orderly, they weren't the pretentious, upscale living quarters he had so often envisioned for his brother, Larry. By comparison, the two-thousand-square-foot ranch David and his wife owned had much more to offer and, without question, cost far less. Of course, he had to mow the lawn each week during the summer and shovel snow daily in the winter, two chores absent in Larry's world. However, the sibling differences he mulled over and over were far in excess of the 2,528 miles separating Three Oaks, Michigan from Santa Monica, California.

David startled when he realized a man standing next to him had been trying to get his attention. "You okay?" the stranger asked.

David masked his rumination. "I haven't seen that kind of bush before," he said, pointing at the low shrubs planted in the narrow strip of earth between townhouses and sidewalks. "Does it only grow along the California coast?"

The stranger was evidently not interested in idle chitchat, so without a word, he turned and walked away down the sidewalk.

David watched until the stranger disappeared around a corner. *I, too, am walking away*, he thought. In fact, he planned to separate completely from his rather typical middle-American life in search of a long-dreamed-of, carefree existence. Never had David thought of himself as a quitter, and even now, he would not admit to himself that *walking away* and *quitting* were the same thing.

★ ★ ★

The southern California coast seemed a familiar place, but one David had only read about in the Sunday travel section of the *Chicago Tribune*. Scattered, black-and-white gulls shrieked overhead. They darted to and fro across an endless pale-blue sky reflected in the ocean's flat expanse, which was only occasionally interrupted by a lazy swell. Except, straight ahead of the ferry's barnacle-encrusted bow, the horizon was empty as far as the eye could see in all directions. A vision of a pleasant South Seas hideaway took form in David's reverie while a distant land drew ever nearer.

As if rising from an enormous mirror, Santa Catalina gradually came into view. Verdant hillsides were a perfect backdrop for the charming harbor town of Avalon. The town sparkled in the late-morning sun like in a fairy tale of lost Atlantis. Whether mere wistful anticipation or pleasurable reality, David had also envisioned his arrival harbor as a Polynesian paradise complete with tall, supple coconut palms swaying before warm and gentle trade winds. Swimmers, sunbathers, and casual townsfolk moved about the slender, crescent-shaped beach separating a tranquil surf from the harbor's weathered boardwalk and narrow waterfront street. *Will this be my long-imagined Shangri-La?* David wondered.

With the hungry eyes of a sailor on limited shore leave, David assessed the village from his vantage point on the upper deck. He inhaled the picturesque scenery. Well-tended but unpretentious homes dotted the green hillsides in a semicircle around a modest business district. Once the Shoreline Ferry moored, he trailed other excited passengers down a short metal gangplank to the wharf's worn wooden deck. A lanky teenage boy scurried through the new arrivals and came straight toward David.

"Mister! Mister! Would you like to book a passage on world-famous Avalon Carriage Excursion? One reservation left."

David stepped back, at once amused and impressed by the young man's youthful enthusiasm. The boy reminded David of himself when he was in junior high school, soliciting the neighbors for odd jobs in quest of enough money to buy a new English bicycle with thin tires.

The young man's startling good looks complemented his gallant manner. He parted his short-cropped, jet-black hair on the left, and his smooth, olive skin and penetrating, dark eyes were highlighted by an eager smile revealing two perfect rows of white teeth. He had seized David's full attention, and he knew it.

"Sir, I can tell you are a gentleman of exceptionally good taste, one who would enjoy an informative journey through the historic streets of Avalon. Learn of its glorious past. Am I right? Only five dollars, sir. Best deal on the island."

Not to be viewed as a naive, easy mark, David asked if the tour was overpriced. He was assured it was beneath the going rate. Then the boy pointed and called out, "Yo, Biscuits!" A well-groomed, small, brown-and-white mare hitched to a nearby four-passenger open surrey bobbed her head and nickered in response.

"Biscuits is magnificent steed that will be drawing your carriage, sir. My name is Kwan Collins, and I shall serve as personal chauffeur and private tour guide."

David succumbed easily to the cheerful sales pitch. After all, he was on a scouting mission, and this particular guide and tour was much to his liking. He explained as such and asked his would-be chauffeur to repeat his name.

"Kwan, at your service. Right this way, sir. Biscuits awaits!" Kwan bowed with the wave of his left hand in the direction of the carriage as Biscuits nickered.

"Lead the way. You can call me Da—" David hesitated. "Dan." David found himself both charmed and entertained by Kwan's confident, animated demeanor, even if it resembled that of a county-fair, midway barker. He also found his own impromptu pseudonym equally amusing, although he had intended to remain anonymous in any case.

"Right this way, Mr. Da Dan! Climb aboard." Kwan flashed a toothy smile.

"Dan will do just fine."

Once the two were seated on the driver's bench, Kwan snapped the reins and charged, "Step lively, Biscuits, click-click."

"One reservation left, hey?"

"Biscuits prefers one passenger, two at most." Driver and passenger exchanged knowing smiles.

For the next hour, Biscuits clip-clopped up and back the two cobblestone streets that rimmed the quaint little bay and, as if by memory, a couple of appealing turnouts. The rhythmic sound of hooves against stone pavement satisfied David; he had found his long-dreamed-of, much-fabled destination—remote and unassuming yet exotic in a mysterious sort of way.

A treasure trove of information spilled from Kwan's lips about the town, the island, and himself. David was interested in all three and quite sure he saw all the village of Avalon had to offer, some things more than once. Everything seemed to his fancy. It fulfilled his necessary criteria: far from home, almost anonymous, and entirely enchanting.

According to Kwan, there were approximately two thousand year-round residents. A couple of For Rent and Help Wanted signs caught David's eye. They, too, would be necessary to follow up on. Listening to Kwan's enthusiastic descriptions of life on Santa Catalina pleased David's quest for a long-desired sanctuary far from the tedium of his everyday life.

The castle-like Catalina Casino stood out as the town's main attraction. Its sheer size seemed out of place given the overall coziness of Avalon. Kwan insisted they stop and take a look inside the spacious auditorium and well-appointed, grand ballroom. A polka band rehearsed behind the drawn stage curtain in preparation for an evening event.

"I often see movie stars here. 'Keep your eyes peeled,' as the mainlanders say." Kwan's enjoyment serving as a tour guide came naturally to him, and pride in his island home impressed David, reminding him of his own personal community pride. Santa Catalina was only twenty-six miles southwest of Los Angeles, yet it felt like a world away.

David was sure that the number of movie-star sightings was exaggerated, as was the grand significance of other locations of, in Kwan's words, "extraordinary importance." However, David played along with his guide and found himself fascinated by the flamboyant accounts of pirates, rumrunners, and smugglers who "plied these waters" surrounding Santa Catalina.

As the tour drew to a close, David still had several questions about the island, especially if it might be his eventual permanent home. Housing and employment topped his concerns. He also wanted to know more about Kwan, who reminded David of a young character from an old Charlie Chan detective movie.

When they arrived back at the ferry, Kwan drew up Biscuits, who required little restraint. Although his tour time had expired, David did not move from his seat next to Kwan.

"Kwan, your knowledge of Avalon and Santa Catalina is impressive. Pride in your home is obvious and a credit to both you and Catalina. You learned this in school?" Cautious with his inquiries, David attempted to flatter Kwan in hopes of continuing their conversation. However, Kwan's answer took him aback.

"I quit school three weeks ago, sir."

"What? Why? You're a bright kid."

"Good schools on mainland. Too expensive."

"You find a way! Nowadays, school is a must if you want to get ahead. Were you born here?"

"Born in Korea. I'm not citizen, and neither is Papa."

"Papa? Who's that? Your father?"

"Sure you really want hear about me? It's nothing special like Avalon and Santa Catalina." Biscuits shook her head, stomped her right hoof twice, and expelled an impatient whinny, as if ready for the barn or pasture.

"You don't look Korean." For fear of being misunderstood or insulting, David lightheartedly added, "Neither does Biscuits!" At the sound of her name, Biscuits again shook her head and whinnied, this time with authority.

"I am Korean, at least mother is, and so is Papa." Out of the corner of his eye, Kwan scanned the dock for potential customers.

David followed Kwan down from the carriage. The two stood next to Biscuits while Kwan smoothed her withers with a hairy curry brush he'd retrieved from beneath the seat. As he groomed Biscuits, he began to tell his story while continuously scanning the area, presumably on the lookout for future business.

It was early afternoon, and the dock was located in the heart of the business district, but the area seemed altogether quiet to David. A couple of fishing boats looked as if they were preparing to take out small charters for some deep-sea fishing. On the far side of the bay, a sailing school taught students how to right small, capsized sailboats, much to the pleasure of the youthful sailors overboard. All outward appearances portrayed an out-of-the-way, relaxed island community. David continued to be impressed with Santa Catalina, as well as Kwan's independent personality and sense of responsibility. To be a mentor for a young man like Kwan would be a pleasure.

"I don't remember Father. Have just few memories of Mema. No pictures. What I know, Papa tell me. He big talker."

"It runs in the family." David patted Kwan on the shoulder. "Kwan must be a Korean name?"

"Yes, sir. Papa tell me Dad was an officer in the American Army. They show up late for big war, and so some were sent to Korea when we were divided between Communist and the South at thirty-eighth parallel. You've heard of it? When Americans left, Father stayed because he and Mema married. I already born."

"I don't understand though. How did you end up here?"

"Papa tell me when war start, we live in Seoul. Father rejoin the Tenth Corp who pushed Communists back. He was in Chosin Reservoir battle with Chinese. You've heard of it? December, 1950, I think. Very cold. Troops called 'The Chosin Few.' They should have called them 'The Frozen Chosin.' Most died. Papa say father froze to death."

"Kwan, I'm so sorry to hear that … it must've been a difficult battle for him and for many others. But I will say that the Chosin Reservoir sounds familiar. I tried to follow the Korean War, but that was over ten years ago. You know, they already call Korea the forgotten war?"

David was drawn to history, especially war stories. He remembered a couple of discussions with his wife and parents about the possibility of reenlisting in 1950 and how they were all opposed, himself included, considering his growing career. At that time, he and his father were in the process of expanding their hardware business, and neither wanted an interruption in their plans.

"Papa not forget. If he has way, I not forget. He talk about it all time."

"Do you remember it, Kwan? The war?"

"Not really, just what Papa tell me. I only toddler then."

"Where's your mother—Mema? And how did you end up here?"

"Mema captured by Red Army as we escape. Papa say she cover for us but never catch up to us. We got away on old freighter. We run from war. I don't remember. We never be able to find what happen to Mema. But maybe someday."

"I'm sorry. So how did you end up here in California?"

"Papa tell me we sail to Formosa. Lots of people sail Formosa. You know, Taiwan now? Maybe a year. From there, I don't know. I remember getting off large boat here in Avalon. They gave me chocolate ice cream cone. Papa got job as grounds keeper for rich lady. I was four. We live on her estate. I'm almost sixteen. Papa eighty-two. He doesn't do much work, but he speaks English a little. Rich lady,

Mrs. Stockbridge, depend on me more. She gave me Biscuits three years ago. She has two other horses I take care of."

"You should be in school; you're so bright, Kwan. Are there schools on Catalina?"

"I need help Papa and take care of Biscuits." Kwan patted the horse's neck, clicked his tongue twice and retrieved a small apple from under the carriage seat. He held the apple in the palm of his hand while he offered it to Biscuits. She gobbled up the apple, slobbering while bobbing her head up and down with obvious pleasure.

"Look! Biscuits agrees with me that you are smart and need to be in school," David said, smiling at the two.

"Maybe someday. Right now, I need you to pay, and Biscuits need another passenger."

David pulled his wallet from his back pocket, found a five-dollar bill and two ones and handed them to Kwan. "The five is for the excellent tour, and here is an extra one for the driver and one for Biscuits. Best deal on the island."

"We thank you, sir. Say, are you for or from?"

"What do you mean, 'for or from'?" David asked.

"A single man. First time. No specific place to find. Experience tell me you run *from*, not *for*. Like Papa and me. I'm right, Mr. Dan?"

David chuckled, pondering the question. Kwan's observation displayed an insight well beyond his years. David stared at his interrogator for a few seconds then simply responded, "Okay." The answer satisfied neither, but both were ready to move on.

"Thank you, sir. You are gentleman of good taste. Speak of taste, you may want to check out Avalon Café." Kwan pointed toward the restaurant and told David to tell them Kwan had sent him. Kwan added that he worked there from five to eight in the kitchen, learning to cook.

Kwan's suggestion tempted David. Having eaten nothing since coffee at 7 a.m., he thanked Kwan and started in the direction of the café. Then he stopped, looked back over his shoulder, and shouted at Kwan to get back in school. "A smart guy like you can figure a way."

Kwan had already cornered two matronly ladies. He assured them of a smooth, relaxed, and informative journey, "best deal on the island." If he heard David's command, it went unacknowledged.

The Avalon Café lived up to Kwan's introduction. David stuffed himself on a delicious seafood platter accented with spicy-hot cocktail sauce and a healthy serving of coleslaw. After eating his fill, and with time on his hands, he decided to meander the streets of Avalon. Again, he liked everything he saw of the quiet island town and its unhurried residents. In many ways, it was a stark contrast to the Midwestern agricultural community he had left behind. Then a stroll near the water's edge brought back pleasant memories of long walks along the shore of Lake Michigan. Eventually, he returned to the dock to wait for the 5 p.m. ferry to take him back to the mainland. Satisfied with what he could expect on the island of Santa Catalina, he looked forward to a relaxed return crossing.

The calm morning cruise from Long Beach had lived up to his starry-eyed fantasy and lent support to move forward with a long-sought but undisclosed yearning. Catalina's relative isolation as a low-key tourist destination, a getaway for a few affluent Californians, and a generally tranquil environment all beckoned David. He glanced at the Bulova wristwatch his parents had given him for his high school graduation. It would not hurt to reconfirm the length of time it would take to cross from island to mainland.

Since his morning cruise, the ocean had become choppy with large white-capped swells nudging the eighty-five-foot passenger ferry from side to side. David held on to the first deck's three-foot-high guard rail as he watched Santa Catalina recede from view. An occasional wisp of salty spray forced him to turn his head away from the wind. At first, the fresh ocean air felt exhilarating but soon brought with it a tinge of discomfort. Being at liberty to move about the deck helped combat a sense of uneasiness David had detected growing in the pit of his stomach. He decided against climbing the stairs for the views from the upper deck where more of the ship's rolling sensation would be felt. Instead, he entered the main central cabin in search of more stability. After a couple of minutes inside, he changed his mind in favor of the fresh ocean air and a rail to hold on to.

In November 1940, near the end of his first year of Coast Guard duty, David experienced seasickness, but that was on the seventy-two-foot Coast Guard cutter *Beaver Island* in the Mackinaw Straits. An early and fierce winter storm caught several weekend yachters by surprise, and the Coast Guard had been called to rescue them. Though David's illness had been short-lived, its memory endured as the worst feeling possible short of death—a condition he never intended to revisit. Yet today, he felt its nauseous tentacles creep higher with each pitch and reel of the ferry.

Several passengers, waddled along the rails of the ferry's two decks. Some grasped the rails in general enjoyment of a marvelous September day. They scanned the water in innocent wonder, as if discovering the ocean for the first time. Three coeds wearing Bermuda shorts with bikini tops held their tanned faces up toward the wind, their long iron-pressed hair flowing out behind. An ever-expanding flock of seagulls winged about the ship's stern where elementary-age children tossed popcorn into the air. Both children and gulls seemed to revel in the airborne meal.

Near the end of this late summer afternoon, a light-blue sky played host to wispy, white clouds. Santa Catalina had disappeared from view, and the California coast still lingered beneath the eastern horizon. Within this tranquil setting, David's uneasiness continued to grow. His seafood lunch schooled forth for a possible return run through his esophagus. *Why had I insisted on a second serving?* His wet knuckles turned white in his near-death grip on the guard rail. He feared Long Beach would not arrive in time to save him.

In an effort to distract himself and ward off an impending convulsion, David fixed his attention on a volunteer convoy of dolphins, the gleeful focus of noisy sightseers along the deck above. More passengers gathered at the rails to marvel at the sleek swimmers whose pewter bodies sliced knife-like through the dark-blue swells. Unfortunately, the playful saltwater spectacle did nothing to relieve David's mounting distress.

Someone shouted, "Whales behind the ship!" David turned to see several fellow passengers pointing. Sure enough, a pod of orcas cut across the ferry's wake less than one hundred yards back. As David watched the glossy, black-and-white creatures, the thought crossed his mind that they or he may be on an endangered species course. However, he lost concentration as throwing-up drew near.

A loud-mouthed upper-deck passenger, more interested in personal attention than attention to the orcas, broadcasted for the entire eastern Pacific, "Now that's what I call cruisin' the coast!" Realizing he amused only himself, he jump-switched to academics but in the same bombastic manner. "The pod of orcas we see, erroneously referred to as killer whales by the less informed, is heading south to calf, most likely in the Gulf of California."

"You don't say," muttered a leathery, old salt attached to the rail next to David. "They're headed south. He got that right."

David wanted to support the critique but knew it was best to keep his mouth shut.

The self-appointed maritime orator continued, "Is it fair to call them American wetbacks?" He laughed but with a conspicuous lack of accompaniment. Other passengers either didn't understand his meaning or didn't want to acknowledge the buffoon. As for David, he felt too sick to care. He stared straight ahead and braced for the inevitable.

The old salt, who appeared to be Polynesian, grumped, "We call 'em *haoles*."

"What's a how-lee?" David slurred. For a brief moment, he tried to ignore the turmoil rumbling up within.

"Haole's what we call a mainlander on Lanai, where I'm from."

"Is that in the Hawaiian Islands?" moaned David while holding his stomach.

"You a haole?" The crease-faced, old man smiled through worn, brown teeth. "Lanai is the most beautiful of the islands. My home. You go there?"

"Not my plan. But maybe—ohhhh!" David gripped the handrail as if his life depended on it. His eyes watered, and against his will, he lurched forward, slamming into and bending his midsection over the restraining barrier. The old man recoiled as a foul-smelling spray erupted from David's mouth and spread with lumpy tracers toward the innocent dolphins skimming the surface below. "I'm sorr—" he began, but before he could fully straighten to apologize, a second oral eruption with equal force and heavier shrapnel thrust him again into the rail. His abdomen cramped, and a yellowish substance oozed from his nostrils, filling him with a drowning sensation.

For a second time, David attempted to straighten himself, but dry cramping heaves would not allow it. He had attracted the attention of other passengers who seemed to find him a more interesting entertainment than the aquatic wildlife. Several now pointed in his direction, but none rushed to help. The hardened Hawaiian was the only one to show concern. "You need coconut milk," he said.

"Ahhh, I'm sick." David wiped his lips and beads of sweat along his forehead with his shirt cuff and sleeve. "What's coconut milk?" His voice again slurred with another involuntary abdominal contraction.

"They sell coconuts to haoles on the dock. You will make it. Only thirty minutes."

"Not soon enough," David said. At that point, he wasn't sure he wanted to make it, just wanted the sickness to end. He nodded at the old man but could manage no more reaction than that. He turned back over the rail, held his stomach with his left hand, and resumed dry heaves, unable to hack up more than a righteous remnant of foul-tasting bile.

Half an hour later, David collapsed on one of the benches lining the Long Beach Pier, eyes closed, forearms on thighs, and forehead held in his hands. When he opened his eyes, he could only stare downward at the worn planks. He could not immediately recall what had happened or how he'd gotten there. A bent and crusty old Hawaiian holding a large hairy, brown coconut in his two hands moseyed down the pier in David's direction.

"Here," he said, holding out the coconut. "Drink this."

David looked up through water-filled eyes without recognition. However, he soon recognized the Good Samaritan as the old man he'd met on the ferry. Confused, he received the coconut and asked, "What am I supposed to do with this?"

The Hawaiian pointed to the hole carved in the top of the coconut. "Drink. Make you feel better."

Eager for relief, David did as instructed, albeit clumsily. Coconut milk leaked from the corners of his mouth and ran down his neck. He did not attempt to wipe off the spilled milk as he held the coconut with both hands.

"I think I'll sit here for a while. Thanks."

"You come to Lanai." The old man shuffled away back down the wharf. All David could do was watch in silence. Then he lifted the coconut for another drink.

CHAPTER 3

Long Beach, California

Twelve hours later, David opened his eyes but did not see the grainy, black, mold outline around the water-stained ceiling tiles above him. He lacked wakefulness. However, as the minutes passed, his awareness grew.

A rhythmic pounding in his head matched the thump in his chest, his heart laboring as if waking had been a strenuous endeavor. *Still dehydrated*, he thought. He felt body aches from head to toe and bruises about his abdomen. Blinking several times to clear the sleep from his eyes, David turned his head toward the light, but the sensitivity caused him to shield his eyes with one hand.

Sunlight streamed through a cloudy window next to the door. As his sticky cranial cobwebs retreated, David realized he was in the same seedy motel room he'd rented a day earlier before boarding the 10:30 a.m. Shoreline Ferry for Santa Catalina. He turned to discover a coconut seated on the bedside stand.

As wakefulness continued very slowly, he tried to trace through the events of the previous day: the quick stop in Santa Monica, the cruise to Santa Catalina Island, Kwan's carriage tour of Avalon, the ill-fated meal, and the blustery return by ferry. In fits and starts, his Santa Catalina day trip came back to him, reminding him of the grainy, sixteen-millimeter newsreels his high school history teacher had shown the class whenever she lacked a lesson plan.

At first, David could barely move more than his encrusted eyes. Plus, he feared rekindling yesterday's nauseating bout of seasickness. Finally, his gaze returned to the bedside stand and the large, hairy coconut. David took a long, slow breath. Behind the coconut sat a shoebox-sized, red, plastic radio alarm clock. Ten minutes after eight.

"Ten after eight?" Panicked, he sat up and grumbled aloud, "Damn it! I'm late." He rolled out of bed but momentarily lost his balance as he tried to stand up and fell butt-first back on the bed. Restarting, he gathered himself up then snowshoed to the bathroom. First order of business: clean his eyelids and remove the foul taste from his mouth. He vigorously brushed his teeth, shaved in a hurry, and showered, each step carried out with lukewarm water. The shower made him more alert. Not perfect but a whole lot better.

After dressing, he examined his souvenir coconut and pondered whether the Hawaiian's seasickness remedy really worked. He hoped to meet up with that old man again. He would definitely cross paths with Kwan. What did the boy mean, "Running *for* or running *from?*" With no time to reconsider, David Dailey was on a mission.

He closed the door on his way out and slid his suitcase into the Chevy's back seat. Then he rushed back into the room, retrieved the coconut, and placed it in the shotgun seat next to him.

It took only a couple of minutes to get to Charlie's Boat & Bait Shop, a business he'd made a mental note of twenty-four hours earlier. Charlie's was next to the southernmost Long Beach pier and ferry-boat landing, the perfect take-off point for a diversionary strategy.

After only a quick view of Long Beach the day before, David was in awe of the size and bustle of the California seaport. Huge cargo ships moved throughout the harbor, while others were loaded and unloaded. Several more ships waited in a queue offshore. It was a robust, economic atmosphere. David shuddered and ducked when a jumbo cargo plane roared low overhead. He could feel the ground tremble as the huge, lumbering plane passed, reminding him of his childhood fear of thunderstorms. Several signs pointed the way to both the McDonald Aircraft and the Douglas Aerospace installations. Clearly, industrial plants specializing in national defense manufacturing were plentiful hereabouts.

David recalled that Long Beach had been built on an active oil field, both on shore and beneath the ocean's floor. The sounds and smells of a thriving industrial center invigorated him and reminded him of being back in Chicago. However, the salty air stirred acrid memories of the boat ride back from Avalon. At that time, his arrival in the bustling seaport passed without memory of anything other than his helpless state of illness.

Now he resolved to forge ahead, determined to be on the 10:30 a.m. ferry. As the sun rose higher, so did David's resolve. No time to waste. He'd seen the finish line, and it was only twenty-six miles away, almost within sight. Ironically, he needed a simple rowboat to launch the final leg of his journey.

"What's up, Doc?" asked the emaciated hippy stationed behind, but lying on, the greasy linoleum-covered counter inside Charlie's. A cigarette balanced above the young man's left ear, partially covered by his scraggly hair, and a mangy goatee protruded beneath his lower lip. David guessed that the kid, like so many of his generation, was a twenty-something in search of an identity and rebelling against his parents. He looked like a cheap, disheveled imitation of Ichabod Crane.

"May I rent a boat? Say, a fourteen-footer?"

"If you gots the bread, I gots the cheese." The renegade's laconic response was delivered with a distinct lack of enthusiasm. However, in time, he did manage to struggle to a full upright stance of about six-foot-four, little more than half a foot below the grimy fishnet-covered ceiling joists. David, though amused by the ungainly youth's colorful manner of speech, knew he would never hire such a creature to work for him. A pleasant vision of his family-owned business flashed in his mind, tidy, clean, and inviting. As much as he sometimes resented being caught up in the family business, he knew it thrived under his supervision.

"How much bread are we talking?"

"Depends."

"On what?"

"What you wants the cheese for, and how long you wants it."

"What do you care what I want it for?"

"Listen up, Doc. If you wants to haul ammo or homemade hooch to terra incognita, that-a-be *mucho dinero*."

"Let's make this easy. I want to go fishin' for two or three hours. What's the charge?"

"You wants a motor? You needs a motor. I gots what you needs if you gots what I needs."

"Can you tell me where I might best catch fish?"

"Yes, buddy."

"Where?"

"About three miles down the shore, near a rocky point. Can't miss it, Doc. Big rocks."

"And you guarantee me fish, eh?" David was satisfied his fishing trip ploy was swallowed hook, line, and sinker.

"If you has the right gear … I gots that too."

"I got all the gear I need. But I'll take the motor."

"Gots-ya, Doc. But don't get too close to them rocks, or the fish'll be usin' *you* for bait."

Chief Ichabod's description of a somewhat precarious fishing location pleased David. He needed to get started right away. "How much for the boat and motor?"

"Twenty-five bills for three hours, boat, and motor—up front. Driver's license for security."

David reached for his wallet. "Hold time, Doc!" The Chief raised his voice along with his right hand.

"What?"

"You gots a fishin' license?"

"I need a license to fish in the ocean?"

"If you wants to fish. It's the law, man. Sign's on the wall."

After considering the various license options listed on a mimeographed sheet of yellow legal paper, David said, "Okay, where can I get a one-day license?"

"I gots the cheese if you gots the bread."

"Okay, okay. Let's go. Give me a license. Do you rent rods and reels here too?"

"Yes, buddy."

"Is there anything you don't sell here?"

"That depends, Doc."

"Okay, okay. Can we settle up? There's a sea bass waiting for me." David pulled out his wallet again, his urgency amplified by the putrid fish smell inside the bait shop. It had stirred his queasy stomach, and he felt a sudden need for fresh air.

"Hold time, Doc."

"What now?"

"Don't gots any boats."

"Listen, Chief, you said you had the cheese."

"Yes, buddy. But not now. All our ships are on the seas. Be here at seven in the mornin'. We'll have your boat and motor."

"Can I rent a boat somewhere else? I need one now, right now."

"Negative. Leastways, not 'tween here and Hog Island."

"Is that in the Pacific?"

The young man lit a Chesterfield and squinted as he blew out a lazy, white smoke ring that drifted toward the open door. "'Bout ten miles south, Doc."

"That won't work." David's quick search for an alternative came up empty. "Okay, I'll be here first thing in the morning." For his plan to work, he needed to rent a boat in close proximity to the ferry.

"If you're not here by seven-thirty, you won't gets the boat. What's your name?"

"Doc! And I'll be here at seven. Scout's honor." David made the three finger Boy Scouts salute, turned, and strode toward the door. But before exiting Charlie's, he turned back, "May I leave my car here in the morning?"

"If you gots—"

"I know. You gots the cheese."

Rocky coast? Three miles? Perfect.

The three-mile drive down to the rocky outcrop the kid had suggested was as crooked as a dog's hind leg and considerably more than three miles by car. David swung into a gas station and coffee shop with no intention of buying either; he needed directions. However, a large black coffee and two Little Debbie Swiss Rolls did clear a few tenacious mental cobwebs and help settle his stomach after yesterday's bout with seasickness. Twice he complained to the coconut who bounced and rolled aimlessly on the seat next to him.

Following the gas station attendant's convoluted directions to Chief Ichabod's fishing hole required all David's concentration. But with some resourceful country-boy reconnoitering, he found the destination. Once David got out there to the water's edge, the kid's description of the area became clear. Large boulders were strewn along the shore in front of low cliffs with sharp, rocky outcroppings. The surf was choppy with four-foot breakers one hundred yards offshore. A pounding surf along the rugged shoreline provided enough hazards to make a fatal accident possible, if not probable. Planning one's accidental death in order to mask one's disappearance into the lap of paradise seemed more literary than real, though, and David tried to steer clear of that sort of thinking.

The area possessed a natural charm, still untouched by the creep of urban sprawl. This undeveloped setting pleasantly surprised David. A wildlife trail paralleled the shoreline, which David could use in the morning to facilitate an undetected return walk to Charlie's and the ferry. The fact that he saw no one either along the shore or on boats out in the water was an added plus. His plan, now timetable amended, must proceed unnoticed if his premeditated disappearance was to be successful.

Following reconnaissance for the next day's bogus fishing trip, David had the balance of the day and, until seven o'clock the next morning, to kill. After considerable thought and a return stop for a second cup of coffee, he decided to drive back up to Santa Monica to better check out where his brother lived. He did not intend to meet with Larry, although that had been his justification to his wife and mother for a solo trip halfway across the country. He simply wanted a sneak corroboration of his brother's lifestyle, one he had so long coveted and even longer resented—a life he was certain his brother had reveled in since high school.

A slow, wearisome drive north required driving straight through midtown Los Angeles. It was far too strange and frenetic to be tiresome. Unfamiliar Asian and Latin American cultures blended with equally unfamiliar, intertwined expressways and cloverleafs choked with urban traffic. David was stressed; he was not accustomed to any of this. However, with plenty of time on his hands, he decided to stop for a leisurely lunch in the heart of LA. That proved to be a longer stop and more expensive than he had anticipated due to his inability to locate a convenient parking place, find a suitable restaurant, and decipher a peculiar menu. By the time he parked the car, he was ravenous. The chicken fajitas were not bad, and the time spent in the Mexican restaurant was a welcome respite from the big-city hubbub.

Following lunch, his return to driving in close quarters accompanied by agitated drivers reignited his anxious mood, especially for his car's welfare. Even though he planned to abandon his beloved Chevy after this trip west, he needed to protect her until the end. Since the day she arrived, special order, he'd maintained his car in mint running condition, kept her exterior washed and waxed and the interior spotless. All who knew David knew he treasured his Chevrolet Bel Air.

A brief scare shook him when a cab driver shouted, "Get the fuck out of the way!" while pounding on his horn and swerving in front of David halfway through a congested intersection. When David realized what had happened, he became even more nervous. Although he navigated through the teeming city streets without any further incident, he despised the confusing, crowded conditions aggravated by the thick and murky air hanging low over the city.

"Relax, Mr. Coconut," he told his silent passenger. "You're not in Kansas anymore." With his right hand, David found the shaggy-haired coconut and rolled him closer. David possessed a well-honed habit of quoting lines from literature and movies, even when he was the only one around to be amused by it.

Shortly before five o'clock, David spotted a sign that read: Welcome to Santa Monica, End of Historic Route 66. He breathed a sigh of relief even as he considered his impending return drive back through the city. Of course, the angelic image of Santa Catalina Island remained, inviting him to the end of his journey.

From the glove compartment, he retrieved the slip of paper his mom had given him with his brother's name and address: *Larry Dailey, 210-A, Olympic St., Santa Monica, Calif.*" Once David entered Santa Monica, he followed signs to the pier and easily found an open parking space in an enormous beachside parking lot. Although tempted by the many amusement-style attractions on and around the pier, he decided to first have a second look at exactly where Larry lived. He felt confident his brother would most likely be out at that time of day. Consulting the metropolitan map his mother had insisted he take, he had no problem finding Larry's circled and yellow-highlighted address. It was now so close and somewhat familiar, he decided to get out of the car and walk.

Discreet and spacious residential streets lined with a few well-maintained, single-family homes and lots of townhouses caught David's eye as a stark contrast to Long Beach and Los Angeles. Stately royal palms shaded every street as balmy ocean breezes swept past the contented tanned faces on sidewalks and porches. And Larry lived just three blocks from the shore. As David walked, he took in everything—the people, their living conditions, the clean air—everything. In vigilance, he kept an eye out for his brother. He did not want to run into Larry. *What a place! Larry's got it made.* David saw it was a paradise by the sea, just as he had anticipated.

Now he walked with purpose, investigating while looking over his shoulder for his brother. He breathed easier when he surmised no one was home at 210-A Olympic St. Taking in the surrounding four blocks occupied his attention for the next hour. In short conversations with three separate people, he asked each if they knew of or had seen Larry Dailey. "A sandy-haired guy, about five-six, approximately a hundred fifty pounds, early forties?"

Responses to his inquiries were abrupt and impersonal. No one knew or had heard of Larry Dailey. Eventually, he wandered back down to the pier and sat down on a park bench, one with a great view of the ocean. On the back of the paper scrap, David now wrote down an amended plan:

1. Pick up boat from Chief Ichabod at 7 a.m./leave license, keys, and car.
2. Approx. 1 hr. to fishing hole, give or take—8:30 arrive.
3. Attach old three oaks sweatshirt to boat, capsize.
4. Approx. 1 ½ hr. to hike trail back to Charlie's.
5. With 2nd set of keys get suitcase from car.
6. One way ticket on 10:30 ferry to Santa Catalina.
7. End of Trail.

After jotting down his escape timetable, he reviewed his plan twice for reassurance. In particular, were there sufficient clues left to reveal the tragedy but not too many to appear staged. He folded the paper and put it in his wallet. Rested and ready, he decided to walk past Larry's house one last time before heading back to Long Beach.

While standing on the corner a half-block down from 210-A, a short, wrinkle-faced Asian woman selling flowers stumbled into him. Taken off guard, he stammered out an apology, although he was clearly not at fault. In a repentant manner, David bought two red dahlias at one dollar each. After paying the flower lady, he asked, "Do you happen to know a Larry Dailey, 'bout forty?" David held up his hand to approximate Larry's height. "Sandy hair."

"Maybe. Who wants to know?"

"I'm an old friend of his from way back in high school."

The flower lady tilted her head to one side. "You sure you're a friend?" She looked David up and down and then glanced along the street as if someone might be watching.

"Friend, that's all. Haven't seen Larry in years," David responded, smiling.

"You're not from California?"

"No, just visiting. Knew Larry Dailey when we were kids."

With head still tilted to one side, she continued to assess David. Then she said, "Always buys one red dahlia. Works hard. That's all I know." The lady spoke matter-of-factly and with no noticeable accent.

"I've knocked at his door, but no one's home. Do you know where I might find him?"

The flower lady tilted her head to the other side and smiled. "You like my flowers? Mr. Dailey always buys my flowers."

Recognizing the solicitation, David said, "May I buy four more dahlias? Half a dozen will make a nice bouquet, don't you think?"

Her eyes brightened. "You betcha, young fella." She searched through a bulky flower box at her feet and selected four more dahlias, wrapped a damp newspaper page around the stems, and secured them with a rubber band. Then she presented them to David.

He handed the flower lady a five-dollar bill for which he received four dahlias and no change. Although he had anticipated a dollar in return, he smiled and accepted the circumstances. She had, indeed, given him some helpful information.

"They tell me Mr. Dailey went to the hospital. That's all I know."

As much as he cajoled the woman, the only additional information David could glean from her was an approximate direction to Santa Monica General. Not sure why Larry might be at the hospital, David determined he would have to find out before returning to Long Beach. Avoiding direct contact should not present a problem. After all, to see Larry in person could and probably would destroy his escape plan.

Might Larry be visiting someone in the hospital or possibly working there? As David drove across Santa Monica, concern for his brother's well-being began to weigh on his mind. If he'd been admitted, there was no benign reason for it, at least no good one David could think of.

Larry had graduated from high school in 1941, two years behind David. David recalled his brother's dogged determination to graduate then leave Three Oaks as soon as possible and head for California. At that time, lots of people were heading out West. Larry's parents were opposed to him going out on his own so early but ultimately caved-in to his strong-willed badgering. However, they insisted David accompany his brother. "You help Larry get settled. The trip will be good for you both."

That had been in the early summer of 1941, twenty-two years earlier. Lots changed in the country and in Santa Monica since then. What had been a sleepy little US Highway 1 beach turnout on the west side of Los Angeles was now a tourist destination along the ever-more-popular Southern California coast. Warm, sunny days accented by fresh ocean air and a perpetual blue sky easily encouraged a year-round outdoor life. Bohemian Venice Beach adjacent to the south and scenic Pacific Palisades to the north drew thousands annually to this West Coast paradise.

David inhaled the idyllic place and time. It was every bit the longed-for object of his imagination. As David looked for his brother's home and then the hospital, the beauty and casual excitement of Santa Monica sounded in his ears like a beckon. Three Oaks was sterile and gray in comparison, like an old, black-and-white movie. Santa Monica was exciting with Color by Deluxe! And Santa Catalina called even louder in David's imagination now.

Over the years, the Daileys had longed for Larry's return. His mother had continued to pray for such. To the dismay of all, though, Larry had never shown the least inclination to move back to their rural village of Three Oaks, Michigan. David expected his brother would never return for anything more than a short visit and then only to gloat over some exotic vacation or grandiose business adventure he had completed or was anticipating.

By the time David arrived at Santa Monica General, his emotions confounded him. He was uneasy with emerging doubts about continuing with his early morning "fishing" plans while at the same time assuring himself to stay the course. When asked for a second opinion, Mr. Coconut declined to comment.

CHAPTER 4

Santa Monica, California

At Santa Monica General, his thoughts focused on concern for his long-estranged brother. David's inability to find a vacant space in the hospital's parking deck, despite countless caution laps around the five-floor facility, served to elevate his concern to a twinge of apprehension. Finally, he managed to park along an unkempt side street clogged with old automobiles, over a half-mile walk from the hospital. As a rule, he avoided parking his prized Chevy on any street, let alone a street in a questionable neighborhood. After only a few steps, he returned to the car to make sure the passenger-side door was secure. While checking the lock, he heard the slam of a screen door behind him.

From a swaybacked front portico came the roar of a shirtless man with a huge stomach protruding from each side of tattered bib overalls. "You block my driveway!" A robust wad of spittle subdivided his declaration. "There'll be hell to pay!"

Although in a hurry, David paused to evaluate the Chevy's position. The back bumper was a good yard beyond the big man's two-track dirt driveway but only half a car length from a damaged curbside fire hydrant in front.

"We're good," David said. With a contrived, cordial wave to the driveway guardian, David struck out to find his brother, leaving Mr. Coconut to guard the car. He hustled past ramshackle tenements, some with porch occupants lounging on mismatched living-room furniture.

The neighborhood was obviously in the throes of urban renewal and the decline that accompanied human displacement.

The well-being of both his brother and now his car compounded David's distress. If Larry had a job at the hospital or was visiting there for any number of reasons, those would be good things. In either scenario, he'd go back to his car and head for Long Beach. But if Larry had been admitted … not a good thing. The latter case might alter his plan. What he knew for sure, now, was a crafty flower lady had sold him an overpriced bouquet of droopy, red dahlias now wilting away in the backseat.

Upon entering the hospital, David walked straight to an information kiosk in the center of a cavernous lobby crowded with weary faces in search of an appropriate place to sit down. Some sat on the floor, others sat on marble, perimeter windowsills. A middle-aged woman, wearing a Depression-era thick floral drape, dispensed rote information. She sat beneath a hat reminiscent of the front wheel of a child's tricycle, festooned with delicate, pink peony blooms.

David was second in line behind a short, stout, black-bearded gentleman. A boisterous fellow, the man argued his case to have a parking deck voucher stamped.

"Excuse me," David interrupted. "I need to locate a patient, my brother." If he could determine Larry was not a patient, it would answer his fundamental question and go a long way toward fulfillment of the hoped-for plan tucked in his wallet.

"Stay in line, sir. I'll be with you in your turn," squeaked the snippy botanical garden. Without looking up, she returned to a verbatim oral reading of the hospital's parking manual.

After what seemed an eternity, the information bouquet bid the persistent man a dismissive "good day" and bobbed her headdress toward David. "Step forward, young man. How may I direct you?"

Surprised by an unexpected upsurge of clove-scented perfume, David momentarily lost his train of thought. Clearing his throat, he asked, "Where can I find Lawrence Dailey? He may be a patient."

"And are you a close relative?" she asked.

"He's my brother."

The attendant licked her rubber-covered thumb and leafed through an admissions directory the size of a Sears & Roebuck catalog. "Let's see D … D-a … here he is. Fourth floor ICU. Next?"

"And I see you too," David said, to which he was greeted by a blank stare. "Sorry." David swallowed. "What does I-C-U mean?"

"Sir, that happens to be our intensive care unit. If you can get in at all, visiting hours will close at eight. No exceptions. Next?"

Jostled from behind, David held his position at the front of the line. "How do I get there?"

The woman pointed to a bank of elevators at the back of the lobby while rubber-necking around David. "Next, please."

David entered the ICU through two sets of double, steel doors. The long, narrow hallway before him was claustrophobic, with only a quick-stepping nurse or two darting in and out of lateral rooms. David's senses became choked with the strange, yet familiar, medical atmosphere—the hushed, hurried voices of nurses; the stinging smell of disinfectant; and the heaviness of imposed quiet. He forced a swallow around a hard lump in his throat.

He had become distracted, his mind racing between worry for his brother's health and the possibility of being forced into abandoning his planned disappearance. Again, he resolved to wait and see.

He walked down the empty hall and turned a corner, where things changed. Several people partially blocked his path. He made his way, careful not to step on a rugged-looking man sound asleep in a camo sleeping bag. Then he skirted three preschoolers at play on the floor, making zooming noises with matchbox cars. Eventually, he found a path through to a cluttered nurses' station. "Take a seat. You will be called," the nurse manning the counter told him.

"But I need to see my brother. How late are visiting hours?"

"Forty-five more minutes."

"What if I'm not called?"

"You may come back in the morning and try again."

"But I won't be here in the morning."

"Sir, please be seated."

David sat down in a faded-green, vinyl chair with no armrests, one of three chairs in the hallway and the only one unoccupied. He looked around the makeshift waiting area but wasn't interested in striking up a conversation. Getting in to see Larry before closing time was top priority. He picked up a coverless *Sports Illustrated* magazine. A table of contents headline reported, "Mantle and Maris, Getting Older." *They're not the only ones*, David thought.

Twenty minutes passed. David gave up hope of being allowed in to see his brother before visiting hours ended. He might lose the night already paid for at the Long Beach motel, and he would have to decide about Santa Catalina and the ferry—then amend the schedule he'd already amended once.

At the moment of his complete resignation to fate, the door to the inner sanctum of the ICU swung open and jolted him out of the doldrums. A tall, fit, no-nonsense nurse marched into the waiting area. Her uniform was starched white from hat to shoes. "Mr. Dailey!" she barked. David looked up and was astonished to see how many more people were now milling around in the congested hallway waiting area.

David stood up. "Yes, I'm David Dailey. May I go in?"

"In a minute, sir." The detail-attentive nurse reviewed her clipboard. "Sir, what is your relationship to the patient, Mr. Lawrence Dailey? And I will need to see identification."

Recalling his earlier encounter at Charlie's Boat & Bait, David pulled out his wallet and handed the nurse his driver's license. "We're brothers."

"Hmm, so say you. And where is Three Oaks, Michigan?"

David held up his right hand to illustrate the map of Michigan, and with his left pinky and index finger, he pointed to the location of Three Oaks and its relationship to Detroit.

"Interesting. That's exactly what Mr. Dailey did. I guess there really is a Three Oaks?"

"Yes, ma'am."

The nurse led David through another set of doors and down another hallway. In a low but firm, cold whisper, she said, "He's resting comfortably under a mild sedative. He's had a long day, several tests. You don't really look like brothers." She gave David a blank but questioning glance.

"We are. I'm just over two years older." It was hard to gauge the nurse's real interest because she maintained a strict, indifferent demeanor.

"Dr. Anderson wants Mr. Dailey to stay with us for at least tonight and will expect to have a conference with the two of you before discharge. You may go in. You have twenty-five minutes. He's in the second carousel on the left."

"How does the doctor know me?" David asked, despite feeling impatient to see his brother.

"Dr. Anderson requires a patient advocate to be present at discharge and to see the patient home safely. I assume that's you, brother Dailey," the nurse said. She turned with her clipboard and marched back toward the nurse's desk.

Larry looked better than expected considering he was a patient in an intensive care unit of a large urban hospital. The order of those events had not been determined. Fortunately, he had broken no bones. David was confused about his brother's condition but still weighing his options for the next day. Should he hang around to care for Larry, or could he steal away to his paradise? He smiled as he thought to himself, *What would Kwan think of my predicament?*

At first, Larry appeared lethargic, probably the result of medication. However, his heavy eyelids snapped to life the instant he recognized his brother. He sat straight up in bed and flashed an enormous smile.

"Who are you, and where did you come from?" Larry half-shouted in a delightful welcome to his brother.

"Oh, just passing through and thought I'd pop in," David responded, unable to mask personal pleasure behind a phony poker face.

"Hey!" said Larry, glancing from side to side. "What did you think of my nurse? I wouldn't kick *her* out of bed, right?" Larry continued his brash, brotherly greeting filled with pleasurable excitement.

The two men shared several moments of frenzied reception, often kidding one another about their sexual prowess or lack thereof. Their excited banter made it hard to understand each other, but neither cared. Their pleasure was mutual and genuine. They unwittingly drew the attention of other unseen ICU patients and staff.

As the initial enthusiasm of their reunion receded, David took a slow look around to make sure a certain nurse couldn't hear him. "Unless there's a nurse here I didn't see, I'll consider your vision impaired."

"Got twenty-twenty. It's my heart they say's impaired."

With that, the brothers vigorously engaged in a round of rowdy kibitzing, something they hadn't done in over twenty years. Each was relentless in his flamboyant, good-natured attempts to one-up the other.

They had not seen each other since 1952, Larry's last visit home eleven years earlier. At that time, they were aloof, standoffish, and each demonstrated little outward interest in the affairs of the other. Some have said that "absence makes the heart grow fonder," but in the Dailey brothers' case, the opposite had been true. Larry had long nurtured an unflattering opinion of his brother as a lazy, hopeless homebody who had taken advantage of their parents when he took over their father's hardware store. As for David, he had grown to resent Larry's desertion of family responsibilities in pursuit of a self-centered, will-o'-the-wisp lifestyle. Each had harbored a long-festering, often bitter jealousy of the other. But now, at least momentarily, those negative feelings were held at bay.

After a raucous ten minutes of laughs, David feared they might be headed for a stiff reprimand. After all, they were in the intensive care unit where calm, serious decorum was the standard. In an even voice, he asked, "Larry, what happened? Why are you in the hospital? Intensive care, no less. You look good though. Could use a haircut …."

"I feel good. Never better! I shouldn't really be here," Larry said, explaining he had fallen off a scaffold while training a couple of Mexicans to be brick masons. "I was knocked cold, flat on my ass. After they revived me, my foreman drove me here where I've been ever since. They tell me I also had a heart attack. They said they needed time for tests and observation. As for the ICU, I don't know. Maybe a convenient empty space. They don't tell you nothin' 'round here." Larry's judgmental assessment echoed all-too familiar for David.

"Surely, you must know something. You had a heart attack, for Christ's sake!" Though impatient to know more, David knew he had better throttle the interrogation. "Well, let's find out all we can then do whatever to get you out of here."

Although he had not seen his brother in over a decade, he still knew Larry by heart—his slapdash nature was still alive and well. David chose not to bring up the death of their father, the victim of a heart attack two years earlier. However, it did weigh on his mind. He hoped Larry's doctor would suggest rest, tell him to tone down the workaholic, go-go-go regime. If recommended, David would forego his clandestine plan, at least for the time being, and insist Larry return with him to Michigan for a while, if not permanently. Meeting up with Larry and Larry's medical condition had torpedoed this morning's intention to disappear permanently.

"From what I've seen, with this hospital area an exception, I like this town," David said. "It's obvious why you would want to stay out here in the warm California sun."

"I don't see much of it, Dave. I work twelve-to-sixteen-hour days, six or seven days a week. And that's a good thing." David perceived both candor and lament in his brother's tone, with a light seasoning of macho exaggeration. He resolved to engage in some form of intervention but was unsure of exactly what that would consist of and look like.

"Me and my partners own and operate a very profitable residential construction company, if I do say so myself. We build in the Los Angeles/San Bernardino area, home construction mainly." Larry listed his professional activities next, including personal ownership of a concrete business specializing in custom driveways, patios, pools, sidewalks, and curbs. "I keep six men going full-time. It's a money machine, for them and for me. Oh, yeah, I'm also a licensed building inspector. Don't have much time for that, but it opens doors and avoids problems," Larry said, accenting his resume with ample dollar sign punctuation.

His voice rose as the list of accomplishments lengthened. Finally, David interrupted, "Income aside, how do you find time for all this? You're making me tired just listening."

As busy as Larry had been, he had still had time for three wives in twenty years, not concurrently but with some overlap. Fortunately, only the first had given him a child. Back in Three Oaks, when David was asked about his brother's marital status, he'd respond, "Larry started out with poor taste in women, and it deteriorated over time, just the opposite of the 'good wine' he boasts about collecting." David never got to know any of his brother's wives, although he had met the first. What he knew of Larry's business life, he heard from their mother, or it was relayed through Jane, David's wife. Every detail of those accounts never failed to annoy him.

As he listened, though, his mind did drift to thoughts of Larry's characteristics they might share. Professional aspirations were a Dailey family trait going back at least to their grandfather who had cleared land for a peach orchard and grape arbor, firsts in their area. And his brother's fascination with women might also run in the male family members.

Aware David was losing interest, or perhaps simply running out of energy, Larry turned his attention to his discharge. His cardiologist, Dr. Anderson, had scheduled a discharge meeting for the next day at 3 p.m., after which, provided all was going well, he would be sent home. He told David he had already talked with his partners to let them know he planned to take a week off.

"Concrete will get laid. I've got contracts for my men lined up for the next two months." He concluded with a few flattering words about his personal financial advisor and accountant and how busy he had kept her. "Now that you're here, I'll call and tell Karen she needn't come by to drive me home." Then Larry's self-absorbed narrative of excellence spewed forth again. As it did, David's interest and positive reinforcement dwindled.

"Listen, Dave, if you'll stay with me a few days, I'd like to show you around, take you to a couple of job sites? I think you'll be impressed."

"I'm sure I would," David said. Then in an attempt to divert his brother, he quite unintentionally blurted out, "Actually, I was hoping you'd come back to Michigan with me. Mom would sure like to see you. Besides, you need to take it easy for a few weeks, maybe a month or two."

"Time-out. You the doctor now?"

"I mean it. Being back home would be good for you." David masked his tepid enthusiasm for such a trip well. It wasn't the plan, but that plan had already been scratched. And though he had only a passing interest in a topographical tour of Larry's business portfolio, David did his best not to let even a hint of resentment show.

"Ahhh, I don't think so. Got irons in the fire, Dave."

"That's your problem, too many irons in the fire. You need a break. We both do. You for medical reasons and me for mental reasons," David said, immediately regretting mentioning his mental state.

Larry laughed heartily. "I told you, I'm fine! Obviously, it's you who needs a break. Got mental problems, hey?" Larry had no clue what David's "mental reasons" slip really referred to. A moment passed, and then a furrow crossed Larry's brow. "Tell me, why did you show up here tonight? How did you know I was in the hospital? Why did you come out here anyway? Don't get me wrong, I'm glad you're here."

"I told you, I dropped by to take you home."

"No. Come on! Why are you here?"

"No, no. Left home five days ago. Told Jane and Mom I was going to see you, see how you were. Jane said it would do us both good, and Mom also wants me to bring you back. Always has. She means well but honestly means 'home for good.' Make no mistake about that." David grinned then repeated, "For good, Larry."

"That's crazy. Ain't gonna happen."

"No one except our mom would ask you to move."

"That's good 'cause it ain't happenin'."

"Hey, consider this: come back with me. We'll drift across the country, have a great time, just like when we came out here before the war. We can do it in four or five days, easy. You can see Mom and stay for as long or short as you like. I'll take you to O'Hare when you're ready, and you can fly back."

The two of them went back and forth, hashing over David's suggestion. Larry was concerned about contracts, deadlines, and dollar signs, while David emphasized their mother's loneliness. "More so since Dad died. Mom really needs to see you, Larry. Come on. You can do this. *We* can do this."

"If I go with you, I've got to be back before October first. What's the date?" Larry asked.

"We can do this, easy," David repeated. "We may be able to leave by Friday. I'll do the drivin'."

"Okay. Let's do it, but be warned, I got to be back by October first. We have two make-or-break construction bids pending."

With Larry's commitment to a home visit, the two of them reverted to happy memories from their small-town upbringing. Larry wanted to know if David remembered smoking in their grandfather's barn and accidentally starting a fire. David raised his voice. "That was no accident! You wanted to know if straw could catch on fire from a cigarette butt."

"I never smoked," Larry said.

"Really? Remember—I'd found a couple of long cigarette butts down at the store, you snuck some kitchen matches, and we headed for the barn," David said.

"I must have proved my thesis. We put it out, didn't we? What about the time you put 7UP in the minister's water glass?"

"Crosby tried to take a drink during his sermon, sneezed, and blew 7UP over the people seated in the front two pews," David said.

"Must have been a good sermon. Everybody got a good laugh out of it, especially Crosby. Remember when he said, 'Somebody's changed my water to wine. A miracle! Did anyone see a couple of angels in the sanctuary before church?' Dave, do you think we ever got away with anything, really?" Larry's enjoyment of the spontaneous walk down memory lane was intense. David thought he sensed an underlying homesickness on his brother's part. If so, he wanted to reinforce it.

"This is my take. What we thought we got away with then, we want credit for now. Like, I want everyone to know it was me who put Saran Wrap under the toilet seat in the women's lounge at the high school."

"No shit! It was you? I knew it. You crazy bastard! You always got away with everything," Larry crowed with pleasure. "I'll tell you this, Mrs. Fanally didn't think it was funny. Remember how she had to go home and change?"

"Did she really cuss out the principal? I heard he laughed at her when she went to the office to report the incident."

"Bet that landed like the Hindenburg," Larry said. "Wish I'd seen it!"

Both men relished sharing nostalgic memories of youthful pranks and indiscretions. Even after so many years apart, an unmistakable familial bond tugged at them.

"Won't take me long to pack. My last wife took the house, the cars, basically everything except two pairs of skivvies and a half pack of smokes. That was all the first two overlooked!"

"I thought you said you never smoked!"

"Not since I entered the hospital. Speaking of skivvies, could you bring me some clean clothes when you come back tomorrow? I'll fly back. Got to be back here in ten or twelve days, if not sooner."

Larry's smug self-satisfaction bothered David. It was a self-centered behavior he'd witnessed as a teen, and it had irritated him then too. He answered, annoyed, "You need at least a month's rest. Recover. Take it easy. And no smoking."

"There you go again, playing doctor," Larry said.

"It wasn't me who got caught playing doctor with Jeannie Meadows," David said.

"Hey! It was her idea. I never could say no to a woman in need." Larry clearly relished that David had just reminded him of yet another glorious youthful escapade.

"There's nothing here that can't wait," David said. "Why don't you sell out? Join me at the hardware store?"

"Hardware?" Larry waved the idea away. "You don't keep a racehorse in the barn. I can't see me shuffling nuts and bolts to redneck plow-pushers. Not when there's a prime tract of San Bernardino property waiting for my shovel."

"Slow down, Larry. I'm not sure you're even up to a cross-country drive. You still smoke? That's gotta stop."

"Look at it this way, Dave. Even if they're telling the truth about smoking causing cancer, which I doubt, I figure we're all going to die anyway. So what's the big deal?"

"Smoke can't be good for your heart, as well as your lungs," David said sternly.

"Lighten up. I'm ready to roll. There's a young lady in Tucumcari who said she'd leave a light on for me. Remember?"

"Larry, my dear boy, that was over twenty years ago. If memory serves, she was at least twenty years older than you, Stone-Age ugly, and we were in Gallup, New Mexico, not Tucumcari."

"Tucumcari. Gallup. What's the difference?" Larry asked. "I can still see tumbleweeds blowing across the street in the middle of those dusty, little desert towns. Let's rock 'n' roll."

David asked, "Remember the tavern we were in that ran out of beer before eight o'clock? Could you believe that?"

"Yeah, I remember. It was one of the few places that never questioned whether I was of legal drinking age. I'd died and gone to heaven ... and then they ran out of beer. Go figure."

"That was the best road trip of my life. Let's do it!" David said. His exhilaration suppressed any reservations or previous qualms about a change of plans.

The sentimental exchange about their 1941 Route 66 experience escalated until the totem-pole-stiff, all-white nurse marched in. "Boys! It's time to give it up. One of you needs to get some sleep, and the other needs to get out of here. It's past time. Now, which is leaving, and which is going to sleep?" She glared wrinkle-free beneath pencil-thin, black eyebrows.

At the far end of the ICU, a sixty-year-old auto accident victim lay with an arm in a cast and an elevated leg held in traction. He was wrapped in bandages from head to toe and wore a neck brace from chin to chest. In a harsh, raspy voice, he tried to shout, "No, no, I want to hear more about the girl from Tucumcari."

Larry shot back, "In a minute. That reminds me." He said in his best Tarzan shriek, "She said I was a sixty-second man! Insisted I hurry back!" Laughing and coughing burst out across the beds within the all-male ICU, and every conscious patient was now wide awake.

Larry reached for the small table near the head of his bed and pulled the drawer open. He took a key from a key ring he'd hidden there and gave it to David. "Here's the key to my house. Do you know how to find it?"

"No problem. I was there earlier."

"You were? Why'd you say you were here?"

Before David could think of an acceptable answer, they were interrupted. Nurse Deadpan snarled as she reached for David's arm. "Say goodnight, Gracie!" she said then escorted David to the ICU exit.

David's walk back to his car through the dimly lit and deteriorating residential neighborhood became uncomfortable. He took vigilant note of every sound and shadow along the way. Two teenage boys ran across the street in front of him and disappeared into a dark alleyway between two tenement buildings. When he found the car just as he had left it, he breathed a sigh of relief, climbed in, and locked the door.

The fifteen-minute drive from the blighted hospital area to Larry's touristy part of town was a welcome release. Larry's house was easy to locate since it was now familiar, straight up the street from the carnival-lit entrance to the Santa Monica Pier.

The sun had gone down before he arrived at Larry's, but David's spirits were up. During the previous twenty-four hours, his state of mind toward Larry had moved from *I couldn't care less* to a rekindling of a long-lost concern for his little brother's well-being. Spending some private time inside Larry's townhouse was bound to provide more insight into his personal life. David was hungry but chose to investigate where he planned to spend the night before rustling up something to eat. In the background, sounds of a lively night scene emanated from the pier and all along the Venice Beach boardwalk.

The neat homes and trendy townhouses pinched together on both sides of Larry's street appeared even more fashionable in the evening lights. Centrally placed front doors at the top of three to five steps were constructed to offer maximum first-floor privacy while second and third stories provided additional living space. David noticed, too, that the street sloped gently upward, away from the ocean still crested by the afterglow of sunset.

David parked directly in front of 210-A Olympic Street, ascended the steps, unlocked the door with Larry's key, and entered a spacious living room furnished with contemporary second-hand furniture. To the right was a prototype Whirlpool kitchen with red Formica countertops and a chrome-rimmed, metal kitchen table and chairs to match. Behind the kitchen was a half-bath, a stairway to the second floor, and a back door that opened to a postage-stamp-sized backyard.

The second floor held two bedrooms, each with a queen-sized bed and a pine-laminated chest-of-drawers with a dark, cherry-stained finish. A full bath separated the bedrooms, one of which featured a twenty-four-inch Zenith TV and a creaky rocking chair. Dull, thick, orange-shag carpet covered all the townhouse floors except for the kitchen and bathrooms, where large taupe tiles covered the floors. David wandered deliberately from room to room, looking in closets and opening dresser drawers. He laid some clothes out on the bed to take to Larry. *So this is where Mr. Success sleeps.*

On the counter next to the kitchen sink sat a black, rotary telephone. David had not spoken with his wife since leaving Three Oaks six days earlier. He decided to give Jane a call and report that Larry might be coming home with him. That message would strengthen his credibility for wanting to go to California alone, a trip Jane had been hesitant to support.

But tonight, Jane sounded happy he called. She said she couldn't wait to deliver the news of Larry to her mother-in-law. She twice thanked David for calling and wanted to hear more about his trip. However, her interest surpassed David's desire to share. Of course, he said nothing about Santa Catalina or Long Beach. He promised to call again before they left for home. His conflicted conscience did not ease with the call, try as he might not to think about the unexpected turn of events in his life.

David's hunger pangs resurfaced and coupled with his eagerness to see more of Santa Monica at night. These combined urges mitigated his feelings of self-doubt and the sense that his envisioned quest was wholly self-centered. As ever, his quest for adventure was revived.

When he asked the next-door neighbor for dining directions, she pointed and said, "Straight down Olympic, cross Appian Way, and you're on Ocean Front Walk. Can't miss it. Lots of places to eat on the left." The festive sounds and smells could not have been more enticing.

The walk from Larry's to the pier took less than five minutes. The air was a waft of appetite-tempting aromas, all sweetened by giant, pink puffs of cotton candy and thick, extra-sweet caramel popcorn. The sounds of people screaming on pier amusement rides added to the festive atmosphere until David could feel a smile spreading from ear to ear.

A tall, white, metal sign with black lettering stood in the middle of the entrance to the teeming Santa Monica Pier. It announced: End Route 66. David reached up and slapped the rectangular road sign then strolled to the end of the pier to gaze out at a dark ocean illuminated by a gold-shimmering moonlit pathway—postcard perfect. It reminded him of how much he and Jane adored viewing sunsets over Lake Michigan.

Casually meandering the crowded ocean-front promenade toward Venice Beach affirmed his dreamed-of destination. He questioned why he so impulsively invited Larry to go home with him and why Larry, with little coaxing, had agreed to travel back to Michigan. David relished the stress-free, casual beachfront location as his concerns for his brother's health, as well as his feelings of self-doubt, receded.

He allowed the animated beach scene to simply wash over him. From first impressions, he thought there must be some kind of crazy costume party up ahead. He could observe no pattern to the way people were dressed, other than multiple perplexing social statements. *Even Mr. Coconut would feel at ease here*, he joked to himself.

There were countless choices of places to eat. Popular music and bizarre noises blasted from sidewalk bars. Venders shouted invitations to passersby. A squadron of bikini-clad promenade roller skaters, revealing more than legal, nearly ran him down. Most attention-grabbing was a gymnasium-sized concrete platform between the red-brick walkway and ocean occupied by oily, iron-pumping bodybuilders, several wearing audaciously feminine costume jewelry.

David asked a fellow onlooker, "What is this?"

"It's the Body Shop, my man! Sun goes down, they pump up!"

To David, it was a sideshow of greasy exhibitionists showcasing their massive muscles.

"That's what's happenin', man. You like?"

David lacked an appropriate response, so he raised his eyebrows, smiled generously, and continued his slow stroll along the seafront.

A sidewalk café with a welcoming sandwich board conveyed a Midwestern appeal. An arty male waiter, who could have been a cast member in *West Side Story*, attempted to tuck David's six-foot-one, well-proportioned frame into a tiny curbside table. "Come on," he said to David. "We can do this, cowboy."

David smiled questioningly, but he considered the table a perfect location from which to observe people. He studied the menu in a conscious effort to avoid gawking at strange-looking characters parading by. They were so close, he could reach out and touch them. He watched but could not be a dispassionate observer like his father had always been.

The waiter interrupted, "Name's Linfield. Happy to be of service."

"Do you really serve burgers and fries here? I see the 'Traditional American Burger' on the menu. You do have pop, don't you?"

"Pop? Whatever you wish, cowboy," Linfield said.

"Do I look like a cowboy? I don't even have a horse …."

"My apologies, sir. It's just that you don't appear to travel in the usual crowd …."

"And what's the usual crowd?"

"That's just it, sir. There's no usual crowd, and you're so … so usual. You dig?" Linfield spoke in a suave and soft voice.

"Make that hamburger medium well. And ketchup with the fries. I dig. I think."

Before David's order arrived, a woman, thirtyish, he thought, walked past. He noticed her clean-cut, attractive figure. She turned, caught him staring, smiled, and motioned that she'd like to join him.

Her forward manner threw David off guard, but the tiny restaurant was packed, and she radiated a mysterious charm. He swallowed involuntarily. "Sure, okay. I mean, yes, please join me." He tried to stand, but she signaled him not to before he could untangle his legs from beneath the cramped table.

"Name's Shelly, and I pay my own way," she said. She pulled out the chair across from David and moved it to one side where she had more room. "We can hear each other better," she said.

"David. David Dailey. Pleased to meet you."

"And I you," Shelly said. "Seems crowded for a weeknight."

"Back home, we call this going Dutch treat," David said.

"Why?" Shelly shook her head and looked straight at David.

"Each party on a date pays their own way. That's my understanding," David said.

"Sounds sorta disparaging of the Dutch as being cheap, don't cha think?

"Never thought about it, but maybe … Lots of Dutch in Michigan. But what about you? Are you from here?"

"Ventura." The tanned, young woman had dark eyes and shoulder-length, straight, brown hair. Personable and gregarious, she asked lots of questions, which helped David carry the conversation. Before they finished his burger and her french green salad, she knew most of his life's story, although he never thought to mention he had a wife.

Twice, they bumped each other beneath the table. Each touch sparked a pleasurable nervousness in David. And he hoped the bumping was *not* accidental. However, it was a small table in a crowded restaurant. Neither party acknowledged the touching with more than a slight foot or knee adjustment.

David offered to pick up the check, but Shelly would not allow it and insisted on covering a gratuity in addition to her half of the bill since she had invited herself. Then she winked and reached for David's hand. "Come, walk with me down to the pier," she whispered. "I'll tell you all about this place," she said playfully as she tugged on his sleeve.

Linfield genuflected, "Happy trails, cowboy."

Their walk became a lighthearted amble, which ended all too soon for David. At the intersection of the pier and Appian Way, Shelly squeezed David's arm as she hailed a cab. "Thank you. Hope to see you again soon."

"Do you come here often?" David asked as she got into the back seat of the cab.

"I run the beach every morning, early. Usually alone. You should try it sometime. Good for the soul." She waved and winked as her driver edged into traffic. Ripples of other times, places, and faces passed through David's head. The Santa Monica setting of beach and ocean reminded him of Lake Michigan but with music instead of majestic sand dunes.

The next morning, David rose and jogged down to the beach as the sun's rays slid through the hills behind him. The early-morning breeze was invigorating. He inhaled the rhythmic sound and smell of the briny surf turning over and over again hypnotically as it ran along the shore. In discovery mode, he explored the shoreline for a mile to the north of the pier. No hint of Shelly, last night's dinner companion. He had not yet given up, though, when three truant, teenage boys carrying surfboards crossed in front of him.

"Hey, man, wanna catch a wave? Cool, man."

"Thanks, but I've never been on a surfboard."

"No problem, man. We'll teach you. It's cool, man."

"How 'bout a rain check, okay?"

"Cool."

"Say, you guys seen a foxy lady running along the water this morning?" David tried to paint a description of Shelly, but his portrait ended up looking more like Natalie Wood.

"Sorry, man. Many foxy fish in the sea ... You cool?"

"Cool," David said without conviction. He'd lost interest in the school-skippers and his vision of a pretty beach jogger. Guilt replaced wistful daydreaming. How had Larry spent the night, and would he be discharged today? David headed back to his brother's place to see if he could find something in the refrigerator.

* * *

Larry and David were seated in a tiny conference room off the ICU entrance when Dr. Anderson rushed in at ten minutes past three. Even before sitting down, the doctor told Larry, "Yours may not have been a major attack, but it's your second." Then, along with more detailed warnings, came dietary instructions to combat high blood pressure and a suggestion for cutting out strenuous physical exertion. "Absolutely no heavy lifting. Get more rest. No smoking, and no alcohol in excess. Maybe a glass of red wine now and again."

"Doc, I'll be a sinking ship with no freight to throw overboard," Larry said.

"Those are only my suggestions," the doctors said, adding, "That is, if you want to live."

"Listen up, Doc. If I follow your advice, will I live longer? I know this: if I stop hustlin', it'll sure seem longer."

If Dr. Anderson was amused, he never let on. After a pregnant pause, he exhaled and said, "You may have a point, Larry. I never know perfectly what to say to my patients. Let us leave it at this: the heart prefers moderate behavior in every facet of one's life."

From Larry's swagger, it appeared he had just won the Kennedy-Nixon debate. "Hey, Doc, is it true that having sex is as good for your heart as running seven miles?"

"I wouldn't be running any half-marathons, if I were you," the doctor said wryly.

"What about a little one-on-one sprint once in a while?" Larry pressed.

"Can't say for sure. Gotta go. Got serious patients waiting." Dr. Anderson smiled at David and bowed to Larry from the neck up as he closed the door behind him on the way out.

For the rest of the afternoon, David drove all over Los Angeles as Larry navigated from the passenger seat. Larry wanted to show David the sights, as well as building projects he and his partners had completed. They capped off the tour with an excessive barbecue dinner at Smoky Joe's Rib House in Long Beach, less than a mile from Charlie's Boat & Bait and the Shoreline Ferry. David realized his trip from Long Beach to Santa Monica the day before had been needlessly convoluted, but he kept that experience to himself.

During dinner and while back in Long Beach, David thought of the time he'd spent there a couple of days earlier. He found himself more relaxed, free of the seasickness and the pressure of the clandestine timetable he'd failed to meet. Internally, he felt relieved and knew it wasn't just because of the delicious plate of ribs Larry had insisted on paying for.

It was midnight by the time the two returned to Larry's townhouse. Once there, they spent a couple more hours sitting at the kitchen table, laughing at crazy stories of things that had happened, or they thought had happened, during their teenage years. Exhausted, they finally turned out the lights.

Neither brother got up until well after eight the next morning. Larry made coffee and served his brother a stale, toasted bagel with aged cream cheese. David was disappointed it was too late to search the beach for Shelly again but happy to find Larry had been telling the truth about travel preparation. It took him little time to pack. However, it was high noon before they turned on to Santa Monica Boulevard where they picked up I-10/Route 66 toward San Bernardino.

"What happened to all the orange groves and grape vineyards I remember?" David asked.

"People like yours truly planted subdivisions and strip malls. Now we harvest money. Still green," Larry said.

"Too bad. Do you know we can take this road all the way to Chicago?" David asked.

"Lots of it's still two-lane. So we need to get moving," Larry said.

"No timetable, please. Let's take our time, enjoy the ride. Remember coming out here after high school?"

But Larry's attention wandered. "We've done work out this way and are currently building a new Ford dealership and may subcontract for some work on an A&P store. If I can get you to come back, I'd like to show you how it's done."

"What's wrong with right now?" David asked, anticipating that Larry would enjoy showing off a little more.

"No, let's get on down the road. Remember that thing about irons and promises?"

"And Tucumcari." David pumped the gas pedal, relishing the sound and feel of the engine revving and car accelerating while Mr. Coconut, now relegated to the backseat, rolled over.

Chapter 5
Amboy, California

"Ahhhh. Where are we?" grumbled a drowsy Larry as he stretched to sit up straight.

"Right cheeeer. Where d'ya think?" David teased.

"Uh, okay, stop with the wiseass," Larry said. "How long did I sleep?"

The highway lay arrow-straight before them, far into next week, empty in both directions. Lifeless sagebrush peppered the skillet-flat plain all the way to distant foothills. A stoic boulder and an occasional bedraggled Joshua tree stood lifeless on an overall weary landscape.

David shifted uncomfortably on the sticky, black leather seat, straightened his arms, locked his elbows with both hands on the wheel, drew in a long, slow breath, let it out easy, and finally turned toward his lethargic passenger.

"You drifted off somewhere north of Cajon Pass. Haven't missed much."

"Tell me something I don't know. Still lost. Where the hell are we?"

"Okay, try this, smart boy. We recently passed through beautiful metropolitan, if not cosmopolitan, Barstow, California. Next, the sprawling megalopolis of Dagget where the 1960 census found thirteen point five persons." David's monotone sarcasm provoked a counterfeit yawn from his companion and a lazy stretch of an elbow behind the head.

"Want me to drive?" asked the bleary-eyed passenger with a shrug. He reversed the window ventilator, leaned forward, and focused the air rush directly on his sweaty brow. "With our late start, we need to make up some time, although I'm not sure we should push this old beater."

"No. You take it easy. We got time. Remember what your doctor said," David replied.

"Doctors will say anything to cover their ass. Scared, confused patients make 'em feel important. I don't plan on checking out anytime soon." Larry leaned his head out the window but failed to escape the uncomfortable, dry heat and quickly drew it back in.

Since Cajon Pass, David had driven in quiet meditation, lost in his thoughts for his brother's health. Having one heart attack was bad enough, but Larry had had two. The fact that heart problems seemed to run in the family heightened David's concern.

"You hungry? The stuff they served me in the hospital would make a hog puke. Besides, I could use a cold beer. Maybe two."

"Are you kidding? Stop where? We'll need gas in about an hour or so. Think you can hold out that long?"

"Gas my ass," Larry said. He went on to explain how gas was hard to find in the Mojave Desert between Barstow, California and the Arizona border. Also, he voiced skepticism that David's car would be able to withstand such a desert crossing.

"Hey! Please don't disparage my ride. This chariot will manage. Secondly, it's not like it was when we came out before the war. Civilization has arrived. The last sign we passed said, 'Gas at Roy's Route 66 Café 66 Miles.'"

"Say what? Ole' Roy's liable to be dead by the time your chariot gets us there. I haven't seen a livin' thing move since I opened my eyes." Larry stared out his open window but didn't bother to move closer to the rushing air. All car windows were now fully open. Larry's sandy, wind-blown, collar-length hair had grown darker over the years. "We're all that moves in this desert. For the next thousand miles, we'd better put gas in this old crate every chance we get. I'm not hitchhiking. Remember what the doctor said?"

"Relax. Like I said, civilization has arrived." The empty concrete two-lane continued to lay dead straight ahead until it disappeared in a shimmer. With a lull in their conversation, David took the opportunity to boast about his coveted 1958 Chevrolet Bel Air. He claimed it was the finest set of wheels to come out of the Motor City since the Model T. He had ordered it factory-direct, fresh off the assembly line. But even David soon lost interest in his subject. A fanciful vision of a Dairy Queen rising up from the desert floor like an oasis stimulated his dehydrated taste buds.

Larry belatedly responded, "If you say so. I still could use a cold brewski. Is that a truck stop up ahead?"

"Come on, you said we needed to make up some time," David noted, ignoring Larry's repeated interest in alcohol. However, a cold beer did sound good.

They sailed past a little grocery store with a lone gas pump by the side of the highway. "I thought someone said we should take our time. Okay, fine. Wake me at Ole' Roy's. And come on, step on it," Larry said.

David pumped the accelerator then sensed the powerful V8 stammer ever so slightly before surging ahead. So minor was the engine's falter, he felt confident it had passed without notice. Not so.

"What's that?" Larry asked.

"Must have got some bad California gas," David said.

Monotonous miles slogged by. The thin, plastic steering wheel became damp and slippery. David repeatedly wiped his wet palms on his pant legs. Hot wind continued to blast through the open windows but provided little relief from the dry-sauna, desert air.

David's physical discomfort was accentuated by perplexing mental unrest. He worried about his brother's medical condition while at the same time envisioning the call of Santa Catalina. In spite of a determined effort not to, he analyzed and reanalyzed his ulterior motive for coming to California, definitely not to visit his brother, as he had worked so hard to convince his wife and mother. Was he in the process of squandering the opportunity to pursue that dream of peace and passion?

Images of Larry and the life David had imagined his brother led infuriated David and had for many years. He was at once judgmental yet envious. *Why should Larry enjoy the good life while I march forward as the responsible son, trudging on as expected? Am I sacrificing my last chance?* David again weighed the pros and cons of a change in his life's trajectory. "Most men live lives of quiet desperation, never daring to take a chance," prophesied his old high-school history teacher. At that time, young David had shrugged it off as the lament of a frustrated old maid. Much later, he discovered it was a bastardized quote from Henry David Thoreau's *Walden*. However, as years passed, that prophecy's echo had grown louder and louder in David's ears. At times, he surely could feel the drumbeat of quiet desperation reverberating in his pulse.

With right hand on top of the wheel and left elbow propped on the open window ledge, he glanced down at the gas gauge. A quarter of a tank left. He pumped the accelerator lightly, and the motor responded with typical perfection. David envisioned how his sleek automobile must look to an observer as it continued hurtling across the desert plain. Impressive!

A loose gravel parking area separated the entrance to Roy's Café from the historic desert highway. David failed to adequately brake before he swerved off the pavement and was forced to slam on the brakes. The Chevy slid to a stop less than four feet from the restaurant's front door.

"Roll up your window!" Before Larry could react, a swirl of coarse, gray dust trailed over the car and drifted into the passenger-side window. At the same moment, the deep waxed shine of David's two-toned, cream over turquoise, Chevy Bel Air coupe faded before his eyes.

"Did you overshoot the runway?" Larry asked in a monotone.

"We were running on empty. I floored it five miles back. If we ran out of gas, at least we could coast a ways. Easy to lose track of how fast you're moving out here in the open spaces," David said.

"No problem. You beat the competition for the prime parking space. Any closer and we'd be seated at the bar. After that, let's hope there is a bar."

"Let's hope there's gas, but I could use a tall cold one too," David said.

They had arrived at Roy's Café, the only sign of life over the last fifty miles. Both were tired, hungry, and also running on empty. At first glance, it appeared to be a mere wide spot in an otherwise drab slab of two-lane concrete. David had done all the driving while Larry struggled in constant search of a nonexistent comfortable position.

From their midday start, they had been on the road steady with the exception of one short pit stop. While passing through the traffic-choked Cajon Pass northeast of Los Angeles, they had stopped at Summit Station for gas, a can of pop, and a men's room visit.

"It's Saturday Vegas traffic," Larry had said. "Once we get past Barstow, we'll be free."

Now, damp with sweat, the two men were anxious to remove themselves from four continuous hours confined in cramped quarters. Both stiff, they untangled their taut limbs from the car and stretched. David bemoaned his car's dust-covered finish. Larry passed gas in a less than discreet manner while shaking his right leg. Neither observed the splatter of a boiling, orange sun hanging low above the road they had traveled. A fine dust lingered in the parched air.

"Where the hell are we? Have you gotten us lost in a God-forsaken wasteland?" Larry's colorful questions, intended as humor, conveyed a less-than-favorable assessment of Roy's establishment. And most empirical evidence supported his inclination.

David took a more measured look around. There was room for a half-dozen cars in front of Roy's Café, with extra parking around the sides and in back. In addition to David's Chevy, only two other vehicles were present. A faded-red Reo pickup from another era lay exhausted directly in front of the restaurant's flickering, orange, neon EAT sign. Resting to the right of the vintage pickup sat a black, 1949 Ford coupe. It featured a brown right front fender panel, two peeling white sidewall tires, and a cracked right taillight. Could one surmise by this scant evidence that the Saturday-night crowd had arrived?

Five small square cabins stood in a semi-circle behind the café with signage identifying Roy's Tourist Court. To the left of the café was a three-pump gas station combination grocery publicized as Roy's

Gas & Livery. One of the gas pumps supported a white crown atop a calibrated, five-gallon, clear-glass cylinder, museum ready. Beyond the business area lay crevassed, hard-baked earth gasping for rain. Three stooped Joshua trees, an intermittent tuft of brown grass, and a disheveled shrub with two or three green leaves seemed right at home in the harsh setting. After a full half day on the road, the Dailey brothers were still in California but a world away from Santa Monica.

In a pretentious Viennese accent, David proclaimed, "Larry, my good man, we have arrived at an oasis deep within the treacherous confines of the infamous Mojave Desert. Perhaps the only sanctuary between here and the end of civilization. I surmise Roy to be the proprietor."

Larry looked sideways at his brother but to no avail. David continued, "Roy is possibly the lone occupant of this unmitigated, arid expanse, save for a retarded rattlesnake and a buoyant buzzard or two. Resourceful creatures they must be! Please, let us tarry not, but enter this fine dining establishment and inquire if we may procure nourishment and an evening's lodging."

"And gas," Larry added.

"You should talk about gas!"

"Dave. You're so full of shit, your eyes are brown. But who gives a damn? I'm hungry. I'd eat the hind quarter of a dead mule if I could find one."

With that, he stood straight and stepped for the door. They both coughed in a vain attempt to clear their dry throats of the dusty air.

Larry started to push through the door, which had a piece of thick, brown cardboard nailed to it with a scrawl in black paint—OPEN. He stopped and said, "Think 'closed' is on the flipside?" To investigate would have done irreparable damage to both cardboard and door since the sign was secured with a six-inch railroad spike.

"Please, what treasures lie within?" David resuscitated his Viennese accent and motioned for Larry to proceed. Larry smirked, indicative of a life-long combative nature.

"Howdy, strangers!" boomed a rugged voice from behind a saloon bar straight out of a Hollywood set for *Gunsmoke*.

"Welcome! Any table or belly up. What's your poison?"

"You heard of beer?" Larry asked.

"Budweiser or PBR? Tap or bottle?"

"Two tall Bud drafts and a couple of menus," David answered.

"Menu's on the wall," the bartender declared with a nod toward the slate blackboard covering the wall opposite the bar. "Two Buds comin' up!"

Three additional patrons were in the tavern. At the bar stood a tall, young man in a ten-gallon, white, Stetson hat and polished, black, leather boots with silver spurs. He tipped his hat to the new arrivals. A Social-Security-aged couple looked up from their table to appraise the entering strangers. The sweet smell of freshly baked bread seemed out of place in the dark, cavernous saloon, but there it was.

Larry and David sat down in the middle of seven round, wooden, tables, each with four mismatched, well-worn chairs. The table condiments included glass salt and pepper shakers next to small, brown, pottery bowls filled with bare, white sugar cubes but only on three of the tables. A tall floor lamp stood at each end of the dimly lit, rectangular tavern. Three evenly placed lightbulbs beneath small, green, metal shades hung from the ceiling above the bar. At each end of the bar sat a small oscillating fan contributing some relief from the oppressive outdoor temperature. A large, cracked mirror covered the wall behind the bar and above an ample liquor display.

Shortly after they sat down, the eager bartender arrived with two sixteen-ounce, foam-overflowing, frosted mugs. David smiled and, after a long pull, smacked his lips and said, "Best I've ever tasted. You Roy?"

"No, sir, Popeye. I work for Roy's daughter, Bessie, and her husband, Buster. Landed here in '47. Been here ever since."

"Buster and Bessie, hey. Sounds like a big-time wrestling tag team to me. We must have passed through here back in '41. Don't remember Roy's. You sure?" Larry asked. He pressed his cold beer mug against his forehead.

"Oh, Roy's was here. So was Roy. Still is."

"Well, tell us, why *Roy's* Cafe?" David asked.

"Bessie tells me her dad, Roy Crowl, and mother ran out of gas here back in '27. They're Oklahoma Sooners, yah know. Never left. Nothin' here back then except sixty-six and the crater. The two of them built most everything you see here in Amboy. They live above the station." Popeye clicked his heels and saluted in that direction. Larry raised an opinion-arched eyebrow.

"Funny, Popeye, we just happen to be out of gas. Maybe we'll stay," David said.

"Speak for yourself," Larry said.

Both men were interested in Popeye's supper suggestion—Bessie's Mojave Roast Beef Sandwich—and so ordered. Before Popeye could place the order, Larry requested another round.

Ten minutes later, the Daileys were treated to thick slices of tender roast beef on freshly baked sourdough bread with an ample helping of mashed potatoes all smothered in rich, dark, onion-laced gravy.

David straightened his plate in front of him. "Looks too good to eat."

"Smells too good not to," Larry said while shoveling a fork-full of mashed potatoes into his mouth. Before he had swallowed it all, he said, "Now, this is what I miss about home." Larry smacked through another mouthful of mashed potatoes while simultaneously grasping his second mug of beer. "I've eaten in the best restaurants anywhere, but I'll admit to missing Mom's cooking, if not much else." Larry was speaking with his mouth full, a habit for which his mother had often admonished him.

While the boys were growing up, a typical supper meal in the Dailey household was announced by Mrs. Dailey at precisely 6 p.m. most evenings. Mrs. Dailey insisted no one start eating until all were seated and a blessing had been offered. David remembered how Larry would cheat, sneaking something before the blessing, and how when scolded for not saying "please" and "thank you," he would respond by mispronouncing those words to the irritation of everyone. Food dishes often congregated around Larry's plate because he failed to pass things unless asked a second time. Larry always gave the impression of being in competition to get the most, first. Being the oldest, David tried to help his parents enforce the rules on his little brother. Even now, Larry was still that willful little boy. Nothing to be done about it.

Nothing much was said as the hungry travelers devoured their meals. Both were ravenous, and Bessie's roast beef sandwiches were delicious. As David wiped up the last bit of gravy with an extra piece of sourdough bread, he asked, "Is Mom's cooking the only thing you've missed about home?"

No answer.

Larry had never expressed an interest in living in Michigan, much less in Three Oaks. He had only returned twice in the twenty-two years he'd been away, and both visits had been short. The first was in the fall of 1942 while passing through on a whirlwind honeymoon following marriage number one. At that time, the parents did everything in their power to please him and his pregnant bride. His mother repetitively shared her desire to be an important part of her "baby's growing family." Such talk annoyed Larry, and he had to bite his lip to keep a civil tongue. Their mother's solicitous behavior toward Larry and his bride annoyed David as well. Although he never said so to anyone, he could never come to terms with his brother's knocking up a girl then rushing into marriage.

No other children were born of this or Larry's subsequent marriages. And the grandparents were never included in their grandchild's life. The first marriage formally dissolved after only three years. The year before the divorce, the grandparents had visited Larry's family in California, announced but uninvited. That visit was remembered by all as an emotional strain and the everlasting lament of Larry's mother. Mrs. Dailey refused to allow herself to even think of Larry not fulfilling a parent's responsibility.

Larry's second trip back home had come at Christmas following divorce number two. His flippant, carefree attitude concerning the failed marriages, plus his lack of parental accountability, bothered fellow family members and deeply troubled his mother, who tried to deflect blame or responsibility away from her son. "I can't imagine what kind of woman would do such a thing! Throw her marriage away and separate a baby girl from her father." When Larry explained both situations only as good riddance, his mother glossed it over as, "He didn't really mean that," or "It could not have been his fault," concluding, "I don't want to hear anything more about it."

Mrs. Dailey had spent a lifetime heartsick over her strained relationship with her youngest son. Since Larry's premature birth, she had suffered what she perceived, and others observed, as unrequited love from her baby. She struggled to internalize her feelings but, given her effusive nature, was never completely successful.

The tall cowboy nursing a double shot of whiskey at the bar strode over to the jukebox spurs jingling. As he searched for a selection, Larry shouted, "Play 'Blowin' in the Wind' by Peter, Paul, and Mary." The cowboy looked over at the brothers and tipped his Stetson then turned back to continue his search.

Larry turned to his brother and said, "I think we were blown in the wind when you almost crashed us into this tavern." His cocksure expression gnawed at his brother. "You ever heard of Peter, Paul, and Mary?"

"Yeah, I've heard of them. But, I think 'Heat Wave' by Martha and the Vandellas might be more appropriate, considering our drive through the desert."

Soon, the clank of the cowboy's quarter could be heard falling through the Jukebox coin receptacle. From the speakers came the soothing music of Henry Mancini's orchestra composition of "Days of Wine and Roses."

"What?" Larry exclaimed. "Ain't that a little highbrow for a place like this?"

"I don't know. I like it myself," David said.

"You would, go figure."

David had always possessed a close and constant relationship with both parents. Following a two-year tour of duty in the US Coast Guard, he settled back in his hometown and, for years, never considered any alternative. At the conclusion of his first year back, he became a partner with his dad in Dailey Hardware. One year later, he married Jane Crossman, a young woman he had known all his life. Jane was the exact person Mrs. Dailey wanted for a daughter-in-law.

"The Crossmans are a fine, upstanding church family. If I'd had a daughter, I'd wish for one just like Jane," she repeated several times at David and Jane's church wedding reception.

David and Jane had fallen in love the year David had returned from the Coast Guard. Although they had grown up together, been playmates during elementary school and lifelong friends, they had never dated much less thought of each other romantically. When they started dating, it was a surprise to both of them. David was proud of Jane's dedication to her new teaching responsibilities and her level-headed, can-do approach to life. Likewise, Jane was smitten with David's mature good looks, sensitivity for the welfare of others, and no-nonsense, serious nature.

Mrs. Dailey had gotten her wish, but to the disappointment of all, Jane and David never had children. Upon entering their marriage, they both wanted and expected to raise a family of two or three offspring. They frequently shared tender thoughts of activities they anticipated engaging in together with their young and growing children. Prospective kids' names and pets' names were bandied about in a good-natured, teasing manner. Unfortunately, those dreams were never to be fulfilled.

From the start, the couple had cultivated their full married life in all other respects. Together, they evolved into pillars of the Three Oaks community and were the pride of both sets of parents. All good, and yet, as the years passed, David experienced a growing sense of having missed out on something. He sensed Jane harbored a similar disappointment, although such feelings were tucked well beneath the surface.

As the brothers finished their meal, Larry ordered another round, to which David reluctantly conceded, "Okay, but that's enough."

"Come on, loosen up, tight ass. A couple a beers will do you some good!" Larry lit up a Pall Mall and blew his smoke toward the ceiling.

"Let me remind you of what your doctor said, 'You need to stop smoking and go easy on the alcohol. Maybe a glass or two of red wine per week.' Wasn't that what he said?"

"Ahh, there you go again. You sound like Mother. Look at it this way, Dave, a few beers and a smoke never hurt nobody."

"You just had a heart attack, for Christ's sake. Seems you'd like to live a little longer, huh?" David said.

"Not without wine, women, and song … and a smoke now and then." Larry smiled self-assuredly as if he had just laid down a universal proclamation for the meaning of life. His logic, ever since high school days, had been habitually presented in similarly slapdash and dogmatic terms.

"It has always peeved me that our parents favored you, especially Mother," he continued. "You were like Davy-Do-Right. 'Be like your big brother.' I heard that a lot. I couldn't stand it. Had to get out of there."

"Where the hell did that come from? That's a crock of you know what," David said.

"The hell it is! She was always bragging on you, telling you how wonderful you were. Hell, I excelled beyond you in everything— athletically, academically, you name it. I worked my ass off, harder than you ever did! Still do. For what it's worth, I bet I even spent more time in that old, redneck church than you. Even so, no one ever gave me credit for anything."

"Don't be stupid. You had a dresser full of awards and honors. Mom still displays a framed, eight-by-twelve graduation picture of you on top of her 'don't touch' china cabinet."

As their voices rose, David became more and more self-conscious. Several more customers had entered the café while the Daileys were eating. All patrons were now spectators to the brotherly squabble, intently so as the brothers' voices escalated.

"I'll admit, you received better grades than I did, but who's competing? You could say I cleared a path for you." At first, David tried to be conciliatory toward what he perceived was a beer-fueled assault, but he failed—couldn't let it go. "However, I've never thought of you as a particularly gifted athlete. We both had fun playing ball. I liked my teachers and coaches and think they liked me, but I don't believe anyone ever favored me over you." David's quiet, even tone did little to conceal his resentment and only served to further incense Larry.

"Oh, yeah? Teachers always told me what a good student you were, how much they enjoyed you in class. Why'd they do that?"

"Don't know. But you're making a mountain out of—"

"Bullshit! You were the original brown-noser. When coaches would see me coming, they'd say, 'Good, we got another Dailey on the team.' I got sick of all that crap! I won more awards and letters than you ever did!"

"Now, Larry, there's nothing older than yesterday's sports page," David said. He glanced at the two couples seated at the table between them and the bar. All four were staring at the brothers.

"And where the fuck did you get that line of bullshit?" Larry shot back. David felt cold stares from the other tables. His brother's health worried him, too, but *the damn fool had himself to blame.*

"Larry, we were all proud of your accomplishments and discouraged when you were so hell-bent on leaving. Especially Mom. She has never given up hope on your moving back home."

"Bull! And why in hell did they have to send you to California with me? Now you're here to take me back? I can take care of myself. I wanted to get as far from Three Oaks as possible and was happy to send you back where you belong. What a chump life! Not for me."

"Enough, Larry!" David feared his brother was on the verge of saying or doing something they'd both regret, and what about the damn fool's heart?

Larry refused to let up. "And those stupid-ass broads in my class, always asking about you. They didn't even want to talk to me. Didn't give a fuck about me, except as just a way to get to you!"

"Take it easy. Your blood pressure must be through the roof."

Larry's face looked like an over-inflated pink balloon. David's self-consciousness spiked right along with their heated argument. They appeared headed toward physical blows, an immature destination. David knew he must derail their quarrel or risk any possible amenable outcome.

Their clash had drawn the disdainful attention of everyone in the place, in particular the distressed bartender who slipped another quarter into the jukebox and turned the volume up. Then Popeye fetched two more drafts and returned to the Daileys' table. "This round is on the house. You two could use a break. Life's too short to worry much about past hard knocks. That's a life I know something about."

"Oh, and how's life out here in the bush, Pops?" Larry asked, his expression aflame with contempt. The bartender undoubtedly had years of experience in dealing with disruptive barroom situations, but for his part, David did not want the Daileys to be an addition to such a list.

"You may call me Popeye," the bartender said in a sturdy, direct response to Larry.

Popeye's upper body tightened as he glared at Larry and then at David then back at Larry. He was a fit, well-proportioned man, only three or four years older than the Daileys. The Marine insignia was tattooed on the outside of a thick right bicep well defined against a tight, white T-shirt. His short, salt-and-pepper flattop exhibited sharp edges. In a firm, husky voice, Popeye said, "May I share a story with you two." Not a request.

Larry turned a sour face toward his brother. "Here we go. A tale of the hard times of Ole' Roy, another Oakie from Muskogee."

Popeye stared straight through Larry. The music on the jukebox ended. Bessie peeked her head over the swinging kitchen door. Several seconds passed without a word until David broke the tension permeating the entire saloon. "We'd like to hear your story, Popeye. And thanks for the beer. It's welcome relief after a hard day in the saddle."

Without breaking his gaze, Popeye picked up the chair between the brothers as one would a baseball bat on the way to the on-deck circle. He spun it around with one hand and sat down backward. He gripped the back of the chair with meaty hands, revealing two muscular, sculpted forearms. He began by pursing his lips.

"You two been in the service?" Popeye asked. David nodded he had. Larry made no reaction. "In the spring of 1941, I joined the Marine Corps down at Camp Pendleton. About the time you boys were coming out here. By August of that year, I'd been sent with the corps to upgrade a small naval air station on an island in the middle of the Pacific, Wake Island—actually an atoll. Do you guys know what an atoll is?"

Larry and David exchanged blank looks. Then Larry piped up, "A saltwater rock?"

Popeye glared at the table. "Close enough. Think of three large coral rocks barely above the surface of the ocean halfway between Hawaii and Japan. Three square miles of nothing but volcanic rock—no fresh water, no food, few trees. Basically nothing."

"Kinda like this place," Larry said. No response.

Popeye continued, "I had become close friends with three guys I'd buddied up with from boot camp. The four of us did everything together. They were my first real friends, guys I could depend on, and they could depend on me. We were like family, you might say. Wake became our island paradise. Sun, clear skies, warm, easy wind, and a bottomless, pure cobalt-blue lagoon between three saltwater rocks, as Larry says. Paradise."

The description of Wake Island and the term *paradise* conjured a vision of Santa Catalina in David's mind. Might Wake Island be an alternative future destination to be considered? From Popeye's account so far, it met most of David's disappearance requirements.

"And we had responsibility. We were the first line of our nation's defense in the Pacific. Wake was the strategic station on a lifeline to the Philippines and China. Not to mention we protected the Pan American Airways relay station to the Far East. I was happy. Three pals. Three squares a day. Not a care in the world. Oh, we'd heard about that European war, but that was a lifetime away from us. We were Marines.

"My buddies and I were assigned to join a work detail to improve the island's air strip. That project turned urgent the day we heard the Japanese had attacked Pearl Harbor and might be headed our way. Still, we were taken by surprise about five hours later when Japanese bombers roared low over the island. No radar, and because of the constant pounding of the surf, we didn't even hear them coming until they were smack-dab overhead.

"Believe me, those bomb explosions got our attention! Panic! Everything blowing up. Fire everywhere. Shrapnel ripped apart soldiers, sailors, civilians—everything. 'Take shelter!' But there was none. We were sitting ducks on a pond, the runway, the target. 'Run!' Run to nowhere. Zeros peeled off, came strafing." With a hand motion, Popeye simulated a plane banking and flying low over the table, shaking as it passed the condiments. "Men blown apart. Machine guns rattling. Zeros so low they appeared to be landing. Their motors snarled, belching oily exhaust. You could smell it. Then gone in an instant!" Popeye again motioned with his hand a plane's smooth flightpath away from the table.

"A smoky haze covered our island. From my place hugging the earth, I got up unhurt but dazed and stumbled towards HQ. Stepping through and over the debris-littered airstrip, I came upon a cluster of bloody, mangled corpses. Couldn't help but look. My buddies, my family, gone. Just gone. Why I wasn't with them haunts me from time to time. I may have been the only person on Wake that day capable of identifying their dismembered, disfigured remains. I'll never forget them, never.

"An officer called us together and organized details to care for the wounded, put out fires. Next, we gathered the dead, loaded them on a flatbed truck, and hauled them to the PX meat locker. It was refrigerated. To have waited until dark would have invited putrefaction and the onslaught of hermit crabs—ugly creatures."

"So did you spend the rest of the war marooned on a remote desert island?" Larry asked.

Popeye shrugged and studied Larry with sympathetic eyes. "If only it were so. We knew they'd be back. HQ radioed for reinforcements but prepared for the next attacks—which came like clockwork each day at noon. We had no sleep. No reinforcements. No way to evacuate, even after we beat back the first invasion attempt. Word came that a relief convoy had turned back. The inevitable was in sight. It was hopeless. Later, they called Wake Island the 'Alamo of the Pacific.'

After two weeks of daily air raids, the second invasion overran us. We surrendered. No one wanted to, but we had no option. None."

David was completely captivated by Popeye's heartfelt story, and Larry had warmed to it. Larry asked, "Popeye, this was December 1941, right? No one will ever forget Pearl Harbor. What happened to you over the next four years? The war had just started for us Americans."

"I'm an American," Popeye said. He sat up a little straighter in his chair, looking questioningly at Larry.

"I mean the US had just declared war. What happened to you, Popeye, the next four years?"

"The Japanese used us survivors as forced labor rebuilding the airfield they destroyed. They had total contempt for us, for anyone who surrendered. You've heard of the death march of Bataan?"

"Yes, sir," David said.

"We were beaten frequently and poorly fed. After about a year, they took half of us to China as slave labor during their occupation there. At first, I welcomed the change, but life was just as bad in China. Living in hell, you might say. After the war, I heard that the hundred men left on Wake were marched out to the end of the airstrip, lined up, and machine-gunned. So maybe I was better off. Anyway, Truman dropped the big bombs, and the Japanese left us in China. End of story."

Popeye raised his eyes and gazed at Larry then David. His whole presence radiated fatigue, as if telling his story, had taken the life out of him. He stood up and replaced his chair under the table.

"Popeye, we want to hear more, and more about Roy's history too. But right now, we'd like to pay our bill and see if we might rent one of your tourist cabins for the night. Speaking for myself, I'm beat," David said. The contrast and similarities between Kwan and Papa's escape from Korea and Popeye's capture and being taken to China meandered through David's head. For the time being, though, he'd put those considerations on hold.

"Sure you wouldn't like another Bud?" Popeye asked.

Both men declined but expressed their appreciation for the hospitality.

"Okay, then, I've put the two of you in cabin number one, twin beds. Let's settle up in the morning, being as the two of you are the last customers." All three men looked around the room and saw it was true; they were all that were left in the tavern. "I think Bessie has already put the cash box away."

Larry and David made eye contact. It was obvious their appreciation of the humble bartender had grown. While they were listening to Popeye's time in the Marine Corps, the tavern had completely emptied out except for a rumpled old dog stretched out asleep beneath the bar. Without another word, the two men followed Popeye around the end of the bar toward a back door. At the door, Popeye handed Larry a key labeled "Cabin #1" and added, "See you two recruits at reveille."

★ ★ ★

The sun streamed brightly through the lone cabin window, exposing a million tiny flecks of dust suspended in the air. David's eyes had been wide open for some time, silently counting blemishes in the suspended, used-to-be-white ceiling tiles. He lay motionless as thoughts of Popeye and Larry zigzagged between his ears. Both men seemed to know they were where they wanted to be. Why was he the one who always wanted to be somewhere else?

Since reuniting in the hospital, David found himself reconsidering his relationship both with Larry and home. For as hectic as Larry's life was, he did seem contented. David asked himself why he wasn't equally satisfied with his, by any reasonable assessment, comfortable life. After all, he was sure he had it pretty good. Be that as it may, the call of Santa Catalina still held him.

David turned his eyes toward the window but quickly turned back, evading the blinding sunlight. If only he could block out his brother's ability to irritate him as easily. Even so, it was worth taking Larry home just to see the look on their mother's face when they walked through the kitchen door. The excitement of the previous forty-eight hours did not lessen but served to sidetrack David's conflicted state of mind. Too many things said and unsaid had both cast a shadow over and highlighted the brothers' separate life paths. In many respects, the Dailey brothers were familiar strangers.

"Are you awake?" Larry's dry, scratchy voice rose from beneath the sheets.

"Well, yes, if not before. How'd you sleep?" David asked.

"I slept like Lincoln after a night at the theater. However, I've been thinking about Popeye. Why do you think he wanted to tell us about his time during the war?" Larry asked.

"I hadn't thought about it that way. At least not yet. He spent over three years of sheer hell, didn't he?" David said.

"You got that right."

"Maybe he regrets the loss of his pals."

"Who wouldn't? He survived though. I couldn't have. Wouldn't have wanted to," Larry said.

"You could if you had no choice. Popeye's a good guy. Not too much older than us."

"Had you ever heard of the battle for Wake Island?" Larry asked.

"Yes, but not much. I like history. Only problem is it's always changing."

"What? History can't change."

"I mean it's only what the current generation chooses to remember about another generation. I guess we didn't choose to remember Wake Island."

"I don't think I'll forget Wake Island. Not now," Larry said.

David wanted to continue the conversation and share some of his thoughts about the role history played in personal and national life. "I love history. It fascinates me."

If Larry had listened to his brother, it was not evident. "You think we should get something to eat before we head out?" he asked. David wanted to continue analyzing Popeye, Wake Island, and the subject of history but acquiesced in the interests of harmony and a timely reunion with the road.

"Well," David said. "I'll bet you five bucks that Bessie is waiting for us in the kitchen."

"Aren't you the high roller? You're on," Larry said. "Let's get up and go see. We need to get rolling."

As they walked from cabin number one toward the back door of Roy's Café, the smell of frying bacon beckoned. A coyote-sized, mixed-breed dog with a shabby, ashen coat loped across their path headed in the same direction. He trotted to the door, rose on spindly hind legs, and punched the latch with both front paws. As the door opened, he entered, whereupon the door swung shut with enough force to relatch itself.

"See that!" Larry yelped. "Guess y'all are welcome around these parts."

David grinned. "Was that the same dog we saw last night? ... Ah, smells like bacon wafting out to me."

Upon entering, they found the dog sprawled out on the floor in front of the bar, exactly where they'd seen him last night. He lifted his head and, with a slight nose quiver, approved of the two men then quickly rested back down with a soft but audible exhale.

A short, stout woman, presumably Bessie, popped her round face over the swinging kitchen door. "Mornin', gents. Take a seat anywhere. I'll get your order in a sec. Coffee?"

The brothers replied in chorus, "Yes," and made their way to last night's table. They sat in the same chairs they had chosen the night before. Other than the dog and Bessie, they were the sole occupants of the café.

"We'd like two cups of your best Amboy coffee!" Larry shouted.

"Only the best for Roy's guests." Bessie had disappeared back into the kitchen but had no problem hearing and responding to Larry.

David watched his brother while he rubbed the thumb and fingertips of his right hand in his face. "Looks like you owe me one Abraham Lincoln."

Larry ignored the gesture.

Popeye entered through the main door. "How you two doin' this mornin'?" From his berth beneath the bar, the dog batted his tail twice against the floor but didn't open his eyes or raise his head.

"So far so good," Larry said. "Sure could use some of that good coffee we've been promised."

"I'm sure it's on its way. Let me get your orders. You two'll need a good breakfast before taking on the crater."

"Crater? What crater?" Larry asked. "We're on a tight schedule. How far to Needles? We gotta get goin' if we ever expect to be in Chicago day after tomorrow."

"Chicago?" Popeye repeated. "Everyone who passes through Amboy must see the Amboy Crater. That includes you two pilgrims."

Bessie surged through the swinging door with a mug of coffee in each hand. As she sat the coffees before her customers, she asked, "May I suggest eggs, bacon, and hot cakes?" Like Popeye, she asked with an assurance in her voice that predetermined approval.

"Sounds good to me. How about you, Larry?"

"Guess I'll give it a try."

After a half hour of back-and-forth with Popeye, and a breakfast that would satisfy half a dozen starved lumberjacks, the brothers agreed to go see Popeye's crater. Neither had ever seen an actual volcanic crater. David had read about the Amboy Crater but didn't let on, not wanting to dampen Popeye's enthusiasm that radiated his passion for everything Amboy.

Popeye split his time talking with the brothers and waiting on two truckers and a female forest ranger. The forest ranger seemed out of place in the middle of a desert, but Popeye's greeting indicated she was a regular. The ranger supported Popeye's nature-hike suggestion for the brothers.

"Do you think Popeye ever meets a stranger?" David asked.

"He for sure never says goodbye to one," Larry replied.

Popeye carried a steaming tin coffee pot as he visited with customers, refilling their coffees, and seeing to their needs. When he observed the brothers were about to complete their breakfast, he headed back in their direction.

"Sure you don't want a little more coffee?" The Daileys agreed they were more than satisfied. "Good, it's settled. You can walk from here. Hobo will show you the way." Popeye sounded more like a tour director than a waiter or bartender. Again, it reminded David of Kwan, his Avalon carriage driver. The sleeping dog jumped to attention at the sound of his name and shook his entire body from head to rump. Popeye pointed and commanded, "At ease, Hobo!" The compliant pooch gave off a short whine, circled twice as if searching for a perfect landing strip and then flopped, with chin on the floor, eyes glued to his master and ears half-perked. "Mind your manners. Our guests haven't finished breakfast." Hobo's eyes followed Popeye into the kitchen, but he did not raise his chin from the floor.

"I don't know about walking. What do you think?" David asked.

Before they finished their third cup of coffee, Popeye trooped back from the kitchen with a canteen of water in one hand and two old hats in the other. "Saddle up, men. You, too, Hobo. I'll point you in the direction. As you see, Hobo wants to scout for you."

Hobo was already on all fours, shaking again from nose to tail, then wildly wagging his tail as he spun his wheels on the way to the front door. He punched the latch with ease and went out. Hobo clearly was on a mission.

"How long did it take you to teach him how to open doors?" Larry asked.

"You mean Hobo? Smart dog. No one taught him. Been with us for … 'bout two years now. Found him sleeping by the door one morning. Since then, we've never locked the doors. Hobo sleeps in front of the bar. Sort of our night watchman … though more of a welcome mat, to tell ya the truth." An affection for the ungainly canine played out in Popeye's eyes. "He pays for his keep by helping Bessie with the scraps."

Once outside, Popeye pointed up the road in the direction they had come from the day before and insisted they take the water canteen and each wear one of his hats. "Up sixty-six a ways, you'll see a trail off to your left. In the distance, you'll see what looks like a flat-top mountain; that's the Amboy Crater. Follow the path. When you get to the crater, you'll see a steep path up. Don't take it. Stay on the trail to the right till you see a shorter, easier path up. Take it."

"How far is it?" David asked.

"Oh, 'bout two, three miles." Popeye scratched his chin.

"One way?" Larry asked.

"I don't know. Should you be walking that far?" David questioned his brother.

Popeye chuckled. "Stay on the trail. Don't step on any rattlesnakes. Hobo will usually alert you."

"Usually?" David asked.

"Rattlesnakes," Larry said. "Dave, I thought you said there was only one rattlesnake in this desert?"

"Oh, there's a sight more than that. But they ain't no bother, usually," Popeye said.

"Usually?" echoed the brothers. They exchanged another questioning glance then repeated, "*Usually?*"

From a short distance up the road, Hobo sat on his haunches and stared back at the three men. Larry shouted, "High-O, Hobo!" The dog sprang up, let out a shrill yip, spun around, and dashed away on up the highway to the west.

"Wait up!" David shouted. Hobo and Larry shared a determined launch, and David refused to be left behind. The mid-morning sun warmed their backs as they started on their crater journey. It was a comical sight: an overly motivated, scruffy crossbreed dog leading two middle-aged men wearing old-timer, worn-out Orange County baseball hats on a safari.

Hobo waited impatiently at the trail cutoff. A clear view of the crater lay straight before them, although the path to their destination was obscured as it bent into dense low-growth sagebrush. Again, Hobo streaked ahead. "Wait up, Hobo!" Larry hollered as he picked up the pace.

"We've already gone over a mile," David said. "I think this may be a bit too strenuous to be fun. You've only been out of the hospital a day and a half. Maybe we should turn around?"

"Get serious. I don't know about you, but I was born for strenuous." Larry beckoned over his shoulder as he forged ahead of his brother. Hobo darted back and forth across the path before them with his nose stuck close to the ground—tail swishing vigorously.

After thirty more minutes of hard walking, they arrived at what looked like the base of the Amboy Crater as described by Popeye. However, it was too massive to fully comprehend. They paused to catch their breath and take a look around. The air was still and hot. David unscrewed the canteen top and handed it to Larry. He took several swallows and handed it back to David, who also took an ample drink. Without relaxing, Larry tramped forward on the trail's right fork with David close behind. Soon, they came to a near-vertical pathway leading skyward.

"Not this," Larry said as he squinted up. Their guide had rushed ahead on the scent of some elusive prey. "Follow Hobo," Larry said. Hearing his name, Hobo stopped motionless and stared back at his followers. The instant they started toward him, he scampered forward, in and out of view, nose low, tail high.

"We're at least a mile from the highway," David repeated. "At least." He shook his head as a bead of sweat dripped from the tip of his nose.

Eventually, they came to a gentler slope up toward a lower summit, and one they could clearly see. Hobo had already found it and climbed fifty feet ahead with little effort. He stopped and, as before, stared back at his two followers. Larry shouted, "Charge, Hobo!" Their chaperone whirled and bounded still higher.

"Do you think that dog's done this before?" David said.

"D'ya think?" Larry said.

The two men paused again to catch their breath and look around at their surroundings. The few trees and low straggly brush had little foliage and provided less shade. With the lack of a breeze, standing still provided no comfort either. They started to climb.

When they reached the crater's rim, they were able to gaze for miles across the desert plain. "It takes your breath away," David said. He turned his face away from the scorching sun and into a faint summit breeze. "It feels like we're in a hot air balloon, although I've never been in one."

"Amazing." Larry walked on a few steps and peered down into the crater. "Amazing! It must have taken a huge meteorite to have blown this hole." He lifted his gaze along to the opposite wall to see the elevation of that portion of the crater's rim still quite a ways above them.

"No, no, my dear Larry," David said as he resurrected his contrived Viennese accent and impulsively seized the opportunity to enlighten his brother. "What we're standing on is the cinder cone of an extinct volcano, possibly eighty thousand years old. We are at a point much lower than the majority of the summit rim, which is approximately two hundred and fifty feet above the desert floor. If you can believe it, we are less than halfway up and in the middle of the volcano's breach. When this side blew, and basalt lava spilled out, it created a lava plain below about the size of one Michigan township. The last eruption was approximately ten thousand years ago."

Following the self-important conclusion of David's mini-lecture, he was shocked to find Larry burning hot and not from the heat of the sun.

"There you go again! How the hell do you know? When did you become the vulcanization authority? Right or wrong, you're still the same pompous asshole! Some things never change." Larry turned his attention back to the crater, his anger palpable.

David recoiled at Larry's confrontation. It had never occurred to him his brother viewed him as condescending. Obviously, his Viennese accent, which he often reverted to unwittingly, had added to his brother's annoyance. Whatever the reason, David tried to smooth things over.

"Sorry. I don't know why I talk like that. Just trying to be funny, I guess. We all like to be in the know, don't we?"

"You sound ridiculous, and it's becoming monotonous."

"I said I'm sorry. Ya know, Larry, sometimes I feel jealous of you, even envy you. Compared to you, I'm so provincial. Sorry, I mean rural, commonplace, even downright dull." Before David was halfway through this well-intended confession, he was already questioning himself as to why he was doing it.

Larry faced David, furrowed his brow, and raised his hands palms up. "What? Why would you be jealous of me? Ridiculous."

Uneasy moments passed with both surveying the extraordinary depth of the crater. After second-guessing himself, David tried again to smooth things between them. "During the time I spent waiting for your release from the hospital, I went to a library and looked up the route we should follow going home. I read about this volcano. Anybody can do that. If I have an off-putting way of sharing information, I apologize." Larry made no effort to reply or even look at David. Whether because of curiosity or avoidance, his attention was the crater's interior contours.

"As for the jealousy ..." David rambled on, mainly to himself. "I'd always figured I'd shown you the way. At least, that was my intention. I wanted to make sure you knew what to expect, what was important and what was not. What classes and teachers to take and which ones to avoid. I wanted you to excel. But when you did, I started to resent it. Eventually, I convinced myself you had an unfair advantage. You weren't special, or whatever Mom used to say. I resented the fact the Mom and Dad always worried about you, even today."

"Say what?" Larry asked. "Ahh, forget it. Let's do a little exploring inside this bowl."

"Sure you should do that? It's getting pretty darn hot." David took a white handkerchief from his back pocket and wiped uncomfortable perspiration from the back of his neck. Both of their shirts showed armpit and midsection discoloration from sweat that had almost dried due to the hot, dry air.

"Look, I can do anything I set my mind to. Stop mothering me! Come on; we won't go too far. I just want to see what it's like. What do you think, Hobo?"

Panting with his large pink tongue hanging out, Hobo sat on his haunches, listening. But he remained beyond arm's reach as he regarded his two charges through brown eyes. When Larry returned his stare, Hobo tilted his wary head to one side and licked his chops. Larry stepped forward to pet the dog, but Hobo jumped back out of reach.

"I'm with Hobo. There's no need to go into the crater."

"I'm goin'," Larry insisted.

Larry led as the brothers started down the cone's steep interior wall. Small rocks and black sand broke loose beneath their sliding feet and tumbled down ahead of them. Their companion stood sentry duty up top, content to watch the would-be mountain climbers.

"Smell something?" David asked.

"What?"

"Sulfur?" David pretended to smell a mysterious odor. He'd seen enough and wanted to turn around for his benefit, as well as his brother's. Their footing was precarious at best, and it didn't look to be improving any ahead of them down the crater's interior wall.

"Come on," Larry said. "Don't be such a chicken shit."

There was not much to see other than ancient lava rocks, loose stones, and coarse sand. As the two slid deeper, David wondered if his new relationship with his brother would end up equally as empty as the Amboy Crater. They did not go far nor last long before Larry submitted to turning around. The hot, suffocating atmosphere within the crater was too oppressive. Even though they had no more than a thirty-five-foot climb back to the rim, they arrived gasping for air. The bills of their hats were damp with sweat. Pant legs stuck to their skin adding more difficulty to every step.

"Suffocating in there, and it's getting damn hot out here," Larry said. The sun beat down from high in a cloudless, blue sky. Hobo, their determined guide, had deserted, no doubt in quest of a shady place to rest.

"At least we can breathe up here," David said. "Have you noticed your sweat seems to evaporate before it runs down your neck?"

"Look at it this way, we're halfway home, and it's all downhill," Larry said.

"Let's drink to that," David said. They shared another healthy drink from Popeye's water canteen in spite of David's initial call for some restraint.

"Hey, Dave, look! There are your buzzards." Larry pointed at two dark shadows lazily circling at crater-top altitude. They were large black vultures approximately a mile away in the direction of the highway.

"Think a car hit something? We'd better get started back," David said. He removed his hat and rubbed his forehead with his right forearm.

"No problem. I don't know about you, but I'm still thirsty," Larry said.

"Let's head for Ole' Roy's. Here, Hobo!" David called. Both men scanned the brush below and called several times, but their faithful guide never appeared.

David flashed a worried look.

"Ahh, he knows his way home," Larry said. "He's probably already stretched out on the tavern floor."

Once they reached the base of the cone, they discussed which direction to take. Larry wanted to explore to the left, explaining the trail obviously continued around the crater's base, and they were surely over halfway around. David thought it safest to return the way they had come but gave in to his brother's logic.

The unfamiliar trail led them through kindling-dry scrub brush and short, spiky, emaciated Joshua trees. As they walked along an ever-thinner path, David watched for the buzzards but could not see them.

"Here, Hobo!" Larry called. It was early afternoon. The merciless sun had reached its zenith and now bore down on the hikers. Both called for Hobo. David hoped the dog had found his way back to the café. The thought passed his mind that the vultures may have been circling Hobo's lifeless body on the highway. The dog seemed to think he owned the road.

"Are you sure this path goes all the way around?" David asked. The footpath meandered through the brush and seemed headed farther out from the cone's base. David started to fear they'd lose their bearings.

"It looks doubtful," Larry said. "Maybe we better go back the way we—" Before Larry could complete the suggestion, a silent, dark shadow then another sailed across the path and scrub ahead. They looked up to see two black vultures silently gliding overhead with necks hooked downward.

"Let's go back," David said and turned around. Now the thought passed through his mind, *If those two birds aren't circling a dead carcass, what prospective meal are they circling?* "My sense of personal mortality has sharpened of late."

"I'm right behind you. Did anyone think two canteens? I need a drink."

"If we make it back to Roy's, I'm a Roy's fan for life," David said. He showed his brother the salt-line of how sweat had dripped off the bill of his cap. However, the cap was almost dry.

"Damn hot!" Larry roared.

"An hour to an hour and a half, I'd guess. Do you want to rest for a while?"

"Not me. Let's keep a steady pace. I need a tall, cold one, maybe three," Larry said.

Once they found the point where they had ascended the crater, they acknowledged it to each other with a blank look and continued on retracing their earlier hike. The buzzards hovered lower but had circled ahead and sporadically disappeared from view. David was sure more vultures had joined their slow death spirals but never saw more than two at a time. Still no Hobo.

They paused to share the remainder of the canteen. Conversation ceased as they conserved their energy. "Here, Hobo," now sounded more like a forlorn plea for help. Their stamina waned, but they were not sweating at all, and their clothes were dry. David kept a close eye on his brother's progress. He remembered Kwan's story of the Frozen Chosen and thought how unlike, but in some ways very alike, their current predicament it was.

Once back at the highway, they could see the sign for Roy's Café and the outline of the gas station and tavern beyond. Without conversation or hesitation, they started to walk along the left side of the highway. Larry stumbled but caught himself and carried on close to normal.

"Have you seen those buzzards?" Larry asked.

"I'm more worried about Hobo. Popeye will be upset if we've lost him. He seems to have a thing for that mangy mutt," David said.

"Ahh, don't worry about that dang dog. He's sucking down a cold beer back at Ole' Roy's right now. Come on, let's pick it up. We're loafing out here." Larry spoke in his typical virile manner but did not pick up his pace, nor did David. Shimmering heat could be seen rising from the pavement ahead, but no oncoming traffic stirred the air.

As they walked single file along the highway's shoulder, David combed both roadsides and beyond for their missing companion, and Larry did the same. "Here, Hobo." There was something endearing about Roy's security guard. If he didn't show up, David was at a loss for what to say, if anything, to Popeye. And what about Larry? He had been walking in the desert heat for over three hours and had drunk no water for well over an hour.

David looked back at the highway behind them. Not a car nor truck nor dog in sight. No buzzards or snakes. Empty.

"Hobo. Here, Hobo. Come here, boy," David pleaded. "Here boy."

CHAPTER 6
Oatman, Arizona

Once the Dailey boys reached Roy's, they headed straight into the saloon where each inhaled a cold draft. No Hobo under the bar. When their mugs were drained, which didn't take long, Larry hustled out the back door to fetch their suitcases while David pulled the Chevy around to the service pumps. No Hobo.

A thermometer bolted in the shade of an outside station wall registered 119 degrees. An old-timer pumped their gas, but David insisted on personally checking the oil, radiator water level, and tire air pressure. He even checked the air pressure of the spare tire housed in a decorative chrome shield attached above the rear bumper. He had paid extra for the custom-built spare tire carrier and was proud to have never seen another exactly like it. When the service stop was complete, David pulled the dust-covered Chevy back in front of the café to pick up his brother, all the time on the lookout for the truant security guard. No Hobo.

Bessie insisted her two boys go take a shower and change their clothes, which didn't take much encouragement. When they returned, she begged the men to rest a spell and taste-test a bowl of her freshly cooked beef stew, a menu choice uniquely out of place in the middle of a scorching desert. Even though the Daileys had enjoyed a bountiful breakfast, both were hungry. Larry negotiated with Bessie, "We'll try a bowl of your stew if you promise it comes with a cold Bud?" The short, pear-shaped cook cautioned him that drinking and driving should never go together. After a stern maternal look, Bessie scurried off to the kitchen.

"So hot in that crater, you could bake a tater!" Popeye bellowed as he entered through the kitchen door. Immediately, he wanted to know what the men thought of their nature hike and his celebrated Amboy Crater. Both Daileys knew what the answer must be.

"Spectacular," David said and, as soon as possible, deflected the course of discussion by asking what the highway looked like east toward Needles. Still no Hobo.

Bessie returned with two hearty bowls of stew and reluctantly told Popeye to fetch a couple of small mugs of beer. She worried about their sunburned faces as only a mother would do. After serving each his bowl of beef stew, she quick-stepped outside to cut a thick green leaf from a potted aloe vera plant she'd nurtured all summer long. When Bessie returned, she crushed the leaf in her hands and rubbed the juice on the necks and faces of the two hikers even while they tried to eat, as if they were her very own children. Neither man complained. Bessie noted Larry was going to have blisters on his neck and possibly on one of his cheeks and forearms.

"Feels good," David said. "I have never heard of this."

"I have. Do you really think it works?" Larry asked. "Say, can you make tequila out of this stuff?"

"I think that's a different plant. Anyway, don't think I'd drink it," Bessie said. She squeezed some aloe vera juice into a small glass jar with the leaf remains and instructed, "Take this with you and use as needed. You'll know when," she said.

In spite of pleas from both Bessie and Popeye to stay another night, the Daileys managed to finish their lunch, thank their host and hostess, and bid them farewell. All four headed out to the Chevy. Bessie cut another leaf of the aloe vera plant and handed it to Larry. "Take this along. You may need it for those blisters headed your way."

It was mid-afternoon, and their goal was to make it to the Arizona border before sundown. At David's side window, Popeye tapped the hardtop with the palm of his hand. "Two hours tops." In spite of their somewhat stressful stay in Amboy, David pledged to Popeye that he'd be back someday.

As they pulled out of the lot onto the all-too-familiar highway, David punched the accelerator and spun the rear tires, throwing up some sand and gravel. He prized the sound of the engine's rumble through the split manifold and dual custom chrome-plated exhaust pipes. In the rearview mirror, Popeye stood at attention in the middle of the highway, saluting. At his side was Hobo, on haunches, ears perked, staring up the road after them. Relief washed over David like breakers on the California coastline. Hobo had returned home, exactly where he needed to be.

"Larry! Look behind. Hobo's back." Both men waved out their respective windows. "Ya know, I come to like that ole' boy."

"Which one?" Larry asked. "Can you imagine trying to make a livin' out here?"

David compressed the gas pedal and accelerated to seventy miles per hour, his cruising speed. The slow, steady fifty-mile climb from Amboy to Cadiz Summit passed without conversation. That included the laconic, brown coconut who had gained a large green aloe vera leaf and a funny-looking little glass juice jar as back-seat companions.

Finally, Larry adjusted his ventilator to redirect the wind flow through the car. Gawking out his window, he asked, "What's with all the rock graffiti?"

David suggested he look in the glove compartment for the roadmap.

Larry struggled with the wind as he tried to unfold and straighten an unruly road atlas. "Says here that it's a tourist tradition to write a message on the stone walls of the Marble Mountains. My guess is we are in the Marble Mountains."

"There should be a law against that," David said.

"What? Being in the Marble Mountains?" Larry asked. Then, realizing his brother's meaning, he continued, "Ahh, I don't know. In LA, we call it public art. Wanna pullover, Kilroy, and write we were here?"

"No. And, yes, I know who Kilroy was."

"Interesting, 'cause no one else does nowadays."

As they cleared the summit, David again pumped the accelerator. The monotonous miles passed like a coal barge plowing up the Ohio River, but according to the map, they were cruising downhill.

They had been on the road for over an hour, yet both believed it would be another two before they escaped the oppressive desert heat. From glitzy Venice Beach to across the motionless Mojave Desert, the world rolled past. For David, California was a menagerie of split personalities somewhat out of focus, especially in contrast to Three Oaks, a quintessential still life of Americana straight out of *Better Homes & Gardens*.

Endless miles passed on. David could not make up his mind. He looked forward to Larry's homecoming but also reminded himself that he personally might not be there to observe their mother's delight. Larry was at best a reluctant traveler, never satisfied or positive he really wanted to revisit his boyhood home. David took a perverse pleasure in what he considered his brother's self-important ignorance.

"Dave, I've been thinking about last night. You know, before Popeye marched us off to war. You want to know why I left Michigan. Make no mistake, it wasn't the knee-jerk decision you may think it was."

"Come on, let bygones be bygones. We've miles to go before we sleep."

"Yes, and I have promises to keep. You still need to hear this."

"*I* need to, or is it a need *you* have for the last word?" The last thing David would ever want was something his brother told him he needed. Larry's snarky manner irritated David to the quick. As much as he dreaded listening to his obstinate brother, he chose appeasement as the better course. He'd listen to him but wait for a quiet opportunity to clarify. It was clear Larry was not to be deterred, so David bided his time.

Larry glared fixedly through the windshield, like an army general surveying enemy lines before marshaling his forces for the next onslaught. Without a cloud in the sky, a tempest brewed within the smooth ride of the Chevrolet Bel Air.

"Remember when you enlisted in the Coast Guard? Everybody thought you were such a war hero? 'Larry, you should follow in your brother's footsteps.' I heard that garbage a thousand times. But we weren't at war, and I wanted no part of the military, much less follow you into it."

"Excuse me, Larry. Allow me to clear up your thinking on the matter of my service in the Coast Guard. I enlisted over two years before Pearl Harbor. You were still in high school, and true, we were not at war, but war had started in Europe and was headed our way."

"So you say. 'You should follow your brother into the service.' 'Isn't it great what your big brother is doing?' 'We need more young men like David, protecting America.' David this, David that, all year long. I wanted to barf."

"Give it up, Larry. What did you want, another plaque, another gold star? How many letters did you have Mom stitch on your varsity letter jacket? They told me you looked like a Christmas tree."

"Give it up, my ass! It didn't matter what I did, what I accomplished. All anybody could think about was *you*. Whenever company came over, all they wanted to do was talk about you. I felt like a doormat. And Ma forever writing you letters, sending you things, and asking Dad and me to write something she could add. I never did and never will." Bitterness seemed to ooze from every pore in Larry's sunburned face. He flailed around, assembling grievances, and David saw that a foul conclusion loomed near.

"You're absurd. I admit, I did look forward to Mother's letters and her oatmeal cookies. But, Larry, I always wanted to know about you, and Mom told me. She was proud of you. We all were. I wanted to come back home from the day I left for basic training. Hopelessly homesick. Did you know that? I bet you never read any of my letters."

"Are you deaf? Never did and never will. I wanted to separate myself from you, and I did. I graduated first in my class. No one even close." Larry shook his head in a haughty fashion reminiscent of World War II newsreels of an arrogant Benito Mussolini addressing the adoring Italian throngs in the street beneath his palace balcony.

"I put in for leave so that I could attend your graduation, hear your valedictory address. If you don't remember, I sure do."

As David spoke, the memory of his brother's speech screeched in his ears. Why had he said things that could have been taken as disparaging toward teachers and classmates? And what about, "No one's going to stand in my way," or "Most people make a pitiful effort in everything they do." Their mother thought it eloquent. Their father reacted with amusement: "No surprises there." David found it a bombastic, self-centered rant and feared people would be offended, if not threatened by his brother's egotistical bluster.

"I remember that you were on the high seas somewhere, keeping us safe, doing your duty for good old God and country," Larry said, sarcasm dripping.

"Come on. The closest I ever came to the war was riding in a boat on Lake Michigan. I might as well have been fishing for perch off the New Buffalo Pier for all the good I did." David reminded his brother that when he'd arrived home on leave, he found Larry already packed for California. They left the day following graduation. David had only two weeks' leave before he had to report back to the Chicago Great Lakes Naval Station.

"I didn't need you holding my hand," Larry said.

"Who said you did? You invited me, remember? And I wanted to go. Didn't we have a great time following this old road from Chicago all the way to the west end of the Santa Monica Pier? We both dove in off the end of the pier." The image of two bold young men provided both with an internal thrill, but Larry exhibited only outward indifference.

They had been twenty-two years younger back then, and each day was a welcomed new adventure. Both young men were full of optimism. David knew there was more of a difference between this trip and the one long ago, more than simple direction.

He continued, "That trip was pure fun. Seeing mountains and an ocean for the first time was like Christmas morning when we were kids." A glimmer of that same emotion showed in Larry's body language.

"Do you remember the hole-in-the-wall tavern we found in Needles?" David asked.

"The Rodeo Roadhouse? I remember that cowgirl who flung a mug of beer at you. Good lookin' trailer trash, I'd say, but judging from what she said about you, she held a low opinion of our mother. How'd you piss her off anyway?" Larry play-acted sympathy for the cowgirl in spite of a Cheshire cat grin covering his pink face.

"You know damn well! You just want me to try to explain it again for your amusement," David emphatically proclaimed in hopes it would placate his moody brother. It worked for the pair of them.

"Well, I doubt anyone would ever believe you, but refresh my memory." Larry's Cheshire grin glowed through his sunburned cheeks now displaying three small blisters. His fair skin had always been something of a family anomaly.

"As I said then and repeat now, I did not request sexual favors from that young lady. Do you think I would have shouted something so gross across a crowded tavern, in a strange town, at a woman I'd never seen before? It was that snaggle-toothed cowpoke seated behind me amongst his snot-snorting, beer-swilling posse."

"Sure, Dave? That booted beauty was pissed and comin' for you. What did you say, anyway?"

"I didn't say a damn thing. *Nada!* Just sat there quietly drinking a beer."

"Well, that's the only time I've ever seen a mild-mannered beer drinker thrown out of a rowdy saloon."

"Simple, Larry. I agreed with the bouncer that it would be best for everyone if I simply left. He never threw me out."

"Sure as hell looked like it. All I know is that herd of thirsty drovers gave the bouncer a big cheer when he escorted you out the door. 'Yeeee haaaa! Get-a-long there, little doggy!'" Larry slapped his leg and stomped the floorboard.

David reacted with a shallow pretense of disinterest. "Larry, why the rush to get to California? What was the draw anyway?"

"No. Had to get out of Three Oaks." Larry's mood again darkened. He sat still as a faraway stare clouded his eyes. "There's something … something I've never told you, anyone." Larry hesitated, as if the rhythmic beat of rubber over highway expansion joints had become hypnotic. Hot wind swirled through the open windows.

Larry resurfaced, took a long, deep breath before he turned to face his brother. "Remember Maggie, Maggie Stevens?"

"Maggie Stevens? Who wouldn't? I remember Maggie. Foxiest girl in the county, maybe the state. I took Maggie to the prom. Most gorgeous woman to ever stroll across the gym floor. She clung to me like her black gown clung to *her*. Those were the days. Every guy there salivated, wishing they could trade places with me."

"That's the one."

"Why would you ask about Maggie? Don't get me wrong, I'm glad you did. I doubt I've seen her more than once since high school." That was a lie, one that had gone unnoticed by a single-minded Larry. Maggie Stevens had occupied a secret corner of David's heart ever since high school.

"I ran into her at Marty's graduation party," Larry said. "Her younger brother, Marty, remember him? Marty was in my grade."

"No, I don't think so," said David.

"Maggie was home from Northwestern and, without question, table grade and knew it. Her luscious body was all me and my buddies could stand. Someone asked me, 'Did your brother get any of that?' I told them, 'I doubt it, but I'd sure like to take her for a test drive.'"

"So? What's the big deal? All guys want that. She was a queen."

"There's more. Maggie came over to me as if I was her long-lost best friend. I had never spoken a word to her in my life. Of course, as usual, she wanted to know all about you, where you were, what you were doing, who you were dating—the usual crap."

"Here you go, Larry. We better change the subject before you get all jacked out of shape again."

"No, it's not what you think. Maggie became interested in me. She kept touching me, rubbing my back. She made me feel like a million bucks. More sophisticated than those high school Harriets I'd gone out with. More my style. Never felt so good. The fact that you had once dated her made her extra tantalizing. All my buds watching, eating it up. I was the main man. Main man! No question."

"That's what you wanted, right? Are you confessing or crowing?"

"There's more," Larry said.

Near midnight, Maggie had asked if Larry wanted to see what her father had given her for her birthday. She took him by the hand and led him through the kitchen into the garage. As soon as she closed the kitchen door behind them, she wrapped her arms around his shoulders and seized him in a passionate embrace. It took Larry by surprise, his first French-kissing encounter, and he all but lost his balance and had to mask his gasping for air.

In the dim light of the garage, Maggie had rubbed her warm nose up Larry's neck until she'd found and nibbled on an earlobe, slowly probing with her warm, moist tongue. In a breathy whisper, she told him, "Come, I want to show you something. Only you."

Maggie had taken Larry by the hand and guided him down two steps into the small, attached garage. With only the eerie light provided by a workbench lamp, Larry was unsure of each step. However, with adrenalin surging through his body, he became an eager participant in whatever his temptress desired.

As his eyes had adjusted to the dim light, it became clearer. "New car?" he stated as much as asked.

Maggie had giggled bouncily and tugged on his arm. "It sure is. My daddy gave it to me for my twentieth birthday. I can't wait to drive up to my sorority house. I don't really need a car at school, but I'll take it."

Awestruck, Larry had concealed an involuntary slow swallow. He had never seen a new car in person, only in magazines. "It's a Che-Chevrolet," he stammered.

"You betcha. A 1941 Chevy convertible from the factory to me. Even has a ragtop to match my hair. Dad says it's not for a little girl, and I'll have to take more responsibility. Do you think I'm a little girl," Maggie had cooed playfully and batted her sleepy blue eyes. She also informed Larry that she knew he was going to graduate first in his class and was sorry she had only graduated third in hers.

Larry had drooled over the neatly folded-down tan ragtop, white sidewall tires, rear-wheel fender skirts, and the smooth, deep-green precious metal finish. It smelled of new leather. "MAGGIE" was engraved in gold on the ivory cue ball affixed atop the long floor-mounted gearshift. An unfamiliar twinge of self-consciousness channeled deep within Larry.

"Isn't it the bee's knees? Jump behind the wheel, Mr. Dailey." Maggie had opened the driver's side door and given Larry a gentle shove to slide inside. She skipped around to the other side and hopped in, sliding up against her driver. "My daddy says we can't take her out until he gets home. Let's pretend. I like parking too. Don't you?" Before Larry could answer, Maggie nuzzled in closer. She lightly put her hand on Larry's inner thigh and snuggled her face between his head and shoulder. A mysterious floral scent lingered in the air. Her warm panting beneath his shirt collar roused a desire for more.

The spontaneity of such an entangled, lustful struggle had been new territory for Larry, although he'd eagerly responded. He luxuriated in Maggie's aggressive, passionate kissing accompanied by ever-heavier petting. They tore off their garments and soon were naked in front of each other. Before he could caress one bare breast in his hand, the second found his mouth. Suddenly, Larry experienced a collision of raw desire and innocent apprehension. Desire won. Their nude bodies struggled for position within the confined quarters of the front seat. As Maggie directed Larry toward her moist private area, he felt an irrepressible euphoric eruption welling up from deep in his groin, ultimately enveloping his entire being. He moaned in sheer ecstasy then tightly clung to Maggie, motionless.

Larry's ecstasy had soon been swallowed by embarrassment. He was at a complete loss for what to say or do. For her part, Maggie was confused and disappointed by her partner's unexpected drawback from their love-making trajectory.

The abrupt termination of pleasurable intimacy had befuddled Maggie, but she'd, unlike Larry, had a clearer understanding of what had happened. A sense of her frustration compounded Larry's insecurity. A minute of silence passed before they attempted to pull apart and reclaim articles of clothing. The comical nature of their effort to get dressed in the cramped quarters of the front seat served to alleviate some of the tension. Maggie tried to cover her disappointment and lighten the somber mood. "This would make a crazy modeling audition," she said. "Don't ya think?" Larry could only manage an awkward smile.

Once fully dressed, Maggie had straightened her mussed hair with her hands. Cheerfully, she insisted Larry promise to drop by about noon the next day. "We'll go for a ride. Just the two of us. Maybe to Warren Dunes? You can drive."

In spite of Maggie's supportive behavior, Larry's anxiety had lingered. He wanted to get out of there, go home. Nevertheless, he wanted to hang around, stay with his new love, and maybe have a second chance. *Is Maggie too sophisticated, too experienced, and perhaps, too rich for me?* He wondered. But he liked her, maybe loved her, and, at that moment, hungered to be with her. He pulled Maggie firmly against him, kissed her neck tenderly, and said, "S-see you at noon."

Maggie had cooed and pressed tighter. "Can't wait." It made little difference. Larry tried to conceal his uncomfortable feelings, but they refused to go away.

Larry completed the troubled story of his Maggie Stevens encounter in a dejected air of defeat, a side of him David had never witnessed. Larry had returned to the Stevens's home the following midday per Maggie's invitation but hadn't stopped. In the driveway were several boisterous college types all clustered around Maggie and her new car. Obviously, they were out-of-towners, strangers. From the end of the driveway, Larry tried to catch Maggie's eye and wave. Maggie may or may not have noticed him, but he thought she had. She was totally absorbed with her company though.

"I got the message. 'Keep movin', country boy.'"

David was quiet for a moment then said, "For what it's worth, I took Maggie out a couple of times before and after our prom date. All she ever wanted to talk about was skiing in Switzerland, sailing in the Caribbean, vacationing at the shore—her snobbish reference for the Delaware coast. You were right. I never got to first base." With that, he fulfilled the need to commiserate with his brother. But Larry's candid talk of Maggie Stevens had disturbed David far more than he let on.

After Larry's soapy confession, they rode without talking for several miles. Then Larry said, "A day or two after the Maggie thing, I swung by Had's Root Beer Stand. It became the school hangout after you graduated. Some of my baseball teammates were gathered at a picnic table out front. Jimmy Howard, who I thought was my best friend, yelled across the yard, 'Hey, ValaDick, a smart guy like you should have been able to close the deal!' They all hooted and slapped Jimmy's back. Other asshole remarks, obviously about Maggie and me, started to fly. But I couldn't play along. I made a lame excuse and left, totally pissed, totally humiliated. I don't know what they knew. Guessing maybe. Had Maggie made fun of me to them? I'm outta there. That's all I knew. Gone!"

It was clear his tryst with Maggie Stevens had hurt him to the quick and still did. More miles methodically clicked by. David searched for something to say but could only think of Maggie, a conversation topic he hoped had run its course. He had secrets of his own and knew they were intimately entwined with his plan to disappear. Neither said a word. Male members of the Dailey family were known for their lack of idle conversation, more than a generational characteristic.

"There's one more thing I'd like to get off my chest." The sound of wind gust and road noise all but drowned out Larry's voice.

"I feel sad for you. Are you sure you want to open another weighty memory?" David then tried to redirect his brother by pointing out that they had already passed through Needles. A signpost announced the Red Rock Bridge over the Colorado River and the Arizona border two miles ahead. "You interested in another roundup at the Rodeo Roadhouse?" David asked.

"Not really. As those cowpokes said, 'Get along, little doggie.' I could use a drink though," Larry said.

As they crossed the Colorado border, Larry spoke up again. "I did attempt to follow you, only you never knew it. It all came back to me while listening to Popeye." Larry explained that immediately following the Japanese attack on Pearl Harbor, he literally had run to the Los Angeles army recruitment post. "Would you believe I failed the physical? How in hell could that happen?"

Larry recalled it had been his left foot, apparently set incorrectly after he'd broken it ice-skating in the fourth grade. He couldn't believe he hadn't been sought after by the armed forces. "I for sure still hold the hundred-yard dash record at old Three Oaks High School." He demanded his brother not tell anyone he had been classified 4-F. "The only thing worse than a 4-F-er was a draft dodger."

"We always wondered why you had never been called up. We knew you were registered for the draft, but your name must never have been called. 'Lucky Larry,' Dad and Mom told everybody."

"No, in my case, it was not just another bureaucratic screw-up. I failed the physical," Larry said.

Larry's male ego knew no bounds regardless of the company he was in. David had usually been a tempering force. However, he made an exception this time and massaged Larry's wound. "We all thought it a little strange, you being such a good athlete and all. Why didn't you simply explain the physical disqualification? No one would have cared."

"Bullshit, David. Everybody cared. Especially so on the West Coast. The Japs and Krauts were coming, remember? The 4-F-ers were slackers at best. At worst, there was something unmentionably wrong with them. Believe me, women didn't want to be seen with a 4-F-er."

David encouraged Larry to forget it; after all it was long ago now, and no one could care less. "Look, we've crossed the Colorado River. Welcome to Arizona."

They turned north through the border town of Topock, Arizona. David spotted a busy roadside diner and pulled over onto the shoulder behind a flatbed load of lumber. Large trucks of all shapes and sizes lined the side of the highway in both directions. Waiting customers clogged the entrance.

"Truckers have a nose for good food," Larry said.

"Give me a tall order of air conditioning," David said. "My sunburn is really bothering me. How about you?" The answer was painted all over Larry's face, neck, and forearms. David retrieved Bessie's jar of aloe vera juice from the back seat, and they each rubbed the soothing liquid all over their sunburns.

While standing in line outside the restaurant's entrance, David pointed toward the sharp border-mountain peaks that had given Needles its name, but he anticipated Larry's disinterest and did not attempt to explain. Instead he said, "Not really hungry, are you?" Larry agreed but suggested they grab a quick beer, maybe a sandwich, and find the head.

The dining area seemed small, made more so because of the crowd and general commotion. They were directed to two empty counter stools but not together. A sleep-deprived long-hauler wearing an old, tattered high school letter jacket motioned to them and moved over so the brothers could sit together. To Larry's chagrin, he then discovered Topock was in a dry county.

They each ordered the Hauler's Special Burger—all the way. Neither knew the specific details of "all the way," and neither asked.

"How far to the Grand Canyon?" Larry asked as their frazzled, grease-spattered waitress hurried on her way to place their order at the kitchen window. She nodded but did not reply. A cool, thick smoky air swirled in her wake.

"If that's where you're headed, you won't make it today," the waitress advised out of the corner of her mouth as she whisked back by. On a return trip, she delivered two burgers and two bottled Pepsis with paper-tipped paper straws rising from their necks. "You'll be lucky to make it to Oatman by sundown. Wouldn't go that way though," she said as she stepped aside to allow the other waitress to pass.

"Didn't look that far on the map," Larry said.

"Ain't far. Just bad road across the rez," said the letter-jacketed high school hero seated on Larry's left. "I just came that-a-way. Road construction." Then he exhaled enough smoke to conceal the Seventh Fleet.

Their waitress encouraged the Daileys to take the bypass through Kingman to Flagstaff and again hurried on her way. The high school hero had disappeared behind a stubborn, blue fog. David appraised the clientele with interest while Larry attempted to request their bill before he discovered the check tucked under his plate.

The Daileys had taken their time while eating, both savoring the cool restaurant air. Larry took the check to the cash register and paid their bill. David left a dollar bill on the counter, which their waitress snatched on her way to the kitchen with a tub full of dirty dishes.

After a restroom stop, the two walked amid the steady rumble of idling diesel motors back to their car. David suggested they take the original road up through Oatman, as it was sure to be a more interesting drive. Larry said he'd rather sacrifice scenery for speed. "Besides, weren't we warned about roads across the rez?" The debate was settled less than five miles down the road when David missed the cutoff to Kingman. They were headed for Oatman, Arizona on the state's original portion of Route 66.

"What did you think?" David said.

"Of what?"

"The restroom."

"You're kidding," Larry said. "That was the largest men's room I've been in since we saw the Tigers play at Comiskey Park. And not sure it wasn't really a fucking rubber museum in poor disguise."

David added, "It was larger than the restaurant." Both claimed to have seen condom dispensers before but never so many in one place. There had been at least eight prophylactic vending machines representing the same number of condom distributors. Name brands were only exceeded by the various sizes, shapes, colors, and other featured amenities of the merchandise for sale. One could have spent an hour reading the advertised advantages and intimate pleasures provided by each of the contraceptive products. Some could have been mistaken for rides at the county fair.

The prominent warning, "Sold Only for the Prevention from Disease," had been displayed on each vending machine and merchandise wrapper. No mention of birth control. Placed in the center of the spacious latrine was a handy change dispenser. Some anonymous frontiersman had scribbled above a long open trough urinal, "Smile, you're on Candid Camera." David found the graffiti hilarious, but Larry had never seen the TV program by that name.

"Did you see the *Buckaroo Rodeo*—"

"Guess what?" David interrupted. He pointed Larry's attention to the road ahead. A flagman stopped the north-bound lane to allow a line of south-bound traffic to use the open half of the highway. They sat there for what seemed an eternity but was closer to ten minutes. The wait time gave David the opportunity to tell his brother about some of the funny *Candid Camera* episodes he'd seen on TV.

For the next eighteen miles, they intermittently crept forward single file between frequent stops. Once through the construction, the highway became increasingly fraught with sharp curves, steep grades, and hazardous driving situations aggravated by bulky dump trucks clogging the narrow two-lane road. Adding both interest and peril were the numerous large gold-and-silver speckled rocks strewn along the highway. They had fallen from overloaded ore trucks hauling iron pyrite, fool's gold, extracted from petered-out gold mines.

Snaking northward into the Black Mountains, the Chevy rarely exceeded thirty miles per hour. The sun sank below the mountains to the west. Several signs encouraged travelers to visit the Grand Canyon. The Daileys discussed the possibility, but the longer they crept forward, the less attractive that option became. Larry complained, "We'll never make it anywhere at this rate. Let's turn around then visit Three Oaks some other time."

After two and a half hours of tiresome, slow progress, they finally saw lights other than those of oncoming traffic. A partially lit roadside billboard read, "Oatman Village Limit, Mayor Al Goodnight." A few widely spaced streetlights provided meager illumination for the road through town, the only road.

"What's that?" David asked.

"What's what?"

"A really large dog, I think, just trotted across in front of us."

"I didn't see anything. Better gas up," Larry said.

David turned into a two-pump, ethyl and regular, Texaco station. It was the only gas station in what appeared to be a rather dreary little frontier outpost. A grubby young attendant sauntered out, enviously eyeballing the Bel Air while wiping his hands on an oil-stained cloth.

"Fill 'er up?" he asked.

"Yes," David said as he popped the hood to personally check the oil. The gas jockey washed the windshield but spilled Windex on the hood. David asked him to wash it off. Total bill was $5.25. David inquired where to find the nearest motel.

"Only one in Oatman. It's surely full by this time. Four cabins."

"Okay then, where's the closest motel between here and the Grand Canyon?"

The attendant scratched his butt, sprayed tobacco juice to the side, and exhibited a most pained expression when it missed his bucket target by three feet. Evidence of surrounding brown spatter suggested it hadn't been his first miss.

"Well, as near as I recollect, well, that-a-be Kingman. Three motels last I heard, maybe four. And there's a tourist court, if it's still operatin'."

"How far's Kingman?" David asked.

"Well." It took the attendant a lifetime to refocus since he couldn't take his eyes off the Chevy. Finally, he drawled, "If you could drive straight, you might could make it in one, maybe two hours. They says there's been a rock slide, but I heard it's open through now."

What little patience Larry had evaporated. In addition to his painful sunburn, the gas station attendant's slow manner of speech irritated him. He demanded, "Listen, we've been on the road all day. We need a place to stay overnight, now!"

The sluggish attendant removed his hat and wiped his brow with the same soiled rag David had borrowed to check the oil. He displayed no sense of urgency. "Well," he repeated. "Name's Earl, and my Aunt Alice has rent a room once in a while."

"Well! How can I find Aunt Alice?" Larry asked.

Earl straightened his hat above a thicket of dark, defiant, steel-wool hair. Then, taking his eyes off the Chevy, he shouted toward the service bay, "Yo, Aunt Alice! You willin' to rent a room?"

Presently, a woman dressed in baggy, men's coveralls emerged from a side door. She slapped her hands twice on her pant legs and adjusted a backward-worn, weather-beaten Chicago Cubs baseball cap.

"I reckon. Five dollars for the night!" she called, but when she saw the two men standing next to Earl, she added, "Apiece! Five dollars apiece!" She pointed toward a two-story, white-frame house straight across the highway. "You can park by the side there. I'll be over directly to get you settled. I've got to bleed the breaks on this Peterbilt first." Without waiting for a reply, she turned and disappeared back into the garage.

"She can bleed my breaks," Larry said under his breath.

The two men were given an upstairs bedroom with one double bed and two windows facing the highway. A large bathroom with a claw-foot tub and pedestal sink was on the first floor down a short hallway behind the kitchen. The lodgings tour was brief, but when Aunt Alice noticed their sunburns, she nodded to David then looked at Larry. "I thought I heard someone say they'd been in the car all day? I didn't see a convertible out there ...."

"You sound like Detective Joe Friday." Larry smiled back at their grease-smudged hostess. "They say sun makes a man thirsty. You know where we can get a beer?"

"Not this time a day. Not in Oatman. But I got something for your burn. It'll help you sleep. That's about all you'll do in Oatman this evenin'." Aunt Alice flashed a knowing expression back in David's direction.

"Thanks," David said. "I'll try anything. I can feel the heat on the back of my neck."

Aunt Alice retrieved a small mason jar of brown salve from the cupboard above the kitchen sink and handed it to Larry. "Rub this on your burn. It's a home remedy. Don't drink it." She held Larry's gaze with an amused sparkle in her eyes, completely comfortable in her grease-monkey appearance.

"I could use some of that. My sunburn has been bothering me ever since we crossed into Arizona," David said.

"Breakfast is at six. Extra blankets on the closet shelf." She turned and disappeared toward the back of the house.

Considering the circumstances, both men slept well. Sunburn ointment coupled with cool mountain air through an open window helped. Larry's burn had blistered in spots but appeared manageable. Neither anticipated taking advantage of Aunt Alice's unexpected, complimentary breakfast. However, they were awakened at 5:30 a.m. by the sound of trucks braking, backfiring, and accelerating through countless gears from Oatman's lone traffic light.

"What's that strange noise?" Larry asked.

"Don't know. Did you hear it during the night? Sorta like one of those old Model A *ahooga* horns," David said.

"Sounded more like Dad sharpening pruning saws behind the hardware," Larry said. "Scraping back and forth, back and forth. Smell coffee?"

They walked down the stairs and into the kitchen at 6:00 a.m. sharp. Aunt Alice, in a fresh pair of blue men's painter's pants, a red-and-gray plaid shirt, and hair pulled back in an attractive ponytail, was holding a platter full of flapjacks surrounded by fried Polish sausages. She motioned for her guests to take a seat at a small round oak table set with three yellow Fiesta plates and matching accessories atop oval reed placemats.

The kitchen, and house in general, seemed an anomaly to David. At first glance, it gave the impression of a Western antique museum, but on closer inspection, it revealed furnishings in first-class functional condition and a warm, inviting stylishness. A brief survey of wall hangings and other adornments portrayed an interior decorator of exceptional taste and a keen sense of family heritage.

"Good morning, Aunt Alice," Larry said with emphasis on *Aunt*. "What a beautiful home you have here."

The hostess beamed. "And good morning to the two of you. Please, call me Al. Only Earl calls me Aunt Alice, although we're really distant cousins. And thank you, my home is my pride and my project. Rather, 'life's mission' would be more correct."

"What is that strange noise we've been hearing?" Larry asked.

"Noise?"

"Yeah, the two-stroke, rasping *ahooga* horn every once in a while," David said.

"Oh, you must mean Rico. He's a burro that staked his claim out back. They're very territorial you know, burros. He takes to braying if he thinks something's amiss. Rico and I look after each other," she said.

"A burro named Rico?" Larry asked.

"Rico's my partner. We go prospecting every now and again. Actually, more like camping in the mountains for two or three days. Rico totes all our supplies."

"You and a donkey, alone in the mountains, for days?" Larry asked incredulously.

"Burros are the remainder of mining days. When the miners and prospectors left, they abandoned their pack animals. Burros roam as they please here in Oatman. You must have seen some on your way in. They meander around Oatman as if it is their private fiefdom."

Al displayed a wholesome western charm and possessed a trim-fit, feminine frame that did not escape either Dailey's appraisal. She set a steaming coffee pot and three matching earthen coffee mugs on the table. "Help yourself."

Returning to the refrigerator, she found a half-pound tub of butter and a glass bottle of Aunt Jemima's Maple Syrup. After placing them on the table, she said, "Dig in, boys. In these parts, we pray after we eat." All laughed at her rugged country pretense. Neither Larry nor David required much encouragement after little more than the Hauler's Special since Amboy. However, it was hard to avoid staring at Al, especially for Larry. There was a striking freshness about her that harmonized with the rugged, mountainous Arizona outback.

Al enjoyed sharing breakfast and conversation with her guests, and they felt the same. At first, there was little talk, attributable to good food and hungry people.

"What's to see in Oatman? I mean, why would someone come to Oatman?" Larry asked in a cordial manner unfamiliar to David.

"As mining declined, neighbors did tend to leave. Looking for greener pastures, I suppose. In recent years, travelers have avoided this stretch of highway. Can't say I blame them. We're surely off the beaten track."

"Yeah, David missed the exit for the bypass, or we wouldn't be here," Larry said.

"I'll admit we haven't seen much since we rolled in after dark, but it doesn't appear there's much to see. Reminds me of a ghost town," David said.

"I'd agree. In fact, waking up here, in this house, reminded me of Dorothy waking up in the Land of Oz. Your home feels, sort of like the start of the Yellow Brick Road," Larry said.

David observed Larry's manner, careful to avoid offense. In fact, a bit playful. From the glow on Al's face, she liked his Land of Oz comparison. So did David.

"Yes, Al, it seems a young person like yourself might be moving on from here," David said.

"For your information, I'm thirty-five and don't plan to move." With a good-natured flair, Al gave the brothers a fleeting sketch of her life. Before she started school, her mother had died while giving birth to a second child, who also died. Then as an only child with no mother, Al was raised by her father who did everything with her. According to Al, "Dad taught me everything I know." Her list of talents included hunting, fishing, prospecting, plumbing, carpentry, and auto mechanics. She had planned to move to Flagstaff and go to college following high school. But then her father died of cancer during her senior year. At the age of eighteen, she inherited and took over a gas station and engine repair shop.

"My business provides a good living. I have plenty of loyal customers, sometimes too many. You met my cousin, Earl. He helps at the station, and I sort of look after him." Then Al flashed a big smile, "And Oatman is not dying. It's coming back. Slow, but faster than my Chicago Cubs, but they'll be back too. The old Oatman Hotel is being renovated and will reopen before Christmas. Other small businesses are scratching out a place for themselves. You'll want to come back in about five years. There will be more than foraging burros roaming our streets. You'll see."

"I believe," Larry said. "I'm going to write to the Oatman mayor and tell him what a fantastic spokesperson you would make for his town."

Al let out a full-hearted laugh. "You could tell the mayor in person."

"I don't think we have time. We're kinda in a hurry," Larry said.

"You should make time. The mayor would be most appreciative," Al said.

"How's that?" Larry asked.

"I'm the mayor."

"Well," Larry said in a Cousin Earl sound-alike manner with no hint of embarrassment. "Mr. Mayor, I think you'd make a fantastic spokesperson for this future tourists' mecca, Oatman, Arizona. In fact, you've already passed that test." Larry winked at Al who smiled and turned her hazel eyes toward David.

"Old gold mines, a renovated hotel, and wild burros, wow. But, as my brother said, we don't have time today," David said.

"When I was eleven, Clark Gable and Carole Lombard spent their honeymoon at the Oatman Hotel. They're naming a suite in the movie stars' honor," Al said.

"I'm going to reserve that suite when I return," Larry said.

"Since the bypass opened, most travelers miss us. That will change. Where the two of you headed?" Al exhibited a pleasant curiosity about where the men were from and where they were going. Her questions were thoughtful and considerate. However, pride in her town and business remained near the surface. She did not plan to move.

"They say 'the last iceman always makes a profit,'" David said.

"Who's they?" Larry asked. "Your history teacher?"

"You got that right. Only, it was *our* history teacher," David replied.

Al chuckled, "Not sure I follow your analogy." And then she said, "There was a time when I'd wish I was going with you. Since Father died, I've pretty much devoted myself to Oatman. They say owning a service station is worse than owning dairy cows."

"Who's they?" Larry asked.

"Never looked at it that way, but I do follow your analogy," David said.

"Why don't you come with us? We've got plenty of room. Just an old coconut rolling around in the backseat," Larry said in jest.

"This girl has never been out of Arizona," Al replied.

"No time like the present. Come with us." Larry continued his put-on.

"Please, don't ask again." Al's voice was business like as she excused herself and took her coffee mug and empty plate to the sink. "Gotta get to work." She wrapped her hair and tucked it neatly beneath her baseball cap then inspected her appearance in a horse collar mirror hung next to the front door. "You men, when ready, may leave your dishes in the sink."

"Today's Monday, and you worked Sunday. Don't you get a day off?" Larry asked. "Maybe you could show us a gold mine or the Oatman Hotel renovations? I'm a building contractor. I'd like to see the possibilities here."

"Sorry, guys. I run a service station. Besides, I promised a trucker to have his rig back on the road by noon." Directing her attention to Larry, she added, "Stick around, and I'll see if the mayor might give you an evening tour. Be sure to close the door on your way out. Don't want some cougar resting in here when I get back."

"Cougar?" Larry asked.

"Thanks, Al, but we're heading out right behind you," David said. He got up and gave Al a ten-dollar bill and thanked her for her gracious hospitality. Following right behind, Larry handed her another ten and teased, "It's time for a new hat. Other than Ernie Banks, the Cubs ain't got much this year. Say, maybe we'll stop at Wrigley Field on our way to Michigan? Want to see a game?"

Al headed out the door. She turned and shouted back, "If you're not stopping at the Grand Canyon, pick up the new road north of here and go east toward Kingman!"

After the door closed, the brothers cleared Al's table. David washed the dishes while Larry dried and put them away. Both men wanted to talk. They analyzed Oatman, its mayor, and her delegated dependents, Earl and Rico. Their conversation was cordial and most complimentary of everything they had seen in Oatman. The primary focus of David's attention was the interior furnishings of Al's house while Larry was interested more in Al and her Oatman aspirations.

"I can tell you one thing," Larry said. "This is Aunt Alice's home, and she ain't leavin'."

"There's something to be said for knowing where you are comfortable. Sort of reminds me of Roy's and Hobo," David said.

David backed out onto US 66, ready to continue the climb northward. Larry was in a good mood. "I like this place. And Aunt Alice ain't so bad either," he said.

"Oatman's not much, and Al's not your style," David said.

"Yeah, I know, Dave, but I'm not so sure you know my style."

"If only it were so," David said.

"Style, Dave? Why the hell do you have a coconut rolling around in your back seat?"

"That's a long story."

"Speaking of stories, how'd you know I was in the hospital—"

Suddenly, their conversation was interrupted by a loud *heeehaaaw* barrage of the most peculiar, but somewhat familiar, sound. The brothers turned toward the rocky hillside behind Al's house. There stood a white-faced gray burro watching them. He lifted his snout to the sky and let out another round of hoarse seesaw hee-haws.

"Rico?"

And that was all there was to Oatman, Arizona—a ghost town in progress ... or maybe not.

CHAPTER 7

About Two Years Ago

The United Methodist Church pews in Three Oaks, Michigan were packed from front to rear, and folding chairs were brought up from the basement fellowship hall and placed along both side aisles. An additional two rows of mismatched auxiliary chairs had been hurriedly set up behind the back pews. All seating was occupied with standing room only in the congested narthex. There had not been an audience this size in the church since the Christmas Sunday School program the previous year.

The steeple bell chimed, and a hushed murmur rippled through the congregation.

Mrs. Elizabeth Dailey, her oldest son, David, and David's wife, Jane, were escorted forward down the center aisle and seated in the first pew on the right, traditionally reserved for immediate family members. A black-robed organist, positioned in the right transept, began playing "Shall We Gather at the River." The now-subdued congregation, made up of all ages, listened in respectful silence—all except for eight women and three men seated in folding chairs in front of the leaded, stained-glass windows along the left aisle. They stood in unison and lent their heartfelt voices to each refrain of the hymn.

As the musical prelude concluded, a minister dressed in a white robe accented by a black clerical shirt and collar rose from the left transept and ascended three steps to the pulpit. His movements were unintentionally amplified by the microphone attached to the podium.

With emotion glistening in his eyes, the pastor surveyed his flock. "Let us bow our heads in prayer," he invited them.

Following the service's benediction, two teenage ushers in ill-fitting, black suits came forward. They led the three Daileys back out the center aisle to the church's double doors at the rear of the narthex. The Daileys prepared to greet their friends, neighbors, and fellow parishioners. The organist played "Bringing in the Sheaves" while the mourners followed in an unhurried collegial fashion toward the Daileys and the wide-open church doors. It was clear the entire congregation shared a somber sense of personal loss.

Forty-five minutes later, the Daileys walked together across the church lawn toward David's car, parked second in line behind a long black Cadillac hearse. David and Jane were dutifully attentive to their grieving mother. For her part, Mrs. Dailey was determined to hold her sorrow at bay, although her grief was profound. She prided her reputation as a model community citizen.

The three walked without conversation. Once in the car, Jane said, "That was a very nice service. Don't you agree, Mom?" Jane looked at her mother-in-law and then her husband, searching for confirmation, as well as rescue from an uncomfortable silence. Jane admired her departed father-in-law, was devoted to her mother-in-law, and was fretful about the fragile emotional state of her husband. Now she found herself seated with a mourning widow and resentful husband. "Oh, Jane, it was *so* beautiful," Mrs. Dailey whimpered. Dabbing her cheeks with a white linen hanky, she said, "Lawrence was so good to us all. He'll be missed, especially by me." She sobbed softly into her hanky.

"You are so right, Mom. Can you believe all the people who came to pay their respects?" Jane said. "And did you notice the line of cars behind us? Don't know if we can all get into the cemetery."

"I remember what my mother always said after every funeral: 'It was well attended.' She always said that," Mrs. Dailey said.

Seated in the middle of the front seat, she pulled David and Jane close on each side. "Everyone is here. And how about those choir members? They didn't tell me they were going to do that."

"Not everyone is here," David said.

"Please, David. This is not the time," Jane said.

"Larry should have been here. No excuse," David said.

Mrs. Dailey sat a little straighter. "David, I'm sure your brother would have been here. He simply doesn't know your father has passed. He would make every effort to be here, I'm sure."

"Mom, you've been making excuses for Larry since the day he was born. You know it's true. Missing Dad's funeral, well, no surprise there," David said.

"David!" Jane said.

Mrs. Dailey's grip on her escorts' arms became perceptibly more resolute. No one spoke during the remainder of the short, slow drive from the church to the cemetery. David followed the hearse beneath the archway into the graveyard. The procession, headlights on, was close behind and trailed well back past the church. The cars and walkers made up the only traffic along the gravel country road. A farmer plowing his field across from the cemetery stopped and turned off the tractor's motor. He climbed down and removed his hat while the somber procession passed.

As she opened the door to get out of the car, Jane said, "I thought the choir stood spontaneously because they were moved by the hymn to join in on the chorus. Did you notice that several in the congregation started to sing along too?"

"It was lovely, simply lovely," Mrs. Dailey said.

"Wine, women, and song! No tellin' where Larry is," David said.

"Please, David," Jane said. She gave her husband a stern look.

"It's inexcusable, Jane," David said.

"Let's go, you two. We've got lots to do," Mrs. Dailey said.

Uncomfortable with her older son's remarks, she cut off further conversation.

Mrs. Dailey directed the three of them to follow the six casket bearers to a white canopy erected in front of a freshly excavated gravesite. The pallbearers were members of the local American Legion post where David and his father had been long standing members.

David's eyes filled with tears as fellow Legionnaires expressed their condolences for the loss of his father. He had always been proud of his father and in many ways had patterned his life after him.

Two years earlier at a birthday gathering, a neighbor said to him, "When your dad was forty, you two could have passed for twins."

He regretted what he said to his mother and Jane about Larry's absence and vowed silently to never broach the subject again. But inwardly, he did not think he could shake his resentment of Larry.

CHAPTER 8
Peach Springs, Arizona

A determined morning sun slithered through jagged mountain peaks to the east. The early start would help them make up for a late start the day before, at least, that was the plan. A road sign—Trailers Over 40 Feet Prohibited—stirred little interest. Armies of saguaro cacti stiffly stood sentry along the steep climb deeper into the Black Mountains. All too soon, the Oatman Highway became a tangle of switchbacks, sheer-shoulder drop-offs, and blind hairpin curves made more treacherous by an up-and-down roller-coaster track. Periodic turnouts with expansive vistas provided intermittent relief from the trying passage through the picturesque highlands. Larry showed little interest in mountain scenery, however, and encouraged his brother to speed it up. David's ears were popping, and the outside air had grown cool as they continued their slow, circuitous ascent.

"Now I understand the warning against driving long trailers on this route," David said. Larry's request for speed was the least of his concerns.

But for his sense of a faint infrequent engine knock, David was pleased with the performance of his automobile over the challenges of this steep road. His repeated glimpses at the dashboard gauges revealed nothing abnormal. He did, however, squeeze the steering wheel a little tighter.

"Did you feel something?" Larry asked.

"No. Why?"

Along the road's left edge soared a vertical stone wall. Conversely, the right edge presented a sheer drop straight down out of sight. Not so much as a caution sign or road safety barrier. Nor were there any extra feet for such either. David's eyes were glued to the road ahead. His two fists bonded to the steering wheel, he naturally guided the Chevy across the center line and ever closer to the inside wall. Although it was a cool morning, he felt sweat droplets running beneath his shirt down his ribcage. All his senses fixated on the winding road.

"You're in the wrong lane," Larry said.

"Lane? Look out your window. Not even a guard rail. I swear, this road's getting thinner," David responded.

"What if we meet someone?" Larry said.

"You got a parachute?" David asked.

"Relax, man. Say, you ever been skydivin'?" Larry attempted to cut the tension.

"No, and I don't plan to start today," David said, tightening his grip on the wheel.

Suddenly, a Rambler station wagon chockful of jumping-jack kids rounded an elevated blind curve not two hundred feet in front of them. David slowed to a walk and eased the Chevy to the right, but still hugging the center line, and held his breath. The two cars passed so close, he swore he could smell the kids' Juicy Fruit chewing gum. The other driver laid on his horn, and Larry flipped him the bird. David agreed with his brother but remained transfixed straight ahead, hands welded to the steering wheel. He exhaled with relief.

The strain of the mountain highway churned David's stomach. He was certain he could feel the pulse of his heart beating in his ears. *Is this what an impending heart attack feels like?*

Larry offered to drive, but David assured him it was his car and he'd drive. He glanced again at the dashboard. The heat gauge needle had buried itself in the red zone. "Damn, damn, damn," David growled. Before Larry could come back with a wisecrack, a Scenic Turnout sign appeared with enough room for several cars to park in a small, almost level, lot. David pulled in and killed the motor.

"What's your problem. You need to take a leak?" Larry sneered.

"Shut up. Listen."

A whiff of white steam rose from beneath the hood. David got out, slammed the door, and lifted the hood. "Damn it! Damn it! Damn it to hell!"

"What's wrong?" Larry asked as he joined his brother in front of a steaming, red-hot radiator. "Forget to check the water?"

"Hell no, Sherlock. Fan belt broke. See?" David pointed to where the fan belt had been. Only a piece of black rubber still dangled on one of the sprockets. Hot vapor hissed and rose from around the radiator cap, but no leak was visible.

"Doesn't look good. Let her cool a while," Larry said as he lit a cigarette.

His brother's nonchalant arrogance coupled with his smoking added to David's angst. Larry casually walked away and wandered over to a metal history board where he read aloud site information that explained the direction to look if you wanted to see three states—Arizona, California, and Nevada.

"Does it tell us where we can get a new fan belt?" David asked.

"Why would anyone want to see three states? Looks like mountains beyond mountains to me. Hey, look there." Larry pointed toward the snow-creased, rocky outcrops on either side of the pass they had just crossed over. Three bighorn sheep made their sure-footed way along a slender stone ledge.

"You ever hear about the ram that committed suicide?" Larry asked.

"No, but I'm afraid I'm going to," David quipped.

"He couldn't make a ewe turn." Larry laughed before he'd completed the punchline.

"Funny. Send him out for a fan belt," David said.

Fifteen to twenty minutes plodded by without a single car passing in either direction. David was unsure what a passerby could do even if they managed to flag one down. His nerves were frayed, so it was good that Larry walked away to smoke by himself. At least the view was spectacular. Try as he might, David was unable to repeat the sheep-sighting or manage to find any others. Tree lines appeared as if belted to the mountainsides at a uniform altitude, a serene and satisfying vista under different circumstances. Now, a simple broken part could end the voyage of both man and machine.

After Larry smoked a second cigarette, he used the towel Mr. Coconut was seated on to loosen the radiator cap. It released more pressure than expected, causing him to recoil. Then he said, "I think it will cool quicker. You still have water, though it's boiling."

"That's sure to happen when you release the pressure. But you know that, right, Sherlock?"

"Of course," Larry sighed.

Another half-hour passed. David considered hitchhiking, but if no one passed, who could he catch a ride with? And which way did he want to go? They hadn't passed anything for several miles, and he had no idea what facilities to expect on the road ahead.

"Fat chance of going anywhere with all this traffic." Larry smirked. He sat on the ground leaning against the historic marker post. Exhaling, he added, "At this rate, I may have to turn around and head back to the coast. Got things to do."

"Think you'll catch the next train?" David asked.

It was doubtful whether either man had prayed, though a prayer was answered when a well-worn, formerly yellow Ford pickup rattled to rest ten feet behind the crippled Chevy. The driver's door creaked open, and out stumbled Earl, hiking his pants while shaking his right leg and extracting a wedgie from his butt. He didn't say a word, just frowned at the car with its hissing radiator.

"I never thought I'd be happy to see this lardass again," Larry whispered out of the corner of his mouth.

"Watch your tongue. This lardass may be our salvation," David whispered back.

"Really? Should we call him Crisco?"

"Refined lard. Now that's a blast from the past," David said.

"Well, didn't expect to see you gents again," Earl said. "Taking in the sights, I suspect?"

"Earl, happy to see you. You may be able to help us. My fan belt broke. Could you take a look and maybe give us some advice?" David asked. Larry gave his brother an expression of disbelief while Earl meandered in for a closer inspection.

"How's your Aunt Alice?" Larry asked.

Earl interrupted his inspection. "She's good. Aunt Alice wants me to go to Kingman and fetch a box of AC Delco sparkplugs and a couple of cases of 10-W-30 motor oil. She wrote it down. See here." Earl held up a slip of brown paper with a numerical list on it. "Well," he continued after a good long inspection under the hood. "Looks to me you be needin' a new fan belt."

"Gee, Earl, are you sure about that?" Larry asked, with deliberate and delayed emphasis on every other word. "Your engine trouble-shooting talent is—"

In an attempt to rein in his brother, David interrupted, "Earl, do you know where we could have a new fan belt installed? We're in trouble here."

"Well." Earl looked back and forth between the Daileys and the still-sizzling radiator. "Aunt Alice could do it, but goin' back to Oatman won't do."

"Well, we don't think so either, Earl," Larry said.

"Might you have a suggestion as to what we can do?" David asked.

Earl turned his attention toward the distant mountain peaks. "Pretty, ain't she?" He dug in his denim coat pocket and pulled out a four-inch plug of Red Man tobacco. In his pants pocket, he found a jackknife, cut off half an inch, and, with his knife hand, put the chaw in his mouth. "Well. Ain't got time to pack you two to Cool Springs and back. Aunt Alice needs those plugs and oil by three. That's what she said."

"Well! We understand, Earl. You're a busy *man*," Larry said. His eyes bored into Earl, but his meaning went unacknowledged.

David knew they needed Earl and did not want Larry to explode and alienate their best chance, possibly only chance. "You are the man, Earl. Think you can help us here? We're kinda in a tight spot and on a tight schedule."

"Well. I might could put a new belt on for you, and we'd both be on our way."

Larry raised his voice. "How in hell could you do that up here in these mountains? Earl, you don't understand. We need to go somewhere; buy a belt that we can use in this car. We need a fan belt and the tools necessary for installing a fan belt. Don't you think?"

"Let's hear what Earl has to say. It can't hurt," David pled. Larry fired up another cigarette and squinted skeptically as he blew smoke skyward.

"Well, okay then. Aunt Alice calls this here truck the Ark." Earl moseyed back to his pickup, unlatched, and let slam down its rusty tailgate. "She told me to put two of most things in the back here. That's why Aunt Alice calls it the Ark. 'Member Noah? We have two Johnson jacks, two cans of Quaker State oil, two Firestone spare tires. We even have spare Clearview wiper blades. They're for your windshield. You need a new wiper blade?"

"No, Earl. Our blades are good, and it don't look like rain," Larry said.

"I only put one toolbox back here, but it's a good-un." Earl slid an oversized, homemade, metal box to the rear of the truck's bed.

"Guess what, Earl? We got a spare tire too," Larry said.

"I reckon ya do. She's a pretty automobile. Bet she cost a pretty penny. But she be needin' a fan belt. I got six and reckon one fits a Chevrolet. Aunt Alice says, 'If it's goin' to be a service truck, some things you be needin' more than two.' That's what Aunt Alice says." Earl's gaze was detached over the heads of the dumbfounded Dailey brothers.

Then the Good Samaritan went to work while the brothers watched but stayed out of his way. After Earl installed the fan belt, he topped off the radiator from a five gallon can of water he reported his Aunt Alice had instructed him to carry. The brothers begged to pay him for parts and labor, but Earl steadfastly refused. Aunt Alice had told him, "You don't accept money from a friend in need." Earl rambled on, "Aunt Alice likes you boys, especially the short one there. She said, 'He knows how to build things.' That's what Aunt Alice said."

David smiled as he caught Larry's eye. Larry shuffled his feet, grinned at his brother, and did a silent fist pump.

They both thanked Earl, shook his hand, and patted him on the back. Earl smiled sheepishly, spit a brown line of tobacco juice downwind, wiped his chin with the back of a forearm, climbed up into Aunt Alice's Ark, and rattled off on his way to pick up some plugs and oil.

Before Earl disappeared around a bend, Larry lit up again. To avoid nagging about smoking, and protect his car, David suggested they relax a few minutes and walk to the edge of the lookout. They gazed out at the wind-swept mountains. The endless rugged panorama served to further lift their spirits. A strange euphoric feeling passed over David, as if he had received a mysterious dispensation and was thereby free to reveal his most private self. "It makes you appreciate life," he said.

"I take back what I said about Earl being four cards short of a straight," Larry said.

David found himself filled with gratitude and appreciation from what could have been a desperate rough country situation. Also, he felt a long-time missing closeness with his brother. He contemplated explaining to Larry his real reason for being in California, a desire he now felt required further appraisal.

"What do you mean, 'appreciate life'? Are we talking Noah here?" Larry asked.

"Look out there. There's a spiritual feel to all this. Don't you think?" David asked.

"Say what? Spiritual? Haven't been inside a church since I left home. Let's go." Larry crushed out his cigarette, and the two men walked back to the Chevy.

They were both more at ease as the road improved with each passing mile, and David surmised amusing thoughts must be swirling in Larry's head.

Out of character, Larry started humming "She'll Be Coming 'Round the Mountain When She Comes." In an absent-minded moment of lost inhibition, David chimed in, and soon, they were engaged in a wildly off-key duet filled with butchered lyrics and unrestrained silliness. Badgering, berating, and one-upmanship all went on sabbatical.

David proclaimed how lucky they were to have met Earl and his apparent caretaker, Aunt Alice. Larry proudly admitted that Earl mentioning, "Aunt Alice said she liked the short one," gave him a rush—that he was "the short one," not so much.

"You remember where we got the idea for calling chubby kids 'Crisco'?" David asked.

"I think it was Coach Fischer. He yelled at us, 'Stop calling fat people lardass!' I don't remember who thought 'Crisco' would be more refined," Larry said. "Probably me."

"I doubt that," David challenged.

David once again became the big brother directing his little brother's thinking. The fact that he had always lived in Three Oaks made him privy to lots of local history and libelous gossip. To David's delight, Larry seemed curious. Neither brother ever let the facts get in the way. The Crisco-for-Lardass story was repeated several times and embellished with each sequel.

"Oh shit! Did you miss the Kingman to Flagstaff cutoff?" Larry asked.

David had become distracted, lost in the reverie of lost youth while absentmindedly following Route 66 signs. He searched for any indication of where they were. When he saw a billboard for Grand Canyon, he knew they had missed the turn and still had been driving north. "I think you're right," he said.

"Right? I guess. Better backtrack. This will take us miles out of our way," Larry said.

"I'm sorry. But it's not that far out of the way, and the road looks interesting," David said.

"Interesting. I've had enough interesting for today! We've got to get movin'. Some of us still work for a livin'," Larry said.

"Lighten up. I work," David said, adding, "This won't add more than an hour or two at most."

David did not let up on the gas pedal, just kept on rolling down an original, now little used, portion of Route 66. Billboards hawking the various attractions of the Grand Canyon fell like dominos as they passed. Larry unfolded the road map and reported they had crossed the Mohave Reservation and were only a few miles west of a place called Peach Springs.

"You think they raise peaches out here?"

"The only thing I know is I could use a smoke. How's gas?"

At first glance, they concluded the best part of Peach Springs would likely appear in the rearview mirror. A sandwich board in front of a feed store announced Headquarters Hualapai Reservation. Larry suggested Hualapai may be sea food. His comment added nothing to the distressed rural crossroads, and David didn't want even the thought of fish. Peach Springs was little more than a dusty, wide space in the road, without a stop sign, traffic light, or even a speed limit sign. In fact, they hadn't seen a speed limit sign since Oatman.

As they continued east, Larry cried out, "Holy shit! We gotta give this a try," as a sign appeared for the Roadkill Café—Stop, Eat, and View the Grand Canyon. David let off the throttle, downshifted, and rolled to a stop in front of the Roadkill Café, the most prosperous establishment they'd seen since Earl and the Ark disappeared down the mountain.

Larry retrieved the jar of ointment Bessie insisted they take with them. It was next to Mr. Coconut and a large aloe vera leaf in the back seat. He rubbed what was left liberally on his face, neck, and arms. David declined, reporting that his sunburn felt lots better. They considered whose remedy was best, Bessie's or Al's? David gave the prize to Bessie, while Larry awarded Earl's Aunt Alice first place.

A five-foot-tall, carved wooden Indian in full headdress and war paint defended the café's entrance. He held a feather-handled tomahawk in his right hand and a fist full of cigars in his left. "Hope they sell firewater here," Larry said. "I could use some smokes too."

The Daileys lunched on buffalo burgers so tough they could have been supplied by Buffalo Bill himself. Larry studied an Arizona map he found on a nearby table, while David read about the Hualapai Indians on the back of the Roadkill menu.

"Since we're in the neighborhood, what do you think about checking out the Grand Canyon, and possibly the Hoover Dam and Lake Mead? And Vegas isn't too far," David said.

"You kiddin' me? Sign said we could view the canyon from here," Larry said.

"I think it's about ten miles north. Here's a picture on the menu, our Grand Canyon view. You can see where we are." David shoved the menu across the table. "You're probably right. We better press on. Otherwise, it'll be snowing in Michigan before we get there."

David told Larry that while they had been at Roy's, Popeye had let him use the station phone to call home. "Jane wished I had called before we left but let it go when I told her I had you in the car. Telephone, telegraph, or tell Jane!" There was pride in David's voice when he said he could hear her broadcast: "'Larry's coming! Dave's bringing Larry! Mom will want all the neighbors in to see you two. I'll help her plan a small reception. Sounds great, Dave.'"

"Well then, let's not keep them waiting. The prodigal son returns." Larry's bravado and authority flew across the table and, like a thirsty mosquito, bored into the back of David's reheated, sunburned neck.

The day's distance had been limited due to their breakdown and the road's endless mountain switchbacks. If ever on the schedule, sightseeing had dropped off the priority list, especially for Larry. However, as the two walked out of the Roadkill Café, Larry stretched his arms above his head and broadcast to the heavens, "Land of the Gods. The Mother Road!"

If outward appearance held any meaning, Peach Springs could never have been mistaken for El Dorado, nor could a cracked and worn two-lane highway be mistaken for the Yellow Brick Road. What little Indian reservation life they had observed from the car windows revealed scarcely a subsistence-producing population.

David glanced into the mirror for one last view of Peach Springs. He had no more than brought the Chevy up to speed than Larry suggested he be careful because there were children playing near the highway. David slowed as he approached three skinny kids, a boy and two girls, taking turns rolling one another down a dirt drive, while curled up inside a discarded truck tire. An undernourished yet barking three-legged dog bounded after them. David came to a complete stop to watch just as the boy in the tire rolled across the highway in front of them with the crippled pooch nipping at the tire.

"Hey, boys! Stay out of the road! You could get hit by a car," David yelled out the driver's side window.

"Cars? Where? Looks like fun," Larry said. "And they're not all boys."

"Right. Maybe their only fun," David added. "But we don't want it to be their last."

The two men sat in the car, watching the kids play. By the side of the drive they were playing on lay two rusting, old automobiles cannibalized of so many parts, it was difficult to identify the makes and models. The drive led up a hill to three small, ramshackle houses with two toddlers standing out front—one crying and the other one naked and holding a baby bottle.

"Let's move on. Wonder how people make a livin' out here," Larry said. David gradually put the Bel Air in gear and began to move on down the highway.

They had cleared Peach Springs by little more than ten miles when David pulled off the highway and stopped. In front of them was a hand-painted sign on a four-by-eight-foot piece of discarded plywood: INDIAN POTTERY 4 SALE.

"What's wrong now? Why are you stopping?" Larry asked.

"You wondered what people out here did for a living," David answered.

"I still do." The surrounding area was just as bleak as the land at their earlier stop.

"Mom loves pottery. Why don't you buy her a gift?" David asked. "Maybe I'll pick up something for Jane."

"You're kidding! Really? I can't remember *ever* buying Mom a gift."

"Even for her birthday or at Christmas?" David asked.

"Don't remember. Maybe. Say, maybe you can trade that coconut rotting in the back seat for a clay pot," Larry joked.

"*Mr.* Coconut to you. And he's going with us," David answered.

Next to a sagging twelve-foot pine plank lined with a variety of brown clay pots sat a leathery Indian woman smoking a long-stemmed, white-clay pipe. As David got out of the car, he waved to her and said, "Hello, there!" She nodded and exhaled smoke she'd been hoarding deep within. With the stem of her pipe, she pointed toward colorful blankets hanging on a clothesline running from the stoop post of a one-room frame cabin to a lifeless ponderosa pine.

While the two men perused the pottery and blankets, a black VW Beatle heading in the opposite direction swerved off the road onto the loose shoulder and stopped in front of the Chevy. Once again, David witnessed a sandy, tan curtain settle over his cherished automobile. A tall, sinewy, bronzed woman with shoulder-length, jet-black hair hopped out. "Hi, Summer! How's business?"

The old woman took the pipe out of her mouth, exhaled another gust of smoke, and flashed a wide, toothless smile.

The tall woman turned to the shoppers and said, "I see you've discovered Summer's Gift Shop. You may have already realized Summer does not speak English? Understands some. Good potter, the best, but those blankets, not authentic. Summer's authentic. So am I. Name's Harmony." She extended her right hand and shook hands with each of the men, who in turn gave her their first names. Harmony seemed as out of place as Man O' War at a county livestock auction.

"Authentic what?" Larry asked.

"I'm Hualapai, same as Summer." Harmony gave them a proud smile and patted the old woman on the shoulder. Then she said something to Summer the Daileys didn't understand. Summer shrugged and grinned but did not take the pipe stem from her mouth.

Harmony appeared to be about the same age as the men, and she was dressed in a below-the-knee, black skirt with a white silk blouse. In fact, she could have been mistaken for a cellist on her way to perform with the Boston Pops Orchestra. Instead, she was talking with two strangers and an old woman who didn't speak English in front of a humble reservation pottery stand.

Larry blurted, "Harmony, who are you anyway? You can't belong here, right?"

David agreed but was taken aback by Larry's shoot-from-the-hip lack of sensitivity.

Harmony laughed then growled with emphasis, "Me Indian! Me belong! *You* paleface!" Then she turned serious and with perfect English said, "Born and raised right here. With the exception of four years at the U of A, I've always lived right here, on the Hualapai Reservation."

"You went to college?" Larry asked, again with noticeable disbelief that furthered David's discomfort.

"That's what they tell me." Harmony laughed again, clearly enjoying the repartee with the naïve White men. "And I am an authentic university graduate with an authentic geology degree. *Entiendo?*" She smiled then blinked at the old woman. "I know, it may all seem a little out of place. I get that from the tourists who are often lost and in need of directions to the Grand Canyon or Las Vegas."

"This paleface wants to know, what does one do for a living around here?" Larry asked. "We haven't seen much more than Peach Springs for the last hundred miles."

Harmony folded her arms then launched straight into a short bio. "As I said, I was born and raised here. A Presbyterian missionary encouraged me to go to college, and so I did. With a geology degree, I thought I could work in the mining industry and did for five years, but the mining here petered out. Now I teach at the Hualapai School in Peach Springs. I don't live far from here, but alas, not in a White man's tepee." She sighed and then flashed a radiating smile at the two visitors.

"Married?" Larry asked. His detached manner amused Harmony as much as it continued to irritate David.

"You interested, mister?" she mocked. "No, not married. You see any eligible braves running around here? You might say that they jumped the reservation. Someday, I may too. Hualapai long for a past, mythical life that will never be and probably never was." Harmony heaved a sigh of resignation. "This is my home. You can't run away from people you love. My students need me, and I them."

Harmony's geniality went down like a spoonful of warm honey. David could worship at her feet. However, Larry's self-importance forged ahead. "I told Dave we had to stop here. Authentic Indians are hard to come by these days."

Larry's loose reinterpretation of facts further annoyed David, a personality trait that needed no encouragement. Poker-faced David added, "Yes, Larry, your intuition is boundless, your sensitivity supreme." Then turning away from his brother, he asked, "Harmony, what do you suggest? My unpretentious brother wants to buy a present for our mother."

Harmony smiled knowingly at David. "All the pots are, as you say, authentic. Summer turns them personally." She turned and again patted Summer on the shoulder. As she did, she noticed her wristwatch. "Oh, darn. Got to go. Nice meeting you two." She bent and said something to Summer in Haulapai. Summer took the pipe out of her mouth then cast another wide, smile in Harmony's direction that was soon blurred behind a nicotine cloud.

Harmony pulled her VW up next to the Bel Air, tapped on the horn and shouted out the window. "Nice wheels. Looks like a real chick-catcher." She beamed and waved goodbye out the VW's open sunroof.

After Harmony departed for Peach Springs, Larry picked out a colorful blanket, while David selected two of Summer's small clay pots, one for Jane and one for mounting Mr. Coconut. The brothers were generous in their payments for Summer's goods.

Early afternoon found the Dailey boys at a Shell Oil service station on the city limit of Seligman, Arizona. While an attendant filled the Chevy with regular, David meticulously checked all other fluid levels, plus Earl's new fan belt. He scanned the area for a place to wash the car but gave up when Larry complained they needed to make up some time. After a quick stop in an around-the-back restroom that established a new standard for laid-back hygienic presentation, they resumed their eastward passage. The distant landscape remained distant, rugged, and soundless with the lone exception of rubber over concrete. David racked his brain for interesting ways to pass the time with his unpredictable companion. At least Larry had stopped complaining about his sunburn. Today, his face was showing a marked improvement.

"Do you list?" David asked.

"List? What the hell are you talking about now, you pointy head? 'Lisp'? Do I speak with a 'lisp'?" Larry demanded, puffed up and self absorbed.

"List! Not 'lisp.' Making lists. Like listing the greatest baseball players, best actors, worst movies, most corrupt politicians," David explained.

"Okay. Let's do it. Name your two all-time favorite movies." Larry's sudden burst of enthusiasm energized David as well.

David responded, "*Casablanca* and *Gone with the Wind*."

In a heartbeat, Larry said they were soupy and mildewed. He then declared *Cat on a Hot Tin Roof* and *Elmer Gantry* were far superior films, especially since they showcased strong performances by Liz Taylor and Burt Lancaster.

"I remember Lancaster's, 'Don't knock it unless you've tried it,' but be real, Larry. Do you think the acting of Gable and Leigh is chopped liver? What about Bogart and Bacall?"

"Sorry, Dave, not Bacall; Ingrid Bergman. Lauren Bacall was in *Key Largo*. And aren't we overlooking *From Here to Eternity*, again with Lancaster, and who could forget Deborah Kerr? She's lucky she didn't run into me on the beach!"

For a brief moment, David visualized Natalie Wood in a black one-piece bathing suit jogging along the Santa Monica seashore. "Hey, I liked *From Here to Eternity*. What about *Psycho*? Jane and I saw it in South Bend last spring. You gotta admit it was good, creepy. Alfred Hitchcock at his best."

"Get serious. The best part of *Psycho* was the posters of Janet Leigh in panties and bra. She was the original 'sweater girl,' ya know, a role she was built for, if you know what I mean."

"Leigh was terrific in the shower scene," David said. "Who could forget that? You probably think she is Vivien Leigh's sister."

"Were they?"

"No, they were not related. In fact, neither was born with the last name Leigh. May I suggest *The Wizard of Oz*? We saw it together just before you moved to California. Remember?"

"Yeah, I remember. I liked it, but the best part was the music and the color. Not really what I'd call a movie."

Discussing and cussing movies and various other subjects served to melt the miles away but lost its appeal the longer they drove on mile after mile. A definite familiarity, if not a similarity, in their likes and dislikes became grudgingly apparent to David. So why the estrangement? Was it necessary? After some thought, he could almost trace back to the exact date at which the two of them had chosen to differentiate themselves from one another.

David had gotten a driver's license, and Larry had still been two years away. Larry wanted David to drive him and a few junior high buddies to the county fair. David refused, not choosing to waste his car privileges on his little brother and his jerky friends. He had already gotten permission from their dad to drive the car to a high school dance that evening, a sure demonstration of manhood in Three Oaks.

David asked his brother if he remembered when they had first been allowed to drive the family car to high school sporting events. "I remember you driving and me always waiting for you," Larry said. "I think you got to drive the car more than I did."

"When I was in high school, there were two of us playing sports. Transportation was probably more complicated. So having me drive helped."

"We sure did play a lot of baseball," Larry said.

David raised a skeptical eyebrow when Larry proclaimed he had wasted his time playing high school sports, but he reverted back to his old self when he said he, Larry, should have been a professional musician. That drove David to near exasperation. "What are you, the original Renaissance Man?"

Larry laughed and said, "Probably." This flippant reply let David know his brother believed it more than he did not.

"If *braggadocious* could be found in a dictionary, your picture should be next to it. You've always been footloose and fancy-free," David said as a familiar pang of jealousy passed through him and a distasteful reflux slunk up the back of his throat.

Attempts to understand his mixed emotions continued to cloud David's mind. He remembered how his mother often bragged about Larry, defended him as faultless. He wondered if his mother ever did this for him when he wasn't around, or if he ever required such promotion at all. Did everyone assume he'd be the one to stay close to home, or had that also been a false presumption on his part? Unfortunately, David's mental state with regard to these matters had reverted to a time-worn resentment.

"Free, my ass!" Larry said. "Never! I got married. Remember? Okay, I *had* to get married—and I know you know that. And with a wife and a bun in the oven, I had to go to work big-time. And I damn sure wasn't coming home or asking for any help!"

Larry sank inward. Furrows rose across his forehead and lines radiated outward from the corners of his bloodshot eyes. He started and stopped several times, as if reconsidering what he wanted to say. Worry wrinkles creased his sunburned face.

Finally, after David had all but given up on the conversation, Larry continued. "I worked full-time at Douglas Aircraft. Paid pretty good, but not enough. I moonlighted every chance I got. Never home. Didn't want to be really. Neither of us wanted the marriage. By the end of the war, we were divorced."

"What happened to her? What about your child?"

With reluctance, Larry explained that his ex-wife had remarried within weeks of the divorce, and her new, older husband had wanted to adopt the little girl. He'd agreed. In the early years, he had contributed some financial support, but it was never required or necessary.

"She landed on her feet, an unfamiliar position for her. Some said she traded up." Larry's half-hearted smile betrayed regret, as close as he'd ever been to humility.

"What has become of your daughter, my niece? She must be about twenty?"

"Honestly, I haven't seen the kid in ten years. I don't think I'd recognize her. She's better off with me out of the picture."

"You got that right. You sound like the prototype for Mayzie in *Horton Hatches the Egg*. Where in the hell is your sense of responsibility? You're the father."

"For what it's worth, Dave, I've never been positive I was the father."

"That's bullshit. Sounds like a cop-out to me. Basically, you're all fucked-up."

David prepared for Larry to come back swinging, but Larry sat detached, a vacant expression covering his face. After a time, he continued, "Ya know, I have thought about baby Sarah. Wonder if she has a good life."

As much as his brother infuriated him, David had to look away from the pitiful sight of Larry's moist blue eyes and red runny nose. For a time, he completely forgot about his plan to run away and wondered if he and Jane could have given a daughter a good life.

In an attempt to back off and lighten the atmosphere, David said, "Well, what else have you been doing for the last twenty years? Mom always showed us the postcards you sent from exotic places. Everyone back home thinks you're a rich man." Though he had never said as much aloud, David always had a burning desire to know the scope of his brother's economic situation and hoped Larry would take the bait.

"You could say that," Larry said as he roused from a melancholy funk. "As for women, not so well-to-do. My second and third wives came and went quicker than an Indian through cheap whiskey. The last one made out like gang busters in the settlement, but that's because I had it to give and was willing to pay to have the bitch out of my life."

"Did she know your financial circumstances before you married? In other words, which head were you thinking with?"

"Which do you think? I'm sure she did, but I'd gotten to the point that … Oh, what the fuck? I didn't give a damn. If you've had one woman, you've had them all. Ha! I'm getting close to that."

David didn't exactly understand Larry's meaning, but it sounded as if he'd made a game of keeping score of his lovemaking exploits. Seemed Larry had a penchant for keeping score. David could not abide what he perceived as his brother's distorted set of values. He was relieved when Larry swung in another direction.

"Moonlighting in forty-two, I discovered the construction trades," Larry said.

"I've heard there's been a real West Coast expansion."

"No shit! It exploded after the war. I couldn't have printed money faster." Larry explained that as an independent building contractor, he never stopped expanding and creating business partnerships, while continually launching new satellite ventures on the side. A workaholic, he became a millionaire in ten fast years.

Sporadically, he would treat himself to an outlandish vacation. "I deserved it," he recalled confidently. He'd light out with what he described as a "lucky female" companion, to some obscure destination most could not find on a map, much less afford. The same was true of the women who had paraded in and out of his life, and whom he took great pleasure in recounting, building up with general compliments, but ultimately defaming.

Larry rambled through a litany of economic successes and romantic conquests. Although impressive, David did not overcome the sting of bitterness he felt toward his brother and the choices he so gluttonously enjoyed. Larry unwittingly affirmed David's deep contempt for Larry's treatment of these many women, but at the same time, Larry's recollections stirred in him an empathy for a shallow life spent in constant turmoil.

In an effort to terminate an uncomfortable monologue, David said, "Well, as Earl would say, Aunt Alice be needin' sparkplugs and some oil." The brothers relaxed in a shared good memory from earlier in the day.

The town of Holbrook wasn't much. They did pass a rather unique motel. It featured several large Indian tepees inviting travelers to spend the night: Have You Slept in a Wigwam Lately? Larry scoffed at the billboard and the tepees, "Doesn't anyone 'round here know the difference between a tepee and a wigwam? Wigwam Motel, my ass!"

David also was amused by the ignorant commercialism and asked, "What do you think Harmony would say?"

"Not authentic!" both shouted in unison.

"That's the kind of woman you need," David said.

"Who? You mean Harmony?" Larry shrugged and frowned. Then he added, "Actually, I'd be more interested in Oatman Earl's Aunt Alice. Something about her, hard to explain."

"They both exuded self-confidence and a loyalty to their place in life."

"Yeah, but there's something more about Aunt Alice ...."

"It may be worth your while to figure it out." David turned on the radio. Static, static, static as he rotated the tuning knob from station to station. The lone exception was a Holbrook evangelist imploring all backsliders—"And I mean you!"—to gather to him and be saved by baptism. "Guaranteed!"

"What do you think?" David asked.

"About what? That Bible-thumping nut on the radio? I don't know how guys like that can sleep at night."

"Probably with someone else's wife," David said.

"Religion is a waste of time and money. Not rational," Larry said.

"It seems to me that everyone gravitates to a belief in something. You often see dying people turn to religion. Religion is a rational inclination, like swimming when you're in over your head."

"What's trying not to drown got to do with religion?" Larry asked.

"It's called living. Bad-mouthing people because they believe in a spiritual life is like swearing at gravity because it's going the wrong way."

"So are you going to tell me that you believe in immaculate conception?" Larry asked with an ear-to-ear artificial smile.

"I'm not answering that question. And I'm not going to argue about religion."

"Good 'cause you'd lose," Larry said.

"I doubt that," David said as he felt a burning need to put his little brother in his place. "Do you remember when you made fun of me because I misspelled 'Sioux' and 'Mackinac Island'?"

"No."

"You did. At the open house, following my graduation," David said.

"I don't think so. Why would I give a damn if you couldn't spell?"

"You did, and several other times. It embarrassed me. I'm sure you knew, and I dreaded the next time."

"I don't believe it, but if I did, it was childish, ancient history. Means nothing," Larry said.

"It haunted me. Still does. I tried to hide being a poor speller—and a worse reader. I don't know why I hated reading in school. I liked learning and got by on the teachers' lectures. It wasn't until after high school that I really started to enjoy reading. I like history and have read every history book I can find. Last Christmas, Jane gave me two leather-bound volumes of historian Dumas Malone's biography of Thomas Jefferson."

"You read them?" asked Larry in disbelief.

"Twice, and I'm anxious for more," David said.

"Okay, I'm impressed. But reading those books will never translate into dollars."

Starting at an early age, the Dailey brothers had displayed divergent personalities when it came to material things. David took care of his clothes and could wear them until he outgrew them. Larry wanted new clothes long before they were needed. Larry wanted everyone to know he had climbed the highest in the hickory tree behind the barn. David wanted to plant rotting hickory nuts to see if they would grow. The boys' grandmother once described them as, "David's a planter, Larry's a harvester."

Larry's indifference coupled with his swaggering materialistic nature stung his brother. When fused with David's intellectual self-consciousness, it resulted in a formula for bitter physical confrontations.

Larry's face showed his cynicism. He said, "Please tell me we aren't still debating religion."

"We're not. But I want to explain a little piece of history I find fascinating. Is that okay?" David asked.

"Well … only if you talk faster than old Oatman Earl," Larry said.

"Okay, here's something for you to consider," David said just as Larry's yawn caused David to change direction. "On second thought, what do ya say we give it a rest," he said as Larry's eyes rolled back in his head.

Thirty minutes later, David slowed to read a sign, Petrified Forest 10 Miles, and woke Larry. "Please don't tell me you want to stop," he said.

"Finally, something we agree on. I assure you nothing new has grown in that forest except another tourist trap full of fresh-cut petrified wood for sale. We stopped twenty years ago. D'you remember?"

"I read something last year about it becoming a national park," Larry said.

Soon, the sun made its slow descent in the western sky, flashing an intermittent blast of white light onto the rearview mirror. The road lay level even though there were rocky ridges, peaks, and buttes on both the right and left. Heavily eroded hills exposed diverse horizontal layers of stratified stone. The combination of lengthening shadows and the sun's reflection off colorful rocky cliffs created an impressionistic wonderland.

David eased the Bel Air onto the shoulder and let her roll to a stop. "I need to take a good look at this."

"What?" Larry asked, emerging from yet another cat nap. "Why are we stopping? I thought we decided to make New Mexico?"

"Check this out," David said as he opened the car door and got out. Larry joined him, stretched, and groaned his disinterest.

"Look at that," David said, pointing to the northeast. The western sun had painted the hills with swashes of color ranging from bright, candy-apple red to dark lavender. "Amazing. Amazing! Where's my camera? Jane would love this."

While the kaleidoscopic panorama fascinated David, his brother saw no traffic and relieved himself on a defenseless, prickly pear cactus. Despite his distraction, the setting was at once lonely, desolate, cool, and yet warm and spirited. David determined his artistic wife must see this place and repeated so to his brother.

"Come on. Let's go. We got to get out of these badlands, or we won't make it to New Mexico before dark."

"Right."

Larry asked to drive, and David conceded for the first time. They needed to clock more miles, and he had grown tired of the driver's seat.

Besides, he wanted to give his undivided attention to the spectacular views. He was enthralled with the color ballet. *Jane would love it. If she was here, she would take a million pictures.* David could almost feel Jane's presence next to him, holding his hand, her soft voice directing his gaze to fine details in the grand vista.

David's respite from behind the wheel was short lived, given Larry's need for speed. His driving style had the feel of dirt-track time trials. Although David lacked a clear view of the speedometer, he didn't believe it ever dropped below seventy-five. The monotonous miles were clicking off though. At dusk, they sped across the state line at Lupton, barely providing David enough time or light to view the border town's prominent brown cliffs.

Larry hustled on at seventy-five to eighty-five miles per hour, faster than David, but the powerful Chevy V8 charged homeward, the miles passing by. Larry slowed to pit row speed for gas in Gallup, New Mexico.

"Are they gaining on us?" David asked.

After refueling, they decided to take advantage of Earl's Famous Restaurant for supper. No relation to Oatman Earl however. The signage billing far surpassed the fare in both appearance and content, but both agreed their meal was a step or two ahead of that offered at the Roadkill Café.

While walking back to the car, Larry said, "I got at least three more hours in me. Let's keep rollin'." David went along with the suggestion, admitting he was tired and sore from riding in the driver's seat. Larry jumped back in the cockpit, and David resumed shotgun. Mr. Coconut had the back seat covered from his position half inside a clay pot. The sun had gone down behind them, and the road ahead was dark. Headlights from infrequent oncoming vehicles provided a small break from the monotony. They didn't talk much. Neither did they notice crossing over the Continental Divide, nor how far they had traveled.

Finally, David broke the silence. "Ya know, I've decided to go home with you. But I'm not in a hurry."

"Come again? I thought I was going home with *you*. You don't mean back to Santa Monica, do you?"

"No, but Santa Monica is calling. I can see why you like living there. I've dreamed about it myself."

"It's not so great. Did you know it used to be known as the Slum by the Sea?"

"Slum? It's a paradise," David countered.

"I guess it's all in what you're used to. But don't change the subject. What do you mean you 'decided to go home with me'? We're headed for Three Oaks, right?" Larry prompted.

"Wasn't my intention," David said.

"Well ... I want to hear your 'tention. Hey, do you hear me, Earl?"

"Right. Well, Earrrrl, we might could find us a room at that there motel up anyways. If they's still operatin'." David gave it his best Oatman Earl but failed to come up to his brother's supercilious standard.

Larry eased back on the throttle and glided to the center runway of a wind-swept junction known locally as Clines Corners. A quaint village, it supported a huge truck stop, or visa-versa, approximately seventy miles east of Albuquerque. What little they could see was battened down tight. It was after 10:00 p.m. on a Monday. Yet a lone orange, neon tube blinked VACANCY.

CHAPTER 9

Elk City, Oklahoma

A steady chorus of reverberating heavy-duty motors accompanied by Larry's hoarse, hacking cough shook David from a deep sleep. With a groggy head and sleepy eyes, his blurred focus was drawn to the stark furnishings of the cheap motel room they had landed in the night before. Rooms: $20 weekly, $6 nightly, $3 hourly. At least they had twin beds and a private bathroom. A hot shower and shave served to further awaken him, but he couldn't loosen up his stiff legs, a reminder of yesterday's marathon car ride along with nagging pain in the back of his head and lower back.

Still bone-tired, he sat back down on his bed to wait. Even though he wanted to get back on the road, another lengthy day in cramped quarters had no appeal. He lacked the energy to push himself or Larry to get started.

From the start of their trip back to Michigan, David had been considering whether he should explain to his brother his real reasons for traveling out to California. At times, he wanted to lay it all out for Larry. At other times, he told himself he'd jeopardize any future possibilities of making such a break if he revealed anything now about his original intentions. *Keep your mouth shut and your options open*, he thought.

From the looks of Larry, he hadn't slept at all. He claimed to have gotten up after midnight and walked across the highway to the Triple XR Bar. He found the tavern swarming with cross-country haulers overloaded with caffeine-spiked testosterone and chock-full

of masculine ambition. In addition to a thirtyish female bartender
endowed with a freedom-seeking bosom, two middle-aged cocktail
waitresses worked the floor, each portrayed an inflated opinion of
personal sex appeal. That opinion was supported by admiring truckers
and translated into healthy tips. That was all Larry could report before
mumbling something about Aunt Alice's sunburn remedy and asked
if there was any left. David cautioned that Al had said it wasn't for
drinking, to which Larry replied he may have had one too many.

"Just one? Don't tell me you went fishin' last night and came home
with a case of crabs."

"Get serious. The only prime cut in that juke joint was behind the
bar. A gearhead bummed a beer off me for which he gave me some
free advice: 'She's the boss man's lady, and he's *real* stingy. Got me?'"

"That stopped you?" David asked.

"You didn't see the boss man. He looked like a deranged Sherman
tank ready to run off its track," Larry said.

David ceased the interrogation. Larry's disheveled appearance
screamed answers he could do without. Watery bloodshot eyes
protruded from a pain-embalmed face reminiscent of rotting tomatoes,
the obvious remnants of an alcohol-laced sunburn.

Once both were ready, they crossed the highway and walked past
the Triple XR Bar on their way to the local breakfast spot: "Ma's
Coffee Pot, Never Closed" said the sign atop the roof. The morning
air provided much needed relief from the claustrophobic motel room
soaked in the stench of stale tobacco and cheap beer. A brisk snap in
the morning air reminded David of apple cider and football season.

"I'm hungry," David said. A dehydrated Larry didn't speak,
only shrugged.

The short morning walk gave David enough time to determine
how much of the reason for his western swing he'd divulge. Larry
had little to say during breakfast and ate even less. His late-night foray
coupled with his persistent hoarseness raised David's brotherly concern
to the point where he reconsidered if the time was right to explain
anything to his brother. However, David needed to talk to somebody

about his emotional conflict in desperate need of release. And, of course, Larry *was* his brother.

A waiter refilled their coffees. "Larry, did you ever wonder why I happened to show up at the hospital? Didn't it seem strange to you?"

"Haven't I asked you this before?"

"Do you still want to know?"

"Maybe. Haven't given it much thought." That was a lie, but Larry was alert enough to consciously downplay his interest in his brother's motives, a muscle-memory behavior he had nurtured since high school.

"Ahh, I wasn't in California to see you. Didn't know you had had a heart attack," David said, careful to choose each word so as not to convey a meaning or incite a reaction he'd regret.

"What? Then why the hell Santa Monica? The hospital?"

"I was in Long Beach. Wanted to catch the Santa Catalina ferry. Intended to sail into the sunset, so to speak."

"What? Why?" Larry asked, more amused than interested.

"Never planned to see you."

"Really? Then why did you show up at my bedside? Don't tell me you wanted to see Nurse Goodbody." Larry let loose a stubborn cough then struggled to clear his phlegmy throat with a swallow of black coffee. He looked around the dining area in search of a waitress and more coffee. Unsuccessful, he turned back toward his brother.

"You okay?" David asked. He leaned heavily on the table, analyzing Larry's compromised condition. Larry rubbed his eyes then stared back. A silent moment followed during which David sympathized with Larry's agonizing hungover condition but said nothing. Then he leaned forward.

"Let me start at the beginning." He repeated that he'd always envied how and where Larry lived. "My life has always been nine-to-five hardware, six days a week and church on Sunday. I'm vanilla, you're pistachio. I want pistachio."

"You want pistachio? I'll give you pistachio," Larry said, rolling his eyes.

"Now who's the wiseass? Shut up and listen," David continued. "Jane's always there. When I go to bed. When I get up. Until Dad died,

I saw both Dad and Mom every day of the week and twice on Sunday. Now just Mom. Even after his first heart attack, Dad helped out at the store, every frickin' day. Couldn't stop him. Nothing ever changes in Three Oaks. Same faces, same overcast sky, year after mind-numbing year. You are liberated. I'm incarcerated."

"Lighten up, Dave! Even you don't know where you're going with this."

"Look." David slid a piece of paper across the table.

"Well, you got that right," Larry said.

"Got what right?"

"My address."

"Turn it over, Dipstick."

Larry turned the scrap of paper over and read while David watched.

1. Pick up boat from Chief Ichabod at 7 a.m./leave license, keys, and car.
2. Approx. 1 hr. to fishing hole, give or take—8:30 arrive.
3. Attach old 3 oaks sweatshirt to boat, capsize.
4. Approx. 1 1/2 hr. to hike trail back to Charlie's.
5. With 2nd set of keys get suitcase from car.
6. One way ticket on 10:30 ferry to Santa Catalina.
7. End of Trail.

Larry studied the paper. Then he scowled and said, "You crazy bastard. I still don't know what the fuck you're talking about. Do you? And why the boat, and sinking it, for God's sake?" Larry cleared his throat as he pulled a fresh pack of cigarettes from his shirt pocket.

"You never listen. I'm trapped in nuts and bolts. I married a second-grade teacher who sings in the church choir. I'm past president of the Valley Moose Lodge. Lifetime member of the American Legion. A church deacon—that's me. Big whoop! I want change. I want a taste of your life." Even as he spoke, David second-guessed each word. However, once started, he was determined to plow forward with his story.

"Santa Catalina fascinates me. As a schoolboy, I knew my Chicago Cubs spring-trained there, and as a man I read about my hero, General

Patton, spending his formative years there. The song '26 Miles' talks about an exotic island off the Southern California coast, complete with palm trees and beautiful women. I decided Santa Catalina would be my South Seas refuge. As corny as it may seem to you, the lyrics 'in a leaky old boat' provided the perfect last puzzle piece."

"There's a wild bison stampede in my head, and you moan about some fuckin' pipe dream pop music bullshit? What's the bottom line? Cut the crap!" As crude as he sounded, Larry was interested in finding out what his brother was up to or had been planning. A throbbing head intensified his impatience. "And who the hell's Chief Ichabod?"

David ignored Larry's last question and continued. "Since my twentieth class reunion, I've fantasized about breaking away. Only problem, I didn't want to hurt anyone. I imagined several departure plans, but each had a defect. I had to escape without a trace and cause as little pain as possible."

Larry thought his brother was talking about divorce, but he was told divorce was out of the question. David went into a long explanation about the negative consequences of divorce while Larry lost interest and cut him off.

"You think too much and are definitely nuts. Go with divorce. Divorce is easy. Try it! You might like it. Sounds like mother at the dinner table, remember?"

"I don't want to hurt Jane or Mom, but it can't be helped."

"Sounds to me like divorce is in your future," Larry said.

David repeated that divorce was not an option, that it would be a more lasting pain to others than if he simply died. "This charade is my cover. It's my plan. If you got a better one, let's hear it." As he spoke, he could not shake the suspicion it was never going to happen. Dizziness momentarily blurred his mental focus. He didn't fear death but did fear never having lived or at least taking a chance.

"You're not getting *my* seal of approval." Larry thought his brother was a dumb fuck and told him so in those exact words. He mocked his "fishin' in a leaky old boat." He evaluated the whole idea as bizarre but concluded, "Dave, everyone *thinks* about running away at some time."

David protested but with a waning tone of conviction. The boat was the best part of the plan. The boat would be found, and when it was, he'd be labeled the victim of a tragic accident. Authorities would trace the boat to the rental shop and from there straight to David. He would be missing and presumed dead. Judging from the pain in his head, lower back, and now the heels of his feet, he may be close.

Jane and his mother would be notified based on the driver's license obtained from Charlie's Boat & Bait Shop. Police would search for his body but would give up after a couple of days. By that time, David would be living in his island hideaway under an assumed name—end of story.

But he had to admit that retelling the plan did not hold as much fascination for him as its formulation had. He admitted, at least to himself, the thrill of anticipation that had whirled through his head as he planned his great escape seemed to lose momentum the closer D-Day came.

"Sounds to me like you want to be the clever coward. But so what? You're out of there, right?" Larry went on to list a wife, a home, a business, and a positive contributor to a supportive community. He told David it was but a small portion of the attributes their mother lauded him for. He concluded, "Every time Mother blew your horn, it pissed me off. I wanted no part of it. But what could be better than the life you have, right where you were cut out to be—a real leader in our hometown?"

A pensive David took his time before formulating a response. He stated again his desire for a change and chastised himself for fear of never taking a chance. He also resented their mother's praise for Larry and believed she kept David where she wanted him to be. "Do you know what it feels like to be left on third in the bottom of the ninth? That's me," David said.

"No, I would have stolen home," Larry said. "You still haven't told me how you came to be in my hospital room."

David hesitated, did not want to be the center of restaurant attention, and refused to be rushed. "When I was sure I could pull it off, I decided to drive up to Santa Monica to locate where you lived.

Mom made sure I had your recent address before I left home. She was so excited I was going to see you. Of course, I wasn't."

"You lied."

"Your flower lady told me you were in the hospital. My intention was to see where you lived, not see you. Sorry. When I discovered you were in the hospital, my immediate plans began to unravel."

"So now you've decided to go back home?" Larry said.

"No, not exactly. I decided *you'd* go back home. I may desert you in Chicago. You couldn't turn back, but I could. On second thought, maybe I'll fly back to LA with you and continue with my original plan. I don't know. I've got to rethink this."

"And you're making me a fellow conspirator? I don't think so," Larry said. "So … where do we stand now?" His hoarse voice softened in an uncharacteristic quality of empathy. "Do you remember Grandpa saying, 'If you have a problem, just slow down and give yourself a chance?' I've always believed Gramps knew more than I did."

"That makes two of us," David said.

"He knew a lot. Let's put it *that* way," Larry said.

"You asked me where I stand. Since the Painted Desert, I've been thinking. As for you, you have to go back home. You need to see Mom, and she needs you." It bothered David to feel so unsure of himself, but that trait had been his life's affliction. He had fought to conceal those feelings of self-doubt. Now he questioned what, as well as why, he had told his brother anything. He wanted a confidant but was uncertain he wanted the one seated across from him. He needed advice, advice unavailable for something he had to keep secret.

From childhood, David enjoyed telling his brother things, knowing things his little brother did not. But this was different, and he was uncertain of how far he should go. Telling a ten-year-old not to belly flop when diving into the old swimming hole was different than sharing intimate adult quandaries. He alone was responsible for his pride, his heart, and ultimately for his personal happiness—not Larry.

"Let's find the car and get started," David said. He wanted and needed more than just a change of scenery, but a change of scenery might relieve his troubled mind—and sore back—he hoped. A tightness rose from off his shoulders as they exited Ma's. The noise and rush of morning traffic provided a boost for the start of day four. More relief came when they hopped into the Chevy and escaped the frantic confusion, sounds, and smells of Clines Corners, the four-way stop intersection of US 285 and Route 66.

Their goal was Joplin, Missouri by sundown. The trip home was taking longer than expected, and a twinge of urgency had taken root. Jane and Mrs. Dailey were expecting them by the weekend. The level highway across expansive barren territory represented a stark contrast from the previous morning's drive through the Black Mountains. A fast ride and lack of scenery helped their speed, but it quickly became tiresome, making the passage of miles seem as slow as the last drop of catsup in the bottle. The Pecos River whisked beneath them as little more than a wide crack in the pavement.

They picked up two hitchhikers in the Tucumcari Tumbleweed, a greasy spoon diner near the Texas border. The hikers turned out to be surfer wannabes heading back to Amarillo College a week late for the start of fall semester. The college boys shared self-absorbed tales of how they met as freshmen in the college infirmary after a white-lightning TGIF party.

Following their sophomore year, they had decided to head for California to find summer work, or so they had told their parents. Summer turned into a whole year spent drifting along the coast between Tijuana and San Francisco, working just enough to keep themselves in beer money. With David's encouragement and Larry's indifference, their enthusiastic reliving of West Coast escapades and nameless amorous conquests continued unabated for one hundred ten miles, all the way to Amarillo. When the young Casanovas were dropped at AC, one said, "Cool 'chine, man, a real chick magnet." Not to be out done, the other added, "We could use it to scout out the fresh batch of coeds. Later."

"Never heard that line before, have we?" said Larry.

"You've got to hand it to 'em, Larry. Those guys know how to live."

"Maybe. They talked so much, I could hardly keep up with the wax running out of my ears. Believe me—that shit gets old."

"You'll have to admit, though, their fun isn't at someone else's expense. I say more power to 'em. Wish I'd done some of that. Maybe there's still time. Whad'ya think?" David said, still basking in the *cool 'chine* compliment.

"Really. Don't believe half of what they said. Those two give credence to legalized abortion," Larry said.

"Come on, Larry. Say, you're not for abortion, are you?"

"Damn straight."

"Never going to happen, especially with our Catholic president," David said.

"Doesn't need to happen. Abortion's already obsolete. Haven't you heard about the pill?"

As the miles passed, Larry's hangover subsided, and his demeanor became less argumentative, more reflective. Listening to his brother's discontent may have played on his conscience, revealing some long-dormant kindred sensitivities.

David pondered the recurrent feelings of resentment he held toward Larry. For years, he'd dreamt of waking up and, instead of going to the store, simply driving away. He envisioned a vagabond, carefree life—no responsibility, no schedule. He'd meet and talk with regular people in ordinary places. Not exactly the life he imagined Larry lived, but a life he'd fantasized over the years. David visualized himself wandering the country like Jack Kerouac in *On the Road*. When he shared these thoughts with Jane, she would casually brush them aside as a midlife crisis. He never told her the daydream began in the first grade when he heard the story of Huckleberry Finn and Jim drifting down the Mississippi on a raft. That was long before Larry left home, before David and Jane married. And long before anybody ever heard of a midlife crisis.

"Larry, you ever heard of Jack Kerouac?"

"Yeah. Just another asshole alcoholic. Good for nothing."

"I don't know. It's not that easy to dismiss his ideas or how he lived them out," David said.

Traveling across the country with Larry had dredged up memories and long-held feelings of envy mixed with personal disappointment.

Why do I mow the lawn? How long can I sell hammers in search of nails? Do I really enjoy volunteering for the annual Octoberfest? And a million other questions about the mundane, repetitive, lackluster life David experienced in Three Oaks, Michigan. He felt trapped, drowning in anxiety, self-doubt, and even martyrdom. If life had already happened, he'd missed out.

"It's that easy. Kerouac's never accomplished a goddam thing. A worthless waste of skin. No sane person wants that for himself," Larry said.

Larry had relapsed into his well-worn, disgruntled self. He could be dismissive and then profane in an instant. It came easy for Larry to say coarse, raw things in an irreverent manner. David believed his brother had clearly never been constrained by the responsibilities of family obligations or the maintenance of a community image. He had never experienced the encumbrances of looking after the needs of others. Larry's only concern was Larry. That was David's belief, and it fed a good portion of his resentment over the years.

Exasperated, David switched the subject to their father's death and to his own disappointment that Larry had not brought it up. Their father had died suddenly two years earlier of a massive heart attack while Larry treated himself to a vacation in the Australian Outback. In Larry's defense, he didn't know about his father's passing until a week after the funeral. However, in view of Larry's recent heart attack, David expected some curiosity about the circumstances of their father's death. If only Larry would recognize the parallel health problems between himself and their father. But there seemed to be nothing there except indifference; it was more important to David than to his brother.

To stimulate some emotion in his brother, David brought up a subject of personal concern for which he suspected Larry would have an emphatic opinion.

"Do you remember Lou Gehrig?" David asked.

"Seriously? I *was* Lou Gehrig. I always played first base. Never missed a game. Just like the Iron Man."

"As a right-hander, you shouldn't have played first any more than a lefty should catch," David said.

"I was the best first baseman Three Oaks ever had. Hit .407 my senior year, stole seven bases, and never struck out." Larry could not stop. "Led the team in RBIs too."

Ah-ha! Larry had swallowed the bait. As suspected, his statistical obsession with childish athletic prowess had not faded.

"How do you feel about death? We talked about ALS, Lou Gehrig's disease, while driving out, remember? Gehrig died in 1941, June." David did his best to show genuine interest in his brother's opinion. But he was all too familiar with his brother's aggressive comeback for the slightest perceived challenge.

"Of course, I remember. Gehrig had just died," Larry said.

"Yes, and Gehrig died a long, agonizing, painful death. What a heroic person he was, toughing it out until the bitter end. He was the true Iron Man," David said.

"Yes, it was too bad. But it will never happen to me and shouldn't have happened to Gehrig," Larry said.

"What do you mean? You had a heart attack, not ALS. We can't control how we die. It's a natural thing."

"No! It's unnecessary, wasteful, and cruel. The fact is, we *can* control when and how we die." Larry's cocksure manner begged for clicking heels and a Nazi salute. A simple question had again led to a full-fledged argument. David believed death was never inevitable, especially in light of current rapid medical advancements. Any end-of-life situation other than natural or accidental death was murder in David's eyes.

"Come on, Larry. What about thou shalt not kill? Remember the Ten Commandments? Or are you one of those free-spirited West Coast atheists?"

Larry's blood pressure could be gauged by his pinkish scalp showing from beneath a full head of fine, light-brown hair. "Get serious, Dave. Struggling in unbearable pain while praying to die is not my idea of life. And there are times when death is absolutely inevitable. Prolonging life in those situations is criminal, plain and simple."

"Ending life by any unnatural means is murder, plain and simple. You don't believe in suicide, do you?" David asked.

"I damn sure do under the circumstances I've stated. Anything else is a cruel and unusual punishment. You remember the Constitution, don't you?"

"I suspect that's how you feel about abortion too," David said.

"Damn straight. It won't be long before the rest of the country wakes up." Larry declared in an authoritarian voice reminiscent of a revivalist preacher.

Their escalating combative discussion continued all the way across the Texas panhandle, a bitter and irreconcilable conflict that served only to pass time and miles. A quarter tank of gas provided a cease-fire opportunity. David pulled into a Phillips 66 station inside the city limits of sleepy Elk City, Oklahoma. His justification was gas, but in fact, both Daileys were mentally exhausted from their contentious, bickering marathon. Larry got out, slammed the door, and stomped off to the men's room around back then went into the station to look for a bottle of RC Cola, all while David asked the station attendant for a fill-up. An armistice was necessary if David ever expected to get Larry back home in one piece. Once out of the car and the confining front seat next to his recalcitrant brother, David started to relax.

As both brothers returned to the car, a rambunctious squad of uniformed high school cheerleaders drove up in a large Pontiac station wagon and parked at the adjoining gas pump. The squad scrambled out and fluttered around the tailgate. The lone gas jockey—Bob, according to his shirt pocket name tag—jogged from the Chevy to the Pontiac, aware he was the object of the team's attention. "How's about a fill-up, Bob?" "Hey, Bob, would you like to take *me* for a test drive?" "Bob, do you think we need an oil change?" "Say, Bob, is your dipstick handy?" With each suggestive question, the girls tittered their wild approval. Not to be outdone, Bob struck back, "That'd be overtime. Y'all know I get laid, I mean paid, more for overtime." Bob reveled in the raunchy banter; they all did.

Before the Daileys got back in their car, David took another snipe at Larry—he couldn't help himself. "So you don't care much about life or death. Tell me, is that why you never made an appearance before or after Dad died? Couldn't be bothered. What about Mom? You ever think about her? Totally devastated. You never showed up. Guess you just didn't give a damn."

"You go to hell, Davy-Do-Right!"

"No! You go to hell, you self-centered, egotistical bastard!" Impulsively, and with both hands, David shoved Larry in the chest, knocking him back.

"Motherfucker!" Larry snarled as he charged back, throwing a wild right punch brushing David's jaw and landing on his right shoulder. David grasped Larry's arm with his left, lunged forward, and clutched him around the neck in the crotch of his right arm. They spun around violently and slammed into the Chevy's passenger side door. Larry kicked the back of David's right knee, causing him to buckle and fall backward but not without bringing Larry down on top of him. They rolled on the concrete, flailing madly in cockfight fashion.

In total rage, the embattled brothers smashed into and knocked over a barrel full of empty, and partially empty, oil cans. The contents scattered and splattered in all directions. Some of the debris smacked into the cheerleaders now huddling between the two cars. Worse yet, the combatants crashed into one of the girls who failed to scurry out of their path. She fell to the pavement screaming. Other team members shouted for help as they rallied around their fallen teammate.

While the Daileys brawled on in unhinged abandon, a now-united team pounced. They grabbed, kicked, and punched, trying to force the two men apart. Two girls had Larry, one by the hair and the other by an arm, pulling in opposite directions. Three others grasped David by the legs and dragged him away from Larry. During the melee, Bob opted for a tactical retreat back inside the station where he observed from behind a picture window cluttered with candy displays.

David staggered to his feet, as did Larry, and they lunged at each other again. This time, however, they were surrounded and held by hysterical, brown-and-white-clad, young women all screaming madly while trying to keep the combatants apart. The team's combined fury exploded, giving no quarter. They punched, kicked, scratched, and shrieked in an effort to stop the fight.

At that point and in the interest of self-preservation, the Daileys turned their individual efforts to defense from the banzai assault of frantic young women. Bob emerged from his bunker and walked out in a show of support for the cheerleaders. With the station attendant's assistance, the family feud was brought under control. Bob stood fast between the two men in an act of feigned gallantry. Unimpressed, one of the team members said, "We got this, Bob. You go take a peek under the hood!" With the exception of Bob, the last comment went unappreciated.

One pitiful cheerleader sat sobbing on the concrete. She wiped at the greasy filth on her skirt, but her efforts only served to spread the dark stains.

As the noise of verbal insults from the spirit section waned, and David regained some composure, embarrassment and humiliation overwhelmed him. Even more so when he saw the weeping young girl now on one knee, leaning against the premium pump. As much to avoid Larry as a sincere concern for the young lady, he moved toward her and said, "I'm sorry. Are you hurt?"

"Oh, I'm okay," she sniffled. Her eyes were so full of tears, she could hardly see the filthy condition of her once-bright cheerleading uniform.

"We will pay for the damage to your uniform," David said.

"You got that right," Larry said. He pulled his wallet from his back pocket and took out a twenty-dollar bill. "Here, I think this should cover cleaning," he said, his voice cracking. Combined with his bruised and scruffy appearance, he made quite a sight. David had to squash a smile. In a stark turn of events, the brothers presented a sincere and cohesive effort in expressing their concern, embarrassment, and apologies to the cheerleaders. The Daileys were united in thought and deed.

The high school coed looked mournfully down at her oil-smeared skirt. Her flushed and puffy face was tear-streaked and dejected. She said, "Maybe Mom can get this out." She looked up at her teammates. "Can we stop at my house on the way to practice? I've got another uniform."

"These old jerks owe Candy a new outfit!" demanded one.

"What would you have us do? What can we do? We are so sorry," David pleaded.

Larry continued, "That's right. We want to pay for any cleaning, damages, whatever we can do. We're sorry. Very sorry." Larry's voice cracked again.

Another cheerleader, apparently the captain, took over. "Judging from the license plate, these two feisty bums are not from around here. I think you jerks need to get back in your car and go back where you came from."

Bob stuttered in an attempt to mediate.

"Shut up, Bob. We'll handle this," the captain said.

Larry pleaded, "You sure? It's our fault. I want to pay at least for the cleaning. Please?" Again, Larry extended a hand, but this time, it held two twenties.

"No," said the captain. "Just leave." She motioned to the others, "Let's go. We'll be late for the team picture." They all piled into the enormous red Pontiac wagon and drove out of the station.

"Good luck. I hope your team wins!" Larry shouted after them. A couple of girls flashed plastic smiles and parade-float hand waves. Another flipped them the bird. The war-torn brothers watched motionless until the red station wagon disappeared down the highway.

David looked straight-faced at Larry. "Does she mean they're number one?"

"Definitely not you, unless it's number one asshole."

"What do you mean, sewer tooth? You started it," David said.

"No, you did. It was your snide remarks about Dad's funeral."

"Okay, I'll give you that, at least when it comes to the funeral. But when's the last time you were home, saw our mom?"

A tilted, bewildered face gawked back at David. "Okay, I'm taking care of that right now. Right?" Larry's expression slowly changed as a smile crossed his battered face. "You've got a purple goose egg on your cheek, and your jaw is all skinned up. You okay?" Larry asked.

David couldn't help but laugh. "Me? It's you I'm worried about. Your shirt is ripped to shreds, and look at your knee—bleeding! You're not getting in *my* car like that."

"You talkin' 'bout me?" Larry lifted David's shirttail. Not a button left, and grease and oil covered his torn pant leg. Also, his right hand was scraped and bloodied. "Follow me," Larry said. "Johns are around back, one labeled Setters, the other Pointers."

"Say what? What do you think that means?"

"I don't know, Dave, you tell me."

"Where did our sunburns go?"

They could not help but smile at each other, and there was a conciliatory tone in their voices. Larry grabbed David by the arm, pretending to help him walk. David resisted and put his arm around Larry's shoulder and pulled him close as they limped together toward the Pointers sign. The small bit of shared camaraderie while cleaning up in the restroom lifted their spirits. David thought of the time in grade school when the two of them came to the defense of a classmate being teased by a group of big kids. Together, he and his brother would never back down—he was confident of that.

"If it weren't for our destroyed clothes, pain, guilt, and embarrassment, I think I'd be satisfied with what just happened. It's a crazy world, but at least no one got hurt," David said.

Larry scoffed, but his eyes sparkled. "You may be right. I think that cheerleader who gave us the finger had our number. For better or worse, we're Daileys."

"Let's get you home," David said.

"Let's change our shirts first. Did you fill her with gas?"

"Yes, and I paid Big Bob. You remember Bob?"

Larry jumped behind the wheel before his brother had a chance. He squealed the tires as they left the station and gunned it eastward through town. His impetuous nature was reflected in his driving, but David was also ready to roll, just as Mr. Coconut was rolling to life in the back seat having toppled over from his perch in the clay pot.

They had gone less than half a mile when David spotted a Squeaky Clean self-serve car wash on the left. He told Larry he had to wash the car. Larry immediately cut across oncoming traffic and came to a stop in the first open wash bay. A Kenworth driver laid on his heavyweight horn with one hand while reminding the Daileys of their cheerleading rank with the other.

For $0.75, they could manually rinse, wash, re-rinse, and dry; towels provided. This was to David's liking, always particular about the correct way to wash the Bel Air. While he tended to his car, Larry lit up a smoke and sauntered across the highway to an A&P Grocery where he bought a couple of packs of Pall Malls and a six-pack of Hudepohl beer. While in the grocery store, the Oklahoma State Highway Patrol streaked by with lights flashing and siren blaring.

By the time his brother returned, David sat behind the wheel with the motor idling—music to his ears. The only better sound was the distinctive rumble of a Harley Davidson motorcycle. He had completed the car wash, careful to eliminate every potential water spot, and had his beloved Chevy road-ready. Mr. Coconut was back in his clay pot perch. Larry returned with a cigarette in his mouth and carrying four bottles of beer.

"No eating, drinking, or smoking in this car."

Larry flicked a butt on the ground and sat the beer on the floor behind his seat.

"You and your rules. I got one for you: go ugly early."

"You still sufferin' from last night's shutout at the Triple XR Bar?"

"In your dreams. You think that damn coconut drinks beer?"

"Mr. Coconut drinks only on special occasions."

David pumped the accelerator and brought his clean machine up to the posted speed limit. The motor purred, the hood gleamed, and the ride was smooth. A clock on the side of the State Bank of Elk City read 6:35. Dusk approached.

"I don't think we can make it to Oklahoma City. Clinton is only twenty-five miles. Ever hear of—" Flashing red and blue lights suddenly lit up the rearview mirror like New Year's in Manhattan, interrupting David's train of thought. "Damn! We got company." The console gauges were good, and the speedometer indicated sixty-five miles per hour, right at the speed limit.

David eased over onto the right shoulder followed by a state highway patrol car with blinding high-beam headlights lighting up the Bel Air. Larry filled the air with guttural expletives. David glared into the rearview mirror, totally blinded. After a long minute, two sturdy officers advanced, one on either side of the Bel Air. The lead officer at the driver's side window said in a rich smooth voice, "Good evening. We've been looking for you two."

"What do you mean?" David asked. "I'm sure we were well beneath the speed limit."

"Excuse me, sir. May I please see your driver's license and registration?" While David retrieved the necessary identifications, the younger officer shined his flashlight through Larry's window.

Larry recoiled. "You got a search warrant? We weren't speeding."

The lead officer thanked David for the license and registration. After reviewing each, he handed them back and said, "Thank you, sir. Everything seems in good order."

"Great," Larry said. "Now, can we get going? We've got places to go and people to see."

The scorn in Larry's speech triggered a response from the second officer. "Please be quiet, sir. We are not done here."

Larry shot back, "We weren't speeding. We're done here!"

The first officer leaned in closer to the driver's window so he could see Larry, "Gentlemen, we did not stop you for exceeding the speed limit. If we had probable cause, and we do, we could search your car. We don't think that will be necessary."

"Then why'd you stop us?" Larry said.

"Please be quiet, sir, please," the second officer requested in such a controlled, respectful manner to appear menacing. With his flashlight, he surveyed the backseat through the window. "Sir, is that beer on the floor back there? Have you two been drinking?"

Before any answer could be given, the officer on David's side requested David to step out of the car. As he did so, David whispered to Larry to keep his mouth shut and stay put. The officers had David walk several paces on the white line along the outer edge of the pavement. They did not reveal pass or fail nor their opinion of the beer in the car.

Larry was invited to join them outside the car. The senior patrolman questioned the Daileys about where they had been and where they were headed. Larry fidgeted but allowed David to answer the questions. The junior officer commented on how nice the car looked. "Your car's very clean. Looks like it's just been washed?" The two officers shared a knowing glance but remained expressionless.

"I prize my car and always want it looking good," David said.

The younger officer impulsively announced that he owned a black '57 Chevy with red leather interior.

"Cool. I'd like to see it. Did you buy it new?" David asked.

The lead officer was about the same age as the Daileys, stood six-foot-four, and weighed about two hundred sixty pounds. He was definitely the man in charge of the interrogation and quickly brought them back to the subject at hand. "You two gentlemen fit the description of a recent complaint. Other than your clean shirts, you both display evidence of a recent physical encounter. And it looks as if your car has just been cleaned inside and out." The officer's explanation sounded too much like a formal indictment for Larry.

"Officer, I think I can explain," Larry interrupted. "There's a misunderstanding here."

"I understand," the patrolman replied. "Please take a seat in the back of our unit. We're taking you two to the county sheriff's office."

"What? What about my car?"

"Please give me the keys. Your car will be taken care of. Now, please, let's go."

"Sheriff? Why?" Larry asked.

"Sir, we'll ask the questions. Please take a seat in back. Let us see if we may find some answers for you." The lead officer's ultra-polite manners would have cast shards of trepidation through Mother Theresa's soul.

Fortunately, or unfortunately, the county sheriff's office was only two miles down the highway in the direction of Oklahoma City. As they rode in the backseat of the patrol car, Larry erupted with vulgar displeasure, calling this action "the sign of a home-cooked Gestapo state." In his defense, both brothers wanted to know what they were being taken in for and were confident they were the victims of some mistaken identity. Neither officer responded.

At the sheriff's office, the troopers handed the Daileys over to Beckham County. David was informed his car had been impounded. When the realization of being arrested and booked for assault and a possible hit-and-run set in, the suspects became bird-dog attentive. They shared an astounded sensation at the mention of suspicion for solicitation of a minor. Sheriff's deputies then escorted them to separate interrogation rooms. Each was questioned about an assault and foiled attempted kidnapping of a sixteen-year-old high school junior. They were made aware of being identified by a gas station attendant as fleeing the crime scene, driving a late '50s model light-green Chevrolet with Michigan plates. The source for the allegations behind their interrogator's questions could not be mistaken: Bob.

During David's questioning, he relied on the plain truth, as ridiculous as it sounded. He prayed his brother did the same. That wish was confirmed later in the evening while seated on bunks in adjoining twelve-by-twelve-foot jail cells.

"Could things get any worse?" Larry asked.

"If we're found guilty," David said.

"Quit the wiseass. Things are serious here," Larry said.

"Finally, we've found something we can agree on."

David told his brother that the detective who questioned him told him witnesses would be brought in for interview first thing in the morning. He had retained a calm surface demeanor. In the best outcome, they would be delayed only a day or so in their return to Michigan. He didn't want to think about the worst that could happen. Strangely, David amused both of them when he said, "Look at it this way: we have not driven out of our way, and we have free room and board."

"Let's hope we cut our expenses for only one night. I can't stand too much good fortune. Wish I'd changed clothes," Larry said. He was still wearing the torn pants from the gas station dustup.

"Wish I'd changed mine too. For however we'd pictured each other's lives, you've got to admit that tonight they are exactly the same."

Both men were hyped-up, and conversation between them bounced back and forth between the cell bars from topic to topic late into the night. However, their dialog always returned to their present predicament. They agreed the problem related to their gas station scuffle but disagreed as to how the pieces fit together. Larry believed that at least one of the cheerleaders must have lied to the police. Physical fatigue eventually won out, and they fell asleep. However, a busy mind and a tightness in his chest resulted in fretful sleep for David. *How did we end up here? What will happen in the morning? Will I ever have another chance for Santa Catalina? Where's my car?*

At exactly 7:00 a.m., a jailhouse trustee raked a tin cup across the steel cell bars to announce breakfast. Through the rectangle slot in each cell door he passed a meal tray of coffee, powdered eggs, and cold, dry wheat toast. Larry ate his breakfast. David only sipped the lukewarm coffee—instant and bad.

At 8:30 a.m., two armed deputies arrived, along with the same trustee who now retrieved the breakfast trays. The deputies escorted the inmates to a tiny beige cinderblock room furnished with one rectangular metal table, five wooden folding chairs, and a domed light fixture hanging from the middle of the cracked plaster ceiling. The outer wall held one small window with closed two-inch wood blinds and a large, framed grocery store color print of the Oklahoma land rush. A Windex-clean inset mirror, picture-window size, dominated an interior wall. They were left by themselves to sit and wait, never told for how long or what to expect.

A few minutes past nine, the county sheriff along with the lead state trooper from the night before, entered the room. Sheriff Buck Hampton introduced himself as well as State Trooper Ben Knowles. "Trooper Knowles has brought in the lady who called in a complaint to Crime Stoppers last evening," the sheriff said. Trooper Knowles nodded recognition in David's direction, and the older brother returned the acknowledgment. A perplexed expression crossed Larry's face. He stared at the large mirror as if he could see through it.

The sheriff informed the brothers that an employee at the Phillips service station was on his way. Apparently, he had seen two men in a Chevy tear out of the station late afternoon yesterday. Also, a young woman who witnessed an assault at that service station was already seated in the outer office. While they waited, the sheriff reviewed driver's license information: *David Dailey, six-foot-one, 185 pounds, brown hair, blue eyes, Three Oaks, MI; Larry Dailey, five-foot-seven, 150 pounds, brown hair, blue eyes, Santa Monica, CA.*

The sheriff's intention became clear right off the bat. He intended to come to a resolution in short order. However, when he outlined the possible charges, Larry jumped up, shouting, "Ridiculous! I want a lawyer!"

"Please be seated," Trooper Knowles said in a low but strong voice. With a thick right hand to the shoulder, Trooper Knowles planted Larry back in his chair with such force, David feared for his brother's tailbone.

"There's an attorney in the outer office pleading to see you two," Sheriff Hampton said. "Going to cost you, though, time and money. You ever met a lawyer who kept his hands in his own pockets?" Sheriff Hampton's meaning was clear, as well as his determination to conduct and control the interview.

During their following conversation with the officers, the situation in question came into focus, as did the evolution of a gross misunderstanding. Larry kept his mouth shut. Each time David attempted to add clarification for what transpired at the service station and the carwash, Sheriff Hampton admonished him, "Please, just answer the questions I ask." Assault, solicitation, flight to avoid arrest, tampering with evidence—fear welled up until a suffocating constriction seized David's chest, and his breathing became labored. Larry sat street statue-like and continued to stare stone-faced into the mirror.

Eternity came and went. Then the door opened, and Officer Knowles' partner entered. Sheriff Hampton introduced Trooper Doak

Knowles who turned out to be Trooper Ben Knowles' nephew. The sheriff said, "What do you have for us, Doak?"

The rookie trooper stood straight and scrutinized each person seated around the table. He obviously relished being the center of attention. "Just as we suspected, sir. The suspects got into a fight at 5:37 p.m. at the Phillips 66 service station, the one owned by Lloyd Wagner on West Sixty-Six Street. In their struggle, they knocked one of the Elk City High School cheerleaders to the ground, soiling her uniform in three places, maybe four—collateral damage, sir. The short suspect reportedly offered money to pay for a new uniform or cleaning expenses for the uniform damaged. The said cheerleaders declined the offer of expenses and left the scene. The suspects departed approximately ten minutes later, according to station attendant Robert F. Spears, and headed in the same direction as the cheerleaders. They spun their rear tires on loose gravel, squealing their tires as they entered the highway. Exhibition-driving, sir. Unsafe driving in any situation, sir—"

The sheriff interrupted, "Doak! Stick to the relevant facts. Some of us have work to do."

"Yes, sir. Sorry, sir. The cheerleader in question stopped at home to change into a second uniform. When her mother asked what had happened, her daughter said she was knocked down by two men at the Phillips Station. That is all the mother reported her daughter said. The victim reported late for cheerleading practice, but she did not miss the team picture. The mother called in the complaint, sir. The suspects washed their car at the Squeaky-Clean car wash and purchased a six-pack of Hudepohl beer at the A&P. David Dailey reported he likes a clean machine. Four unopened bottles of Hudepohl beer were confiscated." Self-satisfaction radiated from every crease in Officer Doak Knowles' fresh-pressed navy-blue uniform.

"That's sufficient, Doak. Take a seat," the sheriff said, pointing to the remaining empty chair.

"Great! So we can go," Larry said.

"Not so fast," the sheriff replied. "You two are guilty of disorderly conduct, endangering the health and wellbeing of others, and littering."

"What about exhibition driving?" asked Doak.

"Okay, that too," the sheriff said.

David turned a stern face toward Larry. A crimson tide rose through Larry's neck. David's eyes shouted the message: *Keep your mouth shut!* David did not want to stay over another night in the Elk City Jail. He intended to be home by Friday.

After a long pause, during which David anticipated being the third Dailey heart-attack victim, Sheriff Hampton decreed, "I understand one of the cheerleaders told you boys to get the hell out of town. I agree. Pick your car up from impound on your way out. There's a fifteen dollar, cash payment, towing charge. We're done here." With that, the sheriff got up and marched out of the conference room, clipboard under his arm.

The Dailey boys looked at each other, thunderstruck. As the two troopers stood, David said, "Hey, Doak, where did you get your name?"

Before Doak could answer, Trooper Ben Knowles slid his chair in and said, "If you can tell me where he got his name, I'll buy you two damn Yankees a man's breakfast."

David was sure of the answer but strained as if in deep thought. Larry said he didn't know but would buy all of them the best Elk City breakfast they could find. He went on to defame the jailhouse menu.

"Slow down, Larry, I got this." Full of confidence, David proclaimed, "Doak was named after Doak Walker, the greatest Detroit Lion running back of all time."

"How'd you know that?" Trooper Doak Knowles asked.

"He thinks he knows everything. Where you takin' us to breakfast?" Larry asked. An air of good feeling swept over the four men as they left in the room.

"Follow us. It ain't too far," Doak said.

The Daileys in the Bel Air followed the Knowleses in their patrol car to The Cattle Drive, a café five miles up Route 66. The sweet aroma of frying bacon wafted on the air twenty yards from the solid oak front doors. All four men ordered the Chuck Wagon Omelet, good and filling. Ben and Doak told the visitors that cattle drives used to come right through the center of Elk City on their way north to the

Dodge City railhead. Larry and David could not have had more fun than they did swapping old sports stories with the troopers from Elk City, Oklahoma. Never once did either brother think about the date or miles ahead, or even Larry's heart condition.

"Doak Walker ran one hundred twenty yards on one touchdown run!"

"Really? Did you know Bobby Layne was a better pitcher than a quarterback?"

"Someone told me Bobby drank six days a week and played football on Sunday!"

"Really?"

"Walker played for and won the Heisman at Southern Methodist."

"Bobby played football and baseball for Texas."

"Where'd you play, Ben?"

CHAPTER 10
Baxter Springs, Kansas

The Oklahoma State Trooper team of Ben and Doak Knowles received a radio message instructing them to go to the scene of a jackknifed tractor trailer. Spilled California citrus fruit blocked Route 66 two miles west of Elk City. Responding to the call forced an abrupt end to the nostalgic sports stories' marathon, but not before Larry lamented how he'd mistakenly turned down a tryout with the Detroit Tigers. Larry's memory had improved over time to the level of remembering things that never happened. David let his brother have the floor and did not contradict or correct.

The Dailey brothers were back on the highway by early afternoon, cruising toward Oklahoma City. Black oil derricks peppered a treeless, flat plain. A dry, invisible wind propelled lonesome windmills and scared up an occasional wispy dust devil. Once or twice wind gusts could even be felt buffeting the Bel Air. Scattered white cumulus clouds rose along the northern horizon in an otherwise empty sky.

When David spotted a dilapidated old farmhouse, he visualized the infamous 1930s Dust Bowl, the scourge of the Texas and Oklahoma panhandles. As much as he wanted to enlighten Larry about the history of the Great Depression, he decided it would be better to simply watch the parched western plains pass on by. A sandy vapor trail swirled behind an orange Allis-Chalmers tractor as it sped across fallow fields toward a stooped, weather-beaten barn. David muttered aloud, "This country could sure use some rain."

"Fat chance," Larry mumbled back.

Larry saw a sign for the new interstate and suggested they take it. "Let's make up for our jail time. This two-lane stuff gets old."

"Not if we get pulled over again."

"Step on it! Four-lane expressways are the only way to travel nowadays," Larry said.

"I know. One has recently opened near home. Saves at least an hour or two from Three Oaks to Detroit. Makes for uninteresting driving though."

"Uninteresting? Really? Dave, we're talkin' speed here."

David took the expressway entrance ramp. True, not interesting but efficient. Oklahoma City flew by, and they merged onto the Will Rogers Turnpike toward Tulsa. After a quick pit stop to relieve bladder pressure and get gas, Larry took over behind the wheel.

"Okay ... boring but faster. Don't you agree?" Larry said.

"Boring? Boredom is a self-inflicted wound injuring the victim in inverse proportion to the victim's intellect," David said.

"Whatever the fuck that means. At this rate, we can make the border of the Show Me State in no time." Larry did not give David's definition of boredom a second thought, if he thought at all. David didn't bother to explain the origin of the Missouri state slogan. He hoped Larry would relax, enjoy the ride. The last thing either needed was another of Larry's coughing jags or, worse yet, another gas station brawl. David watched his brother closely but did not ask how he felt.

David did, however, read aloud a large billboard encouraging travelers to take the next exit: Claremore, Oklahoma, Home of Will Rogers. "Now there's a great man. Did you know they used to call Route 66 the Will Rogers Highway?"

"You know, Dave, for once, I'm going to agree with you. Ole' Will was a funny man."

"More than funny, he was a common man who knew where he came from and where he was going. Wish I could say the same," David said.

"Whatever. A funny man. That's why people liked him."

As usual, David found Larry's dismissive and dogmatic reactions difficult to swallow but knew better than to challenge him. They rode in silence until David saw a sign for Sequoyah. "Hey, Larry, take the next exit."

"Exit? You nuts? We're cookin', checkin' off mucho miles. Why stop now?"

"I want to see Sequoyah," David said.

Larry never lifted off the gas pedal as they sailed past the exit. "Why do you want to see a Redwood anyway? I doubt they even grow here. At least, not naturally—no water. Only in California."

"You think I'm talkin' about trees?" David asked.

"Who knows what the fuck you're talkin' about? You say so much, mostly garbage."

"Listen up, fool. I'm talkin' about the most accomplished American Indian ever. I'm talking about Sequoyah, an illiterate Cherokee who created a written language all by himself. Crippled and an outcast in his own tribe, he was always on his own."

"You open your mouth to hear yourself talk. Not listening. Besides, isn't the only good Indian a dead Indian?"

"Jesus, Larry! How quickly you forget. What about Summer and Harmony?" David's jaw tightened, determined to set his brother straight whether he listened or not. "I'm serious. In the woods by himself, this illiterate Indian created an alphabet, a syllabary. If you memorized his symbols, you could spell every word perfectly. Sequoyah was a great American."

"Really? Could he help you spell, Sir Spelling Bee?"

"As a matter of fact, he could. Present-day linguists can't stand in Sequoyah's shadow. Not a tree, Mr. ValePicktorian. In my mind, Oklahoma should have been named Sequoyah." David swaggered his words for effect and self-satisfaction, much in the pattern of his brother. Larry reacted with a silent, flat affect. Although their words were harsh, their tone had mellowed.

The northern skyline grew heavier and nearer.

"Take the Commerce exit. At least we'll be able to say we saw Kansas," David said.

"Say what? We can be in Missouri in less than fifteen minutes. Bypass Joplin completely."

"Exit now, Mr. Baseball! Commerce is the home of Mickey Mantle, one of your heroes. You taught Mantle to switch-hit, right?"

"The Mick? Really?" Larry jerked the wheel right onto the exit ramp as three or four giant rain droplets smacked the windshield. "Do you think he still lives here? I mean, in the off season?"

"Somewhere in Texas, I think. Is it going to rain?"

"Mantle signed a contract for a hundred thousand dollars," Larry puffed.

"You know what they say about a man who knows the price of everything and the value of nothing?"

David's rhetorical intention was stymied by Larry's cocksure response. "He's rich!"

Commerce, Oklahoma was little more than one caution light, two signs claiming the birthplace of Mickey Mantle, and the Coming Soon Mickey Mantle Museum. Larry wanted to get right back on the interstate, but David insisted they stay on the old highway and continue the few miles north into Kansas. As they passed Mutt Mantle Field, named after Mickey's father, David asked Larry if he wanted to stop and steal home plate.

Larry didn't get it, or didn't want to, but instead came back, "I stole home twice my senior year and once my junior."

"Right."

They crossed the border and arrived shortly in Baxter Springs, Kansas, a small rural town by most standard measures. Sporadic raindrops bounced and beaded on the Bel Air's slick, waxy hood. Due to ever lower, thick, murky clouds, sundown came early. Larry pulled into a Standard service station apparently in the midst of a gas war— "REG. 18 Cents!!" In addition to an inexpensive fill-up, cabins were available around back for $4 a night. The brothers took advantage of both bargains and were directed next door to Miss May's for supper. A clap of thunder rumbled through a troubled sky as the Daileys hustled through the front door to Miss May's Kountry Kitchen. All present smiled in their direction.

Only a few patrons were seated in a cozy dining area decorated in a primitive country-western decor. Separating a high, oblong kitchen window from the main dining room was a long, narrow coffee bar with six cane-backed black tractor seat stools. The lone waitress waved for them to choose any table. They selected the bay window booth with a view of a dark and gloomy Main Street. Black storm clouds had rolled in, totally obscuring the setting sun. The trees lining the far side of the street started to sway in the wind. Before their orders could be taken, a large red fire engine roared up in front of the diner, blocking any possible street view.

"What's with the fire truck? You see any smoke? Looks like rain to me," Larry said.

The fire engine's driver, clad in a white T-shirt, heavy-duty yellow bib overalls, and calf-high red rubber boots, scrambled down from the cab and sprinted to the door as a lightning bolt illuminated the bay window with a silver spear of light, followed by a sharp thunderclap. The fireman ducked his shoulders as he rushed into the restaurant directly behind Larry's bench. Gasping for air he shouted, "Attention, attention!" His eyes, perched toward the sides of a slender face, focused to his left and above the heads of alarmed patrons. He stood straight with shoulders back, giving him an odd dignity despite his fragmented uniform. His startled audience waited.

"What's the matter, Hank?" the wide-eyed waitress asked.

"Listen up! Listen up! Got a call from Columbus Police Department. Flash flood west of here is heading our way." Hank's loud alarm was partially muffled by another booming thunderclap that shook the entire building, rattling windows and dishes. Hank's eyes, along with those of the waitress, opened even wider as he swallowed noticeably. "Spring River risin'! I need help at Brush Creek Bridge! Can some of you come with me?" He caught his breath as he lowered his eyes to scan the dining room but never made direct eye contact. His eager expression receded, there being only nine people present and only two men under seventy.

David instinctively stood up. Larry took a quick look around then followed suit. "Only two?" Hank asked. The waitress untied her apron as she walked over and stood next to the Daileys.

"No, Joan! You stay here. Direct any volunteers to the high school football field. We need help there, bad. I have your number."

Hank swiveled toward David and Larry. "Let's go, men!" The Daileys hustled out the door after Hank and climbed into the high fire engine cab. Once seated with David in the middle, the brothers looked at each other, confused. However, the urgency in Hank's voice and body language affirmed by the angry sounds of a fast-approaching storm filled both with uneasy apprehension.

At the north edge of town, Hank turned the lumbering fire truck left and followed a narrow two-lane concrete road northward. Repetitive jagged bolts of lightning followed by angry rolling thunder tore apart and intermittently illuminated the vengeful heavens. Trees thrashed about violently, and leaves, small branches, and other debris whirled up and across the road in front of them. They rode on the brink of a deluge in a truck that took up more than two-thirds of the roadway. Then, like an avalanche, a vicious downpour collided with the fire engine, pummeling the windshield, and blocking their view. David envisioned an unseen wall of water roaring out of the darkness toward them. But just then a feeling of resolute determination overcame his trepidation, a sensation he'd experienced only once long ago.

"Maybe it's because we're in a fire engine and can't see much, but this road seems too small for this fire engine," David said.

"Original Sixty-Six! Lane and a half! Rainbow Bridge up ahead is original! Maybe the last on old US Sixty-Six!" Hank shouted and turned the windshield wipers up full blast, which provided only brief glimpses of the danger ahead.

"What do you want us to do?" Larry asked.

"Got to save her!" Hank's voice screamed both fear and purpose, while also suggesting he often spoke in too loud a voice.

More by instinct than sight, Hank squeezed the truck across a one-lane bridge and a short distance beyond turned a sharp left into a large, mostly unpaved parking area with a single boat ramp already partially submerged. Hank parked well above the ramp, approximately fifty yards upstream beyond the bridge. Brush Creek, normally no more than forty feet across, roared past at twice that size and boiled beneath the bridge. Bridge clearance was fast diminishing. The noise and power of the rushing water sent a shudder through all three men.

"She's up five feet! May go higher! Don't think she'll make the deck though!" Hank yelled as he reached behind the seat and retrieved two three-quarter length yellow raincoats, two pairs of calf-high red rubber boots, and two large round-brimmed yellow rubber hats. "Here, put these on!"

The brothers struggled in the confines of the cab to put on their coats and boots. They managed but looked to each other for help in deciding what was front and what was back in their unusual-looking hats. Neither put on his hat but held it in his lap.

"What's our assignment?" David asked.

"You two stay here! Make sure storm debris don't build up under the bridge, causing it to dam! If she does, it'll take the bridge for sure and who knows what all downstream! There are saws, shovels, and chains with grappling hooks in the side compartments! Don't think you'll need 'em, but check 'em out anyways!"

"You're not leaving us?" Larry said.

"I'm taking that van yonder and headin' back to the school! We're sandbaggin'!"

"What if we need help?" Larry asked.

"I'll try to send reinforcements! Need to save the school! Don't let her dam! If she dams, she'll fail! Don't let her dam, boys!"

Hank climbed out, leaving the motor running with high beams focused on the bridge. The Daileys watched from inside the cab as Hank's taillights disappeared back across the Rainbow Bridge. Rain fell in sheets, forcing David to try turning the wipers higher. He failed but assumed a position behind the steering wheel. The men continued to search for an unobstructed visual of the bridge with only intermittent success. They were certain, however, that things other than water were passing in front of them then flowing beneath the bridge.

"Don't you think Hank's a little presumptuous? What the hell are we supposed to do?" Larry said.

"Don't let her dam!" David yelled, mimicking Hank in an attempt to cut the tension and enlist support. "This could be a real problem. Are you up for it?"

"You got that right! Born ready!" Larry continued David's Hank impersonation but not with Hank's bravado. A welcomed sense of camaraderie united David, his brother, and their new-found inspiration, Hank.

"Let's stay put until we see a problem. Don't take any chances. Water's dangerous," David said.

"We can't see much from in here. Let's go take a closer look," Larry said.

"You're right. We'll have to do it sometime. Let's go."

Before either man could open his door, the sky lit up with jagged shards of lighting instantly followed by an exploding clap of thunder louder than either had ever experienced. It shook every rivet in the fire engine and continued to reverberate for several seconds. A flame could now be seen flickering halfway up the splintered remains of a poplar tree on the far bank, the innocent victim of a lightning strike.

Before the thunder's rumble subsided, David turned to his brother. "Any second thoughts?"

"No."

"Me neither!"

Both men pulled on their rubber hats and climbed down from their respective doors, immediately pummeled by the vicious downpour. Meeting in front of the fire engine, they stopped to look at themselves. Standing in the direct glare of headlights, in official Baxter Springs firefighter uniforms, the two of them made a comical sight—oversized floppy hats, bright yellow parkas, and tall red boots all shiny-wet in the bright headlights.

A familial sense of purpose warmed each as they shouted through the storm, discussing possibilities of impending challenges and a division of specific tasks. Neither had experienced such a selfless team approach to anything since they had both been members of the varsity baseball team David's senior year. The last game of the season came down to playing their archrival, a much larger school with a far superior record. The whole village of Three Oaks turned out to support *their* team. Most townspeople traveled fifteen miles to the hated rival's ballpark to see the game. Three Oaks won the game two to one. Larry scored one of their two runs, while David made a game-saving catch in left field. The brothers loved their coach who said to the team following the game, "There's no limit to what can be accomplished when no one cares who gets the credit." Those wise words remained the most inspirational moment in David's life.

The Daileys spent the next two hours at war in the hammering rain while assisting an occasional tree limb, along with a wide assortment of other flood debris, to pass safely under the bridge. At times, the gap between the water's raging surface and the bottom of the bridge deck disappeared. Part of an old fishing shack glided atop the torrent, crashed into the bridge, and was sucked under, rising again in shattered fragments on the downstream side.

"I don't think it can be repaired!" David shouted from atop the bridge less than three feet above the furious river's roar. "Bridge rock-solid!" David stomped his feet and could feel water sloshing in his boots.

Larry, who was pulling a tree limb up on shore, squinted up through the driving rain but could barely see his brother before losing his balance on the slippery slope. "Not even by a hardy handy hardware man?" Larry called out at the top of his lungs from a sitting position splattered in mud. He had lost his hat in the fall, and his long hair hung soaked and stringy about his face.

A real scare came minutes later when an enormous sycamore tree, roots and all, approached from upstream like a many-headed dragon. Its large limbs lumbered over in the current like a giant flailing octopus. Once they recognized what was headed their way, the Daileys raced for the chains held in the fire engine's side compartment. Each of them flung a grappling hook around one of the tree's large limbs, and together, they attempted to guide the tree toward shore before it collided with the bridge. Unfortunately, the relentless current moved the massive beast ever closer to the constricted passageway beneath the bridge. Then David secured his chain to a hitch below the engine's front bumper. Larry reset his grappling hook on another branch closer to the creek's bank. But as the hook set, he was jerked thigh-deep into the ruthless water's surge.

"Let out the slack!" David yelled. He quickly grabbed and clamped Larry's line to a second bumper hitch. In a matter of seconds, the churning current drew both slack lines tight and, for the time being, stalled the sycamore's advance. However, Larry had slid deeper into the murky current. Unable to escape the swift tide's clutches, he was swept off his feet. It required significant strength to discover and cling to a partially submerged limb. The current's pressure against the tree limb and Larry's back pinned his chest and shoulders to the limb. All his strength was required to keep his head above water and avoid being drawn under by a fierce undertow.

"Stay away from the chains!" David yelled, but Larry could not hear a thing with water crashing all around and over him, and even if he could hear, he was completely at the mercy of the rampaging stream. "We'll get you out of this," David whispered with determination to himself.

There was no way to gauge the strain on the taut chains and grappling hooks, and Larry's ability to remain stuck to the limb would not last. He could do no more than keep his head above the powerful current. David sensed his brother's strength failing. From the water's edge and as close as he dared get to his brother without being swept in himself, he shouted, "Larry! Let go! Go with the current under the limb! I'll throw you a line on the other side! Let go! Let go!" If Larry became completely exhausted, he might not be able to save himself even if he broke free.

Whether he'd heard his brother's shouts, Larry disappeared below the limb. There was no way of knowing if he'd followed the strategy or had simply collapsed. David waited with rope in hand on the downstream side, shivering as the seconds passed. When Larry didn't pop up right away, he worried his brother may have become entangled in unseen brush below the surface. After what seemed an eternity, while David weighed the possibility of diving in to search for his brother, Larry resurfaced flailing and coughing about ten yards from shore and twenty yards from the bridge.

David threw him the line, and on the second attempt, Larry caught it, but it took every ounce of his remaining strength to hang on to the rope. At least David had a patch of boat-launch concrete beneath his feet and was only ankle deep. Even so, it took all his physical strength to pull Larry away from the current to shore. Once safe on shore, they sat next to each other in the parking lot only a few feet from the turbulent water's edge.

For several minutes, both were silent, totally exhausted. An easy, proud feeling swept over David. It wasn't the sycamore or even the bridge holding sway with him. It was Larry, his brother, for whom he was thankful.

With Larry out of harm's way and the sycamore under control, the creek seemed to level off only inches below the undergirding of the bridge's deck. Relieved, worn-out, and completely drenched in mud, water, and sweat, the two men collapsed next to each other. After a time, Larry tried to speak but panted for air between each word. Their clothes were soaked despite Hank's raingear. Their rubber boots were mud packed. Larry's hat was missing, and David took his off, content to allow the weakening rain to wash over his face.

David got up first and went back to the truck. He checked to make sure the lines were secure. Then he climbed up into the cab and started the engine. When he put the truck in reverse, the rear tires spun. Quickly, he let off the gas and reset the brake, fearing the Baxter Springs fire engine might be pulled in by the current's pressure against the sycamore.

Larry got up and made his way slowly in the truck's general direction. He found and pulled with feeble force on one of the grappling lines. He needed that support to climb the slight grade back up to the fire engine.

"Stand back!" David shouted out the driver's side window.

Larry stumbled on the slippery ground and slid back precariously close to the water's edge.

"Stand back! I'm worried the chain lines might snap or a grappling hook break loose and fly back, hitting the truck or, worse yet, one of us," David called out.

Larry struggled to get back up, staggered up the parking area incline, and, with considerable effort, climbed in by the passenger's door. The truck's tires slid forward ever so slightly but then held as the massive tree began a slow arc-sweep toward the shore. Inch by inch at first, but then the weight of the hefty fire truck overcame the powerful momentum of storm surge against the tree. The taut lines directed the tree ever closer to the creek's bank where the brothers eventually moored it only a few yards before it would have rammed the bridge and blocked the free flow of water and storm debris, Hank's formula for sure disaster.

"If that tree had hit the bridge, goodbye below to Hank," Larry stammered, still gasping for breath.

"You got that right, little brother. When did it stop raining?"

"Dave, I've been thinking. When we're done here, how about you run and get the car and come back for me?" It was apparent he was trying to get a rise out of his brother, but instead, it was a welcomed barb, understood as an attempt to put their near-death struggle with nature behind them.

"Fat chance, big man. In fact, you're not getting in my car anytime soon."

"I didn't think so. I bet you wouldn't let yourself in your car."

"Finally, you got something right," David said. "My Chevy is a piece of automotive art—and it's going to stay that way."

Whether because of frayed nerves or sheer physical fatigue, or both, the two men just wanted to sit still in the din of the rushing water. They discussed the things that might have happened if the sycamore had lodged under the bridge.

"Hank was right, you know," David said.

"Hank!" Larry yelled. "You talkin' about Hank, Fire Chief Hank?"

"Yeah. It was the dam, not the bridge, that was the danger."

"Too deep for me," Larry said.

They agreed then that the Dailey boys had saved the historic Rainbow Bridge and possibly the town of Baxter Springs, Kansas. "From zero to hero in just twenty-four short hours," David said.

The storm's rumble faded as it moved east, and the Brush Creek tide ebbed. After a time, Hank's van, missing a headlight, appeared on the bridge. He pulled up alongside the fire engine and looked up at his volunteer firemen seated in the cab.

"You boys are right where I left you! No problems here, I see," Hank yelled. Hank could see the taut chains hooked to the fire engine and grappling hooks attached to limbs of the massive sycamore tree laying in the creek by the water's edge.

The Daileys looked blank-faced at their fire chief. Then both smiled.

"You boys hungry or just takin' a break?"

Hank looked like a golden retriever with its head out an open car window. Larry looked like a drowned rat with mud-caked pants and long stringy locks half covering his face. David looked no better. Both were war weary. Without question, they both felt far better than they had following their Elk City misadventure. However, David was alarmed at his brother's continued inability to catch his breath.

"Hey, Hank … you did … interrupt … our supper plans," Larry gasped.

"Well, come on then! Ladies Aid's cookin' up something down at the Grange Hall!"

"As my brother too-often says, I was born ready. What's cookin'?" David asked.

"Cook's choice," Hank said. "You drivin' the truck or this-here van?"

"I'm drivin' Big Red," David said.

"Follow me then! Before I forget, you boys did a great job! Yeah, ya know, it really wasn't about saving the bridge! It was about the bridge becoming a dam and then giving way, destroying things downstream!" Hank loved the role he'd played, and he had gained two loyal fans.

"Pretty neat old bridge," David said. Later, they were informed the Rainbow Bridge was one of only three of its kind remaining on Route 66. Important to David, but for Larry, not so much.

David helped Hank reattach the lines holding the sycamore to steel posts in the parking area while Larry watched from the truck's cab. The water level of the Brush Creek had already dropped over a foot and was clearly headed in a safe direction. However, the three men waited another half an hour to make sure.

Larry rode with Hank on the short drive back into town. Hank stopped at the high school to boast about how they had sandbagged around the back side of the school with chat, debris from the closed lead and zinc mines. He radiated pride, as if he had just completed painting the ceiling of the Sistine Chapel. "We had over fifty here filling bags and stackin' 'em around the school's foundation! Water got up to the first row of bleachers out there, from goalpost to goalpost! As they say, the school dodged a bullet!"

"Glad we could be of service, Hank. Next time you decide to have a flash flood, give us a call," Larry said. Then he leaned toward Hank and spoke in a low voice, "I thought sandbaggin' was something you did on a golf course." The perplexed grin on Hank's face indicated he didn't follow Larry's attempt at humor, but he clearly wasn't worried about it.

After David parked the fire engine at the station, Fire Chief Hank Holiday pointed out the Grange Hall. Then he dropped his two volunteers back at Miss May's. Once in their cabin, the Daileys luxuriated taking turns in a slow, hot shower and then a much-needed change of clothes. Once cleaned up, they walked three-and-a-half blocks to a modest, two-story, rectangular, framed building with a brass plaque affixed above the door: Baxter Springs Grange. The quiet air felt fresh and cool, and the clear dark sky was shimmering with a billion tiny stars. The change in atmospheric conditions from their entrance into the rustic Kansas town a few hours earlier was unfathomable to both brothers. The sound of crickets chirping filled the night air.

From the moment the Daileys had entered the ancient hall, they were the toast of Baxter Springs. The holdover Elk City bumps and bruises combined with those acquired fighting the furious flood undoubtedly added to their recognition. Hank announced, "Meet the two who saved our historic Rainbow Bridge!" Townsfolk rushed up and introduced themselves, also taking pleasure introducing their two guests to others. Middle-aged women, and others significant years beyond, wearing knee-length bib aprons scurried about the kitchen and took turns barking directions from behind a broad pass-through counter. Teenagers and younger ones sat and waited tables—family style.

"Where are you boys from? Is that your Chevrolet parked behind Miss May's?" Everyone had to dodge small children chasing about the hall screaming as happy, enthusiastic emotions gripped them— sometimes they were cautioned but never discouraged. Three senior gentlemen seated along a wall to one side clinched crooked pipes in their teeth while thoughtfully observing the cacophony of organized bedlam. The savory smell of roast beef and gravy filled the air.

Preacher Joe was called upon to offer a blessing and did so with mixed success above the familial commotion. Reverend Joe prayed, at least for those who could hear him, with homespun eloquence of how Baxterites had been delivered through the parted seas to the Promised Land.

Larry looked at David, who said, "I think we've arrived." Larry agreed.

It was well past the rainstorm and near midnight before the impromptu community thanksgiving adjourned. David washed and dried dishes with five fellow team members ranging in ages from seven to eighty-one. Larry helped break down tables and sweep the floor. Willing hands were in abundance until the last piece of silverware was in its proper place.

"You boys didn't know you'd have to sing for your supper," said a sweet, little, gray-haired lady smiling and drying the last cooking pot with a homemade dish towel. "Could one of you hang this for me over the cook stove? Seems I've been growin' in the wrong direction lately."

Physically exhausted, but mentally wide awake, neither Larry nor David wanted to leave the Grange Hall and did *not* leave until the lights were turned out. Back in their cabin, they shared stories of the interesting characters they had met and what they had been told about life in the extreme southeast corner of Kansas. Finally surrendering to weariness, David yawned and said, "We ain't in Kansas anymore." For some reason, Baxter Springs and their ordeal had brought to his mind *the Wizard of Oz* and heroine Dorothy's adventure.

"Yes, we are, Dave. We're in Kansas," Larry said.

"Whatever. Get some sleep."

In the morning, the sound of Larry coughing and hacking in the broom closet-size bathroom woke David. He worried about his brother's heart, morning coughing spells, drinking, and smoking. But he resigned himself to the fact that it was all beyond his control. *My luck, I'll probably die before Larry anyway*, he thought.

By the time David was done with the bathroom and dressed, Larry was gone. David found Larry seated on a long wooden plank in front of the gas station, smoking and swapping baseball stories with a couple of diehard St. Louis Cardinals fans. One old-timer sat tilted back against the wall on a rickety Pepsi crate, whittling on a stick with his pocketknife. David asked him what he was carving.

"Oooh, tain't much. Just passin' time."

"I can think of worse ways to pass time." David turned to Larry. "You want to get something to eat?"

Larry took a long squinting drag on his cigarette and said without exhaling, "I'm ready to roll. We can stop on the road and pick up something." Then, smoke streamed in slow motion from his nostrils for what seemed like forever.

"There's high water on the road 'tween here and Galena," the woodcarver said without looking up. "You might better let Joan fix you boys somethin' afore you light out."

"Hey, the sun's out. Air's fresh. Can't be that bad," Larry said. Then he coughed, followed by a throat-clearing salvo of spit that cleared the station's porch.

"Those creek branches feedin' the Spring River can be real tricky," the old man said as he peeled a long curly shaving from his stick. "Where you boys be headin' anyways?"

"We're following old Route 66 wherever she takes us," David said.

"And I'm just tagging along for the ride," Larry said.

Still without looking up, the whittler deduced, "Looks to me like you boys be chasin' your imagination, lookin' for somethin' that never was and ain't never gonna be."

"I'll have to think about that over breakfast. Come on, Larry. Smells like Miss May's got bacon on the griddle." As they walked next door to the Kountry Kitchen, David considered what the old whittler had observed.

An hour later, the Daileys drove out of Baxter Springs, crossing over the now familiar Brush Creek and Rainbow Bridge, whose morning shadow sheltered the hapless and bedraggled sycamore tree they had wrestled to shore a few hours earlier. Its trunk and limbs, now resting in mud more than half on shore, drooped in defeat. Less than a mile beyond the bridge, a flagman stopped them amid the flashing lights of a patrol car and fire engine, both with Baxter Springs stenciled on their doors. A county crew was clearing storm rubble and a couple of stranded cars from the roadway.

"Hey! You boys here to save us again?" There could be no mistake: the flagman was Hank clad in an identical uniform from the night before, except it was a spanking-clean bright yellow. He marched straight up in front of the Bel Air as if he was a general in command of an advancing army. "Give me ten minutes, and I'll have you boys on your way!" Hank said with his typical flare.

Larry turned toward David in cheerful delight. "What can I say? Hank's livin' the dream."

"And so am I," David said. "And so am I."

CHAPTER 11
Atlanta, Illinois

After almost an hour, another yellow-vested flagman waved the proverbial green flag, and the Daileys were again off to the races. Well, not so fast—one lane, one direction at a time, and under caution. They passed by flooded fields and a line of stationary vehicles over a mile long waiting to travel in the opposite direction. Heavy trucks were not allowed to pass over the flood-compromised stretch of highway and were forced to turn around. Difficulty in turning the long tractor-trailers in such confined roadway spaces added another dimension to the traffic delay.

With a full tank of low-priced fuel, the Chevy carried its occupants straight through the heart of Joplin, Missouri. Once they cleared the city limits, the brothers agreed to rejoin Interstate 44 east toward St. Louis, 282 miles. Larry reminded his big brother, "Had we bypassed Kansas yesterday, this would have taken us only fifteen minutes. Remember, I told you so." Larry's lack of conviction satisfied David. It was more "think what we might have missed" rather than a "you did something stupid."

"But we would never have met an old-timer whittling on a stick," David said.

"I'm gonna tell you what, those old guys knew their baseball. Loved their Cardinals."

"And I love listening to a group of old-timers like that, just sittin' around shootin' the breeze. Pay attention or you may miss a gold nugget."

The rolling countryside provided numerous scenes reminiscent of Norman Rockwell's *Saturday Evening Post* covers. Interstate 44 bisected Missouri, passing through pastoral settings of undulating wooded hills and autumn fields. Sprinkled here and there were small white churches, bright-green tractors, and painted barn-side billboards broadcasting the "must-see" Meramec Caverns. Both men were content with the quickening pace of their homeward journey, foregoing several opportunities to rejoin the original Route 66.

As they traversed south-central Missouri, David found himself totally absorbed in the passing countryside. Questions coursed through his head: *How do people here make a living? Why was that tractor surrounded by hip-high weeds abandoned in an empty field? When was the last time the rusting combine harvester was used? What political party is most prominent here? Where does Harry Truman live?* When traveling, or not, David typically asked himself such questions, or anyone handy if they'd listen. Larry did not possess the same interest or "waste his time" on such matters.

After covering countless miles, Larry, somewhat out of character, attempted to start a conversation. "What did you think of Aunt Alice?"

It surprised David that his brother wanted to talk about anything, and he seized the opportunity to needle him a bit. "Just another old mountain maid, I suspect," he said.

"Say what? Get real. She wasn't an old maid. She wasn't old. She gets things done, Dave. And, you'll have to admit, not bad lookin'. I could see camping with her, sharing a sleeping bag."

"Honestly, she was nice enough. I think she is a woman playing out the hand she was dealt. I'll give her credit, though, she wasn't complaining about living in that God-forsaken hole-in-the-wall."

It was clear Larry had been thinking about Al and her obscure mountain town of Oatman, Arizona. It pleased David that his brother wanted to talk about such things, anything really. Also, David enjoyed the amicable conversation. He wondered what may have triggered a softening of his brother's usual pugnacious demeanor.

"I'd like to get to know someone like Aunt Alice. A camping buddy like Rico. That life actually sounds good to me," Larry said.

"You, camping in the mountains with a jackass for a sidekick? Excuse me, but that'd make *two* of you." David found himself pleasantly amused at the picture of his brother hiking through the wilderness leading a hapless pack animal. It represented a stark contrast from his long-held garish image of Larry.

"Seriously, Dave, this may surprise you." There was a long reflective pause then Larry shook his head. "I'm looking forward to getting back home. Hope there's time to spend a couple of days. We should make it by tomorrow night, easy. Don't you think?"

"What'd you say?" David asked. "I thought we were talking about Aunt Alice."

"She told us to call her Al. Know what, I think I'm becoming homesick. Go figure."

"Homesick? Now I'm certain you were in the sun too long, or possibly under the water too long," David said.

"Sunburn's fine. Truth be told, I've been homesick for twenty years. Working and staying busy has helped me to block out those feelings, but they've always been there."

"Are you talking for a visit or for good?" David cautioned himself not to push, but he liked the direction of their conversation and the emergence of a softer side to his brother's character.

"Not sure. We'll see," Larry said.

"Hard to believe what I'm hearing. You've got everything going for you in California. Why the sudden change of heart?"

"As I said, not sudden. Stubborn pride more than anything has kept me going and far from home."

"I don't think you'd like Three Oaks full time, not after living in paradise all these years." David was astounded by Larry's outward position change and by finding himself in the role of devil's advocate with a tinge of reverse psychology. This was one argument he'd rather lose.

"Paradise? Bullshit."

"Having a change of heart, hey?" David asked. Those old familiar pangs of resentment and jealously still lingered beneath the surface. *But, who was it here that was falling victim to the "grass is always greener on the other side of the fence" disorder?*

Larry elaborated, explaining that the only person he knew outside of work was the neighborhood flower lady. He went on to tell of a recent block party held on his street that no one thought to invite him to. His lamenting continued for several miles. It concluded when he confessed to his dread of time spent outside of work as dead time.

"Come on, Larry, it can't be that bad. I'd give my left nut to live single in Santa Monica. Don't tell me I've wasted all these mind-numbing years trudging through life in Three Oaks as the 'good son' only to find out you, the prodigal son, thought you had it bad." David held at bay the urge to commiserate with his brother, not 100 percent sure he could trust him or himself. *Midlife crisis? Right.*

"Have you ever attended a high school reunion?" David asked.

"Where did that come from?"

"I didn't think you were aware, but every other year or two, our alma mater holds a reunion for the graduates of a four- or five-year period, say, those who graduated during the years of 1935 to 1940."

"Sounds interesting, but, no, I've never heard anything about it," Larry said.

"Well, two years ago, weekend after Memorial Day, they scheduled a reunion of the graduating classes of 1937 to 1941—years before the war. Jane and I attended. Remember Jane graduated in forty, between us? It was held at the New Buffalo Yacht Club. Over a hundred attended. Maybe eighty who actually graduated from old Three Oaks High School."

"Was Spit Shine there, or Crisco?"

"Didn't see either. But guess who *was* there?"

"Marilyn Monroe?"

"Close. Maggie Stevens," David said with an unintentional flare.

Larry cast a skeptical eye. Then as realization emerged, "You shittin' me?"

David's gaze reverted to the near-empty expressway, pleased with the vision of Maggie Stevens Fairfax stepping onto the yacht club's broad teakwood deck as the sun had lingered above the Lake Michigan horizon. Old schoolmates tended to gravitate her way, male members for sure. David could feel himself pretending not to notice Maggie and struggling to maintain social engagement with his wife and the two other couples seated at their table. Maggie moved with all the grace of an Oscar nominee promenading along the red Hollywood carpet. There was no mistaking her! If Three Oaks ever had a princess, it was Maggie Stevens. During that fleeting moment in time, a whole constellation of emotion had taken up permanent residence in David's reverie.

"Jane, would you like a drink?" David had asked.

"You just brought us these," Jane had said. Jane held up a glass of pinot noir.

"I mean, I guess, I don't care for this wine. I think I'll go back, get something else. How's yours?"

"I had a sip. It's fine," Jane had said.

"I'll be right back."

David's circuitous route to the bar had purposely intersected with Maggie's path. He avoided encounters with other old classmates. Maggie held his complete attention. Several clever salutations were considered and rejected. To his relief, Maggie spoke first.

"David Dailey! What a nice surprise," she'd said as she reached out and hugged him. Erotic emotions coursed through David as they once had many years earlier. A time and an opportunity he feared immaturity let slip away. He luxuriated in her spontaneous caress and reciprocated for as long as he dared. His eyes involuntarily searched the ballroom for Jane. When once again face-to-face with his senior-year prom date, a warm sensation enveloped him. More gorgeous than he'd remembered, she cast a faint intoxicating scent, arousing long-dormant youthful memories. He was the focus of Maggie's attention, and she was his. Her poised yet intimate manner made him feel alive. Beams of ecstasy pierced him to the quick.

The high school sweethearts had shared small talk, but try as he might, David couldn't recall a single thing they'd said. He did remember an extended shared gaze, one he'd reluctantly ended by asking if he could get her a drink.

"No, thank you. But, David, you must save us a dance. Promise?" Her familiar voice had been made all the more tantalizing when she'd squeezed his hands. "We need to catch up. Don't you agree? This is such a romantic setting." Maggie wrinkled her nose, clasped his arm, and pressed against him.

When David had returned to the table, Jane had asked, "Where have you been? I thought you were going after another drink?"

"What? Oh, I waited forever. The line was too long—"

"Hello?" Larry interrupted David's reverie, aware his brother had become totally distracted. "*Hello?* You are either lost or on the verge of a wet dream."

As David grudgingly regained awareness, he searched to remember exactly what he had divulged to Larry as opposed to simply remembering. A warm blanket of pleasant feelings still enfolded him. He kept his eyes focused on the road and fumbled for a subject change, not sure where they had left off.

"Let's stop for a cup of coffee. You want to drive?" David's unusual offer was not lost on his brother, who was eager to get behind the wheel again.

"Sure. If I drive, we'll be home tomorrow, easy," Larry said.

With Larry in the driver's seat, David slipped back into a trance-like contemplation of his reunion with Maggie Stevens. A struggle between his head and heart ensued, a struggle that had begun during their senior year in high school. Their divergent stations in society, at least from his vantage point, compelled David at that time to hold his true feelings in check. Maggie meant more to him than simply a date for a high school dance. He had placed her on a pedestal, an emotion he had never shared with anyone, not Maggie, not even himself.

Defensively, he shook his head. "There's a place in Chicago I want to take you for lunch. I calculate we'll stop somewhere in Illinois tonight, lunch at the Berghoff in Chi Town tomorrow. Be home for supper," David said.

"Sounds like a plan. First, I'll see if I can get this heap out of first gear." Larry punched the accelerator, more to hear his brother complain than to increase speed. However, with Larry in the driver's seat and ignoring David's renewed interest in passing historical sites, they made excellent time from Joplin to St. Louis. Larry refused all David's suggestions to take in various advertised attractions or for detours back onto the original Route 66. David thought better than to debate his brother, who was on a mission to put Missouri in the rearview mirror and get home to Three Oaks. David liked that.

On the approach to the bridge over the Mississippi River in St. Louis, David couldn't resist explaining to his traveling companion the proposed plan for building the Gateway Arch. They passed with an excellent view of the initial stages of construction. His explanation got only as far as, "630 feet of stainless steel," before Larry let out his patented and obnoxious yawn.

Once safely on the Illinois side of the river, Larry picked up I-55 for Chicago. The rhythmic ride down the spacious four-lane expressway encouraged David again to quietly contemplate the 1961 class reunion and subsequent secret rendezvouses with Maggie. *Will I ever again share special time with Maggie? Escape life in Three Oaks?* Thoughts of Santa Catalina and Kwan resurfaced. How had Kwan said it? Was he running *for* or running *from*? Now Kwan's question seemed even more poignant, yet David had no clear answer to it.

Larry drove all the way to Springfield before giving up and pulling off for gas. A Texaco station attendant filled the Chevy with regular Fire Chief gasoline after which he directed them to follow Business 55, old Route 66, through town. Since David had resumed driving, he followed the attendant's suggestion and took them to visit the Abe Lincoln home and tomb. They were in the Land of Lincoln, and he thought it appropriate since the country was currently commemorating the centennial years of the Civil War. Larry put up only token resistance because it gave him a chance for a much-needed smoke.

David continued on the old highway until they stopped for the night in the sleepy little burg of Atlanta, ten miles south of the Illinois twin cities of Bloomington-Normal. After booking a motel room for the night, Larry drove them to a popular roadhouse, the Old Crow. It featured Chicago-style pizza, fifty beer selections, and a smoky dance floor with jukebox music weeknights and a live band every Saturday night after eight. Both Daileys looked forward to a good time for their last night on the road.

Before entering the roadhouse, the brothers stopped to admire several motorcycles parked in a column on the sidewalk lawn out front. The cycles, all Harley Davidsons, gleamed beneath the lights surrounding the tavern. Larry swung a leg over one and sat in the saddle with hands on the worn handle grips. "Look at this, Dave. This is the way we should be crossing the country!"

David made rumbling sounds and throttle-revving motions with his hands. "I've always wanted a Harley. Look at this one." David called his brother's attention to a shiny, red cycle accented in silver chrome with expensive brown, leather saddlebags strapped over the rear fender.

Before Larry could dismount, two more cycles pulled up next to him. One of the riders yelled, "You think that chopper belongs to you?"

"No, just admiring it," Larry said. He dismounted the cycle but couldn't escape the biker's angry stare nor the loud roar of his cycle's motor. Without incident, the brothers retreated indoors.

An eclectic mix of noisy patrons added an air of excitement inside the Crow Bar, as locals referred to their favorite watering hole. From soft-spoken senior citizens enjoying fried pork chops and corn-on-the-cob, to rowdy college students from nearby Illinois State inhaling watermelon shots, the oversized tavern was plugged-in for a good time. And when a spirited women's tennis team burst through the doors clad in skimpy, white, country-club uniforms, the entire place took on a celebratory atmosphere.

The Daileys looked at each other with large grins. "Last night on the road. Let's make it a good one," Larry said. David agreed.

One of the exuberant team members threw her hands in the air and screamed, "Party time!" Whether the teams' primary intention was to have a good time or be the center of tavern attention, they were on track to accomplish both. David was only slightly more cautious than his brother, and Larry threw caution to the wind. They were going to be home tomorrow, and both were in step with the festive saloon becoming noisier and rowdier by the minute.

Before the two had finished their pizza and second twelve-ounce Ball jar of beer, Larry hustled to the jukebox to assist a couple of tennis players with their music selection. While Larry got acquainted with the young women, David observed six disheveled, overweight men leaning on the bar. Two of them appeared to be scouting the team and possible rivalry.

The two scouts and their four buddies were joined at the bar by three more large men. All wore heavy, black, leather boots, dirty jeans, and matching black leather vests with "Harley Lives" embossed in gold on the back. With their dark sunglasses and silver wallet chains that hung halfway to their knees, David surmised they were members of the motorcycle fleet moored out front.

Before he could reconnoiter more, Larry returned, accompanied by a doubles team and four fresh jars of frothy beer. The noise level in the tavern had escalated to such a level that the foursome had to shout to exchange names. David was never sure whether his designated doubles partner was Sharon or Karen. The young women were both Babe to Larry, and no one seemed to mind.

Names hardly mattered since everyone was yelling over each other, laughing, and having an uproarious, totally uninhibited good time. Suddenly the jukebox throbbed, the crowd hushed, and "Sherry" by the Four Seasons blasted through the speakers of the roadhouse sound system. Several could be heard mimicking the high-pitched vocal cords of Frankie Valli. The volume had been cranked up, and the most eager evening revelers, the attention-seekers, stampeded toward the dance floor, knocking over a hapless barmaid who spilled a plastic pitcher of beer on the floor. One of the college boys assumed the push-up position and pretended, or not, that he was sucking up the spilled brew.

"Now, that's what I'm talkin' about!" Larry shouted. Their two country-clubber acquaintances squealed their support. Larry luxuriated in their unmitigated adoration.

"I love this song!" screamed the young woman who had commandeered Larry. Sharon, or Karen, sprang up, snatched David by the arm, and screamed at him, "Come on, boy, let's dance!" With total abandon they hustled to the dance floor, and for the next two hours, all four engaged in unrestrained frivolity, seasoned with more beer. The climax arrived when "Shout" by the Isley Brothers detonated throughout the building. The entire tavern erupted. The Harley squad was dancing as was the Illinois State crowd after downing a quick shot relay. In unison, the multitudes shouted, "SHOUT!" to the rafters in time with the music. The dance floor vibrated to the beat. Wild party animals repeatedly flung their hands over their heads screaming the lyrics until sheer euphoria reigned. In fact, as the music ebbed and flowed, more than one dancer lost their balance and fell to the floor or into other dancers. No injuries could be felt or reported. By the end of the number, several dancers staggered from the floor clinging to one another in complete exhaustion.

A slow number followed, allowing the party animals to catch their breath. Larry displayed no visible ill effects from the rigorous workout and managed to find a table and occupy a chair. For David, however, the respite was short-lived. He soon found himself locked at the waist with his doubles companion in a midsection-grinding bout that had only a vague resemblance to a waltz. Before the number ended, his dance partner disengaged and pulled him willingly from the dance floor and out a side exit. Larry observed the departure with concern. Once outside, Sharon or Karen put her hands on David's shoulders and gazed knowingly into his eyes. "We needed some fresh air," she said.

Faced with her suggestive expression only inches from his nose, David pulled his seductress into what became a mad, passionate embrace. As their libidos spiraled skyward, the young lady drew back and whispered, "Is there someplace we can go to hide?" David realized only then that they were standing directly beneath two floodlights hung above an Exit No Entrance sign.

"I have a car," David said. With that, he looked around for the Chevy. "Over there," he said and pointed. She smiled and kissed him on the neck. Then she took him by the hand and pulled her willing escort toward the Bel Air.

Without warning, the exit door swung open behind them, and a beefy bouncer snarled, "Back inside you two, or you're out for good!" Alarmed, the couple could see the burly linebacker type was in no mood to negotiate.

"We're just looking for a proper place to have a cigarette," Sharon or Karen said.

"In or out, your choice!" The enthusiastic enforcer relished his job and clearly welcomed any sort of confrontation.

Showing little sign of embarrassment, the couple, hand-in-hand, followed the bouncer back into the tavern. Once inside, they rejoined the table where Larry held court with other team members. Larry had become the main attraction and was doing his best to live up to his legend, if only in his own mind.

David leaned toward Larry's ear. "Did you see what just happened?"

"You mean the bouncer? I sent him," Larry said matter-of-factly without interrupting his feminine audience.

When the Righteous Brothers' rendition of "Unchained Melody" flowed from the jukebox, Larry invited one of his adoring flock to dance. David was relieved to sit it out at the table in general conversation with three of the clubbers who shared in the short respite.

Before long, their attention was drawn back to the dance floor. One of the biker boys tried to cut in on Larry, who did not cooperate, unwilling to share his dance partner. The uncharitable biker clumsily pushed Larry to the side.

"Who the hell are you?" Larry yelled, jumping right back into the biker's face, if that was possible, seeing he was a head shorter than the gentleman making the request.

With that, Larry was pushed aside a second time. "Take a seat, little fella." He was bidden. Several on the dance floor took note of an impending altercation and drew back. The young lady in dispute stepped away from the two men as well, afraid of what was coming and unsure of what to do.

"You go to hell!" Larry shouted as he came back a second time toward the Harley man. Punches seemed about to be thrown, as neither adversary was backing down.

So David rose from his seat and moved toward the combatants. Before he could attempt an intervention, a second member of the Harley Lives gang came boot-stomping across the floor with wallet chain swinging. At first sight, it appeared a tag-team barroom brawl was about to answer the bell. David stood tall but, after viewing the size of the potential opponents, was in no rush for further confrontation. The second member of the Harley Lives posse possessed a six-foot-six paleo man physique, and with one giant hand he pulled his biker brother back and put his other hand in the middle of Larry's chest. Larry's scarlet face reflected his anger but may have been more attributable to his soaring blood pressure than to his wish for a fight.

For a precarious couple of seconds, the warring parties stood still, as did the entire saloon. Then Paleo Man growled, "Break it up, you two! I need to tell you two frisky bitches a story." He took his time while turning his head toward one and then the other, as if daring either man to disagree. The music had stopped. Boisterous patrons became quiet spectators, intently wanting to see what would happen next. "Pay close attention, boys. I don't repeat myself," Paleo said.

David took one more step forward, so he could hear what words of wisdom Paleo had to offer. He wasn't the only interested party. It seemed all the roadhouse clientele desired a story hour and were moving in a little closer to hear.

Paleo started, "A woman's ass and a whiskey glass are marvelous sights to see. But a whiskey glass and a woman's ass made a horse's ass out of me!" He did not wait for evaluation, confirmation, or recognition; he clearly did not care. He shoved Larry aside and escorted his brother back to the bar by the scruff of the neck. People began talking again, and the jukebox resumed as if commanded to do so. Larry turned around and looked for his brother as his normal facial skin tone started to resurface, a sure indication of relief.

When the party of four finally reconvened at their original table, a combined pleasurable sigh of relaxation was followed by a good laugh from all. Larry fetched another round. Karen, or Sharon, asked David if he was married. He considered the question, and even though he had no interest in hiding anything, he wanted to be clever. "Marriage is in the eye of the beholder," he said. Even as he responded, he thought, *That's stupid.*

"That's what I thought," she said. Then she smiled and said, "Me too."

The lights started blinking in the Old Crow, followed by the jukebox groaning to a halt. A bartender bellowed, "It's two o'clock! Good night, my love!"

Larry was interested in extending the evening, but his dance partner had a sudden need to go home to relieve a babysitter. That put an abrupt damper on any amorous aspirations he may have entertained. The brothers were both startled when she called to Sharon or Karen, "Let's go, Shirley! I'm drivin'."

"You sure you should drive?" Shirley asked.

"I sure as hell can't walk!"

As the Daileys walked across the mostly empty and only partially lit parking lot toward the Bel Air, Larry lit a cigarette and looked back at the main entrance to the Old Crow. A group of large men huddled around and then mounted their motorcycles. One of the men jumped on his kick-start and worked the throttle as the engine thundered. Two others followed suit and then two more. In an instant, the air was filled with rumbling Harley Davidson motorcycles. David liked the sound. "Could be us," he said.

"I don't think so. Not this time," Larry said.

The brothers stopped to watch as did the remaining few stragglers. Before the cycles started to roll, the apparent lead rider yelled, "Head 'em up, move 'em out!" The fleet of motorcycles roared to life, peeled off like a squadron of P-38 fighter planes, and accelerated in the direction of the Daileys. The brothers were momentarily transfixed in the headlights of the ghost riders headed straight for them. The motors' sounds became deafening and the headlights blinding. The Daileys stood side by side perfectly still and did not breathe.

CHAPTER 12

Three Weeks Ago

David Dailey was in the backyard putting a second coat of Vintage Simonize Polish on the hood of his treasured Chevrolet Bel Air. The deep rich shine of the Chevy coupe was the envy of the town's high school boys, and more than one had asked if he could take the car for a spin. "Sweet Ride" was what David had christened her. Sweet Ride had never gone to bed dirty since the day she was born, not even with the pervasive, corrosive salt thrown up from Michigan's harsh winter highways. In fact, David had rarely driven his car in inclement weather and never let her sit outside overnight. "Mint condition" was the appropriate label for this prized automobile.

Taking care of an automobile was a habit David had acquired from his father who prided himself on the useful longevity of the vehicles he had owned, none of which had been purchased new.

Mr. Dailey frequently admonished his youthful sons, "You take good care of your car, and it will take good care of you and save you a lot of money. The only thing a new car can do better than an old one is depreciate."

David took his father's advice to heart. He and Jane had managed for years to get by with a 1950 two-door Ford and the store's pickup purchased back when he went into partnership with his father. Be that as it may, he always yearned to buy a new car and *go in style*. In 1958, he purchased a brand-new Chevrolet Bel Air. Chevys were popular, as in, "See the USA in your Chevrolet. America is asking you to call ...."

David relished the attention he drew when he cruised through Three Oaks in his Sweet Ride.

The kitchen door opened, and Jane Dailey walked out and crossed the lawn to where David was polishing the car in the shade of a spreading maple tree. Jane liked their second car too but thought of it more as a luxury than a necessity.

"She looks nice, Dave," Jane said.

She was well aware of how much the car meant to her husband and tried her best not to let his habitual car maintenance annoy her. But she believed that, in recent months, the car had become an unhealthy obsession for her husband.

"Thanks, I've got some new polish I'm trying out. You could brush your hair in the reflection. Look here!"

"Seems like you work on this car whenever you're not working at the store."

"Pays to take care of things," he said.

He snapped the terrycloth towel he was using to remove the dried white polish film and continued rubbing, never looking up.

"You *can* overdo it," she said sharply.

"What do you mean?"

"What's wrong, Dave? Seems you're always busy with something."

"What's wrong with that? Idle hands …" Dave said as he continued to polish the car.

"You know what I mean. You've been withdrawn, moody. What's bothering you, anyway?" Jane inquired.

"Nothing. I just want to wax my car."

"I'm serious, Dave. And for God's sake, it doesn't need another coat of wax. There's an inch of polish on the car now. You just don't seem to want to talk to me."

"It's not that, Jane. The store's been busy. Working on this car gives me time to think, relax. That's all. Besides, I can't shake this tired feeling lately."

"Well, then tell me what you're thinking. I feel I'm being shut out." Jane stood still and waited for an answer.

The sounds of children playing on a swing set could be heard coming over from their neighbor's backyard. Someone was mowing a lawn down the street.

After an uncomfortable period of silence between them, David stopped rubbing dry wax off the car's hood and said, "Okay. I've been thinking about tracing Route 66."

"You've been doing that all your life. So now it's upsetting you?"

"No. I mean I want to go there, Jane. Right now," David stopped polishing and looked at his wife.

"Dave, you know we can't go to California on the spur of the moment. School just started. I only just met my new munchkins last Thursday. Can we wait until Thanksgiving, or better yet maybe Christmas break?"

"No, I mean, I know. I want to go now, alone. Just me," David said.

"Alone? Are you kidding? Since when do you go on a vacation alone, without me?"

"No, it's not like a vacation. I mean, I just want to go. I need to go." David hesitated as if he'd lost his train of thought. Then he added, "Now. See my brother."

"Really? See Larry?"

"If I don't go now, I may never. I'm going, Jane." David spoke in a soft voice but with more force than usual. His mind was elsewhere, torn between what he was saying and what he'd been planning. He was at a loss for what or how to explain more.

"It seems you've already made up your mind. Were you planning to let me and your mother know?"

"Of course."

"When? And when are you planning to leave?" she asked.

"I hadn't decided exactly. By the end of the week. Maybe next Monday." David said.

"End of the week! Monday? Really?"

"I'll make sure everything is covered at the store. We've pretty much taken care of the Labor Day rush," David said.

"And when do you plan to be back?"

"Two weeks, tops," David said, barely masking the enthusiasm in his voice.

"I don't know why you couldn't talk to me about this. But, honestly, going to see Larry is not such a bad idea. He's obviously not coming here. And going alone may be good in some ways. You two have lots to catch up on, bury the hatchet, so to speak." Jane's conciliatory nature was an attribute David and others admired in her and one her students benefited from as well.

"That's kind of what I thought," David said.

"Now, you know the two of us will have to talk to Mom about this. She needs to know, and as you know, she is very concerned about her youngest son. Maybe you might suggest trying to bring him home for a visit? Long shot, I know," Jane said.

"That's kind of what I thought," David said. He could feel himself repeating and searched for something more significant to say.

"Just the idea will cheer her up. If you're sure you've made up your mind, I'll not try to stop you. Let's go over to Mom's right now."

"Jump in," David said. He welcomed the respite from further interrogation and couldn't believe how understanding Jane seemed to be.

As the couple drove the mile and a half to his mother's home, David's mind was choked with colliding thoughts. It was the same route he had traveled a thousand times. Past the same houses, well-kept yards, white picket fences, and waving neighbors with smiling faces. There was always a kid or two on bicycles, a barking dog in a front yard, and a pothole or more to avoid. The same sights, sounds, and smells. He could do this blindfolded. He wondered if the monotony of life contributed to his recent sluggishness.

Lying to Jane and his mother added to his distress. Their conversations always sounded prerecorded. He had never misled or lied to either before and hated himself for doing it now. But what was the alternative? More of the same ol' same ol', or basking in the freedom of the open road, a warm breeze beneath gently swaying coconut palms? How would he ever know the answer if he failed to even take a chance?

CHAPTER 13
Chicago, Illinois

A pounding headache, parched mouth, lips-stuck-to-teeth, and an urgent need to whiz combined to force David to sit straight up in bed at 7:27 a.m. Though muscle weary, the result of a long day on the road and a late night at the Old Crow roadhouse, sleep had been a fretful struggle. He rolled off the bed damp with perspiration and mentally pissed-off for no reason he cared to ponder. Unable to find a light switch, he staggered in the dark to the bathroom, stubbing his toe on an unseen threshold. Relieving himself took longer than usual.

Then he brushed his teeth and shaved in the reflection of a rust-tarnished mirror. After a marathon-length steamy shower, he dressed in yesterday's clothes that held a memory whiff of an anonymous tennis player. With nothing to do except kill time, he collapsed back on the bed to wait for his brother to awake.

There was no hurry. If things went well, they would easily be in Three Oaks by day's end. On the other hand, time was short if David expected to lay out his full intentions, original and amended, to Larry before they got home. After stalling for as long as he could stand, he got up and cautiously shook his brother's pillow. On the second shake, Larry opened one eye. He was not pleased. Bloodshot eyes and wild stringy hair gave Larry the look of a recent shock-therapy recipient. Larry shuffled to the bathroom hacking and coughing in an unsuccessful attempt to clear his congested throat.

"Watch out for the threshold," David said.

A heavy barrage of profanity-laced grumbling followed David's warning, as Larry had neither heard nor heeded it. Then he experienced considerable difficulty shaving because of a dull razor and nicked his chin and jaw, drawing blood in three places. He had to use pieces of toilet paper to blot the bleeding.

When Larry was through in the bathroom a long hour later, he dressed as his brother before him, in recycled clothes. Once ready, he stood at the open door to their motel room in an overstated yet mild display of enthusiasm to launch the anchor leg of their journey. His puffy, red-rimmed eyes and unruly hair were evidence of a hearty evening spent in Atlanta's Crow Bar. Toilet paper snowflakes highlighted with red dots added a circus-clown appearance to his face. David was pleasantly surprised by his brother's humble bid to show enthusiasm.

"Please sit down. I have something I want to share with you," David said.

"Can you share in the car? I want to see if they're harvesting grapes behind Mom's house. Speaking of Mom, I don't know about you, but I need some laundry done." Both men had long since run out of fresh clothes to wear and had each thrown away a torn shirt.

"Please, pull up a chair. The grapes can wait."

"Really? I hope you're going to tell me I got laid last night." Larry flopped himself in a metal folding chair and ran his fingers through his unruly hair. "Were those chicks crazy or what?"

"And married. I'm sure we both got lucky they had to take babysitters home," David said.

"That's not lucky. Lucky is that those damn Harley boys didn't run over us. Remember? Do you think they even saw us?" Larry said.

"Oh, they saw us, all right. Actin' tough. Just wanted to scare us." As they talked about the night before, there was general agreement between them. Even a sense of camaraderie. They agreed they'd had a good time and were fortunate to have survived potential tragedies— the tennis team and the Harley squad—unscathed.

"Whatever. So what's on your mind? I want to be at, what'd you say, Berghoff's by noon. Nothing like good German beer and brats."

After a short pause, Larry put his hands on his stomach, belched, and admitted, "Although, not just yet."

"Is that the style now?" David said.

"What?"

"Your paper-patch chin."

"Oh," Larry said. He felt around his face and rubbed off two blood-spotted pieces of tissue. But he missed a third one, and David didn't tell him.

David took the remaining chair and sat down across from his brother at the small, round, uneven plastic table. The marginally furnished room felt muggy, an apt foreshadowing for the story David was about to divulge—or confirm, as he suspected—to his brother. The relationship between them seemed right, and time was running out. If not before, David felt a burning need, exasperated by a growing tightness in his chest, to share his burden with Larry. *It's now or never*, he firmly believed.

With elbows on the table and clammy hands clasped together beneath his chin, David searched for how to begin. *Never*, he told himself. Never would he ever allow the loose cannon across from him to see his true degree of vulnerability. He knew the conversation ahead would be difficult. As much as he wanted Larry's support, he also needed Larry back home for good in Three Oaks. There were alternatives to both, neither good. His halting preamble was of no interest to his impatient, hungover brother. A lethargic soliloquy on "the proper use of commas" at the foot of Mount Rushmore would have stimulated more interest.

For several weeks, maybe months, or even years, an ocean of trepidation had swelled and roiled beneath the surface of David's mild-mannered appearance. At the same time, fear and indecision had churned deep within his psyche as if it were the forecast of an impending seismic event. For as much as he'd searched for how to explain his dilemma to his brother, words simply failed. He had made half a dozen shaky starts, only to pause dumbstruck in mid-sentence. And now Larry tapped his foot on the curled linoleum floor and glared out the room's lone window, dripping with condensation from the room's cheap air conditioner. David strained to mask his inflamed emotions, but he felt the beginnings of unwanted pressure pooling behind his eyes.

"Spit it out, for Christ's sake! We gotta go," Larry said. "It's almost nine-thirty."

"Slow-up, big man," David said. *Would Larry ever outgrow his hard-guy persona?* David hunted for an alternative verbal approach. Uncertainty haunted him. His brother's irritating, cocksure attitude was mitigated by the comical red tissue dot still displayed on his right cheek. David had to clear his conscience once and for all. It was their last day on the road, and Larry was still waiting across the table.

"Okay … okay, I had an affair," David blurted out but in a flat drone that concealed his genuine passion.

If sympathetic facial appearances could be calibrated one to ten, Larry's ranked a minus five. Unsure if he was heard, David repeated, "I've been involved in an affair … with another woman."

Gritting his teeth, David waited for a response. He wished the silence to stop. It did not. Not a hint of interest, much less compassion, arose from his brother. Larry's blank, red rimmed eyes managed to find David's even though his head never budged and his foot continued its floor rhythm.

Larry belched again. Then he groaned, "So? Let's hope it was with a woman."

"Fuck you, you irreverent bastard." Though coarse, David spoke with a mild manner, not wanting to kindle an argument. "Don't you see? We've been married almost twenty years. I had an affair. Not a closing-time shack-up, or when there's nothing better to do during halftime."

"So what's the big deal? Look at it this way, Dave, you're talking about an American pastime that's becoming more popular every year. You're not the first. I'm not sayin' everybody's gettin' some on the side. I'm just sayin' … probably." Larry shrugged his shoulders and scrunched his face as if comparing paints—taupe or beige?

Larry had no interest in nor could he relate to his brother's anguish. To look to him for empathy seemed to David the second-most foolish thing he'd ever done, but he was determined to finish his story. In a strange way, his brother's casual reaction almost provided legitimacy for his conduct.

"Are we talking about the same thing here? I've been sleeping with another woman. I think it's ruined my marriage, not to mention my life. You could at least give a shit."

"Okay, okay," Larry conceded. "But tell me in the car. It's too humid in here. Let's go."

David, still upset, kept his mouth shut, stood up, and pushed in his chair. He could feel uncomfortable adrenaline draining from his neck and shoulders as if moving toward relief. Before following his brother out the door, he straightened the bedspread, an engrained Coast Guard habit. Once outside, the fresh air delivered a cold jolt that afforded a much-needed lift from what he felt in his initial brotherly revelation.

Larry attempted to cut in front of him at the driver's door, but David blocked him. "No, I'm drivin'! You're shotgun."

Once in the car, Larry became a captive audience. Both men became more relaxed as they rode through town at a leisurely pace. Main Street had a lively business district, indifferent to the passing Chevy and its occupants. The conditions seemed right, and David was determined to share more of his honest thoughts before he got Larry back to Three Oaks.

It did not take long to exit the small town of Atlanta, Illinois. The brothers agreed it would be a smoother drive into Chicago if they took the interstate rather than follow the venerable Highway 66 with its million-plus traffic lights. At first, a smooth ride mattered little to David, but soon, both the Daileys experienced physical discomfort, as much a remnant of the wild night as the increasingly rough pavement. David's state of mind compounded his unease. In a short time, the whole situation had turned his morning-after headache into a pounding migraine.

I-55 provided a generic backdrop easy on David's eyes but did little to thwart the painful throb pulsating between his ears. Even the road noise began to irritate him. As he drove, the pavement became wet, the remnant of an evening shower. David followed other cars at a distance in an attempt to avoid filthy road spray but soon saw it was a useless effort. The wipers served only to streak the windshield with opaque half circles symbolic, he thought, of a life half-lived. A low, gray ceiling hung like a flophouse blanket above the highway, a perfect complement for the gloomy conditions inside the once shiny Bel Air Chevrolet.

They had been on the freeway for less than an hour when traffic started to back up and hurried drivers began swooping from lane to lane as if in anticipation of the white flag at Daytona. David suggested a coffee break. Larry agreed, saying he needed a smoke.

They took the Joliet exit where several signs directed them to Dell Rhea's Chicken Basket. If colorful billboards could be believed, Dell Rhea's was The Most Authentic Stop on the Internationally Famous Route 66—a landmark since 1946. Advertisements seemed to be wasted on Larry who didn't even fake an interest in local history, one of David's prime character traits. However, both were amused by the *authentic* mantle. They never met Dell Rhea, and neither had the stomach for a fried chicken dinner, a remnant of which hung heavy in the air. David's headache coupled with the pungent gag of day-old chicken grease made even the coffee less palatable.

Larry ordered an imported beer, but they both got black coffee, as alcohol was not served before noon due to a Will County ordinance prohibiting such sales. With an attentive audience or not, David launched into a gut-wrenching, at least to him, personal soap opera. He needed to share the internal turmoil that had pushed him to the brink of self-destruction.

"You remember the queen you wrestled with after graduation?"

Larry thought for a brief second then turned to his brother. "Maggie Stevens? Wait a minute ... you mean you've been bangin' Maggie? Wow! Who woulda thunk it? A hot chick like that." He considered his suspicion for a few more seconds then added, "I'll bet she's still table grade."

"How would you know, Mr. High School Harry? And she's not what you think, and not in the back seat, but I'll confess she's still the most attractive woman to ever come out of Three Oaks, Michigan."

Larry smiled as he visualized the memory of Maggie Stevens.

David reminded Larry of how he had had a chance meeting with Maggie at their high school reunion. Without interruption, he paced through the timeline of their discreet encounters. He relished the mental reenactment but recounted it in the staccato style of Detective Joe Friday from the TV series *Dragnet*—"Just the facts, ma'am, just the facts." Nevertheless, Larry was held in rapt attention, nearly mesmerized.

Toward the end of the reunion evening, Maggie and David had danced to the orchestra's version of "Unchained Melody." She snuggled tightly against him and whispered how much she loved slow dancing with him. "This was our special song. Remember?" They took turns whispering the lyrics. All the time, David worried about Jane possibly observing them. Fortunately, one of Jane's old classmates had asked her to dance, and the floor was crowded. David made sure he and Maggie were at the opposite end of the room from Jane.

On the way home, Jane had said, "We should encourage our alma mater to make reunions a regular event." David agreed it was fun to meet and talk with old classmates, especially ones they hadn't seen in a long time.

Yet behind all those words, all the way home, an indelible image of Maggie Stevens had floated among a faceless crowd, casually nuzzling her forehead between David's ear and shoulder until he once again felt her warm breath on his neck.

"Don't ya know, Larry, she showed up at the store the following Tuesday. Tuesdays are always my day to justify inventory, restock shelves, and place new orders. Doug Ackerman, you remember Doug, covered the front and checkout counter while my dog, Hunter, slept next to the garden center side entrance. I didn't see Maggie come in, so she startled me when she asked, 'Which is better, Hamilton Beach or Black & Decker electric toasters?' At that, I dropped a five-pound box of ten-penny nails.

"As I swept up the nails, I kept looking over my shoulder to make sure no one was watching us. I told myself it was nothing, that we were just friends. But my heartbeat said otherwise." David felt light-headed recounting the story, as if he'd been startled, bent down, and then stood up too quickly in that moment instead of just in his tale. He felt a rush, dizzy yet not really. *Strange*, he thought. He rambled on as if in a dream state, reliving the story of his encounter with Maggie.

"Then Maggie said something like, 'It was so good to see you last Saturday evening. Reminded me of those warm nights so long ago.'" David could see himself leading Maggie out into the new garden center and Hunter jumping up, insisting he lead. The dog had squeezed between them, repeatedly bumping against Maggie, begging her for a pet. Maggie patted the graying Irish Setter on his head, and David joined her, much to Hunter's pleasure.

"Does Hunter think we need a chaperone?" Maggie had said in a smooth but teasing voice while smiling up at her old high school sweetheart. They were both a little nervous and gave Hunter the attention he reveled in.

Maggie had claimed she had stopped by to see if she could get David's advice concerning some small home-renovation ideas she had in mind for her beach house. At least, that was what she said Before she was done, she apologized for being such a bother.

Of course, David had assured her she was no bother and suggested he drive over around noon and take a look at what she had in mind. What she might have had in mind tantalized David. He was eager to talk with Maggie in a more discrete setting.

"Terrific! We have a plan," she'd said.

David's mind had raced right along with his pulse. His amorous senses were stroked. *Could she have a hidden agenda?* The moment was provocative in an alluring, forbidden sort of way.

As David relived that special moment in time, he turned toward his brother and asked if he was following the story.

"Sort of. Go on, I want to follow this thing to the climax, no pun intended," Larry said.

After Maggie's "terrific plan" remark, she had invited David to lunch. "This is too special. You sure I'm not being a nuisance?" David could hear her smooth soft voice and his almost cavalier reply. "Honestly, no problem, Miss Stevens." *Her honeycomb manner would have made kamikaze volunteers out of zealous draft dodgers,* he thought. She was so hot, David feared for the survival of his potted geraniums.

"Well then, Mr. Dailey! How about we plan lunch at my house? That's an even better plan." David again heard her enticing proposal and saw her uninhibited vivacious smile. Before he could answer, "Good, we'll do lunch. See you around twelve," her tender yet self-assured style and gymnastics-honed figure had catapulted David's already-elevated libido.

Hunter and David had walked Maggie out the garden center entrance and around the outside of the store to the main entrance, wanting to avoid meeting any other customers. Hunter, now Maggie's best friend, took charge and trotted ahead of the couple. At the front steps, David held Hunter by the collar to keep both animal and master from running away. *She's married. I'm married. Hunter doesn't care,* he thought.

David was amazed how he could remember even the smallest detail of that encounter with Maggie.

"Sounds like my kind of home maintenance," Larry said. "Done a little moonlighting myself."

David shook his head when he realized Larry had entered the conversation. "I guess I'd have to agree with you, Larry, at least on some level."

David quickly reverted back to reliving his encounter with Maggie Stevens as he shared the facts with Larry. Man and dog had watched Maggie drive away from the hardware store. For the remainder of the morning, David was lost in anticipation of his lunch appointment.

After only one wrong turn, he'd located Maggie's beach house tastefully tucked from view along the perimeter of the wooded Warren Dunes Park. He saw Maggie watching from a second-level side terrace. She called out and waved to him. "Up here, David. Hurry, I want to show you something."

David had climbed the curved exterior staircase two steps at a time. He needed no encouragement to hurry. Maggie met him at the top, gave him a brief hug, and pulled him by the hand to a wicker patio table elegantly set for two. He noted she wore a broad gold wedding band on the ring finger of her left hand. He couldn't have missed it. A nervous tension swept through him.

He'd surveyed the façade before he sat down and thought, *What do we have here? Doesn't look like any renovation is needed.* David said, "Your house is beautiful, Maggie! What makes you think you need to change anything?"

Maggie had suggested they discuss all that later. That this was simply a private little lunch shared by two old friends. She thanked him for taking the time to come out to her home in the middle of his work day.

Then she'd asked him to pour the wine, and she'd offer a toast: "Here's to a never-ending unchained melody." They clinked glasses but hesitated, gazing into each other's eyes before sipping their wine.

"I'll always remember that moment in time," David sighed to Larry.

Before they ate lunch, Maggie had led her guest on a quick tour of what had to be the most elegant beach home he'd ever been inside. When they returned to the terrace, she refilled their wine glasses.

They'd sat next to each other. As David sat there with his refreshed glass of wine, he felt a bit out of his element, but Maggie's soothing chatter restored his ease. She asked if it was true that area farmers had been experimenting with wine making. Hers was a sincere interest, and David enjoyed being able to satisfy her curiosity.

He'd confirmed that Michigan farmers were entering the wine industry in a big way and that Dailey's Hardware, Garden & Botanical Center had been the beneficiary supplier of nursery grape plants and arbor-building materials.

Maggie had wanted to celebrate the Daileys' good fortune. She got up to fetch a set of bamboo salad hands and returned with a second bottle of Portuguese chardonnay. David could feel the glowing effects of the wine warming his face. Maggie next uncovered a warm loaf of Genovese rye bread. The smooth sound of the Ray Conniff Singers began to emanate from speakers hidden within a lush yard enclave of rhododendron. From their vantage point on the deck, the lake appeared placid, but David could hear the faint rhythmic, lapping sound of shallow waves against the sandy shore. All his senses were on high alert.

Then he'd told her how nice it was to have lunch with her, but she shouldn't have gone to such trouble. A baloney sandwich on the back steps would have been more than enough for a Dailey.

"Hush," she'd admonished David. "It's been far too long since we dined together." She went on to remind David it was not since he'd taken her to dinner at the Navaho on the way to the prom that they shared such a time. Then she laughed as she pulled her place mat and chair closer to his. Her knee bumped against his. "Are we only old friends? This is special, at least it is for me." She smiled and brushed back strands of hair that had fallen over her right eye. "Let's enjoy our lunch for two."

"Count on me," David had said. He held up his wine glass and looked straight at Maggie until their eyes locked. "It's special for me too."

As David was reliving each second of that encounter, he was unaware of how much he was actually saying aloud to Larry.

A cool, pine-scented breeze had ruffled Maggie's straight blond hair. Again, several strands of hair fell across her face. She shook her head as she brushed them back. The early-summer sun danced playfully in her eyes. "I'd say this is one of those special sand-dune summer days," she said. They clicked glasses again and sipped wine inhaling the moment and each other—"

"Did you get a nooner or what?" Larry interrupted. "Come on! Come on! How many glasses of wine did it take?"

"The wine may have had something to do with the mood, but I think it was a lot more than a glass of wine."

"Don't try to change the subject. We're talkin' bip, bam, thank you, ma'am? Am I right?"

"There you go, thinking with the wrong head," David said.

"I'm thinkin'! I'm thinkin'!"

"Breaking new ground, are we? How about let's get on into Chicago," David said.

"But to be continued. I'm right, yes?"

The motor groaned reluctantly as David tried to start his car. On the second try, the Chevy hiccupped then purred like a sleepy cat on the lap. He revved the motor with two quick pumps on the gas pedal and smiled at his brother.

"Sounds like she's gettin' old. The last time I drove a five-year-old car was at an antique auto show up in Monterey," Larry said. David assured him the Bel Air was as mint as any 1963 Ferrari but might need a new battery.

Heavy traffic seemed to engulf them, the closer they got to Chicago. When they crossed the Tri-State Tollway, with its numerous signs for O'Hare Airport, David could not help but consider how easy his life would become if he jumped on a plane there and simply disappeared. Additional lanes of roadway periodically materialized then vanished for no apparent reason. David slowed in an attempt to protect his car from the rough, uneven, and potholed pavement, and any other unforeseen road hazard.

A battle-tested black Mack dump truck with fourteen tons of crushed limestone in its open-box bed took advantage of David's slow pace and rumbled past. To avoid being hit by castoff stones, David swerved right and back left, cut in front of a second would-be passing car, then streaked out and back around the dump truck. Several motorists blew their horns and shook their fists in angry displeasure at David's speedway maneuvers.

Larry lurched up in his seat. "What the hell?"

"Go back to sleep. I got this under control."

"Heaven or hell, I don't want to go today," Larry said.

"Relax. You getting hungry?"

"Yes, but not for the last supper," Larry quipped.

With a malicious load of limestone glued to his rear bumper, David was driving faster than he wanted. They passed countless construction projects swarming with hard-hatted troops milling around among battered orange-and-white caution cones and lethargic flagmen. Combined with harried and hurried motorists determined to get somewhere first, the whole scene provided for mighty hazardous travel.

Deteriorating pavement added to the older brother's nervous tension. Not so much for Larry. What one viewed as a problem, the other viewed as an opportunity. Larry pointed out endless construction contract possibilities and how the current roadwork was inefficient and of poor quality. "Money to be made here, Dave."

"A fool and his money are easily separated, Larry."

"The same is true for women, Davey boy."

David veered left but was unable to avoid a water-filled pothole. After the jolt, he said, "Chicago'd be a great town to visit if they'd ever get 'er finished." He gripped the wheel with both hands and concentrated on protecting his car as much as its occupants. Cars and trucks were tailpipe to bumper and door-to-door at seventy miles per hour. Exhaust fumes permeated the Bel Air to the extent carbon monoxide poisoning couldn't be far behind, the boys agreed.

Chicago, as usual, was jammed and frantic. Cars streamed past the Bel Air, darting from lane to lane with total disregard for the posted speed limit or work-zones. Amidst the hustle and reigning confusion, David chose not to follow old 66 into town, although he passed two billboards inviting him to do so. Larry hassled his brother about the car not being able to keep up with the urban flow of traffic, to which there was no response—and none expected.

David followed I-55 to the Dan Ryan Expressway then north to the Chicago Loop. Although he'd been in the downtown area dozens of times, he knew finding a place to park would be difficult and recalled how it had always been a source of personal apprehension. Once he reached the section of streets named after dead presidents and then the commercial Loop area, he searched for the public parking deck near the intersection of State and Adams.

As they approached his familiar parking destination, David spotted a vacant curbside slot and whipped in. "This will save us a few bucks and some time. Parking is so damned expensive in the Loop." Before either could open his door, a disheveled middle-aged man stepped into their path, squirted something on the windshield and began wiping.

"Sorry, I don't need my windshield washed," David said, opening his door.

"It's awful dirty. See all this mud." The stranger held up a soiled rag that might have been hoarding a few weeks' worth of dirt.

"Sorry, maybe some other time," Larry said and motioned for his brother to lead the way.

"Boss, can't you help a man's down on his luck? Times be rough in Chi Town. Real rough."

"How rough is *real* rough?" Larry asked.

"Boss, these be hard times, hard times. Yesterday week, the mob done laid off three judges."

"Now that's rough," David said then handed the man two one-dollar bills.

"Bless you, boss, bless you. Imma look after your car. Nobody mess with it."

As they walked, Larry chastised his brother for paying the man off. "He's a con, not going to protect your car. Probably already spent the money on cheap Muscatel."

"Maybe. Maybe not. I figure we saved money by parking on the street," David said.

"That dizzy coconut in the backseat would provide better security," Larry said.

It was only a short, blustery block and a half to the Berghoff, a landmark German eatery. Having skipped breakfast, they were two hungry guys in search of food. More than that, David was relieved to be out of the car and free from wrestling with city traffic and heavy expressway traffic in the midst of critical road transformation.

"You need to see this place. You're going to love it. Great German food."

"And great German beer, I hope," Larry said while exhaling cigarette smoke into the wind.

"Better than that," David said. Before they entered the restaurant, David paused to look around at the blur of activity all up and down Adams Street. The meat packing and railroad hub of the Midwest always featured large crowds of fast walkers moving in all directions, seemingly oblivious to the chaotic noise, filth, litter, and repugnant odors so characteristic of Chicago. The Loop, however familiar and exciting, reminded David of Carl Sandburg's poem about the brutal City of the Big Shoulders. David secretly prided himself as being one of the few readers aware of the ugliness portrayed in that poem. He had earlier shared the poem and his interpretation with Jane, who believed the poem to be an insightful depiction of Chicago. Jane did agree, though, that most people in Three Oaks had probably never heard of the poem. However, unlike her husband, she had never been critical of her hometown's lack of sophistication.

As the travelers stepped toward the main Berghoff entrance, a pale, gaunt waiter dressed in a black waistcoat and a long white apron tied at his waist waved to them from a side door foyer. "This way, gentlemen! You will follow me," he said in a thick German accent. Sporting a salt-and-pepper Hitleresque mustache, he spun hard-heeled and led them down an interior hallway to a second dining room where he pointed to a small table covered with a white tablecloth. Menus were provided before they were comfortably seated. Drink orders were taken and delivered instantaneously, with beer foam still rising and spilling over the lips of glass beer steins. Observing that his customers were not ready to order, the waiter announced, "I will be back to take your orders, gentlemen." His delivery sounded more like a command than a courtesy. Before they opened their menus, the waiter had disappeared.

"Are they always this fast?" Larry asked.

"You will order, and you will enjoy," David said. "Great sandwiches—Reubens, bratwursts. You might want to try their sauerbraten or Wiener schnitzel. Sauerkraut, potato salad always good too."

"You're a regular?"

"Jane and I have eaten here maybe half-a-dozen times. We like it."

The waiter reappeared, took their orders, and served them in less than five minutes. Larry had a Reuben sandwich with potato salad, and David ordered the Wiener schnitzel. Before the men were half finished with their meal, the waiter delivered second steins of beer and suggested what they'd like for dessert before vanishing again.

"Are the Russians coming?" Larry asked.

"The more they serve, the more they make," David said.

"You gotta love German efficiency," Larry said.

David marveled at how his brother's mind worked when it came to business. "Maybe if the Krauts were put to work on the Chicago Autobahn, it'd be finished by now," David said.

"I'm paying for this Reuben, and I will enjoy it," Larry said as he coolly stuffed a fork full of potato salad into his mouth.

"It's good, right? You may remember there are lots of Germans and Dutch in our area of Michigan. Octoberfest is just around the corner. Always a big deal. Bigger every year."

Over German roast coffee and apple strudel, and a momentary Adolf armistice, David continued with the next episode of the Maggie Stevens chronicles.

"Following the beach house get-together, I'd see Maggie every once in a while, usually for some sort of small household repair. If she didn't call me with a request, I'd call her with a suggestion. We both knew it was a charade, but we were having fun. It wasn't long before we stopped pretending to ourselves. Soon, we started saying things to each other that we shouldn't have. Between work and Maggie, there wasn't much time left for home life, and what there was, was filled with excuses, deceits, and outright lies. I became more and more distracted and always half angry when around Jane. I don't know why, just up tight. Maggie and I came here to Chicago once for what I claimed was a mandatory trade show. I could not get enough of Maggie. We made plans. Dreamed. Call it infatuation, love, I don't know. I had to be with her and believed she felt the same. She made me feel good. She did."

"What am I missing here?" Larry asked. "Where's Maggie now? Or better yet, where's Jane? And didn't you say Maggie was married? How did you guys pull this off in little ole' Three Oaks where everyone knows everything about everybody?"

David explained that Maggie had left her husband two years before they reconnected at the reunion but maintained the townhouse on Chicago's near Northside. Her two high-school-aged children were in boarding schools back east somewhere.

"Listen, Larry, we were in love. No doubt about it."

"You had indigestion. She had a handyman."

"Be serious. I knew and believed I was in love."

"I'm serious. Where is she now? Tell me that."

David explained how Maggie had told him she had missed her period. How it felt like being run over by a night train. "It tore me up and us apart. It was hard. I never heard from her and didn't call. Wasn't sure I wanted to. Wanted it to all just go away. It hurt. It still does."

"She had an abortion?"

"No. You'd be happy if she had. You'd like me to look like a complete hypocrite."

"I'm just askin'," Larry said. "No dog or pony in this show."

"Finally, she called me at the store. False alarm. What a relief. Dodged a bullet."

"And have you?"

"What? Dodged a bullet?"

"Continued seeing her?"

"No. At least so far." David lied, but this was one untruth he would take to his grave.

"And Jane?"

"That's a problem. Since the affair started, I haven't been the easiest person to live with. I'm not treating her right, always irritable. Jane and I haven't done much of anything together for the past year."

"You can't ride two horses at the same time Mr. Three Oaks," Larry said.

"You articulate SOB!"

"But I'm right. Right? And if you're not careful, you won't even be riding one—"

The waiter interrupted holding the check. David seized it. The waiter's impatience vibrated. He hovered over David's shoulder. David inquired if he paid at the counter.

"No. I bought your meal, and now you will pay me."

"Oh, that's right," David said. He handed Adolf two twenties. The waiter immediately handed back the correct change already organized for a handy 10 percent gratuity, which David remitted. Larry was curious—a first. David explained that waiters gave tokens for the meals as they picked them up in the kitchen and resold the meals to the customers independently.

"Say what? How the hell does that work?" Larry said.

"Unusual, I agree, but a Berghoff tradition." David looked back to the waiter for validation and an explanation, but he was gone.

The Daileys made their way through crowded dining room tables looking for an exit. Confused by the circuitous route out of the Berghoff, they found themselves in front of a set of thick oak-inlaid doors. A polished brass pedestal supporting a burnt wood engraving announced: Gentlemen Only Bar.

"What's this?" Larry asked.

"Just what it says, I suspect."

"Is this legal?"

"Ask Mayor Daley, he be 'Da Boss,'" David said.

"Let's check it out. A classy bar with no women? Really? I'm buyin' one for the road."

"I'm full," David said.

"Come on. There's always room for one more. Will the boss let me smoke in here?"

They entered and sat down on rich, dark leather stools in front of a massive solid oak bar. Cigar aroma hung in the air with the heavy stillness of century-old tapestry. Although shadowy, the tavern possessed a spotless shine. A red-vested bartender, reminiscent of an a cappella Gay Nineties barbershop quartet, greeted them, "What might ye gents be havin' on this fine day?"

Larry ordered a couple more steins of Old Style from the Irishman. Both men gawked at the old-world beer hall accouterments. Several large, framed paintings hung on the wall depicting full-figured nude women in various positions of repose. With the presence of a cocktail waitress, the complement of the bartender, it was obvious that women could work in the men-only bar but were forbidden to patronize it. Tradition aside, the brothers agreed it wasn't right and would soon fade away just like old soldiers.

After a short pull on his third draft at the Berghoff, David said, "Larry, I'm absolutely sure of what I'm going to do."

"I know—ride off into the sunset and leave us all happily ever after in Three Oaks."

"I have wished so. Planned so. No, I'm going to tell Jane everything. Maggie, the pregnancy scare, the plan to fake death and run away—the whole crazy, bizarre mess."

"So you've decided to take your own life? Big mistake. And speaking of pregnancy, there's something I don't understand."

"That's a switch," David said.

"How come you and Jane haven't had any children? According to Mom, you've always been 'the salt of the earth couple,' America's hope for a brighter tomorrow."

Larry had stumbled, as only he could, on the family root canal. However, it gave David an invitation to inform his brother of a segment of family history seldom discussed.

"A year and a half after we were married, Jane had a miscarriage complicated by a preexisting condition that shot future pregnancy all to hell. And Mom's right—Jane was and is the salt of the earth. She started teaching when I was in the Coast Guard. She was only eighteen but earned a certificate that allowed her to teach in rural one-room schools. When I was discharged, we started planning but put off marriage until the war was almost over. Had to be financially secure. We wanted to do things right and on our own, you might say."

"Sorry I missed the wedding. I was doing the 'arsenal of democracy' thing at the time."

"I'm sorry too. Spit Shine and Crisco filled in for you as my best men. We replaced you with two and a half; Crisco was carrying a few extra pounds of lard at the time."

"No surprise there. I can't wait to see those turkeys again."

"Your chance is near. Anyway, Jane and I had everything we could ever want. I was slated to take over the hardware business, and Jane loved teaching. Ours was a storybook tale in the making. We were the toast of the town, at least in our mother's eyes."

"Your mother mostly," Larry added.

"Be careful, Larry. She's always been proud of you."

"So I've been told."

"Our life revolved toward our expectant family. I built a special bent-hickory rocker for Jane and a baby to nurse in and a wormy chestnut crib. Jane and her mother sewed colorful Mother Goose curtains for the nursery. We didn't tell Mom right away, but at the start of the second trimester, we made the grand announcement. Jane's students gave her small toys and stuffed animals for the baby's arrival.

"Mom immediately started planning for a grandiose shower at the church. She wanted to be a grandmother as much as Jane wanted to be a mother. Maybe more."

"Sounds like our mother," Larry said.

David continued with how he'd spent a long day at the store the Saturday before Memorial Day, an unusually warm day. May had been a busy month for the expanding hardware business, and the holiday weekend had been particularly hectic. Jane had gone to school to draft her letter of resignation, followed by working with a fellow teacher to prepare a year-end party and musical program. When she returned home, she complained of pelvic cramps along her left side and pain in her shoulder. She took a couple of aspirins, and they ate a light supper. Tired, they were in bed by ten.

He'd found it reassuring how their minds worked once they knew Jane was pregnant. They were careful about sex, thinking it could in some way be detrimental to the baby's development. Jane's doctor discounted the possibility.

"In the middle of the night, I opened my eyes, how you do when you think you've heard something. Nothing. Then I heard a low moan, like a cat growling. I lifted my head off the pillow to hear, stared straight at a wall I couldn't see."

The moan had come again, like someone painfully straining. David's senses came wide awake, on edge. Then a shrill scream pierced the dark house.

David had reached over but couldn't find Jane. He bounded out of bed and switched on the bedroom light. Jane was gone. A bloodcurdling screech came from the bathroom down the hall, and he could see a sliver of light from beneath the closed door. "Jane!" he shouted as he swung the door open.

Jane had been on the floor, partially naked, balled up in a fetal position halfway between the bathtub and the stool. She convulsed in pain with her arms wrapped tightly around her abdomen.

A current of panic like a shock wave had ripped through David. Reflexively he yelled, "What have you done?" Tears rolled down her cheeks, and she looked up at him with her face contorted in agony. Such pitiful, helpless eyes. He would never forget the grief and pain in them. He fell to his knees next to the tub and lifted her head and shoulders in his arms as he realized what was happening.

"You're okay. We're going to the hospital," David had told her. She made guttural sounds, and could only nod in agreement. As he carried her to the car, she repeatedly gasped and held her breath, defenseless against the shooting pains.

A week later, David and Jane had been called back to the hospital. A visiting obstetrician spoke with them. "As you know, Jane has suffered a miscarriage. Normally, I'd suggest we simply try again." *Normally* startled both would-be parents. They both wanted clarification and were alarmed even more when the doctor hesitated before continuing to explain. "Jane, you've had an ectopic miscarriage, a tubal pregnancy."

"What does that mean?" David had asked.

"It means that the egg was fertilized in a fallopian tube and stayed there, never making it to the uterus. A fallopian tube was not created to hold a growing fetus, and ultimately, Jane, yours ruptured, and thus the miscarriage occurred."

"So what does all this mean? We want children," Jane had said.

"Normally, I'd say your chances would be very good for getting pregnant again."

"Normally? What do you mean?" Jane had pleaded but dreaded the answer.

"The ruptured fallopian tube was completely severed and is no longer functional. On further examination, we discovered the second tube to be compromised, at least partially blocked with scar tissue, probably due to a previous undetected miscarriage. The likelihood of a future pregnancy will not be easy, but it is possible. So I would suggest that if you want children, keep trying."

Jane had been devastated and cried uncontrollably all the way home. In the days and weeks that followed, she suffered from depression. She lost weight. Mrs. Dailey added to the young couple's anguish when all she could talk about was for them to try again.

Fortunately, Jane's letter of resignation had not been completed, and the start of a new school year was three months away. With time and sheer determination, Jane pulled herself together.

The start of school in the fall had come at just the right time. Both David and Jane threw themselves into their work. The daily routine of responsibility worked wonders for the young schoolteacher and lifted her husband's spirits as well. Their intimate life reignited but with no luck in getting pregnant.

As David recounted the catastrophic train of events to his brother, he relived the life Jane and he had built together. It was a good life, full of good memories and optimistic dreams.

"So you moved on," Larry said.

"I did. But I don't think Jane ever has. At least, not completely."

"What do you mean?" Larry's interest in his brother's life was refreshing in an odd sort of way, and David welcomed the chance to share it with him, even though it was a sad chapter.

"Jane had aspired to be Mother America, and she would have been the best. I'll admit I wanted the white picket fence, tricycles strewn about the yard, an electric train chugging around a decorated Christmas tree, a litter of puppies, and maybe a small pony named Doll. Jane was disappointed by never being able to achieve motherhood. And my sense was that Jane felt she had let me down, that she couldn't live up to my expectations. Nothing could have been further from the truth, but I've always believed she harbored such feelings."

"Did you guys consider adoption?"

"Yes, but it never seemed the same, and the time was never right, not to mention Mom's steadfast opposition to such a consideration. Jane and I have both had productive lives. Finally, after five or six years, we accepted the fact that we would most likely live our lives childless. We never talked about it."

"I wish my first wife's pregnancy and Jane's could have been switched," Larry said.

"Interesting you should say that."

"My advice is to forget everything—miscarriage, Maggie tryst, whatever. Go home and live happily ever after." As wrong as David often thought Larry was, his manner and tone led him to believe his brother sincerely wanted to show support for him.

"Can't, Larry. I've messed things up royally, and I want a clean slate. Jane deserves no less ... and a great deal more."

"What she doesn't know won't hurt her," Larry said.

"It'll hurt me, that's for sure."

"You don't know that," Larry said.

"She may know anyway. I couldn't stand for her to confront me or do something even more drastic," David said.

"Permission or forgiveness, neither appeals to me. If you won't take my advice, I can at least pick up the tab," Larry said.

Larry motioned for the bartender who nodded, "Two more Old Styles it'll be?"

Larry looked at David questioningly then gave up. "No, we'll take our check, thanks."

Unlike the dining room, the Gentleman's Bar did not treat them like cattle being driven through an iron chute to slaughter in the Chicago stockyard. Larry paid the tab, and the brothers found their way, this time, to the restaurant's exit.

When they stepped out of the Berghoff into the impersonal hubbub of Adams Street, the sun's glare caused both men to squint and shield their eyes. David intended to give Larry a fuller explanation of how he intended to approach full disclosure with Jane. However, before he had a chance to start, Larry asked, "Dave, how did you get away with your Maggie fling?"

"Who told me I should forget everything?" David said.

"Just tell me. How did you escape suspicion? Somebody must have known."

"Not sure I did escape. Jane knows. I know she knows."

"How so?"

"Oh, little things she said that had suggestive or double meanings," David said.

"All in your mind. I doubt she knows. You're paranoid."

"When I was packing for California she asked, 'Can you be trusted not to bring back a couple of those fertile Mormon women or easy West Coast girls?'"

"That's just funny, not suggestive."

"Before I left, she asked me if I thought the high school reunions had ended. That's not funny."

"No, that's a question. Are there plans for future reunions? I'd like to go to one."

"And then she said, 'Some time away will do you some good.'"

"So?"

"Don't you see? She meant me away from Maggie."

"As I said, you're paranoid. You know your problem? You think too much. And didn't you tell me you stopped seeing Maggie?"

Larry's lack of empathy, though improving, exasperated David. With hands cupped around a lighter's flame, Larry lit a cigarette. "Didn't we park over there?" He motioned with his head and eyes for them to cross the street in front of a Yellow Cab. The cab driver cut into the curb and stopped directly in front of them anticipating a fare. When the Daileys waved him on, he sped off with little more than a dirty look.

"We parked down that side street on the left, but we don't need the car just yet. Let's walk up to the art museum. Feel the lake air?" David said.

A clear blue sky peeked between the rooftops of tall buildings, seeming out of place above the tormented congestion below. The damp, cool sensation of the breeze off Lake Michigan was invigorating though. Jumping back into the car immediately following lunch and three large Old Style drafts was neither enticing nor good practice for a couple of small-town boys in the big city—at least one smalltown boy.

The casual stroll suited them both, and their amiable conversation was unaffected by the hectic urban discord. Their contentment was mutual for possibly the first time since they left Santa Monica.

"You may not believe this, Larry, but I'm sort of sorry this trip is almost over."

"Let me put it this way, Dave: if you should ever decide to do it again, I'm ready."

The Art Institute of Chicago was only a block ahead and dominated the foot of Adams Street. Jane and David had explored the Art Institute numerous times. Jane loved it, and David had grown an art appreciation there. Art aside, David wanted to be sure Larry clearly understood his personal turmoil and how he planned to address it. He cherished the renewed family connection and support. The brothers sat down in the middle of the expansive concrete steps leading up to the museum's main entrance. David pointed out an L train station down the street where travelers could catch the train to O'Hare Airport. Then he revisited his Maggie Stevens confession.

"Simply put, Larry, Maggie Stevens held me in emotional bondage, by my own choice. She was always on my mind. We collaborated on secret rendezvous, shared discreet hand-held walks on the beach, and discovered romantic hideaways. We even drove to South Bend, in her Austin-Healey, to see the movie *A Summer Place*. Then we christened her beach house, *our* summer place. We exchanged small gifts with unique significance. I gave Maggie the arrowhead I had found while hoeing in Grandma's garden way back when. Maggie gave me an autographed first edition of Margaret Mitchell's *Gone with the Wind*. Everything we did held more meaning for me than ever before—like living out a wish upon a star come true.

"The specter of Maggie's pregnancy hit me like a terminal cancer diagnosis, snuffing out our furtive love affair. I was submerged in a sea of mental guilt and confusion, floundering like a stunned perch at Weko Beach. I had considered divorce but never said out loud, 'I want a divorce.' I didn't. And what if Jane had asked for a divorce? That would've destroyed everything. Ironic, isn't it?

"The notion of suicide also entered the fray. Whether for principle, fear, or the belief that the aftereffects of suicide on the living never end, I rejected it. And as you know, I don't believe in suicide. But to vanish off the face of the earth with a *believable* explanation left behind seemed the best of possible bad scenarios—"

Suddenly, David was interrupted when two police cars followed by a fire engine roared by in front of them heading north on Michigan Avenue, sirens blasting and lights flashing. A third police car peeled off and blocked Adams St. followed by two more firefighting vehicles speeding through the intersection heading north.

For all of five minutes, the Dailey brother watched in awe as intersection activity slowed but never came to a complete standstill. When the squad car blocking the intersection moved on following the others, it did so without siren or emergency lights. All sirens had faded or had stopped. Life resumed as if nothing had happened.

Larry turned to his brother, "Okay, Dave, you may continue. I'm listening."

David looked at Larry and gave him a fist bump on the arm. "Okay. For several years, I'd dreamed of retracing old Route 66, following the road the two of us followed over twenty years ago. Rediscovering places we had stopped or missed on our trip out west. For you, it was freedom, and now it could be for me as well. Putting together a plan for how to disappear on the storied Main Street of America became an amusing, if not pleasurable, obsession. Actually, it helped to replace Maggie in my thoughts. And the physical act of leaving town would help even more, or so I thought."

Larry made no response. He listened with genuine interest, without judgment.

"Let's go get your old car and head for Three Oaks," Larry said. "I want to get there before dark, so I can see if it's like what I remember."

"Slow down. We've got time. I'm telling you, I will not allow myself to go on constantly wondering if Jane does or doesn't know," David said.

"Your decision. How long do you think it'll take to get home?" Once again, their minds were traveling in different directions at different altitudes. But the brothers were the closest they'd been since leaving Santa Monica and maybe even since Larry's high school graduation. And it was now definite: *both* were going home.

"I have one more thing to say." David reached for Larry's arm to restrain him on the step next to him. "Jane and I come to Chicago at least twice every year. Once during the summer to see a ball game or go to a concert and enjoy a nice dinner at some place new. The week before Christmas we come shopping. The Loop's always brilliantly decorated for the holidays. We definitely take in Marshall Fields and come here to the Art Institute. Sometimes, we'll sit right here on these steps and people watch. Watch the guy roasting and selling chestnuts on the sidewalk right over there. When we get cold, which doesn't take long in Chicago, we walk clutching bundles under our arms, down the street to the Berghoff. Every Christmas. And I'm looking forward to the next. And I count on you being here too." David punched Larry again on the arm in exclamation.

"Like I said, Dave, there are fools, and there are *damn* fools. I wouldn't jeopardize what you have by talking too much. But I know it's going to work out for everyone."

"I'm no fool," David said. Larry's body language conveyed a companionship David had longed for. "And to think we waited twenty years and had to travel two thousand miles to find something we could agree on."

"Dave, I know this is and has been a complicated, gut-wrenching situation for you. But being who you are, I'm certain things will work out for the best."

"For all of us," David said.

"Let's hit the trail," Larry said. His voice sounded far away. David could hear the faint rumble of a train slowing as it entered the L station.

"Look down the street. See that white sign up about half a block on the right?" David pointed a finger.

"Yeah. So?"

"Know what it says?"

"You think I can read it from here?"

"It says, 'Historic Route 66 Begins Here.'"

"For us it ends here," Larry said, his declaration delivered in a confident but acquiescent manner.

"I hope it never ends. Jane would love going with us on a trip like this." David could barely hear himself and swallowed in an attempt to clear his ears. *Must be the chaotic noise of the streets of Chicago.*

"Let's go, Dave. There isn't time for another film noir. Besides, we need to be home for supper. Isn't that what our Mom always said?"

Neither man had considered the days were getting shorter, but David could sense it. David remembered Michigan was an hour ahead of Illinois, so they could be pressed to make it for supper, especially if they got caught in heavy traffic.

"You go get the car and swing around here to pick me up," David said.

"Think the old crate'll start?"

"Get serious. I'd just like to sit here a little longer." David was not going to admit to his ever-ready brother that he had a strange but relaxed feeling of drowsiness enveloping him. The trip was almost over, and it would be restful to let Larry drive the rest of the way home.

"You trust me with that antique? Since when? Hope she starts." Larry hustled down the steps and crossed Michigan Avenue over a boisterous pedestrian-choked crosswalk.

David watched as Larry swaggered along the left side of Adams Street until he stopped long enough to light a cigarette directly opposite the Route 66 sign. He saw Larry look up at the sign and thought, *See, Larry? Route 66 begins here.* Larry continued on, his long, sandy hair ruffling in a crisp Chicago breeze. He grew more and more distant and then disappeared.

CHAPTER 14
Five Days Ago

"It is an absolutely jump-down-spin-around gorgeous day!" That was what the meteorologist declared over the noon news broadcast aired on WGN Radio out of Chicago. The weatherman went on to say he was standing outside on the station's eighteenth-floor balcony as he gave the weather forecast. "So I'm fairly certain I've got it correct this time!"

The weatherman had used that attention-getter with positive feedback in the past. While standing under an umbrella in a blustery downpour, he reported, "There's a one hundred percent chance of rain today followed by an uptick in precipitation."

It was a pretty day in Three Oaks, Michigan, as well. Midseventies, light westerly breeze, and a blue sky punctuated with one or two fluffy white cumulus clouds served to cast a tranquil spell over the rural landscape. On such a day, the occupants of the Chevy would normally be full of chatter during their drive home. They might comment on the earthy charm of the countryside they passed through. The hardwood trees had started their colorful autumn pageant and farmers were sowing cover crops over their harvested fields to restore soil nutrients lost during the summer months. There were apple pickers outfitted with sacks climbing tall ladders set against trees with heavily laden limbs. The apple crop appeared bountiful this year. They may have discussed the football season as they passed by a high school where a team was practicing in an open field while a motley-looking marching band paced through formations on the gridiron.

It was a special season of the year, but it was not a happy day for the two women inside the car. The attitude of the happy exhibition outside was not mirrored in the sullen mood of those inside the automobile. Neither woman heard the humorous weather report on the car's radio, nor did they note the glorious scenery pass by. In fact, not a word had been exchanged since leaving the hospital twenty minutes earlier. Both were awash in deep personal thoughts, which was out of character and added to the gloominess of their drive home.

Finally, the car rolled to a slow stop at the end of a paved driveway next to a mailbox painted red, white, and blue. The two women sat silently in the front seat, neither moving. Eventually, the older of the two opened the passenger door, got out, walked around the front of the car, and opened the mailbox. She hastily thumbed through the contents then turned to face the driver who still had both hands locked on the wheel and a foot on the brake. Both appeared tired with glassy, red-rimmed eyes and evidence of salt-streaked cheeks.

The driver rolled down her door window and said, "Mom, I'm going home. There's lots needing tending to do between now and Saturday." She blotted her runny nose with a tissue salvaged from the purse seated next to her.

"Oh, honey, please let me help. I'll call Reverend Rissig as soon as I get in the house," the older woman said.

"No, Mom, you've been up for two straight days and are doing too much. Please, let me handle this. You go in and lay down for a while. You've got to be exhausted," the younger woman said.

"And what about you, Jane? You haven't had a decent night's sleep since David fell, and I don't want you bearing this burden alone. At least come by later and have supper with me. We've lots to talk over, you need someone to lean on."

"My life changed today, and I'm scared," Jane said.

"I can help you. I can relate to what you must be feeling and going through right now. You were there for me when David's father passed. As my mother said to me—and I know it's true—'this too shall pass.'

Make no mistake, we never forget, nor should we. But time has a way of helping us heal. Now, please come by for supper."

"Okay, I'll swing by about six and bring along one of the casseroles that have been dropped by the house. We'll get through this, but we may never get through those casseroles." The two exchanged knowing smiles of reassurance. "You go on now and get some rest. I'll be back around six."

At that, the elder Mrs. Dailey stepped forward and, through the open car window, clutched the younger Mrs. Dailey's shoulders and hugged her tightly. Then she released her and stepped back. "Casserole? Our good friends just want to help."

CHAPTER 15
Three Oaks, Michigan—
End of the Trail

The front tires smoke as the brakes lock up and the car screeches to a halt within inches of a dowdy, blue-and-white Chicago Transit Authority bus packed with disinterested morning commuters. "Damned bottlenecks!" Larry curses while he searches his present surroundings and past memory for an alternate escape route from midtown Chicago. Twenty minutes later, he tosses three dimes into a funneled coin bin at the west-end toll booth for the Chicago Skyway. The traffic pole blinks from red, to yellow, to green and thus releases more horsepower than the entire starting gate at the Kentucky Derby. The thoroughbred sports car rockets forward, beating two Marathon Oil tankers and a shiny, new, black Studebaker Lark to the four-lane merge.

The deeply polished foreign make sprints to the crest of the Skyway and soars Condor-like high above the Port of Chicago. Glimpses of the Loop's midmorning skyline reflect in the rearview mirror. Flowing into the Indiana Toll Road and streaking around the southern tip of Lake Michigan conjures up a happy memory of riding with his young parents aboard the South Shore Line on the way to spend a day at the 1933 Chicago World's Fair. At that time, laying claim to a window seat before his brother could was his sole objective, not viewing the outside world as it passed by. A lot had changed in the thirty years since two small boys got to go on the train to the World's Fair.

The Indiana Toll Road, also known as the Main Street of the Midwest, is a pleasant relief compared to the congested streets and clamorous urban noise left behind in Chicago. However, his nostrils soon become choked with the rotten-egg stench belching forth from the dingy, endless Gary steel mills, the Midwest's man-made version of the Dakota Badlands. One redeeming feature is the expansive blue backdrop of Lake Michigan. "I don't know how anyone can live here," Larry mumbles in a throat-clearing raspy voice. "Uuuhhh, this has got to be America's septic tank." But even as he ponders the ugliness of the scene, images, and aromas of Gary, Indiana, it all brings back pleasant memories of returning home to Three Oaks after a long day in Chicago attending a White Sox's or Bear's game.

With an open road in front of him and no cops in sight, Larry mashes the gas pedal to the floor with space-race determination to be the fastest on the planet. He needn't rush, however, as he has no set schedule and is easily within two hours of his destination. Even so, Larry feels the boyish energy in his muscles, like a horse spying the barn ahead after a long and tiring trip. Larry loves that the motorists he overtakes seem to whisk backward along the highway as if traveling in the opposite direction from him. Ahh! The speed is exhilarating. He feels he is taking off again and even faster than earlier now that he finally has the road to himself.

At the Chesterton travel plaza parking lot, a paunchy, middle-aged man wearing a light-brown Panama hat, pale-green Bermudas, and a flamboyant untucked Hawaiian shirt, leans close to Larry's window and says, "You, my friend, must have been doing a hundred miles per hour when you flew by us a few miles back! Never thought I'd see you again, at least not in this lifetime," the stranger says with a smile.

"You're close! Ninety-five, but she'll do a hundred twenty."

"Whoooa Nellie! You know they can check your speed at toll road exits by the time recorded on your ticket?"

"Why do you think I stopped here? Not for the food. Just killin' time. I'm getting off a few exits up. Headed for Michigan."

"Me too, but I'd need a day's head start to beat you there."

"What're you drivin'?" Larry asks.

"That gas-hog Leisure Seeker RV hooked up at the fuel farm out front."

Larry is amused by his new acquaintance's manner of speaking. The two men, although from distinctly different worlds, visit for the better part of half an hour. They want to know where the other is from, what he does for a living, and why he's going to Michigan. The Leisure Seeker, with wife and kids, is on his way from Naperville, Illinois to the family cabin on Lake Charlevoix to do some swimming and fishing. Larry says he is from California and headed for Three Oaks to spend some time with his brother and widowed mother in the village where he grew up. Both men use their right hands to represent Michigan's Lower Peninsula. They each point to where they are headed compared with their current location.

Shortly after exiting the toll road, Larry crosses the border into Michigan, welcomed by a large road sign: Governor George Romney welcomes you to MICHIGAN—THE WATER WONDERLAND. Two minutes beyond by the side of the four-lane Red Arrow Highway, Larry sees a six-by-six-foot, black-and-white, metal sign: Welcome to New Buffalo, Home of the 1952 State Class D Basketball Champions.

"Not much to cheer about in Boondockville." Larry smirks. Following a quick glance in the rearview mirror, "Damn, give me a frickin' break!" On his rear bumper is the state highway patrol with blue and red lights flashing. Both cars pull over onto the right shoulder and stop.

After an inordinate amount of time, a smartly uniformed state trooper gets out of his patrol car and cautiously approaches Larry's driver-side door. "Good morning, sir. I thought I'd never catch up to you. Welcome to Michigan where we have posted speed limits."

"Good afternoon, officer. For your information, I have a twelve-thirty meeting with an attorney here in New Buffalo," Larry said.

"You're right, it is afternoon. May I have a look at your driver's license and automobile registration, please?"

"Officer, it's twenty-five after. Can't we work this out?"

"Relax, you'll only be a few minutes late. However," the officer looks at the driver's license, "Mr. Lawrence Dailey, along with the speeding ticket I'm going to issue you, I'm going to make an appointment for you to meet with a local constable of the peace. You may plead your case then, not now. If you choose to plead guilty, you may mail in your fine to the address on the summons. If you choose to contest the charge, you must do so in person at the time and place prescribed. You won't want to be late for that appointment."

"No, no, wait, officer! I can explain." Larry is pissed, but he grudgingly swallows his anger and assumes a stoic resignation. While he waits for the officer, who had returned to his patrol car to write out a speeding citation, a road-weary Leisure Seeker honks as it chugs by with its load of happy campers waving out their open windows. An Old Town canoe is haphazardly strapped down on the roof with clothesline rope, and blue smoke curls from a rusty tailpipe. Larry stares at the spectacle in disbelief. "They say it takes all kinds to make the world go round," he grumbles even as he smiles and waves back at the joyful campers on their way up north.

At 12:51 p.m., Larry enters the law offices of Sill, Sill & Hammerschmidt and is greeted by one of the partners. "Hey, there. I'm Bob Sill." Having already observed the bright red Triumph pull up in front of his office, he smiles and extends a hand to Larry, "Since your call, I've been looking forward to meeting you. How may we help you?"

"You don't fix traffic tickets, do you?"

"No, but if you find someone who does, please let me know. It's a regular speed trap from here to the Indiana border."

The young attorney and Larry exchange a firm handshake. "Lawrence Dailey. Call me Larry. You may have heard of the Daileys from around Three Oaks?"

"The name has a familiar ring, but I can't place it."

"I come from the family that for years has owned and operated the hardware store in Three Oaks."

"Oh, yes, Dailey's Hardware and Garden Center. I bought two flowering crabapple trees there for my wife a year ago. They're both doing well. They bloom around Mother's Day."

"Crabapple trees? Great, but I promise you, I'm not here to sell you more flowering trees. In fact, I've never seen this garden center you mention."

"Well you're in for a treat. It's quite impressive."

"I look forward to it."

"Of course, if this is not a sales meeting I'd be interested to find out what's on your mind and how I may help you."

Impatient, Larry comes straight to the point. "My dad died two years back. I was never made aware of the legal settlement of his business and property. At least not to my satisfaction." Larry hesitates in his response, realizing he may appear as a vindictive absentee relative or irate estate claimant.

It doesn't take Bob long to learn Larry did not attend his father's funeral and, in fact, had not spent much time in Michigan over the past twenty years. Larry's explanation becomes halting. He tells Bob that several weeks back he received a phone call from his sister-in-law which was quite unusual. She had never called him before. She wanted to inform him of an upcoming high school reunion she and his brother would like him to join them in attending. During their conversation, she suggested his mother seemed depressed and a visit from him would lift her spirts. Although she never said so directly, Larry believed it was really her husband, David, she was concerned about, and that was the real motive for her request that he make a home visit.

The reason for scheduling a meeting at the law office quickly surfaces. Larry wants to discover the size and scope of his deceased father's estate. More to the point, he wants to know the precise nature of the property division, a division he believes may be problematic. The lawyer appears to understand this type of problem well, all the more so when Larry requests complete confidentiality.

As the meeting draws to a close, the lawyer and his new client exchange contact information, and Larry puts up a $250 retainer fee. Larry informs Bob that to attend his Three Oaks High School class reunion, he will be staying at his mother's home for at least a week.

"When is the last time you talked with your mother?" Bob asks.

"Last Christmas on the phone. She writes me a letter every so often."

"And your brother?"

"Two or three months ago as I recall. But with his wife last month."

"Okay. I'm not sure there's much for me to do here, but I'll look into it for you."

"Right, I just want to know how things stand financially. Please be discreet," Larry repeats. He stands, shakes Bob's hand, and walks out of the first-floor law office.

It's a bright fall day. The sickly sweet smell of tonic water floats in the air. On the sidewalk in front of the barber shop next door, two retirement-aged men are locked in a heated discussion of last night's high school football game.

"Could you believe they threw on fourth down?"

"I repeat, hindsight is always twenty-twenty. At least yours is."

"At least it's not out of my ass!"

"I can't think of another source."

Larry climbs into his car and taps both fists lightly against the steering wheel. *That could have been me if I'd stayed around here.* As he begins to pull away, he recalls how important he once felt when he observed how Saturday-morning quarterbacks cared about *their* local high school team and him by extension. Friday nights were a big deal. With the kindling of boyhood memories and time to spare, Larry turned north. Not a direct route to his old hometown but a drive that once fascinated him. He and his high school buddies branded it The Gold Coast. Now he could take it all in as he cruised by in style.

Red Arrow Highway winds its way north out of the village of New Buffalo and through the tiny coastal hamlets of Union Pier, Lakeside, Harbert, and Sawyer. Famous poet and historian Carl Sandburg spent his most productive years here living and writing among the impressive sand dunes that surrounded his Harbert beachside retreat. Expensive summer homes are hidden from view within the majestic tree-covered sand dunes that defend the Lake Michigan shoreline all the way from Michigan City, Indiana to Traverse City, Michigan.

Aging tourist courts, modern motels, and fair-weather fruit and vegetable stands offer their services to coastline travelers. The locals' livelihoods depend on the tourist trade and vacation homeowners, but they privately refer to those part-timers as FIPs—fucking Illinois peoples.

Numerous out-of-state license plates attest to the seasonal draw of the spectacular fall colors provided by a wide variety of deciduous hardwoods interspersed within an evergreen pine framework. Many of the trees lean eastward, as if they were fleeing a prevailing westerly wind. This natural feature is also visible in the linear rows of plentiful fruit orchards. Fruit and vegetable farms dominate the countryside for more than twenty miles inland, but not beyond the reach of the lake-effect moderation of extreme temperature swings in both the spring and fall. As he approaches the hamlet of Bridgman, he reverses course back south and motors through the rural countryside.

Larry's sleek foreign-built sports car looks out of place as it streaks past peach orchards, grape vineyards, and weathered farm buildings. The landscape conjures up warm, nostalgic memories as Larry rubbernecks to see everything, while recalling his formative years with mixed emotions. His mind is in an earlier place and time when he zooms unobserved through a lone, rural four-way stop.

He throttles back to forty-five miles per hour at the Three Oaks village limit. Coasting along Main Street, he is immersed in a flashback to his high school glory days, now all but forgotten, except when he's home again. It's hard for him to believe that just fourteen hours earlier, he walked out of Chicago's Comiskey Park embroiled in a petty argument with a couple of inebriated Sox's fans over a close call at third base. Gazing about the small town, now much smaller and much quieter than he remembered, he shakes his head.

What's happened here or not?

Larry downshifts and turns into the town's only gas station, more interested in having his car washed than topping-off the gas tank. He had filled up on cheap Indiana gas before crossing into Michigan. A hip young station attendant let out a sharp whistle as he jogs from the lone service bay toward the Triumph.

"Cool 'chine, man. I bet she set you back some major coin!"

"You got that right, *major* coin," Larry says as he climbs out of the car.

"Looks like you'd need a pilot's license to fly this baby," the attendant says.

"Do you think I could get a carwash anywhere around here?" Larry looks up and down the desolate street in the heart of town. A single caution light continuously blinks yellow. He has often described Three Oaks as a one-horse town, but now ghost town seems more appropriate. The total absence of people makes the village resemble the Twilight Zone.

"I'd wash her for free, but as you can see, I'm the Lone Ranger," the attendant says. "What kind is she?"

"Triumph TR3. British."

"Cool, man, coool." The attendant makes a long, smooth motion forward with his right hand.

"Where is everybody? This used to be my town."

"Most gone to the funeral, I suspect. Boss did anyways."

"I grew up here. Don't remember it this small, never this empty. Whose funeral?

"Don't know, man."

"Don't look like you can afford any more casualties. Must be someone important? I probably know or at least knew them at one time."

"You from here?"

"More than you, I suspect," Larry grins. "Left before the war. The big one. Short visits once or twice. Who died, anyway? Sure you don't know?"

"Don't know, man. I've only been here a couple of months. When I quit school, my ol' man said, 'Get you a job or join the navy, one.' So I was headin' out to join up. Got this far. Check these." He flexes both arms out level from his shoulders, fists doubled-up above his head Charles Atlas style. "They call me 'Sailor.'"

"Holy cow," Larry says with lightly veiled sarcasm, more amazed by the bloated biceps than the identical dark purple anchor tattoos they display. "You ever been in the navy?"

"No, but I'm goin'," Sailor said. "How much did your ride cost?"

"If you have to ask, you can't afford it."

"I'm makin' one twenty-five an hour."

"As I said. You know where I can find a good hardware store around these parts?" Larry's poorly contrived folksy voice passes without notice.

"You got that right. Big business, Dailey's Hardware. I'm gonna get me a job there. Right up that—"

"Thanks. I know the way. Catch you later, Sailor." Larry turns and climbs back into his TR3.

"You come back later? I'll clean your 'chine. Say, what's your name anyways?"

"Lawrence Dailey." He starts and revs the engine. "Later, Sailor!" he says as he slips the Triumph into first gear and lets out the clutch.

"Far out!" Sailor calls.

Tires spin with a short squeal from the loose gravel to the tarmac that separates the service station from Main Street. Larry accelerates quickly from first to second for Sailor's benefit, but then lifts his foot and pokes his way toward the north edge of town. He passes the familiar and the now unfamiliar at barely twenty miles per hour. His head swivels right and left. He wants to see everything. A large orange cat darts across the road and ducks beneath a front porch.

Although the hardware store still stands where it did the day Larry graduated from high school, it is now unrecognizable. In addition to an artist's rendition of the Dailey name on an impressive neon billboard next to the street, there's a completely new storefront more than triple the size he remembers. Two large picture windows showcase merchandise while providing a limited view of the store's spacious interior.

The entire edifice astonishes Larry. It's definitely not the quaint rural hardware shop of his youth. The comprehensive hardware supply, trophies, printing, and engraving business is flanked on the right by a half-acre indoor-outdoor Garden and Botanical Center. On the left is an extensive exhibition of farm implements and low-horsepower land and sea recreational vehicles.

"Wow, where did this come from?" Larry blurts aloud. Then wrinkles begin to cross his forehead and fine lines radiate from the corners of his eyes. He slides out of the car and walks toward the main entrance, all the time calculating the monetary value of what he sees. Mesmerized by the grandeur and scope of the commercial enterprise, he's nonetheless drawn to a square sheet of red construction paper taped inside the main entrance window.

CLOSED ALL DAY
SATURDAY SEPTEMBER 28
FUNERAL AT 2PM
UNITED METHODIST CHURCH
INTERMENT SERVICE TO FOLLOW

Larry reads the announcement a second and then a third time. He recognizes his family's church, where he and David were baptized, David and Jane were married, and where he is certain his father is buried. Motionless, he ponders the sign.

A cold tremor creeps through Larry. His wristwatch reads 1:00 p.m.—*Chicago time*. He whirls and sprints to the car, vaults over the door and down into the form-fitted driver's seat. The two miles through the countryside on an ill-paved, narrow road takes less than two minutes. From half a mile away, he can see that a significant event may already be in progress.

The church is a humble white-framed structure with three tall leaded-glass windows on the east and west sides and a heaven-touching steeple above the entrance. Cars, trucks, and two black horse-drawn Amish carriages surround the building and line the sides of the road in both directions. Larry comes to a stop directly in front of the church and double parks, leaving the key in the ignition. A bell peals beneath the steeple as he hustles between cars and up the five concrete steps in front of the main entrance.

A small clutch of mourners huddle in the narthex near the rear entry to a full-to-capacity sanctuary. Larry recognizes his mother and Jane and moves toward them, although he would not have recognized Jane had he passed her on the street. Both women throw their arms around him as tears run down their faces. His mother clutches him the firmer of the two. "I knew you'd be here. I prayed you'd be here! I just knew it."

The fear that reared in Larry at the garden center intensifies. Meeting his mother and Jane like this confirms his worst suspicion. The funeral Sailor had mentioned earlier is the funeral for his very own brother.

After a long embrace, Larry pulls back. Jane blots her enflamed and moist eyes with a tissue held in her left hand while squeezing Larry's forearm with her right. "David wanted me to wake him when you got home. His last words." She barely gets the words out before she cries openly as tears burst forth and stream down her flushed cheeks. She wipes them with her palms. "I'm so sorry," she says. Sniffling, she bumps her head against Larry's shoulder.

"I'm the one who's sorry, Jane. I didn't know. I'm not dressed for this. What happened?" Larry swallows to maintain his composure but keeps a grasp on each woman's arm. Remorse mixed with guilt renders him weak, making him feel he can barely stand. Tears appear on his tanned cheeks. Without the use of his hands, he tucks his cheeks into his shoulders in an attempt to wipe them dry.

"It's good to see you, Jane. I did not expect this though. Wish things could be different. Don't worry about me. It's you and Mom need caring for. What can I do?" He leans in close to Jane's ear and whispers, "How's Mom taking this?" He becomes choked up with painful emotions and can't hold back noticeable weeping. Now the three cling to one another, oblivious to their surroundings.

A young, black-suited usher guardedly approaches them, and in a soft voice says, "Sorry. It's time to go in. Family seats are reserved in the front pew on the right." The organist has already begun playing "Rock of Ages" slowly, even dirge-like.

"I should have a suit and tie," Larry says.

"Hush, you're here and with us. That's all that matters," Mrs. Dailey says. Her thankful determined nature here is testament to her resolute character. She hands Larry a white handkerchief.

Larry turns aside to wipe his face with the handkerchief. He then offers each woman an arm to clasp and proceeds to escort them down the center aisle toward the front of the church. The three family members are visibly the focus of the congregation's attention. As they march forward, Mother Dailey nods a silent greeting to several attendees while Jane fights to maintain her composure by gazing straight ahead at her husband's casket arranged in front of the pulpit. Larry sees several familiar but aged faces. He nods acknowledgment toward two women of his mother's generation who smile expressively then bow their heads. Once seated, Larry whispers to Jane, "When did David die?"

"Monday night," Jane whimpers. "We tried to let you know. I'll tell you more later." Jane turns her face back toward the casket while blotting her eyes and nose with another tissue.

When the organ prelude ends, a solemn-faced minister welcomes the congregation from the front of the church, standing beside the open casket. "David Dailey, our friend, lived his life for family, heritage, and tradition." Murmurs of agreement rustle through the congregation. "However, I feel confident David would agree with today's break from our regular funeral custom. Will Mrs. Dailey's, Jane's, second-grade class please come forward to offer a special musical number?" The minister takes a seat in the pew next to Mother Dailey.

From all corners of the church sanctuary, nineteen children, scrubbed and in their Sunday best, squeeze and scramble out of the pews and hurry forward to form two rows on the steps of the rostrum to the right of the casket. When jostling for assigned positions subsides, the shortest girl in the middle of the front row counts, "One, two, three." And then the children sing "Over the Rainbow."

Jane sobs and leans against Larry. "That's our song. Those are my munchkins."

When their song is completed, the children clamber back to their seats among an appreciative and noticeably proud congregation. Happy smiles and warm hugs abound. The minister again assumes his place at the front of the sanctuary. The church becomes quiet. Vibrant rays of afternoon sun penetrate the colorful west-side windows, giving the spiritual chamber an impressionistic aura.

"That is a hard act to follow. Thank you, Mrs. Dailey's second graders." Then Reverend Victor Rissig opens with a short prayer, followed by a long moment of silence before he starts his eulogy.

"As with all of you, David was a friend of mine." He stops, another long pause. "I, we, will all miss David Dailey. Yesterday, three high schoolers stopped by the parsonage to reminisce with me about their friend, Mr. Dailey. One memory I'll share. It was when David and Jane took their junior high youth fellowship class camping up on the Au Sable River.

"In the middle of the night came a thunderous rainstorm. They were almost swept away when the stream next to which they had pitched their tents crested its banks. They told me they were led rain-soaked in a single-file line through the pitch-black forest holding the hand of the person in front and the person in back of them. David on one end and Jane on the other guided the terrified, soaked-to-the-skin campers through the storm to the safety of the church bus.

"Once all were seated and quiet, jungle sounds began to break the silence from the back of the bus. The deep, dark jungle came alive and so loud you could not differentiate the animals in the herd of wild beasts. The kids never had so much fun imitating and trying to impersonate the sounds of jungle animals. To hear these young people talk about it, well, you could tell they had the time of their lives. The Daileys were, and shall always be, their heroes."

A churn of low voices ripples through the audience, interrupted when a robust voice from a pew in the back speaks up. "Tell 'em about the glider David and you built." It's obvious this story is a well-worn and much-loved piece of community folklore.

"Tell us! Tell us!" chimes a chorus of young people.

"Now that would require self-incrimination, plus outing a fellow conspirator and the would-be glider pilot who I see is seated with us today." The minister gestures in Larry's direction.

Larry waves an acknowledgment then smiles and stands, saying aloud, "I'll take the Fifth, but I still think it would have flown."

Reverend Rissig laughs as do several others in attendance who are familiar with the story of a boy-built glider plane that burned up in a mysterious barn fire. The boys never got the chance to pull the glider aloft behind the Daileys' pickup truck—their declared intention.

"Welcome home, Larry," said Reverend Rissig.

Larry leans toward his mother and whispers, "Isn't that the Vic Rissig we called Spit Shine?"

"It is. He's our *Reverend* Rissig now, and a mighty good one, I might add. Now hush." His mother's quiet but firm command echoes the same managerial manner Larry well remembered, but now inexplicably welcomes.

Reverend Rissig continues his tribute to the character of David Dailey, highlighting his many contributions to the Three Oaks community. The homage is also lightly accented with spiritual references. As he concludes, he says, "About a year ago, David dropped by my office. I thought it odd, but I could see he was deadly serious. It seems he had come across the aphorism, a saying, 'Most men lead lives of quiet desperation, never daring to take a chance.' I confess, I had to look it up. David believed it spoke especially to him, and I could see it had filled him with misgivings about his life. David thought there must be something wrong with him, meaning that he felt afraid to launch out on his own, to try new things, and to go places he only dreamed about, even do something else for a living. He rambled on and on until finally I asked him to stop, 'You're depressing me,' I told him.

"After listening to Dave's lament, we agreed to meet for coffee at Tommy's Place every Monday at seven a.m. Rule number one: each of us had to explain a personal accomplishment we were proud of. Rule number two: each of us had to say something about the other that we liked. Let me tell you I was worried, fearing Dave might run out of good things to say about me before I did of him. Long story short, the exercise and David really helped me!"

Judging from the minister's lighthearted delivery, his intention is humor, but it is lost on his audience. He clears his throat. "Seriously, we helped each other. We looked forward to Mondays, and there were darn few we missed right up until David was hospitalized.

The moral I'd like to convey with this personal anecdote is this: we could all benefit by sharing a little of David's self-doubt. Managed well, as David Dailey ultimately did, it will always push us in the right direction."

When Reverend Rissig's shoulders tremble and he sways back slightly as if his balance is about to fail, an audible shudder ripples through the pews. He steadies himself then casts a distant gaze above his fellow grievers. "In closing, David's family wants to invite everyone to join them for a short interment service at the cemetery, to be followed by a meal provided by the ladies of the church downstairs in the fellowship hall. All are invited. Lastly, the procession to the cemetery, whether walking or going by car, will line up behind the hearse in front of the church. We all know the effort David and many others put forth to establish our Volunteer Fire Department. The new fire engine David worked so hard to procure for the Village of Three Oaks will lead our procession. It arrived yesterday."

A respectful round of applause breaks out, followed by the minister's raising both his hands above his head in a familiar benedictory manner. "Amen," he intones. The organist plays "Amazing Grace" as the parishioners gravitate toward the exit, rambunctious children squirting in-between and around them, racing out the main entrance to see the new fire engine.

Jane lingers at her husband's casket with Larry at her side. After a long minute, Larry says, "David told me he had a minor heart attack several months ago but said he was okay. Did you know that Dave and I had been talking every once in a while?"

Jane pulls Larry to one side as six pallbearers excuse themselves to carry the casket out to the hearse. Two of the pallbearers look familiar to Larry, but one is unmistakable—Crisco. The two old friends point at each other. "Talk later," Crisco says then adds, "Hope you don't mind, I moved your car out of the road."

Jane moves in front of Larry and looks straight into his eyes. "Saw the phone bills. Good to know you two were finally patching things up."

"He called me out of the blue almost a year ago. We started exchanging phone calls, maybe once a month. He gave me an excuse to come home when he told me about the school reunion, and then you called to remind me. Neither of you indicated he was in such bad shape."

"Well, he wasn't in bad shape then, but last Sunday, he had a second, more severe heart attack and was hospitalized. Tried to call you. Apparently, he suffered a third in the night Monday. I tried to get ahold of you again, but I was told you had left for Michigan."

"I must have just missed you. I've been taking my time, checking out some of the places Dave and I talked about, places we remembered from years ago. I definitely was not in a hurry. Didn't know Dave was in trouble."

"Did Dave tell you he researched Route 66? From start to finish. He had mapped the complete route. He was always dreaming, talking about driving that road," Jane said.

"No, and he never told me he had a heart problem either. He did talk about wanting to travel."

"No one knew how critical his heart problem was until this last week. Then David struggled for two days in the hospital, asked about you, babbled things, but was mostly incoherent. At times, it was like he was dreaming, Larry. Mom and I took turns sitting with him at the hospital," Jane said.

"Jane, I wanted to see Dave so much. We did talk about taking a camping trip. Don't know if it was more than two guys shooting the breeze, but it was fun thinking about it. I've never figured out why we couldn't get along—and actually disliked each other, I think."

"Mom said you two were alpha and omega. Just typical siblings, I suspect. Distance may have had something to do with it. I know David became jealous of your lifestyle."

"Trust me, it's not all that great," Larry said.

"I also think that Mom ..." Jane pauses and looks around to see where her mother-in-law is. "Mom wanted you two to be close, proud of one another. She always built you up to Dave. I think she overdid it. It came across as bragging, like one-upmanship at Dave's expense. And it irritated him to the core."

"The same goes for me. So glad he called me. That broke the ice. I planned to surprise Dave by showing up at the store completely unannounced. And holy smokes, what a store! I was looking forward to going to a Sox's game with him just like old times. In fact, I picked up two tickets for a double-header next weekend when the Tigers play in Chicago."

"Larry, that would have been a great surprise. He would have loved it. Mom too. After I thought he had fallen asleep the last night, I told him you were on your way home. He opened his eyes and said, 'Wake me when Larry gets here.' I could sense a smile behind his eyes."

Choked with emotion, Larry stammers, "So so-sorry. I-I should have been here. It's such a shame …."

After consoling each other, Larry and Jane reunite with Mrs. Dailey on the front steps of the church. From there, they observe a long train of cars and walkers moving slowly with the current a short distance down the road and turning right under a wrought iron archway into the graveyard. A bright, new red fire engine is parked on the road just past the archway entrance. Three young boys run across a recently plowed field of foul-smelling, rotting cauliflower, a shortcut to the cemetery. Paradoxically, pleasant memories flood back as Larry inhales the earthy scents he had so long detested.

Jane hurries ahead to catch up with two fellow teachers and a couple of munchkins who want to hold their teachers' hands. Larry walks beside his mother along with several other parishioners down the middle of the road to the cemetery. They reminisce about David, the family, and the hardware store. Larry apologizes profusely for missing his father's funeral.

"You couldn't help that, Larry. You didn't know. We all understood," Mrs. Dailey says.

"But I should have been there, and I'll never forget what a good father we had. And mother too." He squeezes his mother's arm. "What can I do to help you and Jane now that both Dad and Dave are gone?"

"Oh, Jane and I will get along. I do worry about the store though. You know your dad and brother were partners. As organized as David is …" Pensively, she stops. "I'm sure he and his attorney have thought of everything. You must talk to David's attorney, but there's plenty of time to deal with those matters."

A winding two-tire lane meanders lazily through the wooded, well-manicured burial ground. Silver shards of light from an Indian summer sun pierce billowy old maple trees brightly decorated in autumn foliage. Just then, a gust of wind fills the sky with millions of tumbling red and yellow leaves fluttering down upon passive ranks of steel-gray headstones.

Dozens of solemn mourners gather as if pulled by an obscure magnetic force toward a large white canopy engulfed in a profusion of tasteful flower arrangements: gladiolas, lilies, and carnations flourish in the midst. Larry can't help but think of the source and cost of such a floral exhibition.

Out on the road, a radiant jet-black four-door foreign sedan slows as it passes the church and carefully turns in beneath the cemetery archway. The quiet yet powerful engine purrs distinctively. Larry observes the latest arrival with interest. The driver parks on the lawn at the end of a row of cars along the right side of the central lane. Two additional late arrivals follow its lead and park behind.

The sedan driver, a fit mid-thirtyish woman dressed in a tailored gray nurse's uniform, gets out. She strides around the back of the car and retrieves a folded wheelchair from behind the front passenger seat. After securing the chair, she opens the front passenger door and assists the disabled occupant from the car into the wheelchair. She then pushes her patient between the headstones toward the solemn gathering at the canopy.

Larry and his mother stop short of their destination. Larry stands straight, intense. In sports clothes and lacking a tie, Larry feels uneasy. He surveys the impressive assembly. The focal point is a closed casket and an empty grave cavity a step beyond. Two folding chairs remain vacant next to his grief-stricken sister-in-law, Jane Dailey. Three yards behind the new grave site is a large stone marker inscribed Lawrence David Dailey, June 1, 1898–August 5, 1961. *Nice headstone, Dad. I'm sorry I wasn't here*, Larry thinks. Presently, mother and son take their seats next to Jane, facing the pedestaled brown inlaid-cedar casket.

"That is one magnificent casket," Larry says.

His mother leans toward him, squeezes his hand and whispers, "Only befitting for a young man of your brother's stature."

Larry whispers back, "David was a good man and good brother."

"The best," Mrs. Dailey says, wiping her eyes with an embroidered handkerchief. She radiates contentment at having her Larry by her side.

"I drove by the store on my way in. I can't believe the size! Who's going to run it?"

"Hush now. The minister wants to start."

Reverend Rissig, who has been assisting with the placement of the wheelchair, signals that all is ready. He bends and whispers something in Mrs. Dailey's ear, touches Jane's and Larry's shoulders, then takes a position next to the casket. Behind him, fall leaves continue their colorful earthward ballet. The pastor offers a short prayer concluding with an "amen" that is echoed around the gravesite.

He continues, "It is our custom to allow those who wish to place a handful of dirt on the casket to come forward now and do so. There is a mound of soil available here next to the coffin."

No one moves. Then Mother Dailey rises, grasps a handful of dirt, and places it on a flowered garland on top of the casket. Jane follows and is in turn followed by a few more witnesses. When Jane returns to her seat, Larry asks, "How long have we been doing this?"

"Several years now. It's spiritual. You know—dust to dust."

When no other mourners come forward, the minister introduces Mayor Harmony Hillenbrand.

"Good afternoon, everyone," the mayor greets the assemblage. Then she paces through the typical homage niceties and accolades. After several minutes, she comes to what she really wants to say.

"We all know of David's interest in history, especially local history. Remember that old barn on the New Troy Road, been an eyesore for years? Well, it just so happens it was originally built by area farmers way back in the 1880s as Grange Hall. David worked to get a state historic marker to commemorate it and a financial grant to restore it.

"Last we heard, the grant will be rubber stamped. Looks like we'll receive twenty thousand dollars to assist in the restoration. David's idea was that it could be used as a community center. Heaven only knows we need one! If you'd like to be a part of this effort, please see me back at the church following the service."

A supportive round of applause bursts forth. When it recedes, she continues, "David, and his wife Jane, mean a lot to all of us. So true. I'll always cherish what Dave said to me when I told him I wanted to be involved in politics. 'Lots can be accomplished by people willing to do more than their share without regard for who gets the credit.' Seems so simple, but I often think about it, and remember David."

The mayor returns to her place among those standing on the perimeter. Several affirm their agreement while others reach out and pat her on the shoulder or arm as she passes. Reverend Rissig closes with a prayer then repeats his invitation to share a meal and fellowship with the Daileys back at the church.

People begin angling their way out of the cemetery. They pass grave markers, some adorned with flower arrangements and others with small American flags. Almost all are inscribed with familiar family names dating back to the midnineteenth century. The air is dense and still. From the far side of the hill behind the cemetery, a bugler plays taps. As shadows lengthen, autumn leaves blanket the hallowed lawn, thoroughly carpeting the subdued and sacred setting.

Mrs. Dailey walks between Larry and Jane, clinging fast to both. It's her older son's funeral, but having her younger son by her side brings a strange contentment to the recently widowed sixty-five-year-old woman. "There's lots to do, but we've plenty of time. Right now, let's be sure to thank everyone for coming. We have such good friends," she says. Releasing her grasp, she waves to a couple driving out a rear exit.

As the three walk along the lane toward the main archway, Larry sees the nurse pushing her wheel-chaired patient. "Do either of you know those people? Looks like they went to a lot of effort to be here."

Jane turns to look in the direction Larry is facing. "Oh, that's Marguerite Fairfax. She was a classmate of Dave's. Do you remember her?"

"Marguerite Fairfax? Can't place her."

"Her maiden name was Stevens. Didn't you go to school with her brother?"

"That's who that is? What's wrong with her?"

"She has Lou Gehrig's disease. Dave did a lot of work for her out at her lake house. Maybe you ought to go say hello. I'm sure she'd like that. Mom and I'll meet you back at the church."

Larry excuses himself and walks back along the lane to where the nurse is assisting her patient out of the wheelchair and into the car. Neither notice Larry approach.

"Excuse me. May I give you two a hand?"

"Thanks, but we can manage," the nurse says as she skillfully lifts her patient, who appears to weigh less than a hundred pounds, into the passenger seat.

The patient looks up and recognizes Larry, "Why, hello there. You're David's little brother, aren't you?"

"Will you guys ever stop thinking of me as the *little* brother?" Larry says with a smile.

"Old ways die hard, just like some old women." She winces at an obvious shooting pain but continues in spite of a pronounced speech impairment. "Nice to see you, Larry, but I wish it could have been under better circumstances," she gasps.

"It's been a long time—you're quite right. I understand you've had a run of bad luck." Shock flashes in Larry's memory as he comes face to face with Maggie Stevens. She is too old, too decrepit, with lifeless eyes that once dazzled, not the radiant beauty he once gawked at in the English hallway. Hard as he tried, he could not have recognized her. An imitation smile struggles to the surface of her shrunken, bone-jutting cheeks.

"So sorry for your loss, Larry. I really do hate for us to meet again under these conditions." Maggie's speech is slurred with a significant nasal twang. She attempts to brush phantom strands of hair from her face. As she does, her arm jerks, and she clumsily slaps her forehead instead with the back of her hand.

"May I help you?" Larry asks.

"I'm okay. Two years ago, I was diagnosed with amyotrophic lateral sclerosis, ALS. I've been in a downward spiral ever since." Her speech is labored, and her articulation indistinct.

"I'm so sorry." Momentarily at a loss for words, Larry blurts out a change of direction. "I understand my brother had been doing some work for you. Is there any way I could help, maybe take his place?"

Maggie manages another strenuous smile. "David never worked for me."

"He didn't?"

"No." Maggie attempts to swallow several times with no luck. Her disturbed breathing pattern alarms Larry, but it's taken in stride by her nurse. Eventually she stammers, "David called me. Said something about needing my help to organize a reunion. Not sure why he called me. Two years ago, I'd thought he was flirting." Maggie flashes another contorted smile.

"I don't understand," Larry says.

"Nor do I." Maggie tries to take a deep breath and again looks up at Larry. "Casual for your brother's funeral ...." Then she turns and looks straight ahead. "Take me home, Peg."

"Yes, ma'am." The nurse steps around Larry and closes the passenger door in a slow, firm motion. She folds and replaces the wheelchair in back of Maggie's seat. As she rounds the back of the car, she says in a low voice, "Please meet me at Mrs. Fairfax's home at eight p.m." Awash in palpable confusion, Larry nods.

The nurse starts the sedan and drives slowly out of the cemetery being overcome by lengthening shadows. Larry stands immobile as he tracks the taillights past the church and down the narrow road until they disappear over a rise. With the exception of two men tending to the casket's interment, he is all alone.

As Larry starts for the church, he feels a damp, cool snap in the air and smells the sweet fragrance of ripe Concord grapes. His senses are fresh and alert. He looks forward to the community reception and the possibility of meeting and talking with old friends.

The spacious fellowship hall beneath the church sanctuary is bustling and noisy when Larry arrives, a stark contrast to the earlier, more somber church-service atmosphere. Relatives, friends, and neighbors are clearly dedicated to having a jovial time of good fellowship and abundant nourishment.

"There you are!" Larry's mother exclaims as she reaches for his hand. "Come here. I want you to say hello to some folks you may remember."

From that point forward, Larry is shuttled from one person to the next by either his mother or sister-in-law and, at times, by both. Most people express their heartfelt condolences, but in the main, all want to reunite, or meet for the first time, with David Dailey's younger brother.

"So you're the one that got away?"

"Finally, I get to meet the son your mother always talks about."

"You look just like your dad and namesake."

"How's life in the California sun?"

"Coming back to take over the family business, hey?"

Meeting, greeting, shaking hands, and on and on until Larry's cheeks begin to ache from a smile overdose. The assumptions related to moving back and taking over the hardware store catch his attention. Separately, he asks his mother and then Jane about a will or an estate plan. In each instance, he is put off until a more appropriate time and place. He does manage, but with some clumsiness on his part, to get directions to the Fairfax beach house, an appointment he plans to keep, but is unsure of exactly why.

Following the fellowship hall gathering and clean-up, Larry offers to drive his mother home. Jane supports the offer and confesses that she is looking for some time alone in her own house. Mrs. Dailey is thrilled to ride in Larry's sports car Crisco had parked behind the church, and she tells him it is her first ride ever in a convertible. "And only room for two," she says. She is careful not to appear too jubilant.

When they arrive at the family home, Mother Dailey leads Larry upstairs and into the room he once shared with David. Although his mother could not have known for sure that he'd be there, the room is made up and ready for its honored guest. He again explains how sad he felt at missing his father's funeral and how his guilt is now compounded by not being able to reunite with his brother. But Mrs. Dailey does not respond in her usual quick, supportive manner. Eventually, she says, "Larry, things don't always fall the way we want. It's what we do next that counts. I'm just so pleased that you are here with us now."

"You know, Mom, I'm sure you must be right, but right now, I think we should put away the food the ladies of the church insisted we bring home. I might have a piece of that cherry pie before I go to bed."

After refrigerating the church leftovers, the two of them meet in the living room where Larry sits back in his dad's favorite easy chair while his mother sits on the couch. They talk for over an hour about family, the hardware store, and David. Mrs. Dailey asks Larry if he remembers David's fascination with allegorical historical accounts. He said he did not but thought that Jane's munchkins singing "Over the Rainbow" added a special touch to the funeral.

When the phone rings, Mrs. Dailey answers it then turns to Larry and says, "It's a Bob Sill for you. I don't think I know him." She hands the phone to Larry.

"Larry, Bob Sill here." Sill tells Larry that a friend of his with personal knowledge of the hardware store's corporate organization told him that he and his brother each own about 40 percent of the business. This news arouses Larry's interest for more, but he is uncomfortable having such a conversation so soon after the funeral and in front of his mother. He tells Sill he has just gotten home and wants to spend some time with his mother.

"I'll give you a call on Monday," Larry says and hangs up.

A little later, after he and his mother have each eaten a piece of cherry pie, Larry explains he wants to go for a ride to reacquaint himself with his old stomping grounds. He's not completely truthful, but Larry feels an escalating curiosity about the proposed eight p.m. appointment.

"That'd be good for you. Take a lazy drive around. Why don't you drive up to Weko Beach and see the new shelter. You and David always liked going to the beach. They say they're going to build a nuclear power plant up there. Can you believe that?"

"Okay, I'll do it. Don't wait up for me." Larry smiles and hugs his mother who waves for him to go on.

"The kitchen door is unlocked," Mrs. Dailey says.

Larry experiences some difficulty locating the residence of Marguerite Stevens Fairfax. The drive through the thick, wooded sand dunes near Lake Michigan presents more of a tangle than the adventures he remembers from high school. After backtracking twice, he arrives well after sunset, a journey made all the darker by tall trees and an absence of street lights.

Then the nurse he met at the cemetery waves to him from a second-floor deck illuminated by slender torchlights. Her athletic figure is obvious, even in a company-issue healthcare uniform.

"I wasn't sure you'd come, but I wanted to talk with you apart from Mrs. Fairfax," she says.

"Where is Maggie?" Larry asks.

"I usually put her to bed early with a sedative, but she does not sleep well despite it, and is always uncomfortable. My name is Peg, and I know you're Larry Dailey. 'The one that lives out west.'"

"Yes, and I'm happy to meet you, Peg. I'll admit I'm confused. Why are we here?"

"Because I asked you?" Peg says.

"We're beyond that," Larry says. "Please, just answer my question?"

"Okay. Let's start with me. I'm here for two reasons. First, escape from a bad marriage. Second, I'm paid very well by Justin Fairfax the third, a rich jerk," she says. "He shipped Mrs. Fairfax here because he doesn't want to deal with her anymore. Out of sight, out of mind, if you follow."

"Yes, I think I've heard that before."

"Well, it is true, though, that her paralytic condition has stolen her ability to walk and is destroying her ability to speak and eat. We don't know how much longer she has. Even so, Mrs. Fairfax is a proud woman, a fighter."

"You call her Mrs. Fairfax?"

"A professional thing. When we're alone, she insists I call her Maggie."

"Okay, then what brings me here?" Larry asks.

"Because I asked you," Peg repeats, smiling, and Larry can see that she enjoys mischievous banter. "Secondly, curiosity. I'll admit to some of that myself." The two exchange perceptive grins.

"I can't believe that was Maggie Stevens I saw at the cemetery," Larry confesses. "The last time I saw her, she was the rich college girl that could double as Miss America. What happened?"

"I think she told you that a little more than two years ago she was diagnosed with ALS. When she started a steep decline, I answered an ad to be her live-in caregiver. About eight months ago we were shipped here from Chicago."

"You live here?"

"Yes, twenty-four hours, seven days a week. Today was the first time in the past ten days we've been away from the house. What she said to you at the interment service was the most she has said to anyone other than me in the last month. Her paralytic condition has metastasized. Speaking and eating are becoming more and more difficult. Eventually she won't be able to breathe."

"Sounds awful. The two of you must be going stir-crazy."

"That's quite true. I'm in charge of everything around here, in addition to taking care of Maggie. She can be difficult, real difficult, but who can blame her? But honestly, she's grown on me. She doesn't deserve this debilitating disease."

"You know my brother, David, too, then?"

"I met him when we moved in. He built Maggie a ramp at the back entrance. At first, I was skeptical, thought he was another would-be opportunist. But his coming around provided me with a needed break and seemed to lift Maggie's spirit."

"And by that you mean?"

"Maggie becomes more reclusive each day. She's extremely sensitive about her personal appearance. Doesn't want anyone to see her, much less watch her struggle to eat and speak. She loves having me help her dress and put on makeup whenever she expects David to drop by. He has helped her relax. She talks to him, and to me about him."

"Once upon a time, I had a bad experience with Maggie," Larry said.

"I know. She told me."

"What? She told you what?"

"According to Maggie, she had a crush on your brother, wanted to make him jealous. Funny, David never knew about your little tryst with Maggie. You never told him, did you?

"You're kidding me! She told you and maybe David too? What did she tell you, pray tell?"

"Seems almost childish now, but I think he became jealous when Maggie told him about it several weeks ago. Can you believe that? After all these years? Maybe he just pretended to be jealous though. I'm not sure it really mattered to him, at least not anymore."

"How do you know all of this?" Larry asks. He is still unsure of what Peg knows or thinks she knows.

"When he's here, I hear them talking, and when he's not, Maggie tells me everything. Who else? She's a proud woman. Hard to live with at times. But I'd do anything for her."

"Tell me, what was the nature of the relationship between David and Maggie?" Larry asks.

"Like I said, he lifted her spirits."

"You know what I mean," Larry says.

"If you mean more than platonic, I don't think so."

"I guess you'd know."

"Yes, since we've been together, but not the previous ten years or so," Peg said.

"Now you're heading in the right direction. Tell me more."

"Would you like something to drink? A beer?" Peg asked.

"Not right now. Maybe later, after you tell me the rest of the story."

"According to what I overheard and what Maggie told me, they would see each other once every August when Maggie came here with her children on a summer's-end getaway before the start of school."

"It was more than, 'Hello, how are you?'" Larry asks.

"I don't know," Peg says.

"Come on. You know. We're not talkin' platonic here, are we?"

"I'm serious. I don't know. But since last spring, other than myself, David is the only one who has ever taken Maggie outside. They'd go for drives, and once he took her to a drive-in movie in Michigan City. As I said, she liked having him come around. That's really all I know."

"Sure," Larry says, brimming with skepticism. He suspects his brother's choirboy reputation may contain a few blemishes.

"They argued once about assisted suicide. Maggie insists on being in control of the end, but David disagreed. I believe he was trying to keep her hopes up."

"That's interesting. But I've got to find out if David or our dad had any plans for the end of life."

"Are we still talking about euthanasia?" Peg asks.

"I'm interested and do care, but honestly, I have more concerns right now about what's going to become of the hardware store."

"If you're asking about a will and the division of the business, I think I can help you with that too." Peg beams at Larry with a self-assured wiggle. It's clear that she revels in holding his attention.

"You're kidding!" Larry says. Peg's confident manner so early in their acquaintance astonishes him but appeals to him too. And in any case, he wants to know everything she knows about a will and his brother's other life.

He finds it hard to believe Peg, a caregiver, could be so highly informed about his family's intimate financial affairs. Peg informs Larry she is aware of only limited details but says so in a manner that serves to heighten his curiosity. She explains that when their father died, the business was evidently split three ways among the two sons and their mother.

"Just as I expected," Larry says.

Peg tells him that her understanding is that David took over the operation of Dailey Hardware and Garden Center, and he immediately incorporated it—giving himself controlling interest. She was unsure of further details but thought there may be something about a residency requirement.

All Larry's informant knows and doesn't know continues to heighten his interest. However, she also tells him enough to make him at once apprehensive and filled with determination to straighten it all out. Maybe Bob Sill could do that.

The couple's conversation ebbs and flows between illnesses, past marriages, romances, and inheritance, all with an ample flirtatious flavor—at times animated, other times restrained. Time passes unnoticed until Peg hears a moan on the intercom coming from Maggie's room. Larry's Rolex displays midnight, but he can't remember whether he had reset to Michigan time. They agree it's time to say goodnight.

At the bottom of the deck stairs, Larry follows a granite path toward his car. He hears someone call and turns back to see Peg with Maggie on the deck, their heads above the rail, waving to him. "Mrs.

Fairfax says you may visit us again, but you must wear a tie." Peg's smiling face glows in the flickering light from the bamboo torches.

Us? he says to himself then waves back at Peg, who playfully returns his gesture. "A tie, right!" he calls out to the women. When he turns to locate the dimly lit walkway, he realizes he's standing on an engraved granite paving stone with an inlaid arrowhead, "A Summer Place."

Larry winds his way out of the woods along the same narrow, sandy pathway he followed on the way in. He is in no hurry, comfortable in the afterglow of the stimulating visit with Peg. Before he can sink into an analysis of the complexities and challenges of the decisions that lie ahead, and maybe ahead of Peg as well, five white-tail deer bound across the trail. The last, a young pronghorn, stops dead still in the middle of the road and stares directly into the Triumph's high beams. Larry brakes and blinks his headlights on and off. In the next instant, the deer vanishes into the night. He had never seen anything quite like it and, with a shiver, wonders if its sudden appearance might hold some mysterious portent. Larry puts the TR back in gear and proceeds with caution, taking care not to hit a deer or allow an errant tree branch to brush against and scratch his trophy car.

Three Oaks is eerie to him when he arrives; nothing moves except the yellow blink of the lone caution light at the town's main intersection. He pokes on through town and, as if guided by a long-atrophied reflex, turns into the Dailey Hardware, Garden and Botanical Center. Again, but this time channeled by a well-honed defensive habit, he parks at an angle in a parallel space. With the light from a distant flood lamp, his watch reads twenty-three minutes after midnight. *Can that be right?*

He gets out of the car and walks the grounds, once more impressed at how the business has expanded since he had last been here. *Dad and David didn't sit around watching grass grow.* The main building is completely locked down.

Fatigue starts to settle heavy on Larry's shoulders, and he sits down on the store's front steps. The quiet night is clear. The moonless sky is illuminated by millions of tiny white stars. It's a setting rarely, if ever, observed back in an urban area like Los Angeles. "What will I do in the morning?" he mumbles to himself. With forearms on his thighs, he cups his face in the palms of his hands and closes his tired eyes. *I'm not a storekeeper. Especially not in Podunkville, USA.* Time passes, broken only by the intermittent call of a distant hoot owl or two. A damp chill spreads in the night air.

He senses a nearby movement but keeps his head down and eyes closed, listening. When he hears movement a second time, he raises his head. A Lab-sized scruffy gray dog is lifting its hind leg and relieving himself on the right front wheel of his precious TR3.

"What the fuck! Get the hell out of here!" Larry stands and shouts. The dog scrambles half a dozen steps beyond the car, but then stops and stares straight back at Larry. "Go on! Get the hell out of here!" Larry waves his arms above his head. The dog does not move. "Do you know what that tire and wheel are worth? Get!" The dog stands motionless, never taking his eyes off Larry.

"Did I just ask you the price of that wheel?" Larry shakes his head. The only movement from the canine is a slight twitch of a nostril. "Okay, I'm sorry." Larry sits back down. "Come here, boy." He pats his right thigh. The dog does not move, continuing his stoic stare through large penetrating brown eyes—neither scared nor threatening. Just there.

"It's okay, boy. I'm not going to hurt you." The edge is gone from Larry's voice. He pats the step next to him and continues to coax the wary animal. "C'mon, boy. Come here. I want to talk to you. C'mon. You're okay. Come here." He pats the step again but gently this time.

The skinny mutt takes three steps forward. His coat hangs on a frail rack, and his front paws are worn thin. Larry continues to cajole. A slight, if involuntary, wag animates the dog's matted tail. "C'mon, boy. You're okay. No one's going to hurt you."

As the dog moves closer, Larry extends his hand. The dog recoils. "Sorry, boy. C'mon. Come here." Larry pats the step again and the dog steps closer. Larry again extends his hand, but this time much slower and with his palm up. The dog smells his hand and then his shoes. Larry doesn't move, but whispers to his new, would-be friend.

When Larry tries to pet the dog's boney shoulder, the collarless mutt again shies away. A slight rise in Larry's voice causes the dog to step back, sit on his haunches, but with eyes still locked on the seated stranger.

"I don't believe I'm doing this. Who am I talking to here?" Larry says. The dog remains still then tilts his head enough that his right ear hangs limp.

"If you're applying for a job, you've got to have a name. Would my brother take a chance on you? What's your name?" The voiceless visitor with spellbound attention does not move. In the still of the night, man and beast stare at each other until Larry breaks the silence.

"I think ... Chance. Here, Chance."

ACKNOWLEDGMENTS

Over the years, I have talked with countless friends and acquaintances about my desire to write this novel. Without exception, each has supported my intention, several offered helpful suggestions, and a special few wanted to jump into the seat beside me and *hit the road*.

My son, Andy, actually *did* jump in the car beside me, or rather, I beside him, as I rode shotgun in his beloved bright-red Dodge Challenger, an authentic muscle car. Andy picked me up in Chicago where Route 66 begins, and we traced the Mother Road all the way to its conclusion at the Santa Monica Pier in California—a dream fulfilled. Thank you, Andy.

I extend a heartfelt thank you to the following who each contributed their unique expertise and unwavering support through to the completion of this novel: Sally Adkin, resident artist; Alice Joyce, writing confidant; Lorana Kauffman, special teacher; Elaine Taylor, writing group mentor; and the team at Warren Publishing.

Most men lead lives of quiet desperation and
go to their graves with the song still in them.
                                        —HENRY DAVID THOREAU

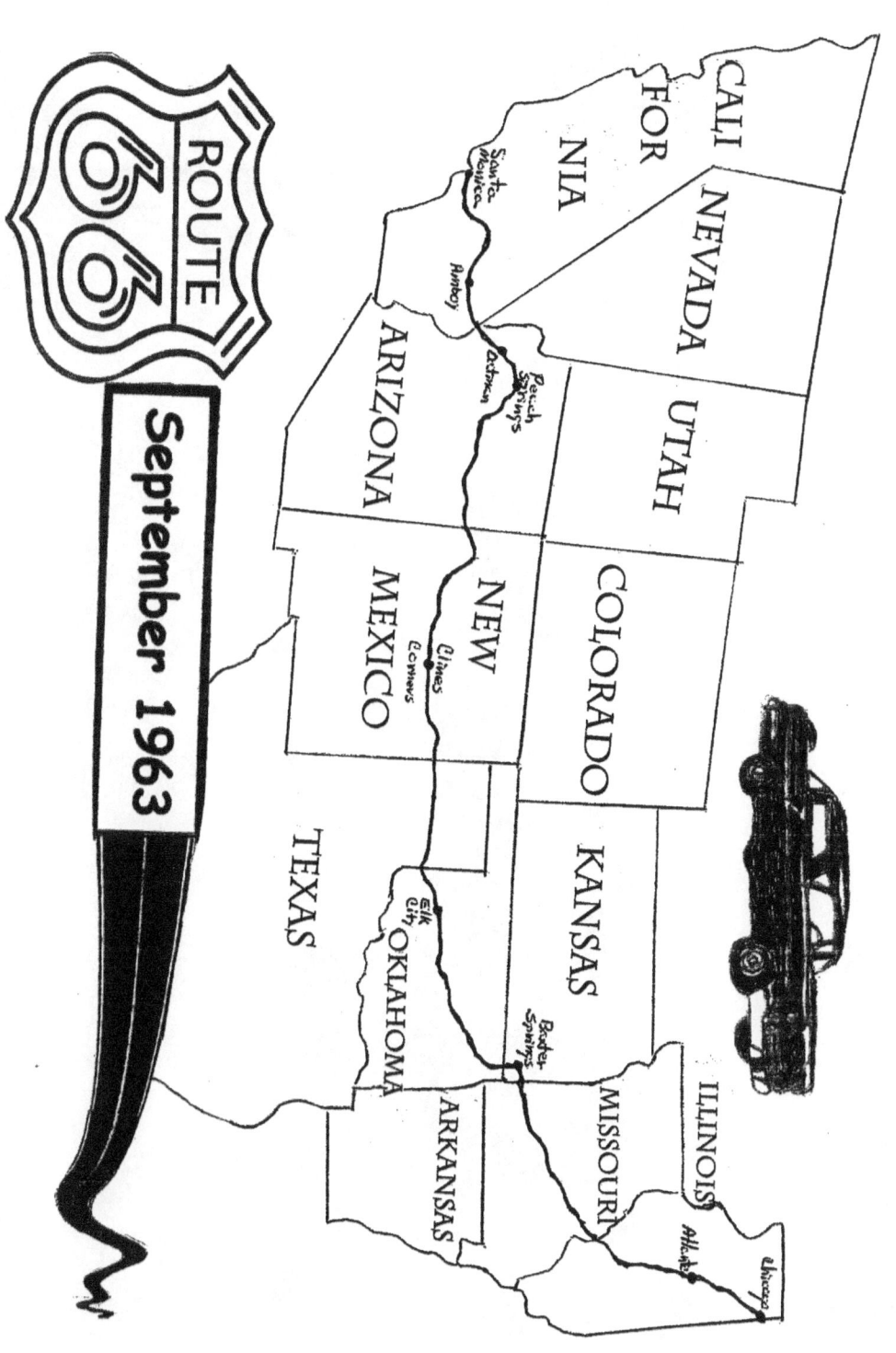

ROUTE 66

September 1963

CALIFORNIA
NEVADA
UTAH
COLORADO
KANSAS
MISSOURI
ILLINOIS
ARIZONA
NEW MEXICO
TEXAS
OKLAHOMA
ARKANSAS

Santa Monica
Amboy
Oatman
Peach Springs
Clines Corners
Elk City
Baxter Springs
Chicago